The
Getaway
Girls

ALSO BY DEE MACDONALD

The Runaway Wife

The Getaway Girls

Dee MacDonald

Bookouture

Published by Bookouture in 2018

An imprint of StoryFire Ltd.

Carmelite House
50 Victoria Embankment
London EC4Y 0DZ

www.bookouture.com

ISBN: 978-1-78681-478-4
eBook ISBN: 978-1-78681-479-1

To female friendships everywhere

CHAPTER ONE

FLOWER POWER

It was on a wet Thursday morning, while she was struggling to attach a daffodil to a sprig of blossom, that Connie McColl recognised the stirrings of restlessness again. Not only that – as a result of her daydreaming, she'd managed to tape her finger into the flower arrangement as well, and swore under her breath as she unpeeled it all. She glanced down at what she hoped was an artistic impression of 'Spring to Life', today's theme, and then studied the fifteen women in the class, all chattering away as they wrestled with bits of evergreen, sprigs of blossom and the inevitable daffodils. They all seemed happy enough. What is it with me? Connie wondered. Single again for nearly three years, so what was there to escape from? I'm sixty-nine, she thought, and I'm supposed to be grown up...

This group of ladies had been disappointed when she'd told them that she wouldn't be continuing with the flower-arranging classes after Easter. Why not? they wanted to know. Why not indeed? Connie wasn't certain herself why not. Was it purely that she fancied escaping the unpredictability of the British summer ahead? But it wasn't just that. In truth, she *knew* what it was. It was her exciting new discovery.

She looked at Mrs Briggs, right there in the front row, who'd plainly given up on her 'Spring to Life', which was now in a state of collapse on the table. She was deep in conversation with the woman next to her, whose name Connie could never remember, about the problems with daughters-in-law. And there seemed to be plenty of them; in fact Connie could have contributed a few of her own.

Connie had enjoyed the classes until now: 'Autumn Leaves', 'Christmas Table Arrangements', 'Here Comes Spring/Summer' and the rest. She had to dream up seasonal names to enhance these Thursday morning gatherings of mature ladies, hell-bent on brightening up their suburban lives under mostly grey London skies.

It was the end of the final lesson before Easter and, as always, the same two women stayed on behind to help Connie clear up the debris: little Maggie scratching away with a nearly bald broom in an attempt to extract squashed catkins from the floorboards, and Gill mopping up puddles of water and discarded leaves on the table tops. Floristry was messy.

'A right bleedin' mess,' confirmed Gill, never one to mince her words, as she attempted to tuck a stray blonde tendril back into its wobbly beehive, which Connie reckoned must have been a real wow back in the sixties.

'Will you really not be doing these classes again?' Maggie asked anxiously. She still had a Glaswegian accent you could cut with a skean-dhu, even after forty years in London.

'I'm afraid not,' said Connie.

Maggie Holmes had admitted that she'd only enrolled in the flower-arranging class because her friend, Pam, was going. Pam said that Maggie needed to get out more instead of hanging around waiting for *that man* to come home. So Maggie did as she was told, and then Pam didn't join because she'd forgotten she was going on holiday and would miss two whole sessions. 'How could you forget you were going on holiday?' Maggie had asked. She herself hadn't had a proper holiday in years and she most certainly would not be forgetting if she was lucky enough to have one in the pipeline.

Maggie sighed. 'So no more Thursday morning flowers then?'

Connie shook her head. 'I don't think so, Maggie.'

'Don't laugh but I never *meant* to sign up for a flower-arranging class,' Gill said. 'I thought I was enrolling for a life-drawing class.'

'A life-drawing class!' Maggie exclaimed. 'Are you artistic then?'

'Not really. I just hoped I might see some naked manly bodies. But somehow or other I clicked on the wrong box, and didn't know how to change it.'

All three of them burst out laughing.

'Aw, Connie!' Maggie went on. 'Who am I going to giggle with on Thursday mornings?'

Connie had become fond of the pair of them, different as haggis and hairspray, in spite of the fact that neither displayed any particular talent for the dainty business of flower arranging. Connie reckoned most of these older ladies came along mainly for companionship and gossip, and perhaps a little therapy woven into their home-going masterpieces.

'Tell you what,' she said. 'I don't know about Thursday mornings but, right now, why don't we go across to the pub and I'll buy you both a lunchtime drink.'

'Hey, thanks, Connie, I'm up for it!' said Gill.

Maggie hesitated only for a moment. Then: 'Och, why not?'

Ten minutes later they'd found themselves a wobbly corner table in the Dog and Duck, where Maggie folded a tissue neatly under the offending table leg. 'There, now,' she said. Maggie was like that: practical. Connie looked round at the gloomy Victorian interior, its walls still yellowed from decades of cigarette smoke, and wondered if she should have suggested finding somewhere more cheerful. But her two companions seemed happy enough.

'Thank you both for all your help this term again,' said Connie as they clinked glasses of wine. 'I'm going to miss you.' She thought for a moment. 'But maybe we should meet up now and again, right here?'

Gill took an enormous slurp of her drink. 'Great idea, Connie, but *why* won't you be doing the classes any more?'

Connie shrugged. 'I don't want to commit myself to anything just at the moment. I'm getting itchy feet and I'm not sure I'll want to stay in London.'

'But where would you *go*?' Maggie, as always, sounded anxious and tired, her skin pale against her faded once-red hair.

'I've got some ideas but no definite plans as yet.' And maybe, thought Connie, it was crazy to plan too far ahead when you were coming up to seventy. The last time she'd felt like this she'd left her husband of forty-one years. She had no regrets whatsoever, although it had taken her some time to recover from the resulting upheaval. Now that the unpleasantness of their bizarre uncoupling – and it *was* truly weird – had passed, the house had been sold and there was some money in the bank, she should really be looking to buy her own place back down in Sussex, near to the rest of her family. Time to be sensible again, perhaps? Oh God no, she thought. Not *yet*.

She knew very little about the other two. Gill, surely the epitome of an ancient Essex Girl, was divorced at least once, had six children, and still eyed every passing male with relish. And she knew even less about Maggie, other than that she lived with some dodgy bloke, had a son on the other side of the world, and never seemed particularly happy. But, against the odds, she'd become rather fond of them both. Connie had realised fairly early on that there was more to each of them than first impressions allowed.

Gill Riley fought against time, tooth (new, white and expensive) and nail (French manicured). 'You 'ave ze 'ands of a woman 'alf your age,' said Mimi at the nail bar as she glued the extensions into place. Mimi's accent rarely slipped, although it was rumoured she originally hailed from Southend. Gill had been a type of model in her prime; not exactly *Vogue*, of course, but then she'd never had to do anything too saucy either, although she'd been asked to do so many times due to being exceptionally well endowed. More top shelf than top drawer.

Now, alone after two husbands and countless lovers, she mourned not only the passing of her youth but also of Harvey, her cat. He'd been her only true and constant companion for years and now he, too, had gone. Gill was, of course, invisible to men, as are all women over a certain age, and she was considerably over that certain age. And feeling lonely.

Nevertheless, she knew how important it was to stay looking good because you never knew just when *he* might show up. And she definitely wanted *him* to show up. But some of these guys online were a complete joke – or they might have been had Gill's humour not begun to run dry, like everything else. She would be seventy next birthday, but she had no wish to celebrate *that*, thank you very much, since everyone except her six kids and their respective fathers thought she was only sixty. Well, she *hoped* they did. Blimey, her eldest, Marlene, at fifty-two, was a grandmother herself! They were scattered all over the place, the six of them, but threatening a mass get-together for her seventieth…

No, she certainly wouldn't be having any of that.

Gill drained her glass.

'I'm empty,' she said, waving it in the air. 'It's my round! Who would like a top-up?'

Connie pushed her glass forward, and Maggie said, 'Same again, but I'll need to go to the loo to make some space!'

As Maggie washed her hands, she stared at her pale reflection in the age-spotted mirror and mourned the red-haired beauty of her youth. Where had 'Miss Pride of the Clyde 1966' gone? She might have been a model, she'd been told, if she'd only been six inches taller, but that was before Dave Holmes swept her off her eighteen-year-old feet with his good looks and gift of the gab. A shotgun wedding, they said. But in 1966 that's what you did; no single mums getting council flats and handouts back then – not in her part of Glasgow at any rate.

She still hated removing her bra. Even after ten years she couldn't suppress a shudder when she gazed at where her left breast used to be. She should probably have had reconstruction surgery, although she'd thought at her age it would hardly matter; but it obviously *did* matter to Ringer.

Ringer had come along three years after Dave's fatal heart attack. He'd taken care of her and Alistair, her son, who was only five at the time. She'd adored him, so much so that she'd even agreed to come to London with him because that was where 'it was all happening', Ringer said. She never once asked where the money came from, because it was better really not to know, but she became an expert at providing believable alibis and hiding his hauls in all sorts of ridiculous places. Sometimes she forgot where she'd hidden them herself. Once she'd even made him turn off the water supply so she could fill the toilet cisterns with banknotes and, when the old bill came rummaging around, she prayed none of them would want a pee.

She lived well enough though. Ringer might not be the most generous of men but he'd got them a two-bedroom ground floor flat with a nice wee garden. But how many times had she dug up these flower borders over the years? When they'd been planting their annuals next door she'd been planting Ringer's bags and boxes, and then covering over the disturbed earth with begonias, or dead leaves, depending on the season. Maggie loved flowers and would have liked a permanent display, but needs must.

Except that lately he'd been meaner than usual with his cash. And his affections.

A friend, Maureen, had seen him up west: 'He'd got this blonde bimbo hanging on his arm and his every bloody word. Difficult to tell her age but a helluva lot younger than him – and us.'

Perhaps the blonde bimbo didn't know Ringer had a partner back in the flat at Rotherhithe. Perhaps he'd told her he was single and, technically of course, he was. Either way it was time for Maggie to take stock.

She dried her hands and went back to join the other two.

Several glasses of wine later they agreed to meet up again just after Easter, 'Right here: same time, same place.'

CHAPTER TWO

THE BOX

Connie walked home along the Thames Path, past the ruins of King Edward's manor house, now no more than a series of small walls. She was fond of that particular spot and stopped to gaze out across the river and take stock of her thoughts. She felt no regrets at abandoning a stagnant marriage or the 'retirement' bungalow she'd never been able to love. She was now ensconced in her elder daughter's stylish London apartment, Diana having moved in with her 'boyfriend'. That's if you could call a man of nearly fifty a boyfriend, Connie thought. 'Partner' was probably more correct these days, she supposed, although she still associated the word with 'take your partners for a quickstep' at the local Palais. All history now, like her marriage. Anyway, 'lover' was a much nicer word.

What Connie hadn't realised was that she might sometimes be lonely, that she might miss her children and grandchildren down in Sussex. They'd all adapted to life without her, of course, which had hurt a little more than she'd anticipated. And she missed her friends too, especially Sue and their shopping trips to Brighton. And their endless discussions over countless bottles of wine about how they'd like to leave their boring husbands and demanding families. Well, Connie had done it, while Sue was still there.

Connie often went down to Sussex, and of course they all came up to London, but there were still some lonely hours to fill when she felt an unexpected emptiness and lack of purpose. Giving the flower-arranging classes helped, but what had helped more than anything was the research into her family history. And that had come about as a result of The Box making its appearance. The Box's contents made Connie feel as if she was reclaiming some part of herself that she'd never known she had.

The Box. Why on earth had her aunt never produced it? Didn't she *know* it was there? Because The Box was only discovered when Connie's cousin was clearing the attic shortly after Aunt Lorna, aged ninety-nine, had finally breathed her last.

'This stuff must be for you,' Judith said, as Connie was about to leave after the funeral tea.

She handed over an old metal biscuit box rusting at the edges, ecru-coloured with romantic scenes of notable Scottish castles on each corner, with 'Crawford's Biscuits', 'From Scotland' and 'For Afternoon Tea' displayed on three banners in the centre of the lid. And inside – along with papers yellowed at the edges, letters in faded italic script and old sepia photographs – was the marriage certificate. The marriage between one Robert Cox and one Maria Martilucci of Amalfi, Italy. The letters were in Italian and, as far as she could make out, from Maria's parents. She'd need to find someone to translate these for her, which would not be easy as the ink had faded from its original colour to a pale yellow and, in places, was indecipherable.

The photos, too, were faded. A young girl with long black hair, all dressed in white like a bride. Maria's first Mass, perhaps? And others of stiffly posed adults beside a large house, tiled and shuttered Italian-style. And a panorama of the sea, which was certainly nowhere around Newcastle. There was a man in some sort of uniform.

As well as the photographs there was a topaz ring, which Connie was now wearing on the ring finger of her right hand.

Connie's Uncle Bill, her mother's brother, and his wife, Aunt Lorna, had taken over when Connie was orphaned at five years old. They'd had four children of their own, so maybe The Box wasn't exactly a priority. 'Stick it in the attic for now,' they'd probably said.

As a result, Connie knew nothing about any box, or about her father's side of the family, other than that he had been an only child, had hailed from Newcastle, and appeared to have no living relatives.

And now, sixty-five years later, The Box had reappeared and Connie had discovered the marriage certificate and her Italian grandmother. An Italian grandmother! And that's when the ideas began to form in her head, ideas that she'd have time to pursue now that the floristry classes were coming to an end. She'd have time to dig deeper into her family's past; this Italian side of the family about which she knew nothing.

*

Connie had sold her car when she moved from Sussex. No need for a car in London, of course, and nowhere to park it, but she missed driving. Perhaps she should think about buying another one and driving down to Italy? She wouldn't be thinking about going to Italy at all if it wasn't for The Box. But, once she discovered what was in it, she couldn't leave it unexplored, so she'd have to go to Italy. But how long would that take and would she have the courage to do it? She supposed she could take her time, all summer if she wanted. The idea had germinated and started to grow.

Then, as she sat in the train heading towards Sussex for the weekend with Nick and the family, it suddenly screeched to a halt. 'Sorry, ladies and gentlemen.' The guard's voice could just about be heard through the fuzzy PA system. 'We've had to stop for a fallen branch across the line. We may be here a few minutes while they clear the obstruction.' There was a general moaning all round and Connie looked out of the window hoping to see the offending branch, but instead became aware for the first time of an enormous caravan dealership that bordered the railway line. She'd never noticed it before but on this occasion, the train being stationary, she was able to read the large banner which proclaimed: 'Special Deal on Motor Homes!' An omen, perhaps? Could she drive a motor home? No, of course not! Forget it!

But then again…

CHAPTER THREE

SOWING THE SEED

On one of her visits to Sussex, Connie told her son about her findings in The Box. Nick knew, as they all did, that she'd been orphaned when tiny and so knew precious little about her father's side of the family. At first Nick had seemed sceptical, unconvinced that the contents of The Box would lead anywhere. But she knew that he, more than the others, worried about her being alone in London. And he admitted to being a little concerned as to what she might get up to next.

'Surely you must have known about some of this before?'

'I only knew her name was Maria because I'd visited their grave up in Newcastle; Robert and Maria they were called. I never met them because they both died around the time I was born. The only information I've got really was from an old neighbour I tracked down when I was up there years ago. He told me my granddad had had a little market stall, somewhere near the docks.' Connie remembered the old boy who was only too eager to tell her about the flour, rice, spices and 'funny foreign things' her grandfather had had for sale. 'See,' he'd said, 'there were lots of foreigners around the docks in them days looking for olives and funny stuff like that.' But he'd made no mention of a foreign wife, funny or otherwise.

'And what I've discovered from The Box,' Connie went on, 'is that my enterprising grandfather had married one Maria Martilucci from somewhere near Amalfi in Italy! I'd love to go there and see if I can find some cousins. Wouldn't that be thrilling? Do you remember we drove along the Amalfi Coast years ago when you were tiny? *So* beautiful!'

'Mum,' Nick said with exaggerated patience. 'You do get carried away sometimes. After all, there must be millions of Martiluccis in Italy and how are you ever going to find out if any are related?'

Connie had little idea, but replied, 'I'd have a lot more chance of finding out in Italy than I ever would here.' And she was fascinated by the idea that some Latin blood might be coursing around in her veins. Surveying her grey-green eyes and less-than-lush eyelashes in her hand mirror, Connie felt a desperate need for some of that traditional Latin lusciousness: the dark eyes, the lustrous lashes and that thick dark hair which turned an interesting steel colour with maturity. Well, at least she had thick hair, although sometimes she had difficulty in remembering what colour it had once been underneath the highlights and lowlights. British brown, if she remembered rightly.

For the first time in decades, after forty-one years of marriage and four children, Connie McColl was free to do as she wished. She went out to Waterstones and bought a *Teach Yourself Italian* book and CD. And then wondered if easyJet or Ryanair flew to Naples. That would be the sensible way to get there. She listened to her Andrea Bocelli CD while pondering the possibilities. Could this be another adventure?

Connie spent Easter with Nick, Tess and the boys. And she spent a lot of that time daydreaming.

*

A week later Connie asked, 'Did you do anything nice over Easter?' as the three women settled themselves at a non-wobbly table near the pub window. It was almost warm enough to sit outside.

'Nah,' said Gill. 'Stayed with my daughter, the one who lives near Margate. Screaming kids everywhere.' She was wearing a too-short skirt and shoes with what looked like four-inch heels.

Maggie took a gulp of her wine. 'No, we didn't do much either. Ringer was out on business a lot of the time.' In contrast, Maggie was wearing jeans and trainers, topped with a purple fleece that drained her of what little colour she had.

Out on *business*, at Easter? Not for the first time Connie wondered about Maggie's partner and exactly what business he was in.

'What about you, Connie?'

'Oh, the usual. A couple of days with Nick and his family, then a day or two with my younger daughter, Lou, and her family. Love them all to bits, but exhausting.' And it was true. In the couple of years she'd been living in London she had definitely become much more tired much more easily. She didn't relish coming up to seventy, but there it was and, as they say, better than the alternative.

Maggie stared gloomily out of the window. 'I think I'm needing to shake up my life.'

The other two looked at her questioningly.

'What's wrong with your life then, Maggie?' Gill asked.

Maggie shrugged. 'It would appear I'm past my sell-by date. Being replaced by a newer model.'

'Oh, Maggie!' Connie and Gill spoke in unison.

Maggie took another large slurp. 'Yeah, well.'

'Men!' exclaimed Connie. 'Maybe it's time you found yourself a younger model too.'

'A toy-boy,' said Gill, 'but don't hold your breath, Maggie, 'cos I've been looking for years.'

'Ringer's five years younger than me anyway,' Maggie said, to no one in particular.

'Why's he called Ringer?' Gill asked.

'Well, he's William really, but his surname's Bell. So, Ringer Bell. That's another story. Not that he does much bell-ringing.' Maggie sniggered at the thought.

'Hardly a campanologist then,' scoffed Gill.

'More of an escapologist,' Maggie said drily.

Connie and Gill exchanged glances, both too embarrassed to ask Maggie exactly what she meant. Connie stared out of the window where an elderly couple were seated at a table on the pavement; he hidden from view by his outstretched edition of the *Sun*, while she gazed sadly into space. Marriage. *Some* marriages. Most marriages? Connie's marriage had been similar, jogging along from years of habit. ('Looks like rain, doesn't it?' 'Will you be golfing today, dear?')

'You're on your own, aren't you, Connie?' Maggie asked.

'Yes, divorced. Just got some money from the sale of the house and from a small inheritance but haven't decided what to do with it yet. I should, of course, be looking at somewhere to buy instead of paying rent.' Connie shrugged. 'I really must make my mind up what I'm going to do.'

'Surely,' said Gill, 'you can do anything you fancy.'

Connie grinned. 'You know what, Gill? You're absolutely right!' She looked out at the rain drumming against the window.

And what I fancy, Connie thought, is some sunshine.

Connie had finally succumbed to her urge and taken herself to have a wander round Get Moving, the motorhome dealership she'd spotted on the day the tree had shed its branch across the train line. She hadn't looked inside any sort of caravan for years, not since the newlywed Nick and Tess had taken themselves off to Spain in an ancient camper van nearly ten years ago.

'You'll hardly be able to stand up or move in that thing,' she'd remarked to her son, six foot two in his stockinged feet, and his well-upholstered wife.

'We plan to be lying down most of the time,' Nick had replied with a glint in his eye.

But these luxurious models were something else. Connie was bowled over by the clever designs, the proper kitchens, loos, showers and beds that popped out of nowhere. You could almost live in one full-time.

Kevin, the eager young salesman, was full of suggestions. 'And you could hang your bike on the bracket back there,' he said.

'My *bike*?' Connie squeaked.

'Well, why not?' Kevin didn't seem at all fazed by his mature customer.

'Why not indeed?' she said. 'But I couldn't afford one of these big new ones. I'd only want a little one for a holiday.'

'Ah, but we have some really affordable used models, Mrs McColl. Have you seen this beauty here? This is La Bellezza, *Italian*, finest model on the market. Four berths, full-sized oven, built-in microwave, nice shower, heating... and you get fantastic mileage. And fuel's cheaper in Europe, of course.'

'It's far too big for me.' Connie wished it wasn't, as it was an amazing motorhome at an almost affordable price. 'And it's left-hand drive as well. I wouldn't want that.'

'But what could be *better* if you're planning to drive on the continent? And it gives you plenty of room for all your stuff. I *know* you ladies like to take lots of clothes on holiday,' Kevin said, nudging her. He looked barely eighteen. 'One size bigger than this and you'd need a special licence to drive it. Hardly been used, has this. One owner, an old bloke and his missus, must have been in their seventies if they were a day. Off to the Costas they were, getting away for the winter and all that. Then, *what* does he go and do? Has a heart attack, that's what. *Kaput!*' He ran his finger across his chest to illustrate this fact. 'Left the old girl down there all on her own. And she couldn't even drive; some relative had to fly down and bring the thing back. It's a real bargain. Massive, innit? Bring your old man along to look at the engine.'

'I haven't got an old man any more, Kevin. The engine will be *my* concern.' Then she realised she might have spoken sharply when she saw his cheeks go pink. 'But I'd appreciate advice on the engine, of course. I'd have to bring my son along to give it the once-over.'

'No problem. The original brochure's in the drawer there, so take it with you if you like and take a few photos as well. Remember, this ain't going to hang around for long, bargain like this.'

'I'll bear that in mind,' Connie said.

Maggie, dark circles under her puffy eyes, had knocked back her large glass of Sauvignon before the other two had had more than a couple of sips.

'Is everything OK, Maggie?' Connie had got to know this nervous little woman well enough to realise that things probably weren't at all OK.

'Yeah, I'm all right.'

'Well, you don't *look* all right,' said Gill with her usual lack of subtlety. 'I suppose it's this Ringer bloke of yours?'

'He doesn't come home very much at the moment,' Maggie sighed.

'Leave him then,' said Gill. 'It's not as if you're married to him, are you?'

Maggie shook her head. 'But I don't know where I'd go.'

'You've got a son, haven't you?'

'He's in Melbourne. Can't exactly pop over there, can you?'

'Why not?' asked Connie. 'Couldn't he help you with the fare, perhaps?'

Maggie shrugged. 'It's not that so much as I'm scared of flying. Here, I'm going to have to have another glass of this – it's the best I've felt all day.'

'My treat,' said Connie. 'Let's all have another one! That's one advantage in not having a car any more.'

'Drunk and disorderly on the Tube instead,' said Gill. 'So what have you been up to, Connie?'

'Well, I've recently discovered an Italian grandmother I didn't know I had. Now I've got a fancy to go out to Italy to find out more about her, and to see if I have any distant cousins over there.'

'You'd better get booking your flight then,' Gill said. 'How long will you be away for?'

'Can't make up my mind at the moment.'

'I met a lovely Italian once,' Gill went on. 'He was called Fabio and he was bloody *gorgeous*. He had to go back home to Italy, but he said if I was ever in Rome I was to look him up.'

'I went to Sicily with Ringer once,' said Maggie. 'Years ago.'

Gill snorted. 'Why am I not surprised? He probably had to report to the Mafia.'

'He's not *that* bad,' Maggie snapped.

'I'm not sure if I'll even be booking a flight,' Connie said, twiddling her glass. 'I might *drive* down to Italy.'

'*Drive!* All that way!' Maggie exclaimed.

'Well, I'm in no hurry; as long as it takes.'

'But you haven't got a car,' Gill pointed out.

'True. But I'm half considering buying a motor caravan. I'd only need a little one. I've even been to look at a few.'

There was a stunned silence before Gill said, 'You'd have to be mad to drive one of those bleeding great things all the way down there on your own.'

'Well, it does worry me a bit but I'm sure I could manage. I *like* driving and I miss it.' Connie hoped she sounded more confident than she felt.

'What would you do if anything went wrong?' Gill asked. 'You'd be stuck there all by yourself.'

There was silence for a few moments before Maggie piped up. '*I'd* come with you, Connie.'

Connie couldn't believe she'd heard correctly. '*What?*'

'I'd come with you. I'm quite good with cars and things. I can change a tyre and do basic stuff on engines. I did a course once when I worked for a garage owner.'

'But it's a great big *bus-like* thing Connie's talking about,' Gill spluttered.

'Well, one engine's much like another.' Maggie seemed unconcerned. Connie couldn't imagine this equally elderly, slightly built, pale little woman doing anything much more strenuous than changing her bed linen.

'Why on earth would you want to go with Connie?' Gill was staring, open-mouthed, at Maggie.

'Because I need to get away and sort myself out,' Maggie said. 'Because it might be an adventure and it might be fun. Because I fancy some sunshine. How many more reasons would you like?' For a moment Maggie had come alive, her face lighting up at the prospect.

'Put like that,' Gill said, 'it doesn't seem such a bad idea.'

Connie, touched by her eagerness, considered this unlikely scenario. She was fond of Maggie but knew little about her, far less whether they could live in such close proximity for days or weeks on end. You'd have to know someone really well, like a husband (not hers, though) or a best friend. Even then it could become claustrophobic.

'Could I come too, then?' Gill was staring down at her drink as if afraid to meet the eyes of the other two.

Connie was beginning to think they must all be a bit deranged. Had they put something in the wine?

Maggie laughed. 'You've started something now, Connie! I bet you never guessed there were so many old bats raring to get to Italy! But why would *you* want to go, Gill?'

'Because I've a big birthday coming up – my *sixtieth*, you know? – and I don't want to be here with my family all duty-bound to give me crappy old lady type presents like bath salts and carpet slippers.'

'You don't look like a bath salts and slippers type of person at all,' said Connie, looking at Gill's layers of make-up and heavily mascaraed eyes. But *sixty* – who was she kidding? The woman was seventy if she was a day.

'Not to mention the fact that there are all these lovely blokes down there. And I'd so like to see Fabio again 'cos I dream about him still. And I've never been to Italy.'

Connie took a deep breath. 'You've certainly given me plenty to think about, ladies. But I haven't made any final plans yet.'

'Well, I can't wait a whole fortnight to find out,' said Gill. 'Couldn't we meet again next week? Will you have decided by then, Connie?'

'Possibly. Maybe. I've no idea. But anyway, why not? No reason why we shouldn't come here again next Thursday – same time, if that's OK?' Connie decided not to mention that she could think of little else.

'OK,' said Gill.

'Fair enough,' said Maggie.

It was too early to raise their hopes, but Connie was becoming increasingly excited at the idea.

CHAPTER FOUR

GERMINATION

Connie tossed and turned, unable to sleep. She envisaged Paris and Nice and Florence and Rome. And Amalfi, of course. But, on her *own*? Surely she'd need someone with whom to share these sights and delights? Someone to look out for road signs and give directions, and perhaps change a tyre – although she couldn't for the life of her imagine Maggie jacking up a motorhome! For herself, of course, she'd only need a little vehicle, with a bed, a mini-cooker, a shower and some sort of loo perhaps. Nothing too expensive either, because she really should be looking to buy bricks and mortar instead of renting Di's flat, even if it *was* only a token amount. She supposed she could sell the motorhome on her return for not far short of what she'd paid for it, providing she could get it to Italy and back in one piece. And there *was* that inheritance from her friend Jeannie, who, Connie felt sure, would approve of such a purchase for what could be an exciting adventure.

For three of them she'd need something much larger, of course, like La Bellezza. She'd looked it up; it meant 'the beauty', and it *was* a beauty. It had stolen her heart, and it was Italian, surely yet another pointer in the right direction. And left-hand drive, so ideal for France and Italy if not for England. It was designed for at least four people, which probably meant a couple and kids. But perhaps she should just go and have another peep at it – not to buy it or anything… Should she take Maggie and Gill along to look at it too? No, no, what *was* she thinking of! Dear Lord, she hardly knew them!

At three o'clock she gave up trying to sleep, got up and made some tea. She studied La Bellezza's original brochure, which she'd taken from the kitchen drawer, while she drank the tea, and then had another look at the photos on her mobile. The brochure was full of details and the photographs were lovely. She had to admit that she'd fallen in love with a big, beautiful Italian. La Bellezza!

Then she considered fuel, and tax and insurance. At sixty-nine the premiums would probably be sky-high. Well, there was no denying that it would be good to share the running costs but, while she might be able to get along with the mild-mannered Maggie, could she cope with Gill? And she could hardly now agree to let Maggie come along without extending the invitation to Gill.

Connie went back to bed and managed to drift off for half an hour before she awoke yet again to thoughts of La Bellezza and her two unlikely passengers. It would be far more sensible to go for the smallest motorhome available and set off on her own. She needn't even tell the other two because it wasn't as if they were close friends. Or, more sensible still, get on an aeroplane, like any normal, sensible person would do. But, thought Connie, I damned well don't want to be sensible! And, because I'm not getting any younger, if I'm going to have another adventure, now's the time!

*

'Gosh! It's *enormous*!' Connie had never seen Maggie so animated.

'Easy to drive and easy to park though,' gushed Kevin, opening the door with a flourish. 'Every mod con you can think of, ladies!' He stood back to let them enter. Give him his due, thought Connie, Kevin did not appear to be daunted at the prospect of three elderly ladies as customers. But, after the Spanish incident, he probably reckoned he'd soon have La Bellezza back on the forecourt yet again for resale. ('Like new, only got as far as Nice, these three old birds!')

'Will you just look at that kitchen!' Gill was opening and closing doors, her elaborate hairdo brushing the ceiling.

'There's probably room for a dishwasher,' said Kevin.

'We wouldn't plan on doing much dishwashing,' said Connie.

'I wouldn't mind; I quite like washing dishes,' said Maggie. This woman was plainly a saint.

'Or a washing machine,' Kevin added, warming to his subject.

'We'd use laundrettes,' Connie said, sitting down on a surprisingly comfortable sofa that, at the pull of a lever, became a nice big bed. Hers, for sure.

'Anyway, we could always wash our smalls in the sink,' Maggie said.

Gill had got as far as the shower. 'I could just about fit in there if I don't put on any more weight.' She patted her enormous bosoms.

Maggie giggled. 'Oh, look, bunk beds!' The beds were installed across the width of the rear of the motorhome.

'Ah, yes, but they're a good size and *very* comfortable.' Kevin patted the lower mattress. 'Go on, lie on that! Isn't it comfy?'

Maggie obeyed, stretching out with relish. 'Och, it is – really, really comfy.'

'And who, exactly, would be sleeping on that *top* bunk?' asked Gill, turning to Connie, who was peering over her shoulder.

'Not me,' said Connie.

'And not me,' said Gill.

Maggie sat up with care to avoid hitting her head. 'I don't mind,' she said. 'I'm the smallest and probably the lightest. There's even a wee ladder there, look!'

No doubting it, this woman was definitely a saint.

'Lots of cupboard space,' Kevin enthused, sliding back a wardrobe door.

'Och, we wouldn't be needing many clothes,' said Maggie, who was also fast becoming a salesman's dream.

'Speak for yourself!' Gill was exploring the large space underneath the lower bunk.

Kevin, in the meantime, was heading towards the front of the living area.

'Now,' he said, 'the driver's seat and the passenger seat both swivel right the way round. Two great armchairs!' Click, click. 'See?'

'Lovely!'

'Right, now I'll leave you ladies to potter around a bit, and I'll be over in the office when you're ready.'

'Is he expecting you to buy it today then?' asked Gill when he was out of earshot.

'Probably,' Connie replied. 'But I'm not buying it until Nick, my son, gives it the once-over. He's got a friend who knows a thing or two about engines.'

'Well, *I* think it's just lovely,' said Saint Maggie.

*

Nick McColl walked round La Bellezza, tapping at wheels and opening up the storages for gas, water and sewage. 'You'll have to empty this every chance you get,' he informed his mother. 'Otherwise it'll stink to high heaven. Especially in the heat.' He wrinkled his nose. 'Although I believe these days the contents turn into little brickettes or something for disposal.'

So far they hadn't been able to prise his friend, Geoff, away from the engine.

'Like new!' he said. 'Top-notch Italian engineering. Can't have done many miles.' He was eventually persuaded to sit inside to check the dashboard. 'Only a few thousand – I thought as much! This thing's hardly run in. How much are they asking for it? Hmm, I think we can get them down a bit on that. Not everyone round here wants a left-hand drive.'

They crossed to the office to meet Kevin and his portly boss, who'd appeared from nowhere.

'Can I offer you a cup of tea? Coffee? Something stronger, perhaps? See what's in the cupboard, Kevin.'

There were polite refusals all round and Connie decided to let Geoff do the haggling since she had no idea how much the vehicle should cost. But she was indeed a beauty. She'd call her 'Bella' for short; 'beautiful'. And she'd certainly like a thousand or two off the price.

Not only did Geoff get the price reduced by a whole five grand but he also explained the finer points about the engine and the controls, and offered to accompany Connie for a trial run to see how she felt about driving and manoeuvring such a monster.

Nick was less enthusiastic about the proposed excursion. 'It's a long way to go with two women you hardly know. And for nothing definite.'

'But it *wouldn't* be for nothing, Nick. I love Italy, and I'd love to see where my grandmother came from. Plus, we'll have an adventure. And enjoy ourselves. Get away from it all. Chase the sun.'

As she spoke, Connie realised this was what she really wanted to do. What had begun as purely research into her family tree was now poised to become an adventure. Another adventure!

Nick put his arm round his mother. 'I've got to hand it to you, Mum, you'll have a go at anything! But, three old birds in a camper van – you couldn't make it up!'

*

Gill's oldest daughter, Marlene, was studying her mother with disbelief. 'Why can't you just go on a nice package holiday like everyone else? Who *is* this Connie anyway?'

'She did the flower-arranging classes. Nice woman.'

'*Mad* woman, more like.' Marlene plonked herself down at the kitchen table and sipped her mug of tea. 'An old woman you hardly know driving a great big caravan. Bloody bonkers.'

'It's not a caravan, it's a motorhome, and Connie's had a test drive and can handle it just fine.'

'She probably can in some quiet backwater round here, but what about them roads in France and Italy? Have you seen the way them crazy Eye-ties drive?'

'No, and neither have you, except on the telly. I'm sure she'll cope and, anyway, we'll just take our time.'

'And what's with *Italy* anyway? What's wrong with Spain? You always go to Spain, Mum. I mean, they all speak English in Spain and you can get proper English nosh.'

'Well, then, it's time for a change. And I've never been to Italy.' Gill thought fondly of Fabio in Rome with visions of them both splashing about in that fountain – whatever it was called – and walking round the Colosseum by moonlight. She wondered if she should write to inform him of her intended visit. But she hadn't heard from him in years, so he'd probably moved. And anyway, better not, just in case they didn't get that far.

'And what about your birthday party, Mum? Bloomin' heck, we've all been planning the thing for months.'

'I *told* you I didn't want a party. I told you time and time again, but you've all got this bee in your bonnets. Anyway you can forget it 'cos we should just about have reached Italy by then. I'll have my tablet with me, so you can all send me them e-cards, or whatever they're called.'

'And you'll never be able to get all that clobber of yours into a caravan,' Marlene went on.

'It's not a caravan—'

'And all your make-up and hair stuff. How'll you survive without Henri doing your roots every other week – tell me that?'

Gill hadn't thought this through properly at all, but she wasn't going to admit as much to Marlene.

'They've got great hairdressers in France and Italy. Most stylish countries in the world,' she retorted.

Gill had had Marlene when she was eighteen. She'd been Gilly Sykes then, a plain child from a large family of better-looking siblings. When the time came to revamp herself with the aid of make-up and bleach, she was the first girl in Basildon to wear a miniskirt; the shortest and tightest into which she could squeeze her ample bottom. That, along with her magnificent boobs, meant that she became popular with the boys for all the wrong reasons and, as the pill was not yet available, the inevitable happened. With guns in their backs, she and the reluctant father headed to the registry office. There followed three years of noisy dissension in a scruffy north London bedsit before Harold came along with his camelhair coat with the velvet collar and his second-hand cars. They had two boys before Harold took himself off to Marbella with a redheaded stripper from Shoreditch. Life was tough until Gill married Peter, a master baker, who took on these three children and put a semi-detached roof over their heads. She went from the breadline to the bun-line, her figure happily expanding to accommodate the freshly baked croissants, bagels and brioches, plus three more pregnancies. But here, at last, was a good guy. She was devastated when he died from cancer at only fifty-five but, for the first time in her life, Gill now had some money to spend on herself and to be able to pay weekly visits to the hairdresser and the nail bar.

But she discovered that the older she became, the more these men of her own age appeared to be seeking a cook-cum-housekeeper-cum-nursemaid to see them through their dotage, and she was certainly having none of that. She'd brought up six kids and looked after three men and now it was Gill Time.

So she did the only sensible thing: she took up bingo and flower-arranging, had 'love never dies' tattooed on her upper arm, and began fancying men twenty years younger.

*

Maggie hadn't felt so excited in years. As she looked through her meagre summer wardrobe she decided it would be easy to travel light; she was hardly high maintenance at the best of times. Most of all, she needed to get away from Ringer. Perhaps *then* he'd miss her. Oh, *who* was she kidding! She hardly saw him these days and she was probably about to be replaced by the blonde bimbo. After all, with one breast and faded looks, what did *she* have to offer? But, damn it, he *owed* her. She'd stood by him, even after the jail sentences and the shady deals, and the police hammering on the door at midnight. And now he seemed to be forgetting all that and Maggie was becoming angry.

She'd tell him only that she was going on a touring holiday, but give no details. After all, what's sauce for the goose... Anyway, she had little idea exactly where she might be going.

*

As Connie had nowhere to park Bella in London, she was grateful when Nick offered to keep the motorhome in his drive until they were ready to leave. It also allowed her to make regular pilgrimages to Sussex to clean and polish, and to stock up with new bed linen, plus crockery and cutlery from the charity shops. It was already beginning to look like home.

Next week Gill and Maggie would accompany her to start loading up their stuff and the following week would be the beginning of June and the beginning of their adventure. She was becoming more and more confident at the wheel too, having taken Bella to

Brighton and back on her own. The left-hand drive felt awkward, although it would certainly come into its own across the Channel, but otherwise it was surprisingly easy to handle and the elevated position of the driving seat provided unbroken all-round views.

Connie's younger daughter appeared as she was cleaning the toilet. If anyone was going to cast doubts on this adventure, it would be Lou – unlike Di, who not only approved of her mother's escapades, but actually encouraged them.

'Are you *sure* you know what you're doing, Mum?'

'Yeah, I'm cleaning the toilet.' She refrained from calling it the loo.

Lou sighed. 'You know perfectly well what I mean – all the way to Italy in a tin can to find non-existent relatives.'

'Well, I'm sure I'll find something.' Connie straightened up and pecked her daughter on the cheek. 'How's Charlotte and her new baby sister?'

'They're fine. Andy's home today so I came over to see if I could help. Dad, of course, thinks you've gone bonkers.'

'Dad would.' Since Roger hadn't understood her in forty-one years of marriage, there was little chance he'd start now. She hadn't seen him much since the divorce. And she felt, in her bones, that Lou still believed the marriage had crumbled because her mother had taken herself off for a few weeks. Unlike her siblings, Lou flatly refused to believe what had really transpired, finding it impossible to imagine how her parents had suddenly found themselves incompatible after so many years of marriage.

'Well, it was bad enough you taking off all round the country for weeks on end, but this is even crazier.'

'I had a lovely time then and I intend to have a lovely time again. Would you pass me the bleach – it's on the floor behind you.'

'I must say this is all looking very nice. Very compact. But Nick says you hardly know these women. Not like they're lifelong friends or anything.'

Connie placed the bleach into the tiny cupboard and straightened up. 'We're only going to Italy. I'm not marrying them.'

'What if—'

'What if we don't get on? Then I'll send them home and carry on solo. Would you like a cup of tea?'

CHAPTER FIVE

DEPARTURE

Don turned up with a magnum of champagne the day after she emailed him to let him know she was going to be away for a few weeks. Connie had met Don on her 'liberation' trip. He was ten years younger than she was and very *very* sexy – a terrific lover but lousy husband material. Still, you can't have it all, so just as well she wasn't looking for another husband. Tall, dark and handsome; an overused cliché, Connie thought, but that's *exactly* what he was. He was nearly sixty now but his hair was still dark, with interesting grey bits at the sides. She was pretty sure he didn't dye it because, surprisingly enough for such a good-looking man, he wasn't particularly vain.

It wasn't just his looks either, or his great charm. He *listened!* He actually seemed interested in what she had to say and then *remembered* it. A unique specimen of manhood. He was a retired airline pilot, and Connie reckoned he must have made many air stewardesses very happy indeed. It hadn't made either of his two wives particularly happy though and now, twice divorced, he had no intention of being tied down again. He'd certainly enlivened the second half of her trip.

She was surprised at the immediacy of his visit and wondered briefly if it had been wise to tell him of her plans.

'Don't tell me I'm mad,' Connie greeted him, 'because, for certain, most of my family think I'm nuts.'

'I don't think you're nuts at all,' he replied, uncorking the champagne. 'It's what I've come to expect of you. You were never likely to be sitting around with your knitting or your cocoa, or your Saga bloody holiday.'

'Send all geriatrics abroad – isn't that what Saga means? Well, I am going abroad but I still don't think I'm really *ready* to be old.'

He handed her a glass of fizz and Connie noted yet again his beautifully shaped hands and nicely manicured nails.

'And I don't think you ever will be,' he said with a little sigh. 'Well, at least let me drive you and your friends down to Sussex.'

'No thanks, Don, really. I need today to myself to get ready and then tomorrow morning we'll get the train. It won't do us any harm to get used to roughing it.' It was a shame really, because the other two would be well impressed, Gill in particular.

'*Roughing* it!' he exclaimed, picking up the brochure. 'I've lived in flats with fewer facilities than that thing!'

Soon, she thought, I shall set off like a giant snail with my house on my back. But even the snail has the sense to travel solo, not share its precious space with two comparative strangers.

'Perhaps,' he said, 'I might pop out and join you somewhere. Rome, maybe. That's if I can push my way through a queue of Italian admirers!'

Rome! Will we ever get that far? she wondered.

'That would be nice,' she said vaguely.

After Don had left she wondered if she shouldn't have been more appreciative of his offer to drive, and also to meet up with her in Rome. He was a ladies' man, but nevertheless he was a good friend. And an excellent lover. And he'd stolen a tiny bit of her heart. But she wouldn't be holding her breath about him appearing in Rome.

Then Di had appeared with an electric kettle and an enormous box of teabags. 'These are Waitrose's poshest. And you'll be able to use the kettle whenever you plug in to some electricity, Mum. Remember, you won't be able to get decent tea over there.'

Of her three surviving children, Di was – as always – the most supportive and enthusiastic.

'Go for it, Mum!' she'd said when Connie informed her of the plan. 'I hope to God I'll be having adventures too when I'm coming up to seventy. And don't worry, the flat will still be here for you when you get back, and don't come back until you're good and ready!'

Connie had also received a card from her ex-husband. 'I hear you're off again,' Roger wrote in his careful italic script. 'Haven't you "found" yourself yet?' It was precisely because she had 'found herself' that she was free to go where she liked and do what she wanted. Connie sometimes wished that all this had happened years earlier but, never mind, she was still only sixty-nine and, thank God, relatively fit. Was the world her oyster? Silly cliché, that! The world was much more like the carrot, dangling seductively in front of her nose.

She was ready to go.

She'd packed most of her stuff into Bella already: the torches, the spare batteries, a set of screwdrivers, the first-aid kit, her Kindle loaded up with books to read, and CDs to play on the state-of-the-art sound system. She'd chosen an eclectic mix, unsure of the others' preferences but well stocked up with Andrea Bocelli. She'd always loved Italian opera but it wasn't until she'd accompanied Di to his concert at the O2 a couple of years back that she became a dedicated fan of the popular tenor. As she listened to 'Una Furtiva Lagrima', the urge to get to Italy grew stronger and stronger. She wouldn't be shedding any tears, furtive or otherwise! On the contrary she was becoming more and more excited, if a little nervous at times at the prospect of everything that might go wrong. 'Connie McColl,' she told herself, 'think positive! You're made of tough stuff, you won't be alone, you'll cope and you'll have fun!'

*

Gill positioned herself in front of her well-lit mirror in preparation for her night-time routine. She undid her hair and set it on large rollers; she cleansed; she toned; she moisturised her face; and then she shaved her legs. She nicked her shin as usual and stopped the flow with a bit of tissue. Tomorrow was a special day. They were meeting at Connie's flat at 7 a.m. to catch an early train from Waterloo, settle themselves into the motorhome, and then be on the ferry at Portsmouth by lunchtime.

She'd already deposited most of her clothes in the vehicle, taking up three-quarters of the storage space allotted to her and Maggie. Fortunately Maggie didn't appear to be bringing much, and Connie had her own wardrobe space at the front. Now, somehow or other, she had to cram all the toiletries, make-up and hair stuff into one little bag. How was someone her age supposed to survive without the hair colour, the eyelash curlers, the cleansing masks, the serums and all the rest? For sure no one had seen her make-up free in years. She found some eyebrow dye and shoved that into the bag too.

Not for the first time she wondered how she'd survive in a glorified caravan, sleeping in a bunk bed with a nutty Scotswoman overhead and bossy Connie at the helm. Her family was right: she must be crazy. Not only that, it was already costing a small fortune in holiday insurance and driving insurance. Connie had insisted on that because, although she herself was going to be doing most of the driving, what if she became ill or had an accident? But Gill hadn't driven much in the past forty years, and didn't intend to start again now on the wrong side of a vehicle the size of a bus, and on the wrong side of the road to boot. But in spite of her doubts she was humming to herself, 'We're all going on a summer holiday' – how she'd loved Cliff Richard in that film!

She set her alarm for 5.30 a.m. but didn't expect to sleep much. Let's face it, she thought, I'm excited. More excited than I've been in years.

*

Maggie hadn't seen Ringer for days, but he reappeared as she was packing her bag.

When she told him that she was leaving the following morning on her touring holiday, he yawned and said, 'That's nice. How long will you be away?'

Maggie had no idea. 'Oh, some weeks. I'll text you.'

'Yeah, you do that.'

She felt tears prickling behind her eyes. Damned if she was going to cry, but he hadn't even *asked* who she was going with, or where, or if he was even bothered about her going without him, all of which would have been unthinkable even a year ago.

'I'm out tonight, babe. Probably back in the wee small hours. What time are you leaving?'

'I'm leaving here just after six in the morning.'

'Six! My God! Well, you'll have to wake me up to say goodbye if I'm back by then.' He was fidgety and preoccupied which probably meant he'd got a job lined up. 'I won't disturb you then when I get back; best if I sleep in the spare room.'

It had been a while since he'd been out on a job and Maggie wondered what he was up to. He'd be needing money to spend on the blonde bimbo, damn her. He'd also taken to the spare room a lot lately and Maggie felt another alien wave of anger. After giving up thirty-eight years of her life to this man, she suspected she was now being discarded like an old pair of slippers.

She finished her solitary supper, washed up and watched an hour of *Big Brother*, then went to bed, aware of her early start in the morning. But sleep eluded her as she tossed and turned and tried to keep her mind blank. Still awake at 4 a.m., she was almost ready to get up to make herself a hot drink when she heard Ringer coming in and shuffling around in the kitchen.

He wasn't one for being domesticated at the best of times so she wondered what he was doing as she heard cupboard doors being opened and closed – even the *oven* door. She was sure it wasn't for cooking. Then she heard him close the spare room door behind him and, after about ten minutes, the sound of his snoring reverberated through the wall.

She got up quietly, taking only a few minutes to get ready and then, picking up her passport and her nearly empty holdall, tiptoed into the kitchen. She'd drink coffee until it was time to go. After she filled the kettle she checked the cupboards to see what Ringer might have been looking for but nothing seemed to be out of place.

Maggie sat down with her coffee. Ringer had been on a job last night, she was sure of that. She was almost ready to leave when she remembered the oven; she'd heard him opening it. She herself was the one who'd suggested the oven as a good 'holding point'.

A canvas bag filled the entire interior, and it was a *big* oven. Maggie eased it out gently and undid the zip, staring at the used notes – wads and wads and wads of them. Must be thousands and thousands, she thought. Why shouldn't *she* have some of that? Come to think of it, why shouldn't she have *all* of it? If he wanted her out of his life, he could damned well pay for it. As far as Maggie was concerned this was a divorce settlement; she was his common law wife after all. She needed some acknowledgement of all the years she'd stood by him, the trials, the prison visits, the time spent on her own waiting for his release. Yes, he owed her, and now she was going to collect. She jammed as many notes as she could carry into her holdall and then, as an afterthought, got a backpack from the hallway and stuffed that full too. Just as well she'd been travelling light in the first place. She hadn't left much for the two-timing bastard – but why, she thought, should I leave any at all? She lifted up her T-shirt, removed her prosthetic breast and filled the space in her bra with two wads of tenners. Then she replaced the empty canvas bag back into the oven.

Terrified he might wake up, she took a quick look round, picked up both the bags and left, closing the door quietly behind her. Maggie knew there would be no going back, not now. She'd often wondered if she'd ever have the courage to leave, but now she knew she had because that was exactly what she was doing.

*

Connie looked at the clock. Five to seven. There was just time for a quick check round the flat. Had she unplugged the fridge, turned off the gas and ensured there were no marks on Di's gleaming worktops? The other two would be here any minute.

First to arrive was Gill, fully made up and coiffed even at this unearthly hour, with an enormous bag. 'Oh, just a few last-minute bits and pieces.'

Five minutes later Maggie, supposedly travelling light, staggered in with a holdall and a backpack bulging at the seams.

'That looks heavy, Maggie.' Connie was concerned for her fragile friend. 'Can I help you carry something?'

'No, no, I'm fine,' Maggie replied, gripping all the handles tightly as they left the flat.

'Has Ringer given you some farewell goodies then?' Gill asked.

'You could say that,' Maggie replied.

Connie felt choked at saying goodbye to her family. Nick and Tess presented her with two bottles of Bombay Sapphire gin while Tom and Josh, aged seven and five, had made her a brightly coloured 'Good Luck' card and were worried about when Grandma would be coming back.

'Will she be away a long time, like before?' Tom sounded anxious.

'No, she won't be away too long, *will* you, Mother?' said Nick.

And then Lou had appeared with the two little girls and a large lasagne and a bag of salad. 'You'll need something to stick in the oven this evening, wherever you get to,' she said, leaving Connie feeling tearful, and not a little apprehensive, as she drove away.

Connie would have preferred Maggie to be in the passenger seat as they headed towards Portsmouth. But Maggie had been reluctant to move from the rear.

'I just need to reorganise my things,' she said. 'I'll sit up front later.'

'I wonder what's got into *her*?' murmured Gill as she fastened her seatbelt. 'She said she didn't have much stuff.'

Then Maggie had seemed hell-bent on staying in the motorhome for the crossing.

'You can't stay down here, Maggie,' said Connie, as they parked nose to tail among countless caravans and motorhomes on the car deck of the ferry. 'They don't allow it. You've got to come up and they'll call us when it's time to come back.'

When they eventually persuaded her out, Maggie got herself into a complete tizz about locking the doors.

'Are you *sure* they're all securely locked?' she asked Connie for the umpteenth time.

'Yes, of *course* they're all locked,' Connie replied. She demonstrated the handles. 'See?'

Maggie's air of preoccupation continued above deck when Gill asked her what sort of coffee she wanted.

'Coffee?'

'Yes, coffee. You know, dark brown stuff, comes in a cup, with or without milk and sugar?'

'Oh, sorry. Yes, just with milk, please.'

'Grab a table then.' As the other two joined the queue Gill asked, 'What's got into her? She's gone all peculiar.'

'I expect it's something to do with that Ringer,' said Connie.

When they finished their coffee, Connie persuaded them to come up on deck. 'Come on!' she said. 'Let's wave goodbye to Blighty; it'll be a few weeks before we see her again!'

Connie felt an almost childish surge of excitement as the ferry left Portsmouth harbour and made its way past the Isle of Wight. They were finally on their way – Le Havre, France, Italy!

'We'll just have a snack,' she said to the other two, 'as we have Lou's lasagne to eat later and we can't afford to be splashing out before we even get to France.'

'Why don't I treat us?' Maggie said, as she returned from the currency exchange with a large wad of euros.

'Why would you do that?' Gill asked. 'We agreed to split costs, didn't we?'

'Yes,' Maggie went on, 'but I'd like to, 'cos I've just had a little windfall.'

'A windfall?' asked Connie.

'How little?' asked Gill.

'Oh, quite a bit.' Maggie was studying her nails with sudden interest.

'What – you've not won the lottery?' Gill laughed.

'Well, not exactly.'

'Oh, was it a scratch-card then?'

'Yes, that's it. A scratch-card.' Maggie looked relieved.

Connie and Gill exchanged looks before Gill asked, 'So why on earth didn't you tell us earlier?'

Maggie shrugged. 'I didn't like to. Anyway,' she said, 'we'll be able to have a few wee treats. Now, anyone want to come with me to look at the shop? I'm completely out of perfume.'

The crossing was relatively smooth but not warm enough, in Connie's opinion, to sit on deck. While Maggie and Gill wandered off to explore the boat's facilities, Connie bought a newspaper and found a seat. She glanced at the headlines but, after a few minutes, gave up trying to concentrate, her mind suddenly full of what-ifs and whys. What if, at this late age, she found she couldn't cope with driving on the right again? What if they couldn't find somewhere to park tonight? After all, they hadn't pre-booked anything anywhere. What if she had problems reversing Bella and hit something? Why had she made herself responsible for transporting two women she hardly knew across half of Europe?

I'm a positive person, Connie thought. I'll be all right. I'll cope. And I've got The Box with me, to remind me of why I'm making this pilgrimage. If my grandmother, Maria, was alive surely she'd want me to do this, to visit her birthplace, to try to find out about her life before she came to Newcastle? She wondered if Maria's parents had ever got over the shock of their daughter marrying a foreigner, leaving their shores and probably never seeing her again.

And then there was the ring. It was a stunning topaz, a magnificent orange with pink undertones, set in a plain gold band.

She'd taken the ring to a jeweller, as at first she hadn't been entirely sure what the stone was. An imperial topaz, she was told, the best kind. Apparently the ancient Romans associated this gem with the sun god, giving it the power to protect and heal. And it was a November birthstone. Did Maria have a November birthday? Well, if she didn't, Connie did!

'*There* you are!' Gill had reappeared. 'Maggie's just treated me to some perfume! And, guess what, we can see the coast of France!'

Connie folded up her newspaper and her daydreams. 'That's good.'

'Maggie's gone to the loo, but she'll be here in a minute. Oh, Connie, I'm beginning to feel really excited! We're actually *doing* this!'

'Yes, we're actually doing it,' Connie agreed with some feeling, as she viewed the French coast from the window alongside her chair.

Maggie sat inside the toilet cubicle and contemplated what she'd done. Now she needed time to herself, to reflect and to wonder how Ringer might be reacting. He was most likely going ballistic. She should spend as much of the money as possible, just in case he *should* come after them – although that was highly unlikely, because how would he know where they were going when she didn't know herself! But Maggie had never had this kind of money to spend on herself before and she was going to enjoy every minute of it, although she was no fool and knew she had to hold enough back to make some kind of future for herself, because she certainly wouldn't be returning to Ringer. There must be enough hidden away to make for some sort of escape. But, in the meantime, she'd stick with the scratch-card story and enjoy spending.

It was good of Connie to let her come along and Maggie wanted to treat her. Gill, on the other hand, was a silly old boot, but harmless enough, and Maggie thought the biggest favour she could do for her was to try to persuade her to visit a hairdresser, probably in Paris. She'd treated Gill to some perfume to add to the collection of assorted cosmetics and treatments in the drawer beneath the lower bunk. She only hoped Gill didn't snore.

It was none too warm but Gill decided to go back on deck to watch the rapidly approaching French coastline. She was the only one who seemed genuinely excited; there was Connie looking at her newspaper, and Maggie in the loo or somewhere when they should be out here, excited like her. This adventure had certainly got off to a good start, with Maggie treating her to that lovely bottle of Obsession. And tonight they'd be camping on French soil, which was another new experience. Gill had been to Malaga several times, but that was different. You got on a plane, looked down at the clouds for a couple of hours, and then you were there. Very nice it was too, but you didn't see much in between. Now they were going to see every stone on the road and probably experience the French lifestyle! And then there was Italy, and all those good-looking, dapper men! She'd feel like the proverbial child let loose in the sweet shop! Quite different from your two-week package where the only people you met were other Brits, all looking for sunbeds and fish and chips.

Gosh, she thought, I haven't set foot in France yet and already I'm feeling this is where I'm meant to be!

CHAPTER SIX

LA BELLE FRANCE

Connie squinted against the late afternoon sun, gripping the steering wheel and concentrating hard on the road ahead. It was several years since she'd driven on the right and it took a bit of getting used to again, although it was definitely an advantage having a left-hand drive vehicle.

'Keep right, Connie! *Right*-hand lane, over *there*!' ordered Gill, the navigator, from her sea of assorted maps. The satnav lady was, in the meantime, doling out instructions in the background.

'Inside? Outside? Nearside? Offside? I can never remember which is which at home, far less over here.' Connie was beginning to feel stressed, hemmed in by the heavy crawl of traffic leaving the ferry at Le Havre. She'd feel more relaxed when the traffic thinned and she was on their chosen route which, hopefully, would get them somewhere to the east of Paris.

'Get into that middle lane *now*!' ordered Gill a little further on. As Connie obeyed, Gill asked, 'What the hell is Maggie still *doing* back there?'

'Goodness knows. Something's definitely up with her. We'll find out when we stop for the night, which'll be soon, I hope. It's been a long day.'

'I wonder how much money she won on that scratch-card?'

'I don't know. But why would she be so peculiar about it, and why didn't she tell us earlier?'

'You'd have thought she'd have been bursting to tell us news like that; I know I would!' Gill pointed towards the right. 'There's the sign for Paris off to the right! We're heading the right way, yippee!'

'Good navigating,' said Connie.

'Great satnav,' said Gill.

Andrea Bocelli was singing 'Canto della Terra'.

'You like this sort of stuff?' Gill asked, prodding the CD player.

'I *love* this sort of stuff,' Connie replied.

Nearly two hours later a little voice from the rear announced, 'I've just seen a sign for camping ahead. About four kilometres, I think it said.'

'How far is that in miles?' Connie shouted back.

'No idea, but it doesn't sound far.'

Sure enough, about two miles further on there was a large 'Camping' sign pointing to an exit road.

'Here we are!' yelled Connie, turning off. 'Let's just hope they've got a pitch for us. Thanks so much for your navigational skills, Gill, you've been a treasure.'

'Are you knackered?' Gill asked as she folded up some of the maps.

'Pretty much. It's been really hard work driving this great big thing, *and* on the wrong side of the road.'

Le patron had an office at the entrance to the park which, at first glance, appeared full, with caravans, motorhomes and camper vans packed in regimental rows.

'Bonsoir! Alors, I 'ave one space just for you. For 'ow many nights?' The balding proprietor wore his few wisps of grey hair neatly tied back in a ponytail, had a droopy moustache and sported a badge proclaiming his name to be Raoul.

Connie looked at Gill. 'What do you think – two nights? Three?'

'Why not? Make it three.'

Maggie had suddenly appeared and was leaning over Connie's seat. 'This is a nice out of the way sort of place, off the beaten track. No one would look for us here, would they?'

'Why on earth would anyone be looking for us?'

'Oh, they wouldn't – I just meant we all said we wanted to get away from it all, didn't we? Anyway, let me pay.'

'There's no need, Maggie...' Connie began.

'No, I insist.' With that Maggie withdrew a bundle of euro notes from her shoulder bag. Raoul, pocketing the cash, said, 'Come, Mesdames!' and led them round the corner into a further park where Connie surveyed, with some trepidation, a space between a British camper van and a German caravan.

'Voila! And, over here' – Raoul indicated a large building about a hundred yards away – 'we 'ave ze toilets, and ze showers and ze shop. All for you!'

'Merci!' said Maggie, suddenly animated.

Connie backed carefully into the space and turned off the ignition with relief. 'So far, so good. That'll give us two clear days here. Paris, here we come!'

'How will we get there?' Gill asked.

'We'll find a bus, that's what we'll do. I'm not driving this thing up the Champs-Élysées, I can tell you.'

'We could have a taxi,' Maggie put in.

'A taxi! Blimey, Mags, just how big was this windfall of yours?' asked Gill.

Ignoring the question, Maggie said, 'I'm heading straight for that loo over there and then I'm going to shower.'

'Great idea,' said Connie as she plugged into the power supply. 'I'll do the same and then we can sit down with some gin and tonics and put the lasagne in the oven. Voila – we 'ave ze electricity.'

It was quite late and so they had the showers to themselves. It was dark by the time they finally emerged, and then Connie pulled down the blinds and popped the lasagne into the oven.

'Now,' she said, 'this loo here is only to be used for emergencies and for wees during the night. At all other times we use any toilets we can find, even if it's in a field or a hedge, or whatever. I really don't fancy emptying that tank too often.'

They nodded in agreement as Gill dispensed the drinks and Maggie arranged the salad in a glass bowl.

'It's damned hot,' stated Gill, fanning herself with one of Raoul's publicity brochures. They'd left the door wide open, but there was little movement of air.

'We'll sleep with the windows open,' said Connie.

Maggie was looking anxious again. 'Will that be safe?'

'Will *what* be safe?' Gill had turned on her. 'Do you honestly think someone is going to squeeze through these windows to ravage us three old girls? Get real!'

Maggie put down her glass. 'We'll keep the door locked at night though, won't we?'

'Yes, of course.' Connie studied her for a moment. 'Are you carrying a *lot* of money then, Maggie?'

'Well, yes, a few pounds.'

'How *many* pounds exactly?' asked Gill.

Maggie swallowed. 'Well, about a hundred thousand.'

'*What?*' Gill slammed down her glass and Connie's drink went down the wrong way.

When she'd finished coughing she stammered, 'A hundred *thousand!*'

'Yeah,' said Maggie.

'From a *scratch*-card?' asked Gill.

'Yeah.' Maggie opened the oven door. 'Look, the lasagne's ready!'

'A hundred thousand pounds! Wow! That's great, Maggie! I presume it's in the bank?'

'Well, no,' Maggie said as she dished up the lasagne. 'I've got it with me. Only because if I leave it in the bank Ringer will spend the lot. We have a joint account, you see.'

'So, you're telling me that you have a hundred thousand pounds *here*, in Bella?'

Connie's appetite plummeted as she realised they were now sitting ducks for any thieves around. So that was why Maggie was so worried about locking doors and things!

Maggie sat down opposite her. 'Don't worry, Connie, we can have a lovely time with this money, stay in top hotels if we want!'

'But Maggie.' Connie put her head in her hands. 'Couldn't you open another bank account or something?' She watched as both Maggie and Gill wolfed down Lou's lasagne. Why was she the only one worried? She might be exhausted but she felt sure she wouldn't sleep a wink.

'Don't you worry,' Maggie mumbled through a mouthful of food. 'There's no problem. I've hidden the money all over the place. And I can carry quite a lot of it. We're going to have a great time spending it. I have never, never had money like this to spend on myself before, and I want to enjoy it. And I don't want to give Ringer the opportunity to get his hands on a single pound of it.'

Getting into bed was something of a major operation. Everything had to be stowed away before the sofa was transformed into Connie's bed, and then Gill had to decide whether she would sleep on the lower bunk or on the narrow divan alongside Connie's. Connie prayed she'd choose the bunk.

'I'll try the bunk tonight,' Gill said eventually, 'because I'm so bloody tired I could sleep standing up. That's if it's not filled up with bank notes.' She grinned at Maggie.

'No, it isn't, but I have put a layer of them underneath the mattresses, and some in my stowage, and my bra, and my money belt and my shoulder bag. And a few other places besides.'

As Maggie got ready for bed, Gill said to Connie, 'This doesn't seem right somehow.' She was dismantling her beehive, which had been askew for some hours. 'If it was me I'd have opened a bank account before I left.'

'Well, maybe we can persuade her to do that. They must have British banks in Paris.'

Connie just wanted to go to bed, but first she tapped out a quick email to her children telling them they'd got to the Paris area safely and all was well. At least La Bellezza was living up to expectations, and the bed looked comfy and inviting. In fact, everything worked more or less as it should. Everything, that is, except the loo door, a fact that was brought home to Connie and Maggie when Gill became the first to check the plumbing just before they went to bed. There followed much thumping and shouting.

'What's wrong with *her*?' Maggie asked crossly.

'Are you all right?' Connie asked through the door.

'I can't get *out*!' Gill wailed.

Connie turned the handle and the door opened to reveal a red-faced and distressed Gill.

'Good Lord, Gill, you only have to turn the handle!'

'I did, I did! But it wouldn't open!'

'Right, try again,' Connie ordered, shutting the door firmly.

There was more clicking and clunking. 'It won't open!' Gill repeated.

Connie opened the door again. 'Come out, Gill.'

They exchanged places. Connie went in and closed the door.

'You're right,' she confirmed. 'It won't open from the inside.'

Maggie got up from the settee and rummaged around in the cutlery drawer. 'I know the screwdrivers are in here somewhere.' Then, finding them, she spent the next ten minutes fiddling with the handle on both sides of the door before giving up.

'We'll get it fixed somewhere,' Connie said, with visions of Maggie, who appeared to have the dodgiest bladder, having to be rescued throughout the night. 'In the meantime, just try to remember to leave the door ajar whenever you go in there.'

CHAPTER SEVEN

GAY PAREE

In the morning Connie sat up in bed, rubbed her eyes and consulted the clock. It said 8 a.m., and then she remembered it was 9 a.m. over here. She'd slept badly, unable to turn off her turbulent thoughts. The bed had been comfy but it was too warm for the duvet she'd brought along and she'd kicked it off during the night. Now it was already hot, the sun sneaking its way in around the edges of the blinds. She swung her legs out of bed, opened the door in the hope of a breeze, and just then a tousle-haired Maggie, with Minnie Mouse emblazoned across her T-shirt nightie, came tiptoeing in.

'Oh, I'm glad you're awake, Connie. I could murder a cup of tea.'

'Me too,' said Connie. 'How did you sleep?'

'Not bad. But, my *God*, doesn't that Gill *snore*! I've never *heard* such a racket. It took me nearly an hour to get off and then I suppose I must have got attuned to it. She's quietened down a bit now.'

Connie had been hearing a snorting sound, which she'd assumed was coming from somewhere outside. 'Well, Maggie, in that case I won't want her in here near me either.'

'Perhaps we should draw lots,' said Maggie, depositing teabags into two mugs, 'and get some ear-plugs as well.'

'But Maggie, I'm so worried about all that money. What on earth are you going to do with it all?'

'*We* are going to spend it, that's what we're going to do.' She fiddled with her phone. 'I'm trying to get the BBC news, just to see what's going on back home.'

At that moment, an almost unrecognisable Gill appeared, her hair hanging round her shoulders, and clad in a pink silk nightie. Apart from panda-like smudges round her eyes she was barefaced.

'Morning, Gill, how did you sleep?' Connie asked with a grin.

'Hardly slept a wink.'

'Well, you sure didn't *sound* like you hardly slept a wink,' Maggie said with some feeling.

'What do you mean? *I* don't snore!'

'Must be the excitement of the trip then,' said Maggie. 'A one-off, perhaps?'

Looking at the unembellished Gill, Connie wondered how long it would take her to be ready to face the world again. Apart from the panda eyes, Gill looked younger and prettier without the layers of make-up and the starchy hair.

'Shall I pop across to see if they have any nice French bread or croissants for breakfast?' Maggie asked.

When Maggie disappeared outside, Connie said, 'Gill, I'm still worried about all this money hidden around everywhere.'

'I don't intend to lose any sleep over it,' Gill said, making herself a cup of tea. 'You worry too much, Connie. Poor Maggie deserves a break, you know. We really should just help her to enjoy it. We can have a lovely trip now, and not worry about dosh. Just think of her as our rich friend!'

Later Maggie, having fetched the croissants, came back and downed another cup of tea, said, 'Gill's been hogging that mirror back there for over half an hour. Just as well it only took me five minutes to get ready.'

Connie thought how pretty Maggie must have been once; petite, ivory skinned, beautiful red hair. Had that wretched Ringer drained the very colouring out of her? Serves him right that he can't get his hands on her scratch-card money.

Fifteen minutes later, fully made up and beehive in position, Gill reappeared, like a galleon in full sail, in an enormous turquoise kaftan.

'Wow!' said Connie. 'Aren't you the glamorous one!'

Both she and Maggie were clad in cotton T-shirts and cut-offs. As always in the summer, she'd dabbed on a little tinted moisturiser and applied some mascara, an operation that took about five minutes. Maggie looked exactly the same as when she got out of bed.

'Well, we're going into *Paris*, aren't we?' Gill said defensively, looking at them both with some disapproval.

Maggie had begun to look anxious again. 'Maybe I should stay here.'

'This money,' Connie sighed, 'is going to give you no pleasure whatsoever if you insist on standing over it from morning to night. I promise we'll lock everything up securely.'

'Why don't we *all* take some with us?' Maggie suggested. 'Come on, ladies, shove a few notes in your purses, or your bras, or somewhere.'

They were all excited at the prospect of Paris. Connie had been several times, beginning with that so-called educational school trip. (She and Helen Palmer had 'escaped' from the orderly crocodile in Versailles and, as a result, got 'lost'. It had been difficult to convince Miss Sims that this was accidental, which, of course, it wasn't.) Maggie's one and only trip to Paris had been with Ringer in the early days of their relationship, when they were still besotted with each other, and had seen more of their bedroom than they had of any of the sights. And Gill had never been and was probably the most excited of the three.

The last time Connie had visited the city had been with Roger to celebrate their silver wedding anniversary. Four culture-packed days, including Versailles again (no chance to stray this time), with hours and hours in the Louvre. Roger was a committed tourist although mercifully it had proved impossible to fit in every museum and art gallery on his list. But they had had some lovely meals and she had been permitted a couple of hours to mainly window-shop, her only purchase being a blue silk scarf from Monoprix.

Connie knew this visit was going to be quite different.

'Today,' Gill announced, 'we should go to Montmartre and look at all these naughty clubs and things.' She'd acquired a pile of leaflets and had decided to become their self-appointed guide. 'And we can visit the Sacre Coeur, of course, for our bit of culture.'

They took a taxi because, according to Raoul, the bus only came twice a day, and sometimes it did and sometimes it didn't. '*C'est la vie*', with much Gallic shrugging.

The taxi deposited them at the Sacre Coeur, the three marvelling at its beautiful, imposing white exterior and panoramic views of the city. They wandered round the hushed interior and then emerged, blinking, onto the southern viewpoint, silenced by the magnificent view.

'Will you look at *that*!' exclaimed Connie. 'I'd forgotten just how spectacular this is! I haven't been here for years.'

And there it all was; the panorama taking in the Eiffel Tower, the Arc de Triomphe, Notre-Dame – the lot. Paris was magical. Then Connie noticed, next to Maggie, a beautiful young couple, arms entwined around each other, the girl tanned with long, shiny, copper-coloured hair, and the boy tall and dark, with brooding good looks. Connie felt a pang of pure envy – how good it would be to be young again!

Gill nudged her. 'Penny for them, Connie?'

'Oh, just wishing for a moment that I was their age.' Connie indicated the young couple with a nod of her head.

'The thing is,' said Gill, following her gaze, 'we didn't look *anything* like that when we were young, did we? We didn't have tight jeans and crop tops, or whatever you call them.'

'We didn't have much in the way of tans either,' Maggie chirped in. 'Certainly not in Glasgow. And I had one of those awful frizzy perms.'

'When we went dancing at the Palais,' Gill went on, 'they were all Teddy boys. Draped jackets, drainpipe trousers, suede shoes and enormous sideburns.'

'I expect you had a similar hairdo to what you have now,' said Maggie, eyeing the beehive.

'What's that supposed to mean?' snapped Gill. 'Of course it wasn't the *same*.'

'I liked the way it looked loose this morning,' Connie remarked.

'*If* it was cut into a good shape,' added Maggie, unaware that Gill was glaring at her in fury.

'What's this?' Gill was seething. 'Are you having a let's-get-at-Gill day? Just because you've got all that bloody money doesn't make you a style expert. When's the last time you went to a hairdresser, or a beauty salon or anywhere else that might improve *your* appearance?'

'I don't go to any of them,' Maggie retorted. 'I cut my own hair and, because it's quite curly, no one really notices.'

'Ladies, ladies!' Connie felt the necessity to mediate. 'You're both lovely in different ways. Now, if you've had enough of this view, how about some lunch?'

As they headed down the steps she wondered if they were going to bicker all the way to Italy. Maggie wasn't as mild-mannered as she'd originally thought. Had Nick been right? Was it at all possible for three elderly and diverse ladies to co-exist in such a confined space and not drive each other nuts? Well, it was far too late to do much about it now.

Lunch, and the wine that accompanied it, soothed any ruffled feathers and soon the three of them were planning to see some of the seamier spots of Montmartre. Later they'd do the Eiffel Tower and have a wander up the Champs-Élysées. Tomorrow they would do the Louvre and the Musée D'Orsay and introduce a little culture into their trip. There seemed to be a dearth of taxis and Gill suggested they use the Metro to navigate their way towards the Barbès-Rochechouart area. They emerged from the Anvers station to a maze of cobbled streets, bars, kebab shops, and all manner of sex shops and peep shows.

'You wouldn't want to be around here at night,' Connie remarked.

'I'm not feeling that safe right now,' said Maggie, hugging her bag even more tightly.

'No dodgier than Glasgow on a Saturday night, surely?' scoffed Gill.

'Now, don't you two start again!' said Connie. 'And just look at this old place here!'

'That,' said Gill, consulting her guide, 'is, or was, the Elysée Montmartre theatre, which was the oldest can-can dance theatre in Paris. Now, according to this, it's falling into decay, and they're not kidding, are they? But, follow me; the Moulin Rouge is at the other end of this street.'

None of the other buildings appeared to be crumbling but there was a certain air of degeneracy about the place. Although the streets were wide and clean there was still a feeling of seediness.

'I daren't look in some of these windows,' Connie exclaimed, having done just that and still reeling from a lurid display advertising sex shows. 'Not exactly subtle, are they? And I really fancy a cold drink as I'm so dry.'

'Plenty of bars round here.' Gill was squinting in one of the windows. 'But this one is definitely dodgy.'

They peered into several other smoke-filled interiors. Nobody appeared to have told the French that they should be smoking outside.

'This one looks OK,' Maggie said. 'Loads of women in there, so it should be safe.'

Connie asked for two beers and a Coca-Cola.

'You are Eenglish?' asked the pretty barmaid.

'Yes, yes, we are. More or less,' she added, looking over to ensure Maggie was out of earshot. Maggie seemed engrossed in her phone.

As Connie looked around she realised she couldn't see a single male; it must be a 'ladies only' establishment, she thought.

'Ees your first time here?' The barmaid passed the drinks across the counter.

'In here, yes,' Connie replied. 'But I've been to Paris before, some years ago.' She was conscious of the barmaid's lingering glances in their direction.

'Maybe now,' said the barmaid, running her tongue across her top lip, 'you will come more often.'

As Connie placed the drinks on the table, Gill, beaming, said, 'That woman over there has just told me how beautiful I look.'

Maggie slammed her phone down on the table. 'Are you sure she's not got a white stick?'

'Here we go again!' snapped Gill.

'Leave it, you two!' Connie said, feeling distinctly uncomfortable as she looked around. Already disconcerted by the barmaid's manner, she was now aware of at least a dozen pairs of female eyes swivelling in their direction. 'I think we should drink up and get out of here as quickly as we can.'

'It seems OK to me,' Maggie said, wrapping herself round her shoulder bag again. 'You don't think we could be mugged, do you?'

Gill, cottoning on, caught Connie's eye. 'Shagged, more like,' she said.

'You don't mean…?' Maggie was gulping down her drink.

'I do. Let's get the hell out of here.'

Just then an elderly woman, clad in a black trouser suit and sporting a collar and tie in spite of the heat, approached their table. 'Eenglish, yes? May I join you?'

'No, no, we're just leaving.' Maggie was standing up, draining her glass and looking towards the door.

'We have an appointment,' Connie said, doing likewise.

'Tout suite,' added Gill.

The woman shrugged her shoulders as she walked away.

Outside on the pavement Maggie said, 'I've never downed a drink in a bar so fast in my life!'

'Me neither.' Gill let forth a loud belch.

'And you don't have to be so *vulgar*,' said Maggie.

'You're just mad 'cos none of them fancied you!' Gill retorted.

'Let's find a taxi,' Connie said, laughing.

As they headed in a taxi towards the Arc de Triomphe, Maggie took the opportunity to read the email again while Connie and Gill enthused at the sights.

You bitch! Don't think you can get away with this. I'll get you if it kills me.

Maggie read it for a third time, then deleted it. She switched her phone off; she'd only have it on when she wanted to make a call, as she certainly didn't need to worry about messages such as this. Anyway, he hadn't a cat's chance in hell of ever finding them in this vast country. Still, she'd probably be on the lookout for maroon-coloured Lexuses – if he came across in his own car. Would he dare? Well, he might if he got the number plates changed. And he had a mate who could change them in a matter of minutes. Then she wished she hadn't been so snappy with Gill. She'd find a way to treat her and be especially nice to her, and anyway it would be a good idea to start spending as much of that money as possible.

Half an hour later, as they were wandering along the Champs-Élysées, Maggie espied a hair salon.

'Gill,' Maggie said, 'do you fancy having a hairdo? My treat.'

Gill looked confused for a moment.

'Go on,' Maggie urged. 'I didn't *mean* to be nasty to you earlier. I'd feel so much better if you'd let me make it up to you.'

'Oh, I can't let you do that!'

'Of course you can! And, like I said, it would make me feel so much better.'

'Well, in that case, thanks Maggie, that would be great.'

Maggie withdrew a bundle of notes from her bag and handed them over. 'I know you like your beauty treatments and I want to share my good fortune.'

As Gill disappeared into the salon Maggie said to Connie, 'With a bit of luck they'll get rid of that awful beehive. It's not even straight – the Leaning Tower of Pisa's got nothing on our Gill!'

Connie laughed. 'She's desperately trying to hang onto her youth, I think.'

They walked a further few yards, exclaiming at the beautiful window displays, before Connie stopped in front of a boutique window. 'Will you just look at that?' she said to Maggie, pointing at the dress on display.

'You can have it, you know, whatever it costs,' Maggie said, as she and Connie gazed at the sea-green dress. It was understated, elegant and cut to perfection, and it stood alone, like a sculpture, against a cream velvet background.

'That is so *you*!' Maggie said. 'And that green would enhance the colour of your eyes.'

There was nothing so vulgar as a price on display.

'There's a saying somewhere,' sighed Connie, 'that if you need to ask the price, then you can't afford it.'

'But we can,' Maggie said. 'I have the dosh.' She could see how much Connie wanted the dress.

'I admit I'm sorely tempted, but wherever would I wear it? No, Maggie, no, but thanks for the offer.'

'We'll find somewhere for you to wear it. There's no law that says you can't try it on. Come on!'

'I feel far too scruffy to go over the doorstep!'

'Listen, it's your *money* they're interested in – come on!'

Hesitantly Connie followed Maggie across the threshold and into a cool, perfumed, subtly lit interior.

'Bonjour!' A mahogany-coloured saleslady rose reluctantly from where she had been sitting at a large, ornately carved white desk. She was stick-thin, immaculately made up, and wore a black dress, pointy shoes and a disdainful expression. Connie appeared dumbstruck.

'My friend loves the dress in your window,' Maggie said.

'Eenglish!' The woman looked from one to the other.

'My English friend,' Maggie said with mock patience, 'would like to try on that dress in the window.'

The saleslady's eyes widened. 'You know the *price*?'

'No,' said Maggie, 'we don't. So, please tell us.'

'Ees nearly five 'undred euros, Madame!'

Maggie could hear Connie gasp. 'That's fine. I thought it might be a bit more. What size are you, Connie?'

'I can't…'

'I'm thinking a size sixteen, maybe,' Maggie went on, standing back and studying Connie.

'Well, yes, I'm usually a sixteen but—'

'So we'll try the sixteen, please. If I remember rightly that'll be a size forty-four.'

The saleslady appeared to be taken aback as she gazed at her two T-shirted customers.

'I will find ze *largest* size,' she said pointedly, before disappearing behind some panelled doors.

'I can't let you do this,' Connie whispered. 'This is ridiculous!'

'You are going to have that dress,' Maggie replied, 'and that's that. No more arguments! But I'll need to come into the changing room to get some of these notes out of my bra; they've been scratching me all day.'

'I 'ave ze forty-four and it is ze biggest size we 'ave,' said the woman, reappearing with the dress on a hanger. 'You are *most* fortunate,' she added.

Connie, holding the dress at arm's length, headed for the changing room.

'I hope I'm not too sweaty,' she said to Maggie, as she removed her T-shirt and examined her armpits. She fanned herself for a moment, then removed her jeans and slipped the dress over her head.

'Wow!' said Maggie a few minutes later, when Connie emerged into the shop. 'That dress has your name on it!'

The dress looked beautiful, and so did Connie. Its lines skimmed her body and gave her the immediate appearance of having dropped a dress size. And the colour accentuated the green of Connie's eyes and flattered her skin tone.

'Ees very nice,' the saleslady conceded.

As Connie re-entered the changing room, Maggie came in behind her, pulling the door across before hauling up her top and extracting a load of notes from her bra. 'I'll just go and pay.'

By the time Connie came out, holding the dress carefully, the saleslady was actually smiling.

'So bootiful!' she enthused. 'Ees perfect for you.'

She made a big performance of folding the dress in reams of tissue paper while Maggie peeled off the appropriate number of notes.

'That's made her day!' Maggie said as they left the boutique with a large, classy carrier bag embossed in gold writing on navy blue.

'I don't know how to thank you,' Connie said. 'It's the most beautiful dress I've ever had. Or am ever likely to have.'

'Listen,' said Maggie. 'You've bought Bella, you've brought us along with you, and this is just a way of saying thank you to *you*. I haven't done anything to *earn* this money, I've just been lucky.'

As they continued walking, Maggie wondered how long that luck would last.

Connie was increasingly worried about the cash Maggie was so desperate to spend. She'd let Maggie pay for the site fees, the taxi, the lunch, and now this ridiculously expensive dress. But, dear God, she did love the dress. It was so beautifully cut that no one would ever know that Connie McColl had a flabby tummy and chunky thighs. That's what you paid for, of course. And she didn't remember Gill arguing when Maggie suggested the hairdo.

'Can we take a taxi to the Rive Gauche?' Connie asked, consulting her watch. 'Gill's going to be a couple of hours yet.'

And so they made their way to the Paris of an earlier Bohemian era, of artists, writers and philosophers, now an area of beautiful boutiques, houses and galleries. And where artists still displayed their works on the pavement, and Connie espied a small watercolour depicting a French village scene. She loved the blue-shuttered houses, the cypress trees and the market where lots of tiny ladies, Lowry style, were buying their vegetables. In particular she loved the colours; the hazy blues, misty greens and golden stone of the buildings.

'Ooh!' she gasped.

'How much?' asked Maggie.

The artist – middle-aged, pony-tailed and smoking furiously – looked at them, narrowed his eyes and, without removing his Gauloise, said, 'Two 'undred euros.'

'We are not Americans,' Maggie informed him. 'That's *far* too much!'

'I was only admiring it…' Connie protested.

'I like it too,' Maggie said, 'and I'd like to see it adorning one of Bella's walls.' She turned her attention back to the artist. 'One hundred euros, maximum.'

'Non, Madame. Non, non, *non.*'

'Anyway, where would we put it?' Connie asked, trying to imagine where there might be a few inches of wall without a mirror or a cupboard or a window.

Meanwhile the artist was studying Maggie, his eyes still narrowed. He removed his Gauloise and sighed loudly. 'One 'undred, seventy-five.'

'One hundred.'

Again, much Gallic shrugging. 'Non, non, *non*!'

'I am Scottish. Écossaise – comprenez? We like value for money.'

'I am French. So do I. Lowest price, for you, is one-fifty.'

'I'm happy to pay one-fifty,' Connie whispered. She was aware that she'd hardly spent any of her own money since they left England. But neither of them were paying any attention to her.

Maggie moved closer to the artist. 'You know it's not worth a hundred even. But, look, I will give you one hundred and twenty-five right now. Pronto!' She began to count out some euro notes.

'Is not enough!'

'Then we will go.' She took Connie by the arm and was about to walk away.

'OK, OK!' he called after them. 'One 'undred twenty-five. How you say – robbery in the daylight?'

Connie's legs were aching as they waited outside the salon for Gill to reappear. 'Do you suppose she's had it cut?' she asked Maggie.

'Not a chance.' She peered in the window to see Gill coming towards the door. 'Oh my God!'

Gill's locks were now a silvery-blonde, as opposed to the previous brassy yellow, which was an improvement; but the beehive had been replaced by an intricate upward display of curls and ringlets, which was not.

Gill looked quite coy. 'Nice, isn't it?'

'I like the colour,' Connie said tactfully.

'Why didn't you get it *cut*?' Maggie demanded.

'Because long hair is far more feminine,' Gill snapped.

Maggie snorted. 'You look like an aged can-can girl. Whose idea was it to have all these curls?'

'Mine,' said Gill.

Connie walked round to survey the back view. 'Will it stay like that until tomorrow? Anyway, as long as you're happy, Gill.'

Gill was eager to change the subject. 'What's in all these bags?'

It was early evening when they got back to Bella and Maggie announced she wanted to 'pop along to the shop'. She returned fifteen minutes later, followed by Raoul dragging a trailer loaded with packages.

'Four folding chairs, one folding table, one green and white awning,' Maggie announced. 'You like?'

'I like very much,' said Connie, who was still trying to find the best spot to display the picture.

'Raoul had them on sale. And it all folds up into this big canvas bag thing, which can be stowed where the bikes would go, if we had any. It'll only take minutes to set it all up and then pack it away again.'

Connie was overwhelmed but pleased at Maggie's generosity; this could prove to be a real boost to their cramped living quarters, particularly once they were out in the French countryside. There wasn't enough room in Raoul's site to set it all up properly, so they ate supper inside with the door and windows open. It was an oppressive evening; you could feel the threat of thunder in the air. They ate bread, cheese and pâté, washed down with wine. Maggie was relaxed once she'd discovered her hidden caches were intact.

'That Raoul's quite attractive,' Gill observed as she dug into the Brie.

'That droopy grey moustache would put me off,' said Connie. 'Probably got last night's dinner still stuck in there somewhere.'

Maggie rolled her eyes. 'Whatever turns you on, I suppose, Gill.'

'He's not in the same league as Fabio, of course,' Gill continued. 'Now *that's* sexy.'

'When did you see him last?' Connie asked.

Gill screwed up her eyes. 'Oh, about twenty years ago. He was working in London for a big Italian car company but then they transferred him back to Rome.'

'He's probably fat and bald now; I should forget him if I were you,' Maggie said.

'Would it be all right if we asked Raoul over for a drink?' Gill asked tentatively.

Connie lay back on the divan and closed her eyes. Why hadn't she bought that tiny single motorhome and set off on her own?

'He just seems a bit lonely,' Gill went on. 'Shall I go over and ask him?'

Maggie sighed. 'Well, OK, just for half an hour or so. If that's OK with you, Connie?'

'Provided he knows when to leave,' Connie replied with feeling, as Gill set off.

Shortly afterwards she reappeared, coming carefully through the door so as not to dislodge the silvery-blonde masterpiece atop her pink, flushed face. She was clutching two bottles of wine.

'What's this?' asked Connie. 'We already have plenty of wine.'

Gill placed the bottles on the kitchen work surface and plonked herself down.

'We've just been chatting in the shop and, do you know, he's really nice when you get to know him. I felt a bit sorry for him 'cos his wife left him a year ago, so I felt he was some kind of kindred spirit. And he was so pleased to be asked.'

'I bet he was,' said Maggie.

Raoul, looking more dapper than usual with neatly groomed hair and moustache, appeared at the door brandishing yet another bottle of wine.

'Bonsoir, Mesdames!'

'Bonsoir, Raoul! Have a seat.' Gill accepted the bottle of wine and continued pouring glasses of Merlot, while Raoul squeezed his bulk behind the table and helped himself to an olive.

'It would have been nice to sit outside,' Maggie said with some feeling. 'But you haven't left enough room to swing a cat between us and the Germans.'

'You 'ave a cat?'

'Pay no attention to her,' Gill said. 'We certainly don't have a cat.'

Raoul pulled a face to accompany the Gallic shrug. 'I no 'ave cat either. And is very busy here. I no like to turn anyone away because in winter no one comes, so how you say, I must make the harvest when the sun is shining.'

'Quite so,' Connie agreed, raising her glass. 'Here's to your sunshine!'

Raoul stayed for nearly two hours, regaling them with tales of warring couples, spurned lovers, cross-dressers and the completely mad – all on his campsite, every year, without fail. Then, when he'd got up to go, Gill, who'd been flirting with him all evening, said, 'I'll just walk along with you for a few minutes because I need to cool off, and it's so hot in here.'

Gill didn't reappear for well over an hour, by which time the others were in bed, Connie exasperated and Maggie paranoid at not being able to lock the door. When Gill did finally return and the door was locked, Connie relaxed and mulled over the events of the evening. Was this then to be the pattern of their trip? Gill flirting with every man in sight and Maggie panicking about her money? She was the one who'd agreed to bring them along so she supposed she'd better get used to it.

CHAPTER EIGHT

SOUTHBOUND

In the morning, Connie studied the least-faded photograph in The Box again. The three men sported most impressive moustaches, formal suits, high collars and tightly knotted ties. The four women all had upswept hair (no beehives), blouses with leg-of-mutton sleeves, long skirts and startled expressions. Were her great-grandparents there? She looked at the other photograph of the man in some sort of uniform. Could that be her grandfather? She didn't recognise the uniform at all.

She read as much as possible of the letters, translating as best as she could from her small Italian dictionary, but it was impossible to understand the grammar. And the word 'Marigino' kept cropping up, and there was no such word in the dictionary. Was it someone's name, or a place, or what? Or something to do with the sea, perhaps?

Connie didn't know where to begin. If only she had some contact in Amalfi! She'd googled 'Martilucci', Maria's maiden name, and found the clan scattered all over Italy and beyond. The only one in the entire Campania region seemed to be in Naples and, when she clicked on that, up came a different name altogether: E. L. Pozzi, Via dei Pellegrini, Napoli. Who or what was this E. L. Pozzi? Perhaps she'd send an email or phone again when they got closer to their destination. She'd tried phoning before leaving London, receiving a torrent of Italian from some woman, who'd then hung up. No, it would be better to go there in person. Otherwise, what was the alternative? Knock on every door in Amalfi and ask if anyone remembered the Martilucci family? Why had it not occurred to her to seek the help of some Italians and do more research before she left England? The friendly family at the local Italian restaurant could probably have helped her.

At the same time Maggie, cautiously switching on her phone again, received an email from her friend Pam to tell her that she'd had a visit from Ringer.

You wouldn't believe how much he's missing you already! He was so worried that he'd lost your itinerary and he was really interested in the motorhome. He wanted to know what kind it was and everything, so I showed him the photos you sent me because there was a lovely one of you and your two friends beside it. He wanted me to forward that one on to him, so I did. He said he'd love to fly out and join up with you somewhere for a few days for a nice surprise! Isn't that lovely, and here's you thinking

that he doesn't love you any more! But he obviously does.
Forget the blonde, it was obviously a one-off!

Love and hugs,
Pam

Maggie felt sick. The photos she'd forwarded to Pam had shown Bella from several angles, a few of which clearly displayed the registration number. And good likenesses of the three of them. But, so what? There was no way he could find them in this enormous country with its labyrinth of roads and autoroutes, and millions of caravan sites. But, still…

On her way back from the toilet Maggie popped into the shop, hoping to see Raoul. He was there, chatting to the baker who'd just arrived with a box of rolls and a box of croissants.

'Ah, Maggie,' he said, beaming with pleasure. 'I enjoyed very much last night.'

'You're very welcome, Raoul,' Maggie said. 'But I wonder if I might have a word in your ear?'

'Oui, oui, of course.'

Maggie cleared her throat. 'It's just that, if a man should call in here asking for us, please say you have never seen or heard of us.'

Raoul looked confused. 'You are not here?'

'Correct. We are not here, and we were *never* here. The thing is, Raoul, that I am escaping from an unwanted lover.' She wondered then if she'd overdone it, even allowing for him being French.

'Ah!' he said. 'So you are not here, never here?'

'Exactly! And, Raoul, we are leaving today.'

'Today? But you have paid for another day.'

'It doesn't matter. We don't want any money back. But we are leaving today.'

Raoul shrugged. 'I am sad. I love you ladies. I love that Geel. I would like that you stay.'

'Yes, well, I'm afraid that we won't be staying. I'm really sorry, because it's very nice here, but we must go.' He looked crestfallen. 'We will come to see you on the way back!'

She could see him brightening up.

'When will that be?'

'Not too sure, Raoul. But let's have your email, and we'll contact you. And can I give you my phone number so if anyone does call to ask where we are, please let me know.'

'Avec plaisir,' said Raoul.

When Maggie got back to Bella with the rolls and croissants, the other two were drinking coffee.

'I hope you don't mind,' Maggie said, 'but we must move on today.'

'Why would we do that?' Connie asked, putting down her mug. 'We were going to have a bit of culture today, like the Louvre and everything. And we've paid for another day.'

'Yes, I know, but Raoul has made a bit of a balls-up with the booking,' Maggie lied, 'and he shouldn't really have booked us for three nights. He's very sorry.'

'Has he given you the money back?' Connie asked.

'Yes, no problem. And we can do the Louvre and everything on the way back, can't we?'

'Come to think of it,' said Connie, 'that's probably a better idea anyway. It is rather crowded here at the moment.'

'Well, I don't want to go,' said Gill. 'I like it here. And I like Raoul.'

'We'll see him again in a few weeks on the way back,' Maggie said. 'That'll be much better because then you could stay on a bit longer if you liked, since we'd be fairly close to home.'

Gill considered this for a moment or two. 'Oh well, I haven't much choice, have I?'

They ate breakfast in comparative silence, after which Gill decided she was going to have a shower before they left.

Gill took her towel and sponge bag and, bypassing the shower block, headed straight for Raoul in the shop.

'I'm so sorry you leaving!' he said.

'Well, it can't be helped. I believe you have another booking or something this evening?'

Raoul looked mystified. 'No, I have no other booking.'

'But, Maggie said…' Gill stopped. 'What exactly *did* she say?'

Raoul shrugged. 'She say if a lover comes looking for her I am to say that no, I have never seen her, or any of you, not in my whole life. That you were never here. *Never!*'

'Is that so?' said Gill.

Although Connie hadn't drunk as much as the other two the previous evening, she insisted they didn't leave Raoul's campsite until lunchtime, to give her system a decent drying-out period before tackling the drive south. They'd agreed to take the Autoroute des Anglais to the east of Paris, eventually taking them down through the Burgundy region ('without a doubt!' they'd all agreed). They'd head towards Dijon, and then take the Autoroute du Soleil south. They'd divert as necessary to hopefully find unspoilt countryside, vineyards, and places for Bella to stay overnight. And thoroughly confuse the satnav lady.

After a night's sleep Gill's Parisian coiffure was unrecognisable and, although she'd made some attempts at restoring the beehive, it was collapsing in sections even before they set off.

'Didn't you tell him how much that hairdo cost before he started running his fingers through it?' Maggie asked.

'I'll pay you back your bloody money,' Gill snapped, before Maggie cut in, 'No, you won't. Just promise me that, before we get to Italy, you'll let me cut some of that lot off.'

Gill snorted. 'Not likely!'

Connie sighed. 'Don't start, you two. Now, let's talk about today. The idea is that we head for Lyon, which is supposed to be a good halfway point between here and the Med. We could take the main autoroute, which is very busy at this time of year, or we can look for some alternative routes and enjoy the scenery.'

'Let's do that,' said Maggie. 'I like the idea of being off the beaten track.'

'This is hell,' Connie stated, wondering yet again what she'd let herself in for. They hadn't taken the main autoroute, but this one was bad enough. She remained, constant and careful, in the slowest lane, surrounded by manic drivers cutting in front of her and around her.

Maggie, now her navigator, was doing her best to decipher signs and distances while, behind, Gill slept spread-eagled on Connie's divan.

'I don't think we should try going all the way to Lyon today,' Maggie said, noting Connie's tension. 'But we could perhaps find somewhere near Dijon. And why don't you let me drive for a while?'

Reluctantly Connie let Maggie into the driving seat. She knew that Maggie had a much stronger constitution than her frail appearance would indicate, but she still hesitated. But Connie's back was aching and she was finding these long drives stressful and tiring. I'm sixty-nine, she thought; I'm entitled to get knackered sometimes.

Maggie was a natural. She adjusted the seat to her own lesser dimensions and then set off as smoothly and calmly as if she'd been driving large motorhomes all her life. She never fails to amaze, Connie thought as she relaxed in the passenger seat. And it would be such a relief to share the driving. But not with Gill, she thought. *Never* Gill. She rooted through her CDs. Andrea Bocelli's 'Sogno' would do the trick.

'We're pretty well in the Burgundy region now,' Connie said. 'And we are most definitely going to be boosting the local economy this evening.'

'Most definitely,' said Maggie.

'How far now?'

'About five hundred kilometres and six hours to Lyon, according to the map,' Maggie continued, 'and that's without any hold-ups.'

'We'll head towards Dijon then. Three hours will be more than enough for this afternoon.'

Maggie thought a lot about Ringer as they drove along the tree-lined road, with scintillating glimpses of vineyards through the foliage. Ringer was not a bad man as criminals go; not a vicious man, just damned greedy. He might well chase after his ill-gotten gains but Maggie didn't think he'd harm them physically, although she couldn't be sure. It was an awful lot of cash. She wasn't afraid of him; only of losing the money and, with it, this wonderful freedom that she hadn't even realised she wanted. She was loving every minute of this journey. No more worrying about the relationship and the blonde bimbo; no more worrying about money because she knew there was enough there to fund some kind of future for herself.

She could afford to be generous on this trip but she'd still be keeping most of it for herself.

They found a signposted turning to Montbard and were finally able to look around and savour the panorama of vineyards. It was early evening when they came across Les Hirondelles: whitewashed walls, green shutters and a sign, in English, which proclaimed 'Superior Burgundy Cuisine, Superior Burgundy Wine'.

'Sounds like us,' said Maggie as, with some relief, she drove Bella into the little car park.

Gill had woken up and was tidying up her beehive and applying lipstick. She yawned. 'Are we stopping already? We're not in Dijon yet, are we?'

'Yes, we are stopping,' snapped Connie. 'While you've been snoring your head off back there we've been contending with hellish traffic, and we're hot and tired.'

'Perhaps the owners can tell us if there's a campsite round here somewhere,' Maggie said. There were several cars parked at all angles, but no sign of life.

'Probably still in the middle of their three-hour lunch,' Connie remarked as she rapped on the door. Finally they heard footsteps approaching from inside and the door being unbolted and slowly opened, bringing them face to face with an Adonis. He was forty-ish, tall and golden-haired with the most amazing blue eyes and a slightly lopsided smile.

'Oh, wow!' said Gill, bringing up the rear.

'Bonsoir!' said Adonis.

Connie cleared her throat, hoping not to have to rely on her schoolgirl French. 'Parlez-vous anglais?'

'Ah, yes,' he said, 'I do.' His eyes crinkled fetchingly as he smilingly surveyed the three women in front of him.

'Um, well, we wondered if we could eat here? Manger, ici? And if there was somewhere to park our motorhome?'

'Yes, of course, you can eat here after one hour.' Adonis consulted his watch. 'My wife will prepare dinner for eight o'clock. And we have a field right there, through the trees. You see? You can be there.'

'Oh, thank you,' said Connie, relief flooding through her weary veins. She turned to the other two. 'No more driving tonight – to hell with Dijon. Who needs their mustard anyway?'

'I am called Étienne,' he said. 'Come with me.'

Étienne's field was little more than a tract of land sandwiched between a dusty olive grove on one side, and an orchard on the other. And all around were acres and acres of vines.

'We 'ave no toilets out 'ere,' said Étienne, as he led them in. 'No water, no electricity. This will be OK?'

'This will be fine,' Connie replied. Which was true. They'd filled up with water at Raoul's, they'd have to use the toilet if necessary, they had candles, they had solar panels and they had bottled gas. They also had a restaurant right on their doorstep.

'Ooh la la! What a dish!' said Gill, gazing after him as he walked away.

'And young enough to be your son,' said Connie.

'Your grandson, even,' added Maggie.

Gill sighed. 'Why is it that it's considered OK for an old guy to have a girlfriend young enough to be his daughter, but it's considered weird if an older woman has a young boyfriend? Tell me that.'

Connie was filling the kettle and thinking of the sexy Don Robertson. 'So much for equality, Gill.'

'We'll put it to the equal opportunities board when we get home,' said Maggie.

'Anyway, I seem to remember him referring to his wife,' Connie put in.

Gill snorted. 'This is France. They do that sort of thing all the time.'

Étienne's equally attractive wife was called Lisanne, and she was as near to cordon bleu as you were likely to get in the middle of rural France. There were aperitifs and crudités, served outside under a rustic pergola overgrown with wisteria, then a goat's cheese concoction with caramelised onions, coq au vin ('from heaven,' sighed Connie), tarte au citron and some amazing cheese, all washed down with an endless flow of superior Burgundy. Apparently Lisanne cooked a feast each evening for as many people as had booked, and in this case there were eleven, all seated round one long table in the oak-beamed dining room with its stone walls and enormous log-burner.

'I suppose it must get a bit chilly here in the winter,' Maggie remarked.

They were the only Brits, along with two French couples who spoke no English, two German girls who did, and a charming Norwegian couple whose English was on a par with the Queen's. It made for a lively evening with much arm waving and laughter. One of the Frenchmen, who was in his sixties and looked like Charles Aznavour, plainly considered himself to be a comedian and enlisted the help of Étienne to interpret his jokes, most of which were lost in translation and, the more incomprehensible the jokes became, the more everyone laughed to the point of hysteria, while the wine continued to flow.

Apart from the Frenchman's jokes, the German girls' cycling tour and the Norwegians' annual escape from the far north, much of the conversation centred on wine, and on the three mature British ladies heading all the way to Italy, accompanied by at least six different ideas on how they should get there. Advice was not in short supply. Connie mentioned that she'd prefer to avoid mountain roads and passes and head due south, and so they were advised to head for Avignon and then follow the coast. Then there was much jabbering and arguing in French on the best way to get there, avoiding traffic hot-spots, tolls and busy roads, along with several sets of scrawled instructions.

Full of good food, good wine and mild hysterics, the three teetered their way back to Bella by moonlight.

'That was one great meal,' said Connie as they staggered inside. She fumbled for the matches and started to light some candles. 'And God, don't we all look beautiful by candlelight!'

'We *are* bloody beautiful,' Maggie said.

*

Connie woke early, aware of yet another hangover, richly deserved. She resolved to cut down on these alcohol-fuelled evenings, even if they were in France's most famous wine-producing region. Today, she decided, they were going nowhere. She would try to send emails or, at the very least, she must text the family.

They had enough supplies to get them through the day, and the lovely Étienne had offered to sell them some milk and fresh bread, if necessary. As she looked out of the window she saw the two German girls dismantling their tent. Now they might have this little field all to themselves.

Connie enjoyed being on the move, even here in France where she found driving much more stressful than at home. For forty-one years she'd mostly stayed still, bringing up the family and running a small floristry business. There had been, of course, the Annual Holiday. This event frequently involved driving both in Europe and further afield, and always involved worries about the kids – *Where* had Nick got to? (Surely he'd been standing right here just a minute ago?) And Diana with the runs after those dodgy moules! Then there was Ben befriending every dog that ambled in their direction, with the accompanying fear of his being bitten and infected with rabies. And what about little Lou, who refused to eat 'funny food' and was averse to sleeping at night? And not least there was Roger, her then husband, deciding where and when they were going and shouting at everyone to get a move on.

It wasn't until she'd taken off alone three years ago in Kermit, her little green Ford Escort, that she realised how enjoyable it was to be travelling with no family responsibilities, no schedule or timetable, and the added plus of making new, and often unlikely, friends.

This trip was, of course, different. She wasn't alone for a start, but she was in a position to decide where to go and when, because after all Bella was hers and *she* was in the driving seat, proverbially at least. And she certainly hadn't *asked* these two to come along. She was beginning to realise that the aim of this trip was not so much to find family in Italy as it was about the *getting* there. And presumably the getting back, although she couldn't begin to contemplate that far ahead yet.

She could hear no movement from the other two, only some gentle snores from Gill, which Maggie had presumably become accustomed to, much to Connie's relief. She did not relish the idea of sharing her precious bedsit area.

She filled the kettle and placed it on the stove to boil before ambling out in her nightie to survey their surroundings. It was another beautiful morning, already very warm, the air scented (could that be wine?), and a dog barking somewhere in the distance. They'd set up the table, chairs and awning on arrival the previous evening and Connie sat, for the first time, in one of the canvas chairs. It was surprisingly comfortable. I want to stay here for a bit, she thought, stretch out in the sun and do absolutely nothing.

She made a cup of tea and returned to sit outside, joined after a few minutes by Maggie, with Alka-Seltzers fizzing furiously in a glass.

'No more alcohol,' she muttered, '*ever.*'

'Can't wait to see how soon you change your mind.' Connie smiled.

Maggie sank into one of the chairs. 'And why is there always powder left undissolved in the bottom of the glass?'

'Don't know. Probably the same reason there's always a teaspoon left in the washing-up basin and a sock missing from the washing machine.'

Maggie leaned closer. 'I'll tell you something interesting now,' she whispered. 'Gill has *false teeth*!'

Connie laughed. 'No!'

'Oh yes, she does. I suspected as much because she keeps a covered mug by her bunk at night and she never wants to talk after she's got into bed.'

'Well, that doesn't mean—'

'Yes, it does. This morning I had a quick peep in the mug while she was snoring away, and there was her set of gnashers smiling up at me.'

'Poor old Gill. I sometimes wonder how much of her is real,' Connie said.

'That reminds me of a joke.'

'Go on, then.'

'There's this newly married couple on their wedding night. First, the bride removes her wig, then she takes out her teeth, discards her falsies and unscrews an artificial leg. Then she says, "I'm ready, darling." He says, "Well, chuck it over. You know the bit I want."'

Connie laughed. 'When I was young nearly all the grown-ups had false teeth. They'd get to forty or fifty and get the lot taken out. It seemed to be the thing to do.'

'And then have a nice, frizzy perm.'

'And squeeze into their corsets,' added Connie.

'With suspenders dangling.'

They sat quietly sipping their tea before Connie said, 'I'd like to stay here today. As the kids would say, it's time to chill out.'

'I'll need to dig out the suntan lotion,' said Maggie. 'And my cover-up swimsuit.'

'What on earth are you covering up? There's nothing of you.'

'Since we're talking of imperfections I might as well admit to mine.'

'Which is?'

'I had my left breast removed ten years ago.'

'Oh, Maggie, I'm so sorry. I'd no idea.' Connie tried not to look at Maggie's slim frontage in her cotton nightie.

'That's because I wear a bra with a falsie in the left side. Correction: I *used* to wear a falsie on the left side. Now I fill it up with a roll of banknotes and you'd be amazed how much I can squeeze in there.'

Connie wasn't sure whether to laugh or cry, but then realised Maggie was laughing. She felt an enormous rush of affection for Maggie, and Maggie must be fond of her too, to have confided this secret.

Gill, predictably, emerged in a bikini, her enormous top half precariously contained by the pink cotton, the lower half stretched tight across her generous hips. She topped this outfit with an enormous white sunhat.

'My hair's in a bit of a mess,' she sighed.

The other two, spread-eagled on towels in their modest one-pieces, regarded her with awe, as she doused herself in suntan oil. She appeared to be fully made up under the wide brim of the hat.

'You should *never* put your face in the sun,' she advised, looking at them with disapproval, 'if you want to avoid wrinkles.' With that she flopped down, none too gracefully, on her beach towel.

'So, where did these Italian relatives spring from, Connie?' Maggie asked, as she smoothed Ambre Solaire on her legs.

'The fact is I honestly don't even know if I've got any,' Connie replied. 'It's only that when my aunt died I discovered a box from her attic full of stuff about my dad's side of the family, which I knew nothing about, and I discovered my grandmother – my father's mother, that is – was Italian.'

'Surely you knew that before?' Gill said.

'No, I didn't. I was only five, you see, when my parents were killed in an accident. And my grandparents died around the time I was born.'

'Oh, Connie!' Maggie stretched across and patted Connie's shoulder. 'Oh, poor you! To lose both your parents at five! However did you cope?'

'Well, my mother's brother took me in to live with his brood of four. I'm none too sure my aunt was very pleased with the arrangement, particularly as Uncle Bill spent most of his time in the oil business in Nigeria, and so she had to cope with us all single-handed for most of the year.'

Connie well remembered being at the bottom of the pecking order; well fed, well clothed but often a little lacking in love and attention. How she'd looked forward to Uncle Bill's visits home!

'So what have you found out about the Italian grandmother?' Gill asked.

'Only that she was called Maria Martilucci and she came from somewhere near Amalfi. That,' she added for Gill's benefit, 'is just south of Naples. So I did some googling.'

'And?'

'And there are Martiluccis scattered around the country who may, or may not, be related.'

'How interesting!' Maggie said. 'I think that's *so* exciting. And you're due some nice relatives, Connie, aren't you? After losing your parents like that when you were just a wee girl! And you've just got divorced, haven't you?'

'Well, yes, but I can't really complain about my life. And I have my lovely kids.' Connie decided not to mention her beloved son, Ben. I'll tell them later when we know each other better, she thought.

'Five years old!' Maggie repeated. 'You poor wee girl!'

'What about you, Maggie? Don't you miss your son, him being so far away in Australia?' Connie asked.

'Oh yes, I do. We Skype regularly, but it's not the same.'

'And you wouldn't consider flying out there?'

'I've flown around Europe, but for the whole time my heart is pounding and my knuckles are white with clutching the armrests. No way could I do twenty-odd hours. No way.'

'Sometimes I wish one of mine would emigrate somewhere.' Gill sounded wistful. 'I'd love an excuse to go to America or Australia or somewhere. None of yours are abroad, are they, Connie?'

'No, they're all in England,' Connie replied. 'And I'm not sure I could bear it if any of them decided to emigrate. Then again, I suppose the hardest thing about being a parent has always been letting them go.' She thought of her son Ben again. She missed him so much.

She was lucky, she supposed, living close to Di in London, and with Nick and Lou and their families only a train ride away in Sussex, close to where she herself had lived for all of her married life. Connie recalled the endless babysitting, the taking to school and the fetching from school, because Nick's wife worked and Lou had never been much good at coping with anything.

But she'd had no idea how much she'd miss them. She visited often, but the little ones, though delighted to see her, had new friends and new babysitters now.

Grandma had moved to London, and life had adapted and moved on in Sussex.

The sunshine was making them drowsy and before long Gill was snoring and Maggie was sighing deeply with her eyes shut. Connie decided she'd had enough sun and stood up, looked around, and decided to go to explore the little orchard and enjoy the shade of the trees. Somewhere in the distance she could hear the sound of water gushing. It wasn't likely to be a waterfall in an area like this, but it was worth exploring. As she turned a corner between the lines of trees, she found her host, stripped to the waist, brandishing a hose.

'Étienne!' Connie exclaimed.

''Allo! As you can see it is necessary to water. These are young trees, you see.'

All at once Connie felt sweaty, frumpy and lumpy in her demure Marks & Spencer black one-piece, and she was about to turn round, wave and walk away when he said, 'If you and your friends would like a cold shower, this is your opportunity.'

The thought of saving some of Bella's water supply and the soothing cold water on her sweaty body was too much to refuse.

Squealing, laughing and feeling about twelve years old, Connie danced under the jets of icy water.

Maggie wasn't asleep. As soon as Connie had disappeared into the trees, she switched her phone on again and checked for messages. *The man came and I tell him you not here, you never here. He driving Lexus, colour of wine*, Raoul had texted. Oh God, how did he know to go *there*? There are loads of sites round Paris. But I'm not going to let this get to me, she thought. I'm having such a lovely time.

Gill woke up and waited until Maggie laid down her phone. She cleared her throat. 'What about this "lover" of yours then, Maggie?'

Maggie sat bolt upright. '*What?*'

'This lover of yours who just might come looking for you, the one you told Raoul about.'

Maggie took a deep breath. 'Oh,' she said after a minute, 'just some guy I used to know.'

'Why would he be looking for you?' Gill persisted.

'Well, it's a long story. Very boring.'

'It's Ringer, isn't it?'

'Whatever gave you that idea?'

'I'm not stupid. I can put two and two together.'

Maggie snorted. 'Making five as usual. *Wrong* as usual.'

'So, where did that money come from, Mags?'

'I *told* you. From a scratch-card.'

'And I think you're telling porkies. Swear on the life of your son that you won every penny of that money on a scratch-card.'

Maggie sighed. 'Well, not *exactly*.'

'Not exactly? How exactly would that be?'

'Well, I know you'll find this hard to believe, but I found it in the oven just as I was leaving.'

'In the *oven*?' Gill stared at her open-mouthed. 'How on earth do you manage to cook up cash? You must let me have the recipe because it sure as hell isn't one of Delia's.'

'I think Ringer thought it was a good place to store it overnight.'

'My God, Maggie! And where might Ringer have got it from?'

'A bank, I should think.'

'Do you mean that he *stole* it?'

'Well, yes. He didn't exactly tap it out from an ATM, Gill.'

It took a moment for Gill to fully absorb this information before she said, 'I don't expect he'll be well pleased?'

'No,' Maggie replied. 'He's not.'

'Is he likely to come after you then?'

'Yes,' Maggie replied bluntly. 'He's already on our tail.' She checked her phone again. 'But for God's sake, don't say anything to Connie.'

'Bloody hell!' exclaimed Gill, as Connie, dripping wet and laughing, appeared from the orchard.

CHAPTER NINE

CUTTING REMARKS

They stocked up with water at Étienne's where, before their departure, Lisanne appeared with a homemade apple cake and a bottle of fizzy Blanc de Blancs. 'You are such *brave* ladies,' she said. 'I must tell Maman about you; she not ever hardly leave the kitchen.'

Wise woman, Connie thought, looking at the other two squabbling about who was sitting up front and who wasn't.

On the way, they found a small supermarket where they bought some wonderful-smelling bread and a cooked chicken, along with some big, juicy peaches. And where they also filled up with fuel and visited the loo.

'You *make* yourself go now,' Connie ordered. 'Otherwise you'll be looking for a field somewhere, because we're not carrying *that* around in the tank with us.' More squabbling followed about not being able to do such things to order. 'People get heart attacks straining when they don't really need to go,' Gill informed her.

They were feeling very jaded, and still a little hungover, when they spotted the layby, screened by trees, off a remote minor road somewhere just north of Lyon. The only sound was that of birdsong and a tractor in the distance. Maggie and Gill had colluded in their navigating in order to avoid the centres of large towns and cities. They were heading in a southerly direction, with occasional tantalising glimpses of the Rhône, and Connie agreed that Lyon wasn't a priority, delightful though it undoubtedly was.

'We'll probably make Avignon tomorrow or the next day,' Connie said, as they assembled the awning and the chairs on the grass alongside. 'This is such a lovely spot and so private.'

Now, as the three settled themselves in the canvas chairs, Connie noted that her freckles were rapidly reappearing, and that they all looked decidedly pink. Only Gill's face remained chalk-white under the large brim of the sunhat, which she insisted on wearing all day.

'I bet your fellow – Ringer, isn't it? – is missing you now you've gone, Maggie,' Connie said. 'He'll realise now how much you meant to him.'

'That only happens in chick-lit,' Maggie said, quickly recovering her composure.

'Why ever did you take up with him in the first place?' Gill asked with a wicked grin. 'Didn't you know he was a villain?'

'No, I didn't at first,' Maggie replied. It had taken some months for her to realise that Ringer did *not* do night shifts at the local factory, and then only because the police came banging on the door. It was the first of many such visits.

'So why didn't you leave him when you found out?' Gill persisted.

'Because I loved him,' Maggie replied.

'Just that?'

'Just that, Gill. I've only ever loved two men in my whole life: my husband, who I lost to cancer, and Ringer, who I'm losing to the blonde bimbo. I'm very dull, very faithful, never had affairs.'

'You must be feeling terribly hurt now, Maggie, if he *is* being unfaithful,' Connie said.

'Well, I was hurt at first, but then I began to get angry. And it's not like me to get angry. But, you know, I've stuck by him for the best part of forty bloody years. I agreed to have no more kids because he didn't want any, I've covered up for him, provided alibis, found places to hide his bloody cash. And, when that failed, I visited him in jail, and struggled on alone for months on end. And I never, ever – not once – asked him where he'd nicked the money from. I didn't want to know, you see, so that when the police questioned me I could honestly say, hand on heart, that I'd no idea.'

There was a silence.

'I'm not really a bad person,' Maggie added.

'I think you're a lovely person,' Connie said with feeling.

Maggie lay back in her chair and lifted her face to the sun. 'You should get some of this on your face and hair, Gill.'

Gill, clad in a voluminous pink sundress, patted the brim of her hat. 'This stays on until I find a half-decent hairdresser.'

'I'm sure there'll be lots when we get to Avignon,' said Connie.

'Or I could cut it for you,' Maggie offered. 'I'm quite good at cutting. Honestly.'

'I don't want it cut,' snapped Gill.

'It would take years off you. *Years.*'

'No.'

'Let's have a look at it then. Just a *look.*'

'No, it needs washing.'

'We can wash it for you, can't we, Connie?'

Connie nodded. 'We've plenty of water.'

'And we've nothing else to do,' Maggie added.

Very, very slowly Gill raised up her hands to the brim of her hat, then gingerly lifted it off. The entire process reminded Connie of some state unveiling ceremony. Gill had tied up her hair in a topknot, having plainly given up on the beehive. Maggie got to her feet to examine it in detail.

'God, Gill,' she said, running her fingers over it. 'It feels like *wire*.'

'It's only lacquer,' Gill said with a sniff. 'It brushes out.'

'You must be using gallons of the stuff,' Maggie said as she wrestled to remove several elastic bands, countless hairpins and an elaborate bejewelled hairclip.

'Why am I letting you do this?' Gill groaned.

'Never mind that. We need a brush, a sodding strong one.'

'There's one beside my mirror. But there's no need—'

'Oh yes, there is,' Maggie interrupted as she went inside. 'Although I think I'm going to need one of these wide-toothed metal jobs they use on dogs. Long-haired dogs.'

Gill sniffed again. 'She's always having a go at me,' she said to Connie. 'I mean, just *look* at her – you'd think she was some kind of beauty!'

'Gill,' Connie said gently. 'I think it's because she's genuinely fond of you and wants you to look your best.'

Gill's reply was cut short by the reappearance of Maggie, waving a blue brush. 'This it?'

'Yeah,' Gill muttered.

'I'm not sure where to start.' Maggie was trying to undo what remained of the topknot. 'This thing's starched into position. When did you brush it last?'

'I don't remember. Probably a couple of days ago—'

'You don't *remember*! Tell me you're kidding!'

Smelling trouble, Connie got to her feet. 'Calm down, you two. I'm going to put the kettle on. Tea? Coffee?'

When she returned with two mugs of coffee, Maggie was still struggling to remove the final tangles from Gill's hair, with the accompaniment of much swearing and yelling.

'It's longer than I thought,' Connie observed.

'It was even longer than this,' Gill informed her, 'before they cut a couple of inches off in Paris.'

'And half of what's left wants chopping off,' Maggie said, holding a long strand up in the air.

'No,' said Gill.

'You can't keep on starching that outdated tower on top of your head. Not at your age.'

'Sixty is the new forty,' Gill replied.

'Come off it, Gill! If you're sixty I'm the Queen of Sheba!'

'Look, Gill,' Connie interrupted before they could begin arguing again. 'Why not just tie it back in a ponytail or something until we get to Avignon?'

'It's like bloody straw,' Maggie continued. 'Which is down to all that back-combing and spraying you've been doing. Look, you're in the middle of nowhere, so why don't you just let me cut some off and then we can wash and condition it. If you don't like it it'll have grown again by the time we get to Italy.'

After some sighing and lip-chewing, Gill agreed that perhaps an ever-so-tiny, teeny-weeny bit off might be acceptable, until Maggie appeared brandishing the kitchen scissors.

'You're not going to use those ruddy great shears!'

Connie was trying to decide whether Gill's pink face was due to its unaccustomed exposure to the sun, or to plain fury.

'It's all we've got. Sit still.'

'I want a mirror!'

'You can have a mirror afterwards, not now.' With that Maggie lifted up a length of hair and cut off what appeared to be a good six inches. Connie gasped.

'What's she done?' Gill demanded, watching Connie's face.

'I'm cutting off your split ends,' Maggie replied. 'All of them, and boy, you're going to be grateful to me!' She continued cutting.

An hour later Gill still wasn't talking to Maggie.

'Honestly, Gill, you look years younger already,' Connie said truthfully. 'Now, come with me and we'll wash and condition it.'

This operation involved using the shower, removed from its lofty wall connection, rinsing in cold water, because Connie was anxious to save as much gas as possible, a lot of shrieking and two very wet women.

'It's so much easier when you wash your hair while you're showering,' Connie remarked, as she sat Gill outside again and towelled her hair. She began to insert giant rollers while Gill, finally allowed a mirror, dabbed at her smudged mascara.

Maggie looked up from her paperback. 'What that hair of yours needs now is layering.'

'Don't let her anywhere *near* me again!' Gill yelled at Connie.

*

Maggie decided it was wisest to keep out of the way and had been staring, unseeing, at the same page in her book for some time. She was thinking of Alistair, her son in Australia. He'd come back with his Aussie wife and their two tall tanned teenage daughters a year ago, and had rented a flat because there wasn't enough room in Ringer's place for the four of them. And anyway, Alistair didn't go too much for Ringer. Never had. This, in spite of the fact that it was Ringer who'd fed and clothed him after Dave's untimely demise. Alistair had left the flat as soon as he got the place at Bristol and rarely came back, preferring instead to spend the holidays with university friends.

Maggie loved her son dearly but later realised, and always regretted, that she'd given less of her time and attention to him than she had to Ringer. Then she'd been heartbroken when Alistair emigrated to Australia. For a time, she nurtured the hope that she and Ringer might go out there too, but it had to be on a boat because Maggie was terrified of flying. Twenty-something hours – absolutely not! However, there was no way either that Ringer would even contemplate the idea, not even for a holiday. Weeks and *weeks* it would take them to get there on a bloody boat, he'd ranted, and weeks to get back again. London was where he wanted to be and London was where he was staying.

This was not the first time he'd been unfaithful, far from it. Somehow or other she'd always managed to forgive him, take him back, make excuses for him. 'It's just his nature,' she'd explained to her friend, Pam. Pam said it would always be his nature and the older he got the more he'd be lusting after young flesh. She told Maggie she should get out, right now, and not wait until she got ditched. And he was a bad lot anyway, everybody knew that.

When Maggie retired from her office job and was at home for most of the day, she became aware of Ringer's comings and goings – particularly the goings. The more she was available for him, the less he seemed to want her. After a while, her hurt turned into anger and she even began to consider moving out. She hadn't much money of her own and hadn't felt ready, either mentally or physically, to consider a retirement complex, complete with wardens and batty old ladies. Even battier than the ones she was with now.

They found the layby so peaceful that they camped there for a day and a half and saw no one. The only sound came from distant traffic and their sole visitor was a large black and white cat who arrived from nowhere, staying only long enough to purr with enthusiasm while they fussed and petted him. Then, turning up his nose at the proffered milk, he stalked away through the hedge and disappeared.

'That's cats for you,' Maggie grumbled, pouring the milk away. 'Full of appreciation.'

'He must belong to somebody round here,' Gill remarked. 'But we haven't seen a soul.'

'At times that was just as well,' said Connie, remembering their expeditions, armed with toilet roll, round nearby trees and hedges.

'It'll be a bumper year for crops,' Gill observed.

'We'll find a proper campsite next time,' Connie said. 'With electricity and hot showers.'

'And nice, flushing loos,' Maggie added.

*

It was agreed that no trip through Burgundy would be complete without a visit to a winery. It was also agreed that, since there would hopefully be a great deal of 'tasting' of the local produce, they probably shouldn't be driving. Much to Connie's relief, Maggie offered to be in the driving seat. She'd save her taste buds for any samples they might acquire – and only when they stopped for the night.

They set off dreaming of dark, damp underground cellars, stacked with barrels of local nectar, little pipettes at the ready. Connie had done her research and knew that they'd be given the cheapest wine to sample first before the quality would improve. They should spit them all out, of course, which Connie had no intention of doing.

Then they discovered three things. Firstly, they should have booked tours and tastings months beforehand; secondly, the well-known wineries didn't particularly welcome visitors (why would they when they could sell more than they could produce?) and, thirdly, the very few that did have signs outside welcoming visitors only welcomed them mid-morning or late afternoon. Plainly nothing must interfere with lunch.

Just when they'd given up hope of finding anything, they came across a tiny, ancient, rustic winery with a scrawled sign outside proclaiming, 'Bienvenue les Visiteurs!' Maggie pulled in to what had to be the car park but seemed to contain mainly agricultural vehicles and machinery.

The tiny man inside was equally ancient and rustic, and spoke no English. He did, however, deliver a torrent of very fast French along with much tapping of his watch and shrugging of his shoulders.

'I think he probably wants his lunch,' Maggie said.

'Then why's he left that sign outside?' asked Gill.

Maggie grinned. 'Are you going to ask him or shall I?'

The cellar, *l'homme ancien* indicated, pointing at a large trapdoor in the floor, was *fermé*. Then he indicated a selection of bottles on the dusty shelves.

'We want to taste!' said Connie. 'Goûter!'

'Taste!' Gill shouted, clearly of the opinion that if you spoke loud enough, foreigners would understand you.

They all made smacking noises with their lips, but he was having none of it. Did he expect them to buy a bottle without even tasting it?

'Non!' said Connie. 'Non, merci!' She turned towards the other two. 'Time to move on, I think.'

'There was a nice-looking restaurant in that village we passed a couple of miles back,' Maggie remarked. 'And it had a sign outside, in English, about sampling their incredible selection of wines.'

'Sounds like us,' said Connie.

'We'll continue heading due south,' Connie informed Maggie later, replete with boeuf bourguignon and several glasses of wine, as she flattened out the creases on their map. 'And I'd like the next stop to be somewhere near the Gorges du Verdon, which I've been reading about.'

'What on earth is that?' Gill asked.

'It's France's answer to the Grand Canyon, I believe,' Connie replied.

Connie had read that the Gorges du Verdon were considered to have some of the most dramatic scenery in all of France, particularly if you were kayaking, a fact she couldn't resist mentioning to the other two. And, because it was a tourist spot, there should be lots of campsites around. Not only that; it was well on the way to the Mediterranean and the Côte d'Azur.

'What about Avignon?' asked Maggie. 'I've always wanted to dance on that bridge.'

'We'll get there somehow if it's only to see you do just that,' Connie replied.

Maggie got into the driving seat while Gill remained behind, surveying herself in her hand mirror and running her fingers through her newly shorn locks. Although Gill wouldn't have admitted it to Maggie, Connie was sure that she was quite taken with her new image. To emphasise the fact, Connie said, 'I can't get over how *young* that haircut makes you look, Gill.'

Maggie snorted. '*When* did you say your birthday was?'

'I didn't,' said Gill, putting down the mirror. 'But it happens to be in a fortnight's time.'

'We should be in Italy by then,' said Connie.

'And *what* age did you say you were going to be?' Maggie asked as Bella's engine roared into life.

'I didn't,' Gill snapped from behind. 'But, since you obviously want to know, I'll be sixty.'

'And the rest,' Maggie murmured as they drove away. 'Perhaps the shorter haircut will allow some fresh air to reach her befuddled brain.'

There was less traffic on the road than previously and, after agreeing the route, Maggie kept Bella at a steady fifty miles per hour in the slow lane while cars and trucks overtook at breakneck speeds. All except one.

*

After about thirty minutes Maggie said, 'Connie, can you see a car behind us in the door mirror?'

Connie squinted out of the window. 'Yes, why?' she asked.

'Because,' Maggie replied, 'it's the only vehicle in the whole of France that hasn't tried to overtake us.' It was maroon coloured and it was a Lexus. She couldn't make out the registration, but it was British, and doubtless not the registration he used to have. And it was driven by a solitary man. She began to feel her hands become sweaty on the wheel and palpitations hammering in her chest.

'It's probably some old Frenchman out to buy his paper or play boules.'

They drove along in silence for some miles.

Then they saw the sea of red braking lights ahead, and all the traffic filtering across into the slow lane. A green van had moved into the space between the Lexus and Bella.

It took twenty minutes to crawl to the point, about three hundred yards ahead, where a Renault and a Toyota had concertinaed into each other. The two drivers were arguing furiously with extravagant arm waving, whilst a solitary gendarme rationed the flow in both directions. As Maggie approached, the car in front was waved through before he raised his hand to them in a stop sign.

Maggie had to lose Ringer. If it was him. She took a deep breath, ignored the gendarme and accelerated past.

'God, Maggie, he might have our number! Why on earth did you do that?' Connie asked.

'He hasn't got time to make a note of it and I'd had enough of crawling along,' Maggie replied as the traffic gathered speed. That had to be Ringer, but how could he know…?

Gill, who'd been dozing behind as usual, leaned over their seats. 'What's all the bloody noise about?' she asked. 'You woke me up.'

The scenery was becoming much more dramatic and Connie, programming the satnav and studying the map, said, 'I reckon we're getting pretty close to where we want to be. We're definitely east of Avignon, near Manosque. There's a sign ahead showing "Caravan Sites", plural. Should we turn off, do you think?'

'Yes, we should,' said Maggie, who had cramp in her left foot.

They drove into a valley bordered with enormous hedges of hydrangeas, ranging from palest to deepest pink and cornflower blue.

'Unbelievable!' exclaimed Connie. 'When I think of how I used to be so proud of mine when they got up to waist height! And I thought they thrived on sea air, but we're not that close to the sea here.'

At the entrance to each caravan site there was a sign advertising yet another further on. When they reached the fourth, and the signs had run out, Maggie decided it was safe to park. The signs at the entrance, in German, French, Italian and eccentric English, informed them of 'Good Rates per Nicht – Every Fassility'.

'I think we'll have a nicht or two here,' Maggie said in her most pronounced Scottish accent.

'Must have known you were coming,' said Connie.

CHAPTER TEN

A NEW ADMIRER

Gill insisted they parked close to the toilets, showers, shop and cafe, with ample space to erect their awning and set out the table and chairs. As Maggie massaged her cramped toes, Connie watched a British-registered Land Rover expertly reverse an enormous caravan into the next-door space.

'He's done that before a few times,' Maggie remarked.

They'd just sat down outside on their canvas chairs with a bottle of wine when their new neighbour appeared.

'Lawrence Portland-Smythe at your service! Just call me Larry,' he announced. 'Lieutenant-Colonel, retired. Haw, haw!' He was tall and tanned, with closely cut white hair and a bristling moustache. And not a day under seventy. The three gazed at him in amazement.

'I'm taking the old gal down to the Med. Planning to leave her there for the summer.'

'Your wife?' Connie asked.

'No, no! Haw, haw! No, she passed away years ago; tripped over the cat, hit her head on the walnut chiffonier – a goner. Bit of a shock at the time.'

'Yes, I imagine it was.' Connie exchanged glances with the other two.

'No,' Larry prattled on, 'I'm talking about Felicity – Felicity's my *mobile home*.' He indicated the monster next door. 'I say, I seem to have mislaid my bottle opener. Wonder if I could perhaps borrow yours?'

'Why not join us?' Gill had suddenly come alive.

'I say, that's awfully decent of you. Don't mind if I do. Let me get my bottle.'

As he bounded off to find his wine Connie said, 'Honestly, Gill, do we *want* to hear him blathering on all evening?'

'He's probably lonely,' said Gill.

'Well, you'd do all right if you could snare him,' said Connie. 'You could stay with *Felicity* down at the Med all summer!'

'And invite your friends,' added Maggie. '*Haw, haw.*'

Larry reappeared brandishing a very expensive bottle of wine.

'Better have our naff stuff first,' suggested Maggie, pouring him a glass. 'I'm Maggie, and that's Connie, and this here is Gill.'

'Pleased to meet you,' said Gill with a glint in her eye.

With a great deal of bowing, he shook hands with them all in turn before settling down on the grass.

'Why do you call it Felicity?' Connie asked.

'After Felicity Kendal, you know, lovely gal. Always fancied her rotten. Still see her in those wellies, hmm! Haw, haw. *The Good Life*, you know?'

'Well, this one's called Bella,' Connie said. 'Short for La Bellezza. Italian.'

'Bellissima! Speak a bit of the old lingo when necessary! Now, tell me where you're all going. It's not every day I come across three such charming and beautiful ladies in an Italian motor-thingy in the middle of France.'

'We're going to Italy,' Gill informed him, edging her chair a little closer to where Larry had camped himself.

'Italy, eh? Golly! On your hols? *Lovely* country, Italy. Are you interested in art and sculpture? First rate, all of it. You can get tickets for the Uffizi on the internet, do you know? And opera? You'll have to see *Aida* in Verona, an absolute must! And…'

The thing about Larry was that he required few answers to his questions, but just kept wittering on. Connie noted Gill's eyes sparkle with adoration. He's a little out of your class, Gill, she thought as she and Maggie exchanged amused looks.

'Haven't you ladies got any husbands?' He plainly expected an answer to that one.

'Not one!' Gill said cheerfully. 'Although we've had a few in our time, haven't we, girls?'

'Just the one,' Connie said, conscious of the fact that Larry's eyes kept returning to her.

'One's normally enough,' said Larry. 'Haw, haw. I say, this isn't bad wine!' He took a large gulp. 'Italy, eh? Well, you're about halfway there I suppose, to Ventimiglia anyway. But you've a fair way to go after that down to Florence and Rome. Do you like this area? I do; first came here forty years ago. No, I tell a lie, must be forty-five years ago! Still enjoy the gorge though, quite spectacular. Love all of France, so civilised, amazing food, if you know where to go. There's a terrific restaurant just a mile or two up the road. You must try it. *We* must try it. I say, your glasses are empty, do try some of mine!' He stood up and poured four generous measures.

'We'd love to try your restaurant,' Gill enthused, studying the tanned, skinny legs emerging from his khaki knee-length shorts. 'And perhaps you could tell us where we could get a tour of the gorge? Connie and Maggie need a rest from all the driving.'

Larry's gaze turned to Connie again. 'Is it *yours*? And you're driving all the way? Incredible! Well now, as we've become chums, I know exactly how you can get a tour of the gorge. Be at the Land Rover there at seven o'clock sharp tomorrow morning, and we'll have a *wonderful* day. It's a bit of a drive, but worth it. Wonderful! And I know another terrific place to eat—'

'That's so kind of you,' Connie interrupted, 'but we really—'

'No, no, I insist! *Absolutely!* Such fun! I know every twist on the road, and there's lots of them, haw, haw.'

As stereotypes go, Connie thought, he's perfect. Straight from the casting department. 'Golly', 'chums' – did anyone speak like that any more? And who, in God's name, had walnut chiffoniers?

'This is the best bit!' Larry roared, as he navigated another hairpin bend somewhere near Castellane. 'Amazing, isn't it?'

Maggie was beginning to feel nauseous.

He'd insisted Connie sat in the front, while a sleepy, disgruntled Gill and a paler than usual Maggie got slung from side to side in the back at every bend. There was no denying the views were spectacular; the early morning sun warming the rocky sides of the gorge to pink and gold, and throwing little diamonds into the sparkling turquoise-green river below. There were viewing points on the edge of the cliff road from which to look down on the river and take the obligatory photographs.

'Sheer drop!' Larry announced, peering over the edge of a precipice.

Connie, who admitted she wasn't keen on heights, stood well back while Gill inched tentatively forwards and Maggie stayed close to the Land Rover.

'Are you OK?' Connie asked.

'I'm not feeling a hundred per cent today,' Maggie muttered. 'And he's going round these bends like a bloody maniac.'

'*You* are sitting in the front from now on,' Connie insisted.

Maggie grinned. 'I'd rather take a chance on being sick!'

'Best time of day!' Larry pronounced as they got back into the Land Rover.

Maggie had repositioned herself in the back. 'Do you think you could drive a wee bit more slowly, Larry?' she asked.

He gathered up speed. 'Feeling a bit Tom and Dick?'

'She'd be better in the front,' Connie muttered.

'Not at all!' Maggie noted Larry placing a restraining hand on Connie's knee. 'I'll slow down a tad. Keep the window open, Maggie. Fresh air's all you need.'

As they passed the next viewpoint, Maggie let out a scream.

Connie swivelled round. 'What is it?'

'Oh, nothing, Connie. It's just me being silly.'

Gill leaned across to her. 'Are you sure you're all right, Maggie?'

Maggie dropped her voice so that Connie couldn't hear her over the roar of the Land Rover. 'I think I just saw Ringer!' Maggie placed her hand over her mouth.

'What?'

'Ringer! In that layby, back there! A maroon Lexus like his and I'm sure it was him standing beside it.'

'Come on, Mags! It could've been *anyone*,' Gill said. 'You couldn't have seen his face clearly.'

'Well, no, because he had his back to us, thank God, looking at the view. But I know his *shape*.'

'Must be millions of men that shape,' Gill retorted. 'And what on earth would he be doing out here?'

Larry was surveying Maggie in the rear-view mirror. 'I say, what exactly are we talking about?'

'It's just that Maggie's not feeling too good,' Gill shouted as the Land Rover swerved to the left. 'Please, just look where you're going, Larry.' She dropped her voice again. 'It wasn't him, Maggie! Maggie—'

Maggie had stuck her head out of the window to disgorge the contents of her stomach.

'Slow down! Stop!' Gill was tapping on Larry's shoulder. 'Maggie's being sick!'

'Not in the car, I hope,' shouted Larry, braking suddenly.

'I told you she should be sitting in the front,' Connie said.

'I'm OK now.' Maggie had settled back in her seat. 'I just need you to stop somewhere so I can walk around outside for a bit. Get some air.'

'I know,' said Larry, pulling into another observation point. 'We'll go down and have a swim, shall we!'

Maggie had clambered out and was inhaling great gulps of air, Gill at her side.

As Connie got out to join them she said, 'It's a lovely idea, Larry, apart from the fact that we haven't brought bathing costumes and Maggie's feeling ill. Do you think we could just have a slow, steady ride back?'

On the way back to the campsite, Larry did drive more slowly. However, Connie didn't have much chance to enjoy the spectacular scenery due to being distracted by Larry's hand snaking onto her knee at every opportunity. Gill looked fed up, presumably because it was Connie's knee and not hers. Although Maggie appeared to have recovered from her travel sickness she still seemed distracted, constantly looking over her shoulder. Perhaps she'd been spooked by the dramatic drops and precipices of the gorge, Connie thought. And so it was with some relief that they returned to where Bella was reposing in the afternoon sun and Maggie, having checked that no one had broken into the motorhome, took herself off to her bunk for an hour.

'I say, would you like to see inside Felicity?' Larry asked Connie.

'Oh yes, please,' replied Connie. 'We would, wouldn't we, Gill?' She nudged Gill.

'Oh, definitely,' said Gill.

Connie was almost as impressed with Felicity as she was with the gorge when Larry showed off the luxurious interior of his caravan. The lounge even had a built-in quadrophonic sound system, the almost full-sized kitchen-diner was equipped with every conceivable gadget, and the separate bedroom had a double bed and a wall of wardrobes.

'Very comfy,' Larry said, patting the bed. 'Wonderful, comfortable mattress.' He nudged Connie. 'Anytime you get tired of that little bed next door – haw, haw!'

'My little bed's perfectly fine,' said Connie, retreating backwards and colliding with Gill.

'More than I can say for mine,' said Gill hopefully.

'Oh dear,' said Larry, 'never mind.' Then, indicating his well-stocked bar: 'Still don't know where the hell I put that bottle opener though.'

Gill looked as if she was about to say something, but thought better of it.

'You could live in there full time,' said Connie as she stepped outside.

'I fully intend to, every summer,' said Larry. 'I'm heading for a site near Nice. Can't rely on sunshine back in Blighty, can we? Haw, haw.'

They turned down Larry's offer of dinner, citing Maggie's 'indisposition'. Yes, they'd had a lovely day, thank you, but they were having an early night. The man was exhausting.

'Never mind, I'll give you a lift into Avignon tomorrow,' he said. 'I'm lunching with my ex-sister-in-law, would you believe? She lives down here. If you can amuse yourselves for a few hours I could pick you up again late afternoon, what?'

'That would be great, Larry,' Connie agreed.

A couple of hours later all three sat in their nighties drinking iced coffee and trying to keep cool. They'd pulled the blinds down in case Larry decided to do some 'window shopping'.

'It *can't* have been Ringer you saw in the gorge, Maggie,' Gill whispered to Maggie when they got into their bunks. 'How could he possibly know where we'd be going? Just as well we were in Larry's car though. But, if it was him, how come he was there, and parked, even before we came along?'

'Well,' said Maggie, 'he's probably been following us and watching us for days.'

'If it's bothering you that much,' Gill continued, 'perhaps you should look out for him and hand over that bloody cash, so we can all be shot of him.'

'No,' Maggie said very firmly. 'He's not getting a penny of it back.'

'But—'

'He's never done an honest day's work in his life and he's always rationed my allowance so I've had to go out to work every damned day while he lives like a king. In nearly forty years he's never once offered me the security of marriage, and now he's dumping me for a newer model. This is my pay-off – my pension, if you like. Sorry, Gill, but he *owes* me.'

Maggie lay sleepless and thought about Ringer. Had he not chosen a life of crime he might well have been a business tycoon, making millions, operating just inside the law and living in the Bahamas or somewhere. With an endless supply of blondes hanging on his arm.

In the early days, he'd told her about his apprenticeship in relieving the public of their money. He was Wee Willie Bell from Foundry Street who'd been selected by the gang of seven-year-olds to lure unsuspecting housewives to their doors with the order: 'Go on! Ring her bell!' They chose posh areas; big detached houses and – hopefully – husbands at work.

The woman would smile down at this angelic-looking scamp, who'd then engage her in a long conversation, punctuated by the odd tear and sniffle, about his missing cat/dog/mother, while the others tried to get in through the back door to root around for her purse, or pocket anything they could find. They weren't particularly good at it and often came away with nothing. Or else the woman would cotton on and phone the police, by which time, of course, they'd be miles away. You had to be able to run fast and be adept at hopping onto moving buses – and hopping off again – before the 'clippie' got to you to take your fare.

Like a slippery little eel, Willie Bell dodged the law. His good looks were undoubtedly an advantage and why he was chosen to be the decoy. 'Go on!' they said. 'Ring 'er bell!' This stock phrase defined his identity.

And he'd always been successful with the ladies, who gladly assisted him to spend his ill-gotten gains. Maggie knew he was anti-marriage, having come from a broken home himself, and he'd insisted, 'You wouldn't be wanting any more kids anyway, would you? One's enough for anyone.'

On reflection, it was probably better not to have had Ringer's child.

Now she might no longer have Ringer, but she did have his money, and he plainly wasn't going to let that go. That was the reason he was following them, but how had he managed to track them down? She thought it might be a good idea to ring Pam.

'Pam?'

'Yeah, is that you, Maggie? Where are you?'

'We're well down in France, near Avignon. I just keep wondering if you'd given Ringer any other details of our route?'

'Mags, I didn't *know* your route.'

'So there's no way he could have known where we stayed a few days ago?'

'Of course not! And anyway, you didn't know yourself where you were going! But he did say he was going to pay you a surprise visit somewhere so perhaps he's guessing where you might go. But listen, did you know the police were after him?'

'Already?' Maggie said.

'Yes,' said Pam, 'something to do with that Bluett's Bank robbery. They've caught a couple of them and now they've got all the names, but I can't believe Ringer would be involved with that… I mean, I know he's a bit of a villain at times, but not with big jobs like that.'

'This is a long story, Pam, and I won't go into it now.'

'Why don't you give him a ring? Give yourself peace of mind?'

'Yeah, good idea, Pam.'

Maggie switched off her phone and waited outside until Connie went to the loo so she could chat to Gill.

'What I don't understand,' said Gill, 'is how he knew where we'd *been*. I mean, we didn't know ourselves where we were going and there's loads of routes down through France. However did he find Raoul's place?'

'No idea,' said Maggie. 'None at all.'

'Let's just call it a coincidence,' Gill said. 'He probably spent days checking every caravan site in the Paris area before he got to Raoul's.'

'That'll be it,' said Maggie, trying to sound more confident than she felt.

CHAPTER ELEVEN

SUR LE PONT

Connie had read that Avignon, on the left bank of the Rhône, was the seat of the Catholic popes for most of the fourteenth century, and that the Palais des Papes was still there. It also had a cathedral – and a very famous bridge.

Larry, true to his word, had transported them right into the centre. He hadn't stopped talking all the way from the campsite. 'Hope you gals will behave yourselves! Watch out for those old Froggies, haw, haw.'

They headed first for the beautiful old bridge.

'I've got to see this thing after all the times we had to sing that bloody song in school,' Maggie said, insisting they walked out to the end of the bridge and back again.

'After all that it's only *half* a bridge,' said Gill.

'But it's so beautiful,' Connie said.

'We don't make people pay to walk across our bridges,' Gill grumbled, fanning herself with the *English Guide to Avignon*.

Connie was taking photos on her phone. 'I wonder why this bridge is so famous in the UK?'

Maggie shrugged. 'I don't suppose the French do much singing about our bridges. "Sur le Pont de Humber", perhaps?'

'Perhaps they go more for "London Bridge is Falling Down",' suggested Connie.

'The French would enjoy that, since they've never liked us much anyway,' Gill snorted.

'Now, we must all do a wee dance,' said Maggie.

'Why?' asked Gill.

'It's what you do, "Sur le Pont d'Avignon". Now, will we dance separately or all together?'

'I'll do my "mum-dancing",' Connie said, wiggling her hips.

'I'll do the Highland Fling,' Maggie said. 'Haven't done it in years. Here we go!'

'Nuts, both of you!' sighed Gill, giving her hips an experimental sway.

People had now begun to stop, raising their phones and cameras to catch for posterity this vision of three mature ladies doing some appalling dancing.

'Is Craig Revel Horwood here?' shouted one very British voice as the three collapsed in laughter.

'Haven't done anything so daft in years,' Gill remarked as they left the bridge.

'Then we should be dafter more often,' said Maggie.

It was when they were heading towards the Palais des Papes that they noticed Zizi. And Zizi was able to offer Gill an immediate hair appointment.

Both Connie and Maggie were constantly telling Gill that she looked younger and prettier without the 'awful beehive', but Gill was still having difficulty in coming to terms with her shorter cut. But Maggie, wielding those kitchen scissors, had left Gill's blonde locks looking noticeably uneven.

Monsieur René was free, said the receptionist as she consulted her watch, because the lady who should be here at this very minute had to cancel, due to her baby arriving unexpectedly early. 'It arrive thees morning!' she said.

As Gill was about to say 'how lovely' or something apt, the receptionist sighed. 'So 'orrible to be in ze 'ospital with ze bad 'air, no?'

'Oh, quite,' Gill murmured.

'Right then,' said Connie, as Maggie shoved a fistful of euros into Gill's bag. 'We will meet up outside the Popes' Palace in two hours' time – OK?'

'Yeah, fine,' said Gill, heading towards a very dapper Monsieur René.

Monsieur René surveyed Maggie's hairdressing efforts and made a sound like 'eough', which only the French can make, and which plainly expressed disdain.

'Non, non, *non!*' he added to emphasise the point, as he lifted Gill's tresses aloft with his fingers. 'We 'ave much work to do 'ere.'

One hour and fifteen minutes later Gill emerged, in a state of shock, and a hundred euros poorer. She was shorn, and layered. Her hair had never been short or layered in her life before. But everyone in the salon had crowded round to say how beautiful it was, and what miracles Monsieur René had performed. Gill had stared at this unfamiliar woman in the mirror and wondered how many years it would take to grow again.

She felt wobbly and light-headed as she stood outside and tried to see her reflection again in the glass of the window. She had forty-five minutes to kill before she met up with the other two, and now she badly needed some coffee. And probably something alcoholic to lessen the shock. Brandy perhaps.

Gill found the little cafe in a cobbled alleyway between Zizi and the palace. There was one free table under the awning, beside a potted palm. She ordered a coffee cognac and wondered if she had the courage to look at herself in her handbag mirror. She rummaged in the interior of her bag.

'OK if I share your table?' A nice-looking man had appeared from nowhere and was smiling down at her.

'Yes, yes, of course!' Gill shut the bag quickly and gave him a coy smile.

'Thanks.' He sat himself down opposite her. 'My God, it's hot, isn't it?' He was quite dishy. What was his accent – Irish, perhaps?

'Yes,' she agreed. 'It certainly is.' She adjusted the top of her sundress to ensure her bra wasn't showing. Perhaps if he concentrated on her bosom he wouldn't notice her upper arms.

'Don't I know you from somewhere?' he asked.

'I don't think so,' Gill replied. Now, that's a well-used chat-up line, she thought hopefully.

He studied the drinks list. 'This is such an interesting place – have you been to the palace?'

'No,' Gill said. 'I've been to the hairdresser's.'

He glanced up. 'And very nice you look too!'

She sipped her coffee. 'Thank you. Are you British?'

'Oh, yes,' he said. He didn't elaborate further. 'I'm Bill, and you are—?'

'I'm Gill. Nice to meet you.'

'Well, Gill, how do you fancy another drink?'

'That would be very nice, Bill.' She gave a little giggle; this new hairdo was making her feel quite coquettish. And Bill wasn't at all bad; stocky, crew-cut greying hair, nice blue eyes. Probably a little bit younger than she was, unless she'd been *really sixty*, of course.

He summoned the waiter. 'Deux cognacs, s'il vous plaît.'

'Oh, you speak French!' Gill cooed admiringly. She lifted her hem slightly; after all, her legs were still good.

'Only the basics, nothing complicated,' said Bill breezily. 'Anyway, what's a lovely lady like yourself doing all alone in a place like this?'

'Well, I'm killing time really. I'm meeting up with my friends in about thirty minutes.'

'That's a shame,' he said. 'Because I was considering a visit to Châteauneuf-du-Pape, and it would be so nice to have company.'

'Isn't that where all that lovely wine comes from?'

'It certainly is.'

Gill had a thought. 'Are you here tomorrow?' She had no wish to share this nice guy with the other two, but perhaps they could be persuaded to go looking at more palaces and things.

'I may be on the move tomorrow.' He sounded vague. 'I'm hoping to meet up with some friends too.'

'Oh well, never mind.' Gill felt a tiny wave of disappointment, dreams of 'Gill and Bill' fading rapidly.

'Tell you what,' Bill said, leaning towards her across the table. 'We could always go to Châteuneuf this evening. Ah, but what about your friends?'

'I'll give them a call,' Gill said, unearthing her mobile from the depths of her bag. Then: 'Oh bugger, there's no *signal*!'

'Look,' said Bill. 'Why don't I just come to pick you up this evening? Where exactly did you say you were staying?'

'I didn't,' Gill replied. 'But I've got it written down somewhere.' She fumbled in her bag. 'When I get a signal, I'll phone Connie – that's one of my travelling companions – and get the exact directions. I'm not very good at that sort of thing. We're on a campsite, you see, because we've got a motorhome.' She stood up and waved the phone around.

He appeared to be studying her avidly. 'Connie, did you say?'

'That's right. We're going to Italy in Connie's motorhome.'

'You are? That's really interesting. I'd like to hear lots more about that.'

'Do you drive a motorhome then, Bill?' Gill imagined a model containing an enormous double bed.

'No; that's my car over there.' He pointed at a maroon-coloured Lexus parked a good way along the street.

'A Lexus,' Gill repeated. Oh my God, she thought, could this be Ringer? 'Nice cars,' she mumbled distractedly.

'Yes, they are. Good and reliable. And fast.'

A Lexus! And now she was fairly certain she could detect a Scottish accent. Could it be Ringer? What a bloody idiot she was! She should never have given him any information. She was beginning to feel faint as she stood up.

'Thanks for the drink, Bill. I'd better go meet my friends now.'

'Well, I'm coming with you,' he said, draining his glass. 'Otherwise how will I know where to pick you up? You aren't going to be able to get a signal on your phone round here, are you? Anyway, I'd *really* like to meet them.'

'Why don't I just take your number, Bill, and I'll phone you later to give you directions.'

Was it her imagination or was her regarding her closely? '*Where* did you say you were meeting them?'

'Um, well, I didn't,' Gill stuttered. 'But look, I'm desperate to spend a penny. Can you wait for me while I pop inside to find a loo? Then we can go there together. I won't be a minute.'

She was aware of him watching her as she made her way into the dim interior of the cafe. She bypassed the not-very-nice toilet and almost collided with the waiter, who was emerging from the kitchen with a tray of coffees.

'Oh, sorry! Sorry!'

'Madame,' he said, 'you *cannot* go into ze kitchen…'

'*Please!*' she said, edging past him. 'Is there a way out at the back there?'

'Yes, but—'

Gill didn't wait. She hadn't moved so fast in years as she rocketed through the kitchen, tearing past a couple of open-mouthed staff and out through a door at the rear into a dustbin-lined alley. She looked desperately in both directions. Please God, she prayed as she turned right, let this bring me out somewhere recognisable! And while you're at it, God, please let him still be waiting at the front!

She emerged via a narrow passageway, just across the road from Zizi, and not far from the palace. Then she began to run again. I'm going to have a heart attack any minute, she thought. The sweat was trickling down between her bosoms and the straps of her new gold sandals were digging into her feet, which had swollen with the heat. Neither she nor the sandals were designed for sprinting.

'Oh, thank God for that!' she panted as she saw Connie and Maggie waiting a short distance away, watching her in astonishment.

'You don't have to run, Gill,' Maggie called out. 'You're not late.'

'*Love* your hair!' exclaimed Connie.

'*Hair?*' Gill was gasping for breath. 'Oh yeah, my hair.' She'd forgotten all about her hair. 'Never mind that, we have to get away from here, *now!*'

The other two exchanged looks. 'Whatever's the matter, Gill?'

'I'll tell you if I ever get my breath back. Come on, *pronto!*'

Gill had told Connie that a guy had made a pass at her, and he looked menacing, and she'd been afraid. Connie was mystified. It wasn't like Gill to be put off any man so easily, so he must have looked very *very* menacing.

Now that Gill and Maggie were sitting outside, wine glasses in hand, Connie decided to have a few minutes to herself and withdrew The Box from the drawer underneath the settee which doubled as her bed. She looked again at the dark-eyed, dark-haired Maria in her white dress and wondered what she might have looked like in later life, as there appeared to be no further photographs, not even of her wedding. Perhaps Maria and her grandfather had eloped? But how had they met? No package holidays in those days, when only the very rich ventured to Italy on the Grand Tour. Well, she'd contact this Pozzi person when she got to Italy. As he or she probably only spoke Italian, delivered at machine-gun speed, she'd need to befriend someone to help with the translation. She'd only got as far as the future tense in her *Teach Yourself Italian* book. 'I will come to Naples tomorrow' was unlikely to be very useful in establishing who this Pozzi person was and how he or she might be connected to these elusive Martiluccis.

Even with her reading glasses on, Connie found it difficult to decipher the faded writing on the letters. Perhaps one of those little magnifying glasses would help her to read the faintest pen strokes. She'd look up the word and go shopping for one as soon as they got to Italy.

'Describe him again,' Maggie ordered, as she and Gill sat under the awning with large glasses of Burgundy. Connie was inside and Larry had gone out with the sister-in-law again, much to their relief.

'Well, he was average height – a bit taller than me.'

'Go on.'

Gill was massaging her blistered feet. 'And he had a sort of crew-cut.'

Maggie frowned. 'Ringer's head is normally shaved.'

'I suppose it could have grown a bit since we left,' Gill remarked. 'Particularly if he wanted to *look* different. Blue eyes, quite good-looking. He was wearing shorts and—'

'Shorts! No way!' Maggie interrupted, shaking her head. 'His left leg's badly scarred; he never wears shorts!'

'And he was wearing a stripy short-sleeved shirt. And a Rolex. I noticed he was wearing a Rolex.'

'Well, yes, he has a Rolex, but so have lots of people,' Maggie retorted.

'Not lots of the people I know,' Gill said. 'And I'm pretty sure he was Scottish, although he didn't sound *very* Scottish. Not like you.'

Maggie was chewing on a nail. She was well aware that Ringer could tone down his accent if it suited him. And that's exactly what he would do.

'Oh God!' moaned Gill. 'I've just remembered I told him I was travelling with someone called Connie in a motorhome heading for Italy.'

Maggie groaned inwardly. Trust Gill, she'd tell any man anything to get herself a date. Well, if it was Ringer, she thought, then he's certainly going to be on to us now. And, fond as I am of Connie, I don't know how she'd be likely to react if she knew.

'I think Connie might go to the police,' Gill said, as if reading Maggie's mind, 'if she knew what was going on. No need for her to know, is there?'

'What on earth are you two whispering about?' Connie asked, appearing out of the doorway.

'I'm just trying to convince Gill how nice she looks with short hair,' Maggie said. 'And she's still arguing about it.'

CHAPTER TWELVE

GRASSE

At breakfast the following morning, Gill was clearly having some difficulty in coming to terms with the fact that her admirer's intentions may not have been entirely romantic. *If* it was Ringer. And, if it wasn't Ringer, she'd let a very fanciable man slip right through her fingers.

'Perhaps I should have stuck with him,' Gill lamented to no one in particular.

'Never mind, Gill,' Connie soothed. 'He probably had a wife and six kids somewhere.'

'*I've* got six kids,' Gill retorted.

'Yeah, well, perhaps he had halitosis,' Maggie added helpfully, making a face at Gill to tell her to shut up.

'It's all very well for you two,' Gill said. 'You've left your bloke behind, Maggie, and you're not bothered about meeting anyone else, are you, Connie?'

'No,' Connie replied. 'Not after forty-one years with the same person. I'm enjoying my freedom.'

'But,' Gill persisted, 'don't you sometimes just feel the *urge*, the need… you *know*…'

'I only feel that sort of need when I'm with a person who turns me on,' Connie said. 'And there aren't many like that around, particularly at my age.'

'Haven't you fancied *anyone* since your divorce?'

Connie grinned. 'No, not so much *since* my divorce as *before* my divorce. That was one of the reasons why I decided to leave Roger.'

Maggie and Gill both turned to stare at her.

Gill finally found her voice. 'So where is he then, this fancy man?'

'In Cornwall, probably. That's where he lives.'

Connie thought again about Don Robertson, as she often did; his tall, toned body, his dark eyes, his wry sense of humour.

'Connie,' Maggie said patiently. 'You need to tell us all!'

'Yes, you do,' Gill added. 'You know all about *us*. All we know about *you* is that you were married *forever* and you know how to arrange bloody flowers!'

Connie hadn't realised that she'd spoken so little of herself. Did they think she was a bit boring? Just another old Silver Single, or whatever elderly divorcees were called these days?

'OK, I'll tell you then. My marriage was stagnant. Yes, that's the word – stagnant. So I decided to take myself off in my little car, and leave them all to it, while I sorted myself out. I drove all the way up to the north of Scotland and back again.'

'And did you decide what to do?' Gill asked.

'Oh yes, but only on account of the people I met and the experiences I had on the way. They all helped me to see life more clearly, what was important and what wasn't. And it was on this trip that I met Don.'

'Don?' said Maggie. 'Let's hear about him!'

'Well, sex with Roger was, by this time, non-existent. And it never bothered me unduly because I'd stopped fancying him and it had never been great anyway.' She paused. 'I met Don briefly when we were roped in as extras on a film shoot, and then, shortly after that, my car broke down just outside Inverness. And guess who came along in his Merc to rescue me? Tall, dark, handsome, and ten years my junior!'

'Wow!' said Gill.

'I had no choice but to accept his offer of a lift. My car had given up the ghost and I thought I'd take a lift to the nearest station and then head back home. That, of course, would have been the sensible thing to do.'

'But you didn't do the sensible thing?' Maggie asked.

'No, I didn't. I'd stopped being sensible.'

'Hallelujah!' cried Gill.

'He said he'd give me a lift home – via the scenic route.'

'I'll bet!' said Gill.

For a brief moment Connie was back in Arisaig on Scotland's stunning west coast, with its golden sands and panoramic view of the islands: Skye, Rùm, Eigg.

'The weather was glorious, and we found this beautiful place. And we made love.' Connie paused. 'And I'd never experienced anything like it in my life! *Never!*'

They both stared at her expectantly.

'And then?' Maggie asked.

'And then we had a few magical days together. And then I left him behind.'

Gill looked thunderstruck. '*You left him behind?* Why the hell would you do that?'

'Because I didn't want to fall in love with him,' Connie replied, aware for the first time that this was, in fact, the truth. 'He was a ladies' man, a lotario; he'd been married and divorced twice and everywhere we went the women were ogling him.'

'Sounds good to me,' sighed Gill.

'It wouldn't have worked in a million years. We both knew that. But he'd awakened in me feelings, physical feelings, that I never knew existed! And, for that, I'll always be grateful. Always. But he was just one of the experiences I had that made me realise I didn't have to endure a dull, boring marriage.'

There was a moment's silence before Maggie asked, 'And you've never set eyes on him again?'

'Oh, just occasionally,' Connie replied, smiling. 'When he comes up to London we sometimes have a day or two together. In fact, he was with me for a day shortly before we left.'

'And that's enough for you?' Gill asked.

'That's enough for both of us,' Connie agreed. 'But I might just see him in Rome.'

It would be fun to see him in Rome, she thought, but not as important as it once would have been.

'You must all come with me to Nice,' Larry said, looking directly at Connie, as he tapped on their door a little later. 'Once I've got Felicity nicely settled I'll be free to take you gals around, what?'

'Well, of course we'll call to see you,' said Connie. 'But now we want to go to Grasse, for the lavender. And Gill wants to go to Cannes.'

Larry guffawed. 'Cannes! Bloody place is full of poofs and posers, and the film festival's over, you know.'

'I'd still like to go,' Gill said. 'I've always fancied going to Cannes.' She no longer fancied him though. Apart from the fact he'd set his sights on Connie, he was such a bore, always trying to organise them. And that posh accent and haw-hawing were getting on her nerves. He sounded like someone out of an old British wartime film; you couldn't believe people ever spoke in those precise clipped accents.

'I can't go dragging Felicity round half of Provence,' Larry sighed. 'But promise you'll come to see me in Nice. Promise?'

They all nodded solemnly. It didn't do to argue with Larry and, anyway, they could make it a very short visit.

'There are so many places you won't be able to get to with that bloody great thing,' he said cheerfully, with a nod in Bella's direction. There followed an exchange of numbers and much advice from Larry on where they might park Bella.

'This isn't Brighton or Bournemouth, you know,' he said, 'you're not going to find zillions of caravan sites.' He was probably right. 'Anyway, you'd better head for the Luberon if you're set on all that lavender.'

They waved goodbye to him with sighs of relief, as he towed Felicity out onto the road.

'He means well,' said Maggie.

They arrived at the perfume capital of the world at exactly the right time, with the fields of lavender in full, glorious, scented bloom.

It took Maggie's breath away. She'd always loved perfume; even as a little girl she'd help herself to her mother's Evening in Paris or Yardley's Lavender, both of which she considered to be the height of sophistication. In later years, she'd sampled most of the well-known perfumes before settling on Chanel No. 5. You couldn't go wrong with Chanel No. 5 and Maggie had treated herself to the perfume in Paris. Not the eau de parfum, but the real deal. And several bottles at that.

In Grasse, they bought sachets and oils and soaps and lotions. They visited the International Perfume Museum, and even discovered that jasmine and roses – the key ingredients of Maggie's Chanel No. 5 – were grown in protected fields around the area.

They were unprepared for and completely mesmerised by the sight and smell of the unbelievable purple miles of lavender, which seemed to stretch to the horizon in every direction.

'It's the best time,' they were told at one of the lavender farms. 'From now until the middle of July, before the harvest. And the tourists.'

'There's no shortage of tourists now,' Connie remarked. 'So heaven only knows what it'll be like next month.'

'And in August,' Maggie added, 'when everyone in France goes on holiday.'

Most of the lavender farms were family-run and, having asked the elderly owner's permission, they left Bella in the tiny car park of one of them, where fortuitously it was well hidden from public view.

They strolled along the roads between the fields, breathing in the scented air, the only sound being the tinkle of sheep's bells in the distance, and the occasional bleat of a goat.

'Wow, it's hot!' Maggie exclaimed, collapsing onto a grassy bank.

'My feet!' moaned Gill.

It was *always* Gill's feet. She should get herself some decent trainers, Maggie thought, instead of all those ridiculous strappy sandals.

Just then some goats made a fleeting appearance.

'Perhaps we can get some goat's cheese,' Maggie suggested.

Connie stretched out her legs. 'Good idea!'

'Horrible stuff!' said Gill.

'Well, you don't have to eat it,' Maggie retorted. 'I'm sure we can find you a bit of mouldy old cheddar somewhere.'

Gill snorted.

'You're putting on a little weight, Maggie,' Connie remarked. 'And it suits you.'

'It must be contentment,' said Maggie. She was pleased because she'd always been on the skinny side. And yes, it might well be contentment because, for the first time in years, she felt relaxed and happy. What was it, she wondered, that someone had once said? That it wasn't the destination that was the best part, it was the *getting* there. That, of course, was before the days of being herded like cattle through airports. Now she didn't even care too much that Ringer was on their heels and might well catch up with them, because she was hopeful she could outwit him and, besides, she had enough cash in her bra alone to get well away.

She'd always been clever. When she got her Highers in school the teachers all agreed she should go to university. She hadn't gone, of course, because the family couldn't afford it, and then Dave came along. But she'd have liked to study law; the legal system fascinated her and sometimes, when she was watching courtroom dramas on TV, she wished she'd managed to get on the right side of the law.

'It'll be dark soon,' Connie was saying. 'We should be moving.'

When they got back to the little car park, Bella was the only remaining vehicle. As they were unlocking the door, they heard the sound of a tractor approaching and recognised the farmer driving it.

'Excuse me!' Maggie got to him just as he turned the noisy engine off.

'Oui?'

'Could we stay here tonight? Ce soir? S'il vous plaît?'

He jumped down and studied the three of them for a moment. 'Pourquoi? Why?'

'Because it is getting dark and we have nowhere booked to stay tonight. Comprenez?' Maggie gave him what she hoped was a sad, appealing look. 'We are three ladies, all alone. And we will pay. Money. Argent!'

She wondered if he'd understood. Finally, he stepped forward and held out his hand. 'Yes, for tonight only. I am Claude.'

He had white tufty hair and very blue eyes. He nodded as they all shook hands solemnly.

'I am Maggie, and this is Connie and Gill.'

'Ma-gee,' he repeated. Then, as an afterthought: 'You have food?'

The French, Maggie thought, always get their priorities right. 'Yes, yes,' she replied. 'We have food. We'll be no trouble.'

'Ask him if we can use his loo,' Connie murmured.

'You have a toilette, Claude?'

'Of course!' He paused and shrugged. 'Maybe it is not so clean. I am alone, you see.'

'Let me clean it for you!' Maggie said eagerly, as the other two gawped at her in astonishment. 'I'm good at cleaning, Claude!'

'She's good at everything!' Connie added.

'He wasn't kidding,' Maggie said later, wiping her brow, as she replaced the toilet cleaner and bleach. 'But at least we can use his loo now without feeling guilty.'

'Or catching something nasty,' added Gill, who was busy chopping onions. 'Or forgetting not to shut the door and getting stuck inside.' She still managed to get stuck in there, at least once a day. It was proving difficult to remember not to pull the door shut behind her.

'And he's letting us use his electricity supply,' Maggie added. 'I've paid him for everything so he's a happy bunny.'

Connie was slicing mushrooms and adding generous amounts of red wine into the minced beef simmering in the cooking pot.

'Tell him he's welcome to join us if he fancies some spag bol,' she said. 'Except actually its tagliatelle-bol because no self-respecting Italian would dream of having *spaghetti* with bolognese sauce.'

'Perhaps he won't eat Italian,' said Gill. 'Some of these French are supposed to be peculiar about everyone's food but their own.'

'He'll jump at the chance,' Connie said, stirring the pot. 'He's got his eye on Maggie.'

'Och, what nonsense!' Maggie said, going noticeably pink. 'He just knows a good loo cleaner when he sees one.'

Claude had no hesitation in accepting their invitation to supper. Connie reckoned he couldn't have cared less what nationality the food was; he ate with relish, rarely taking his eyes off Maggie. When he spoke, usually with his mouth full, he told them how much he missed having a woman in his life since his Marianne had died.

'Four years ago,' he mumbled as he shovelled in another forkful of pasta. 'And I make all this lavender for her, for Marianne.' He waved an arm to indicate his domain. 'My father like to grow it, I like to grow it, and later my elder son will return from Marseille and he too will grow it.' He gazed sadly at Maggie. 'And now I only grow it for the tourists.'

'Maggie loves lavender,' Connie said, winking at Maggie. 'That's why we're here.'

'When I was young we had one wee lavender plant in our back yard,' Maggie said with a faraway look in her eyes. 'My mam would put bunches of it in the wardrobe to keep away the moths, and then she'd put some in the airing cupboard so the sheets and towels would smell nice.' She turned to Claude. 'It reminds me of my mam, and when I was a wee girl in Glasgow.'

Claude wiped his mouth. 'You are from Scotland, Ma-gee?'

'Indeed I am.'

'Ah,' he said. 'The music of Scotland I like very much. I have in the house a record of Jimmy Shand and his band, brought to me from Scotland. You would like to hear?'

'No, no, Claude, but thank you very much for the offer,' Maggie said hastily, trying to ignore the others' snorts. 'Fact is, we're all pretty tired so, if you don't mind, I think it's time we said bonne nuit.'

Half an hour later as they got ready for bed, having trooped in and out of Claude's loo, Maggie said, 'Poor man, he's just lonely.'

'Perhaps he frightens the ladies away with that Jimmy Shand record,' Connie suggested.

Maggie grinned. 'Nothing wrong with Jimmy Shand. And you know how the French like their accordions.'

Before Claude trundled away on his tractor the following morning he gave them directions to 'the farm of my son'. This son lived a very short distance from Cannes. He was sure that Jean-Paul would be happy to let them park there, and that they would like to buy his vegetables and his wine.

'They probably need their loo cleaned,' Maggie murmured as he waved them goodbye.

'This talent of yours could probably get us parked all the way to Italy,' said Gill.

'Ah, but he did fancy her,' Connie put in.

'You missed your chance there,' Gill said. 'You could have spent the rest of your days sniffing lavender and feeding him pasta.'

'And listening to Jimmy Shand,' added Connie.

And they all giggled at the thought.

CHAPTER THIRTEEN

CANNES

Claude's son, Jean-Paul, and his wife, Amélie, had a small farm very close to Cannes. There was a vineyard, an olive grove, an assortment of fruit, vegetables and poultry, and a large, woolly dog of indeterminate breed called Guy. There was little doubt about Guy's masculinity as he seemed intent on mounting everything in sight: the table leg, Connie's leg, Maggie's leg, Gill's leg. Guy was not picky.

Apparently Claude had telephoned ahead with his approval of the 'so-charming lay-dees', who needed somewhere to park and who would pay, of course, and would very likely buy eggs and fruit and wine. Although Jean-Paul spoke reasonable English, it took a little explaining from Maggie to make him understand that they would prefer not to be seen from the road.

'Why?' Connie asked. 'What does it matter?'

'Traffic noise,' said Maggie. 'It always keeps me awake.'

Eventually he got their drift, shrugged, and found a spot for Bella well concealed behind a cluster of farm buildings. And with the added bonus of an outside loo, which had Maggie digging out the bleach again.

Connie was relieved to stop for a few days; to wash Bella down, if she could borrow a hose, and to examine her for bumps and scratches. She still had problems reversing the vehicle, which had resulted in a few minor scrapes, but fortunately there seemed to be no dents.

Apart from Guy's unwanted attentions it was an ideal spot, from which they could walk into Cannes where, at the station, there was a regular train service all along the Riviera coast, all the way to Italy.

'We should stay here for a few days,' Connie said. 'It only takes about forty minutes to get to Nice and Monaco. Let's face it, we don't want to be parked too close to Larry, and that's if we could even find a site at Nice.'

'Take your choice between two randy males then,' Maggie said. 'Guy or Larry?'

'Oh, give me Guy every time,' Connie replied. 'He's quite happy with a table leg and a biscuit.'

'I'm surprised Larry didn't make a play for you, Gill, with that new hairdo,' Maggie said.

'I don't need Connie's cast-offs,' Gill retorted.

'He was never exactly cast-*on* as far as I'm concerned,' Connie commented. 'And I think he'd have driven you mad in a very short space of time, Gill.'

Although she'd never admit it to the other two, particularly Maggie, Gill was very pleased with her new look. Her short haircut did, as predicted, take years off her, and she'd cut down on the make-up too – partly from necessity, as it kept sliding off in the heat. Besides, she'd acquired quite a tan. Her kids would hardly recognise her! And she felt happier than she had in years. And that, she thought, always puts a smile on your face and a bounce in your step, even at seventy. Well, she might as well admit it: she *would* be seventy shortly, and she was beginning to realise that it might be preferable to look young for seventy rather than old for sixty.

Anyway, there was no fooling these two. She should never have let them see her passport, which she'd thoughtlessly lifted out of her shoulder bag, along with everything else, when she'd thought she'd lost her purse back in Avignon, which of course she hadn't.

Maggie had grabbed it with the speed of light. 'I love looking at people's passport photos,' she said. 'God, Gill, that beehive did you no favours!'

So they *knew*. But she was only a couple of months older than Connie and a whole year younger than Maggie, so there was nothing much to worry about.

Up to now Gill had spent very little of her own money and had a fierce urge to do some shopping. Cannes was, after all, one of the playgrounds of the rich and famous, and must be stuffed with enticing boutiques. Not only that, Maggie had given her a wad of notes before they went to bed last night and had said, 'Go on, buy yourself something, Gill. And thanks for being so supportive about Ringer and for not telling Connie.'

She'd lost a little weight, she had a new hairdo, and she could hardly wait.

'I'm going to go on ahead,' she said to the others. 'I want to have a good look round the shops.'

'OK,' said Connie. 'Let's meet up at the marina at midday, say. I've borrowed a hose, so I'm going to wash Bella down before I go anywhere.'

Jean-Paul pointed her in the right direction and Gill set off. 'Just keep the sea to your right,' he'd instructed her.

It was all so beautiful: the incredible blue of the sea, the dark pines and the vivid flowers, all set against the dark grey-blue background of the mountains. The walk took longer than she'd reckoned because she kept stopping to admire her surroundings and then got a bit lost finding her way to the centre of the city, it being considerably larger than she'd expected. But, oh boy, it was worth it! Lovely shops, expensive of course, but at least they catered for ladies with large bosoms. They probably get a lot of them round here, Gill reckoned, thinking of all those bikini-clad starlets. And so, for once, she had no problem in finding two dresses that fitted her curves.

She had an hour to kill before midday and couldn't afford to spend any more money, so she headed towards the marina. She loved looking at yachts, imagining who might own them, and what they might be like inside. And there were plenty of yachts here, each one seeming intent on outdoing the one next to it. They were sleek and beautiful, as were the few people she saw on their decks: suntanned, bare-footed, with sun-*kissed* hair – not sun-*bleached* – and there was a huge difference. Several hundred euros' worth of difference.

Il Delfino caught her eye. It was one of the larger craft, painted in blue and white and flying an Italian ensign. Wow – what a boat! Gill stopped and stared just as a bronzed young man, clad only in very tight white jeans, appeared on deck.

'Hey!' he called out. 'Come on board! You must be Gill!'

Gill looked round in confusion. There was nobody else there, but how did he know her name?

'Yes,' she stuttered, 'but how—'

'Come on, then,' he said impatiently. 'Let me show you around quickly. I am Pietro.' He spoke perfect English with a very attractive Italian accent.

As if in a dream, Gill, clutching her carrier bags, wobbled her way across the little gangplank. She'd give a lot to see inside, but how on earth did this guy know her name?

Her new friend glanced down at her feet. 'You're not wearing spiky heels or anything, are you?' He indicated the expensive wooden deck.

Gill shook her head, glad she'd decided to wear flat shoes for her walk into town. She was tingling with excitement. Just wait until she told Connie and Maggie about this! She must be looking even better than she thought!

She followed him across the deck, bypassing the enormous salon, which she very much would have liked to see, and into a wood-panelled, elegant dining room, the polished table set up for twelve lunches. She hardly had time to savour her surroundings before he said, 'Come, now! I'll show you the galley!'

Gill would have liked to see the salon and the bedrooms in this floating palace, but perhaps he'd show her those after the kitchen. Maybe this was some sort of tour and she was the last person who'd shown up. Perhaps she'd be joining the others later.

She followed him down the staircase into a long, streamlined galley kitchen, where two suntanned, blonde-haired, giggling girls in tiny tops and shorts were busy chopping vegetables.

'This,' Pietro said, with a wave of his hand, 'is Céline and Fifi, and they will be assisting you today.'

Assisting her? To do what? As she was about to ask what the hell was going on, she realised, with consternation, that the boat was moving. Where she could see the yacht moored alongside only a minute or so ago, there was now only sea.

'We're *sailing*!' she exclaimed.

Pietro looked at her as if seeing her for the first time. 'That,' he said drily, 'is what boats do.'

'But I need to get off!' Gill shouted. 'I'm meeting my friends in a few minutes!'

There was silence. The girls stopped chopping and turned to look at her.

'What are you talking about?'

'I need to get *off*!' Gill repeated. 'You'll have to take me *back*!'

Where the hell were they going? Was she being abducted?

'You *are* Gill, aren't you?' Pietro's voice was heavy with exasperation.

'Yes, but where are we *going*?' Gill stared out in panic at the receding coastline.

'You're our chef for today?'

'*Chef!*' Gill leaned against the work surface for support. 'Chef! Are you kidding? Is this some sort of bloody joke?' I'm definitely going to be having that heart attack any minute now, she thought.

'No, it is *not* a joke!' Pietro shouted, getting red in the face. 'You are supposed to be cooking lunch. Why else would you be on board?'

'Because you asked me,' Gill snapped.

'Because you said you were Gill! And you have these bags of vegetables, no?'

'I *am* Gill! And I have bags of dresses!'

'Then you are the *wrong* Gill!'

Pietro was pulling at his hair, by which time the girls were clutching each other in hysterics.

'This is no laughing matter!' he shouted. 'Dio mio, we will have to go back! We have no cook! They will go crazy!'

With that he disappeared up the steps, two at a time. There followed raised voices, much scuffling and a distinct change in engine noise.

Gill, speechless, stared at the uncut courgettes and peppers on the galley worktop, while Céline and Fifi wiped their tears of laughter with kitchen towel.

'She's late,' Connie remarked, consulting her watch. 'Heaven only knows how many outfits she must be buying.'

'Never mind,' said Maggie. 'There must be worse places to wait. Will you just *look* at some of these yachts!'

Connie indicated a bench. 'We might as well sit down. My feet are complaining. It's not that it was a particularly long walk, but it's the heat, I think. My ankles didn't used to swell like this years ago, did yours?'

'No, they didn't. And I didn't need to keep looking for loos either.' Maggie's first priority was always to find a toilet, which inevitably meant buying a drink at a cafe just to use their facilities, and which rather defeated the object since she then had to go again shortly afterwards.

'Never mind,' Connie said. 'We look better than that old girl over there.'

The old girl in question, surrounded by carrier bags, was short and fat, with cropped grey hair, and she filled every inch of her checked trousers.

'Perhaps she's waiting for her boat to come in,' Maggie giggled.

Connie looked at the glamorous young people on their decks. 'She'll wait a while.'

'Have you ever been on one of these yachts, Connie?'

'No, never. Have you?'

'No, but I might be able to buy a little teeny one now!' No, I wouldn't, she thought. This showy lifestyle wouldn't be for me.

'Hey, look!' Connie pointed out at the entrance to the marina. 'Look at this beauty coming in!'

They both gazed in awe as the sleek blue and white yacht came slowly in and moored in the empty space directly in front of them.

'"Il Delfino"; that's Italian for "The Dolphin",' said Connie, fresh from her studies.

'Wow!' said Maggie.

At that moment an attractive but very angry-looking young man, clad only in tight white jeans, leapt ashore brandishing a rope. He shouted at the woman with the bags, who nodded.

'Well, he doesn't exactly look like a barrel of laughs,' Connie said. 'And what about the old girl! You can never tell from appearances, can you?'

Having secured the boat at the little walkway, the young guy retreated as a large, bald, mahogany-coloured man emerged from the main cabin, accompanied by an ordinary-looking woman with a couple of carrier bags.

'*She* doesn't look much like a jetsetter,' Maggie remarked. 'She looks a bit like Gill.'

'Yes, she does. And I bet Gill would give her eye teeth to be on a yacht like that!'

'Her false teeth, you mean!' Maggie said, and they both dissolved into giggles.

Now the bald man was shaking the woman's hand and she seemed to be waving at them.

'Why is she waving at us?' Maggie asked, screwing her eyes up against the sun.

'Because I think it *is* Gill,' said Connie.

'You're having me on!'

'No, I'm not. Are we hallucinating or something?'

'Coo-ee!' Gill called out. She stepped ashore, shaking the hand of the woman with the bags, who then went promptly on board.

'I've just had a lovely glass of champagne!' she said cheerfully as she joined Connie and Maggie, who were gawping at her open-mouthed.

'What in heaven's name were you doing on a boat like that?' Connie asked.

Gill filled them in with the details. 'I didn't know they were looking for a cook,' she said. 'I thought he just wanted to show me around.'

'Why on earth would he want to do that?' Maggie asked.

Connie was still laughing and wiping her eyes.

'Dunno,' Gill said. 'What's so funny, anyway?'

'You are!' Connie spluttered. 'You're priceless!'

'So, what happened when this Pietro discovered you were the wrong Gill?' Maggie asked.

'Well, he went ballistic. But it wasn't my fault, was it? He had to go up to tell Sir Somebody that he wasn't going to get any lunch if he didn't turn the boat around. But Sir Whatever-his-name-was was ever so nice to me. He told me all about how he'd chartered the boat for a fortnight from some rich Italian car magnate. He just thought it was all a big joke. He was full of apologies and gave me a lovely glass of Bollinger while we came back to the marina. I wish I could find myself a man with a yacht like that!'

At this, both Connie and Maggie howled with laughter again. Then Connie stood up and gave Gill a hug. 'What would we do for entertainment without you?' she asked.

CHAPTER FOURTEEN

NICE

The day following Gill's mini-cruise, they boarded one of the many trains heading eastwards along the coast to Nice, where Larry was to meet them at the station. Connie had informed him on the phone that they'd just like a stroll along the Promenade des Anglais and a wander round the old city, knowing that Larry would have plans for Vence, and the mountain villages.

'He means well,' Connie sighed, gazing out at the incredible blue of the sea from the train window. 'He just likes organising people.'

'Bloody bossy more like,' said Gill.

'And he drives like a maniac,' Maggie added, with memories of the gorge. 'And you can bet your boots there'll be loads of twisty mountain roads round here.'

Connie had been here before. 'Some are,' she confirmed.

'And he also wants to get your knickers off,' Gill informed Connie.

'Oh, that's a bit of an exaggeration,' Connie replied. 'And I can assure you he hasn't got a cat's chance in hell.'

'He'll try,' warned Gill.

'He's *very* trying,' Maggie added.

At the station in Nice, Larry hugged them all in turn, Connie longer than the others, planting wet kisses on hastily turned cheeks as he aimed for their mouths. He beamed at them, resplendent in his Fred Perry shirt, baggy khaki shorts, and short grey socks underneath his brown leather sandals.

'I thought today we'd do Nice,' he announced, as they strolled along the promenade. Everyone here looked healthy, tanned and casually elegant behind their outsized sunglasses. 'And tomorrow we'll go up into the mountains, because there are some places you gals simply *must* see. And then there's Monaco of course; terribly vulgar and lots of ghastly people live there, but worth a look around nevertheless. Wonderful casino though, if you have a million or two to get rid of, haw, haw. You can pass a week round here very easily.'

'We're not staying a week,' Connie said firmly. 'Only a couple of days. We want to get to Italy.'

'What's the hurry?' Larry asked. 'Italy will still be there next week.'

'We want to get there for my birthday,' Gill piped up.

'Why?' Larry stopped in his tracks. 'What's wrong with France?'

'*Nothing's* wrong with France,' Connie replied. 'It's just that Gill fancies having her birthday in Italy.'

This was news to all of them as Gill's birthday, just a week or so away, had not been discussed in any detail, other than that Gill wanted it kept very low-key. There had been no word about Italy. Until now.

Larry gave one of his derogatory snorts.

'But we appreciate all your kind offers,' Connie added. 'Perhaps we'll be able to see a few more places on the way back.'

'And when will that be?' Larry asked.

There was complete silence as they all stopped and looked at each other.

'I've no idea,' Connie said truthfully.

'We don't want to think about that,' Maggie said.

'I'm not sure I'll even want to come back,' sighed Gill, gazing around at her spectacular surroundings, the sea and the city sparkling in the morning sunshine.

Larry gave an exasperated sigh.

Connie couldn't imagine him ever going anywhere without a strict timetable, always knowing where and when he was going, and the exact date he'd be coming back. Just like Roger, her ex. How very sad, she thought, when it isn't necessary at all. And how very liberating this trip is, that we haven't even thought about coming back!

'Is Felicity happily settled?' she asked politely, as they headed into the shadowed streets of the Old City.

'Oh yes, my dear,' Larry replied. 'Charming spot. I shall take you there later for tea.'

'That's very kind,' Connie said quickly, silencing the about-to-protest Gill with a glance.

The man meant well. Here was another lonely soul, and how sad that none of these eligible old boys had fallen for Gill yet, she being the only one actually *looking* for a man. But, try as she might, Connie couldn't for the life of her imagine a more unlikely duo than Gill and Larry.

And she'd quite forgotten how charming this city was. Larry accompanied them with a non-stop running commentary, which was constantly interrupted by one or all of them heading into the little shops. Connie and Maggie had each purchased a colourful Provençale tablecloth, and Gill had found a filmy white top. These shopping detours were punctuated by much sighing from Larry. Connie and Maggie would gladly have spent more time in the picturesque and colourful Marché aux Fleurs, but Larry shepherded them on relentlessly.

'It's only flowers,' he said dismissively, before leading them to the cathedral in all its baroque glory. 'Now, here lie the remains of the martyred Saint Reparata,' he informed them. 'Would you like to hear her story?'

'Another time, perhaps,' Connie said, following the other two, who were hastily heading for the door.

Outside again, Larry consulted his watch with a worried frown on his face.

'We mustn't be late for lunch,' he said.

'Why?' Connie asked. 'Have you booked somewhere?'

'Of course!' Larry replied shortly, and off he headed through a maze of tiny streets, some of which were little more than alleyways with cobbles underfoot, crowded and noisy. Clothing, jewellery, shoes, fruit and vegetables were all displayed in windows, doorways and stalls.

Connie would have liked to browse around there for a while but, glancing at Larry's face, decided against it.

It was there that Maggie saw the dress. It was dark brown, linen and sleeveless, and dangled alluringly from the doorway of what appeared to be a particularly chic boutique. Maggie supposed she really ought to have a dress. Most women had a dress. At the moment, her wardrobe consisted only of T-shirts, shorts, trousers and one cotton skirt.

'That would really suit you,' Connie confirmed.

'It would, wouldn't it?' Maggie stood back for a minute. 'I haven't bought a dress in *years*.'

'Time you did then.'

Maggie was aware of Larry gnashing his teeth, determined to stick to his self-made schedule.

'Look, you all go on,' she said, determined to keep the peace. 'I'll catch up with you shortly.'

'We'll be at La Bouche d'Or,' said Larry, pointing vaguely ahead. 'It's only a couple of minutes' walk.'

'You OK with that?' Connie asked. 'I can stay if you like.'

'No, no, you go with him, for God's sake! If I can't make up my mind we'll come and look at it again on the way back.'

Maggie continued to gaze longingly at the dress before venturing inside. She'd need a smaller size.

'Ah, oui, plus petite!' The saleslady reappeared within seconds with the smaller size. 'You try!'

And so Maggie found herself in a tiny changing booth with a tarnished mirror and barely room to turn around. With difficulty, she donned the dress and emerged into the tiny shop in search of a better reflection. And she liked what she saw in a non-tarnished mirror. She glanced at the label; it was a lot of money for such a simple dress. Well, I have a lot of money, she thought happily.

'Eez beautiful,' said the saleslady. 'And now you need ze shoes! I have here ze pair which will be perfect!'

Maggie stepped into some high-heeled gold, silver and bronze sandals, which looked exquisite with the dress. How on earth did that woman know her size?

And she wasn't finished yet. 'Now,' she said, 'I have ze necklace you must wear.' She then produced an elaborate metallic concoction, which matched the sandals and set the dress off to perfection.

Maggie pirouetted some more. There was no denying it; she looked good. Connie would be proud of her. All she needed now was some make-up and a hairdo.

'Yes, I'll have it all,' she said.

'Everything?'

'Everything. And, this dress, does it come in any other colours?'

'There is also ze cream, and ze red, and ze—'

'I'll have the cream, please.'

The woman appeared confused. 'You want ze cream, and not ze brown?'

'I want them both,' Maggie replied, heading back to the changing booth to remove some notes from her bra.

'And ze shoes, and ze necklace…?'

'Everything!'

'Ah, oui! Certainement!'

Maggie, carrying a large bag, emerged from the tiny shop having been kissed on both cheeks by the jubilant saleslady. What extravagance! What the hell! And they were going to Italy, so who knew what opportunities there might be to wear these dresses. And hey-ho, she thought, there's another few hundred euros you won't be able to get your sticky fingers on, Ringer Bell! Not unless you've taken up cross-dressing!

She pushed her way through the throngs of tourists in the direction the others had taken, half hoping there might still be some sign of them, but of course there wasn't. They'd probably have ordered their meal by now, with Larry in charge. Maggie decided to go straight ahead. She could always phone if she got lost. What was the restaurant called? Something 'gold'?

There were fewer shops here, so she could imagine Larry legging it and shepherding them along, determined to deprive Connie and Gill of any further retail therapy. It was a long, narrow street with tall, ancient buildings and large, ornate wooden doors. There were columns of nameplates alongside countless doorbells, signalling a more commercial area. Would Larry really have brought them up here? Perhaps not. Maggie stopped and looked around, finding herself alone on a road going nowhere that she could see. It felt dark and oppressive and, in spite of the heat, Maggie found herself shivering. Just then her mobile rang. She'd switched it on in case she needed to call Connie. And this most likely would be Connie, thank God, she thought.

'Connie?'

There was a moment's silence and then a familiar voice that she had no wish to hear said, 'I know where you are, you bitch. And I'm coming to get you.'

Maggie froze. How on earth could he know she was here? She clicked the phone off and leaned against a wall. Then it rang again. She didn't recognise the number but, with shaking fingers, she felt compelled to listen.

'Are you there, bitch? Don't think you're going to get away with this. I'm going to take you and your nasty little caravan apart – just remember Kenny Flynn.' And he was gone.

Maggie, thoroughly frightened, began to retrace her steps along the now deserted street. Was he around here somewhere? Would he suddenly emerge from one of these sinister-looking doorways? Suddenly this whole street seemed dark and forbidding, and she began to run, back towards the sunlit square. Dear Lord, had he been following her? Of course not! He must be bluffing.

But she *did* remember Kenny Flynn: a small-time criminal, who Ringer had poetically described as 'greedy as shit'. Some years back he'd gone along with Ringer's gang on a Post Office raid and had unwisely headed off with most of Ringer's share of the money. Ringer went ballistic and spent several weeks hunting Kenny Flynn down. Later Maggie was never able to work out whether or not Ringer had managed to retrieve his loot, but she did remember Kenny Flynn had come to a sticky end by falling into a large vat of glue in an East End warehouse. Ringer, of course, denied all knowledge of who had killed Kenny.

Maggie looked around frantically as she emerged into the square. People were still strolling in the sunshine, children were shouting, a dog was barking, and somewhere someone was playing Edith Piaf's 'Non, je ne regrette rien'. Still shaken, she clicked on Connie's number and, with great relief, got directions to La Bouche d'Or, which was only a couple of minutes away. She found them sitting at a table outside, shaded by banks of hydrangeas and dangling greenery.

'Did you buy the dress?' Gill asked, surveying the large bag.

'Yes,' replied Maggie, relieved to sit down. 'Two dresses, in fact.'

'Two!' Gill gawped.

'And sandals, and a necklace.'

'Good for you!' Connie exclaimed. 'High time you treated yourself!'

Maggie, still thinking about the telephone calls, wondered if the cost of 'treating herself' might be too high. If Ringer really *was* around here somewhere, it almost certainly would be.

As Connie studied the menu she was conscious of Larry's leg pressed against hers. She moved hers away, and he followed with his. She wished she'd been wearing trousers; at least then she wouldn't be quite so aware of his hairy skin.

'The food here is sublime,' Larry informed them, rubbing his leg against hers. 'You simply must have the moules, and the salade niçoise, and the fried zucchini flowers, of course.'

'We have to eat *flowers*?' Gill looked from one to the other in consternation.

'Zucchini flowers – deep fried and stuffed with ricotta, quite delicious,' Larry said airily.

'That's courgettes to you and me,' Maggie said quietly.

'They sound very interesting.' Gill's sarcasm was barely disguised.

'Come on, Gill, be adventurous,' Connie said.

Gill rolled her eyes. 'Right,' she said, 'fried flowers it is.'

But she would not be persuaded to eat the moules marinière. 'Ugh!' she said. 'I can't eat anything slimy out of a shell!'

'Not very adventurous, your friend, is she?' Larry murmured to Connie.

Gill might not be very adventurous, Connie thought, but, in the few weeks since they'd left England, she had blossomed. Apart from the haircut and the tan, she'd managed to lose some weight and, more importantly, she'd softened a little. She swore less, laughed more and, although she and Maggie still bickered occasionally, it was with humour and a certain amount of affection.

'Gill's all right,' Connie murmured.

'If you say so...' Larry pressed closer to Connie. She pulled her leg further away. She was now almost sitting sideways. Maggie eventually cottoned on to her plight, and obligingly moved along to give her some leeway. Maggie was very quiet and seemed rather twitchy, constantly looking around as if she was expecting someone, Connie thought. She was definitely not her usual self.

The moules, in their creamy sauce, were beyond delicious, as was the famed salade niçoise, which even Gill, who professed not to care much for fish, demolished at speed. And they all ate the fried zucchini flowers, washed down with a great deal of excellent Bordeaux. Then Gill made some reference to the courgettes being left rampant after their deflowering, which set them all off into alcohol-fuelled giggles, particularly Maggie, who seemed to be on the verge of hysteria. Only Larry wasn't laughing; he adopted the expression of a long-suffering parent unable to control his unruly offspring.

'Are we having pudding?' he interrupted. 'I fancy the tart myself.'

At this the three became hysterical.

'The tarte au citron,' Larry explained loudly above their laughter. Several heads had turned in their direction from nearby tables. Plainly annoyed at such frivolity, he moved his leg away from Connie's and continued to study the menu avidly.

'You have your tart, Larry, and I'll just have some coffee,' Connie said, wiping her eyes.

'Yes, coffee's fine,' Maggie confirmed. 'And maybe a nice wee brandy to go with it?'

Connie thought Maggie looked like she could do with a brandy. 'I'll have Cointreau then,' said Gill.

'Well, why not?' Connie added. 'And, as we're almost in Italy, I'll have a Limoncello.'

Seeing the expression on Larry's face, Maggie said, 'Don't worry, Larry, we're paying our way, aren't we girls? We had this little windfall, you see…' She gave a small smile and looked around distractedly.

Climbing up the Colline du Château didn't seem such a brilliant idea on full tummies, after too much wine and with Maggie's bags. They navigated the worn steps with care, and further giggling after Gill's sandal fell off and she had to descend half a dozen steps to retrieve it.

'No wonder I'm losing weight,' Gill puffed, while Larry soldiered on ahead, waiting with a look of long-suffering patience at the top.

'Look!' He spread his arms at the panorama below because there it was, in all its breathtaking glory: the sparkling blue and turquoise of the Baie des Anges, the beach, the Promenade des Anglais, the marina and the city, glittering in the afternoon sunshine. And flowers everywhere.

'Well worth the climb,' Gill conceded as they fished out their cameras and phones.

Larry was studying his watch again. 'We must be off in a minute,' he said. 'I'd like to get to Felicity by four o'clock at the latest.'

'Surely Felicity won't mind if we're a bit late,' Maggie said. 'We're not in any hurry, are we?'

'We've stopped hurrying,' Connie explained to Larry. 'We just do what we feel like doing, if and when we feel like doing it at all.

That's the whole point of our trip.' And it suddenly dawned on her that it was, that time had become unimportant.

Larry frowned. 'I thought the point was that you were going to meet relatives in Italy?'

'*If* they exist. We'll get there eventually. This week, next week, sometime, never.'

'And I want to look at the view for a bit longer,' Gill added. 'Will you just look at those yachts!'

'Don't let her anywhere near a yacht, for God's sake,' Maggie said.

It took ten minutes to walk to where Larry had parked his Land Rover. It was a foregone conclusion that Connie would sit in the front seat, where she kept as much distance as she could from Larry's wandering hand, caressing her thigh each time he changed gear. They climbed up and away from the city to a thickly wooded area, eventually turning into a driveway and a car park. From there they walked along a path through the pines, to what looked like a small village of very large mobile homes, Felicity included. Each unit was screened from the others by trees, and formed a large semi-circle facing a giant swimming pool. And from there, through the trees, was a panoramic view of the sea.

'Wow!' said Connie.

Larry looked pleased. 'I think Felicity will be very much at home here.'

He led the way to where Felicity was sited, accessed by a path of tiny white stones.

'Home from home, what?' Larry pronounced as he unlocked the door.

'This is great,' said Gill. 'But I need to pee. Are you plumbed in?'

'Of course it's plumbed in,' Larry retorted, pointing to the relevant door. 'Now, let's get the kettle on.'

As he fussed around in the kitchen area, Connie and Maggie took stock of their surroundings. It seemed enormous after Bella's modest dimensions. It was luxurious but spartan, and a ray of sunshine was highlighting a network of cobwebs in one corner. It lacked a woman's touch, Connie felt.

There was a copy of *The Times* lying on the table. 'May I have a look at this, if you've finished with it?'

'Of course,' Larry replied. 'It's several days old. Take it with you – no good to me!' He was fumbling about in the cupboards.

'Let me help,' Connie offered, all at once feeling a little sorry for him.

'Perhaps you'd be kind enough to get out the mugs,' Larry said, 'while I look for the biscuits.'

As Gill emerged from the toilet she said, 'I fancy having a quick look round that pool.'

'I'll come with you,' said Maggie, plainly feeling surplus to requirements. 'Too many cooks and all that…' She nudged Connie as she headed out of the door.

Thanks a bunch, Connie thought, as she set out the crockery on a colourful tray Larry had unearthed. The tray, which featured a bright blue sea and sky, white sands and emerald fields, with pink blossoms positioned coquettishly round the edges, proclaimed 'Northumberland'. Connie wondered on what day of which year the artist had depicted Northumberland in such tropical glory.

She was suddenly aware of Larry's close proximity.

'How about a little kiss?' he asked, facing her with his hands on her shoulders. 'While they're admiring the view, what?'

'I don't think so, Larry,' Connie said, backing away.

'Oh, come on, old girl!' he persisted. 'At our age we don't get so many opportunities for a little hanky-panky, what?'

'I am really not looking for any hanky-panky,' Connie said slowly and clearly, as she tried to extricate herself from his embrace.

He was strong and persistent. 'Just a kiss,' he pleaded, 'for now. But perhaps we could lose the other two tomorrow?'

'*No*, Larry!'

Now he had her pinioned to the wall, his lips seeking hers and his right hand seeking her breast.

'GET OFF, PLEASE!' Connie turned her head to one side to avoid his lips while frantically trying to push him away and remove his hand. As she edged towards the work surface she managed to extricate herself for a moment.

'I like a woman who puts up a fight,' said Larry through gritted teeth.

It hadn't put him off though. As he tried to kiss her again, Connie said, 'I'm going to shout, Larry, and really loud! Think about your neighbours!' Because this was outrageous, in broad daylight and with the other two due back any minute!

He tried again to grab her by the shoulders in a clumsy embrace.

'Get off, Larry!' Connie shouted at the top of her voice.

He backed off. 'OK, OK, keep your voice down!'

They could hear footsteps on Larry's path.

'Tea ready yet?' Gill asked cheerfully as she bounced in through the open door.

*

The next evening, sitting outside Bella, Connie was relieved to know there would be no more Larry, having told him so in no uncertain terms. She enjoyed these evenings with purely female company, when they sat outside to eat supper, drink wine, fall asleep. And they chatted. Gill spoke of her husbands and lovers and Maggie spoke of happier days with Ringer. And Connie realised that she felt more relaxed and content than she had in a long time. Because, in spite of their differences, they were all getting along just fine.

During the day they'd taken themselves to Monaco on the train, where Gill spent most of her time going on about how crazy it was to have a station 'in the middle of a bleedin' tunnel'. Maggie said it was all exactly as she had expected, with the high-rise buildings and the yachts and, if it wasn't a tax haven, who would want to live in what was, after all, a millionaires' skyscraper estate? Connie thought it had a certain charm with some noteworthy buildings, particularly the casino, and so many beautiful flowers everywhere. Best of all, they'd managed to avoid lecherous Larry.

Now, as they sat sampling some of Jean-Paul's finest vintage, Gill said, 'At times like this I'm really glad I'm not married any more.' Seeing the raised eyebrows of the other two, she added, 'I don't mean that I wouldn't *like* to get married again, 'cos I would. But there's something very nice about being free, sitting here getting gently sloshed with you two.'

'It's what's known as friendship,' Maggie informed her.

'Do *you* like being free, Connie?' Gill asked.

'Yes, I do. I love it, but it can be a little lonely at times. Not with you two around though.'

'Were you *really* married for forty years?'

'Forty-*one* years,' Connie said.

'Blimey!' Gill said. 'That's a life sentence! Except you'd have got time off for good behaviour.'

'Some people wouldn't be able to turn their lives upside down after all that time,' Maggie said. 'They'd just soldier on. I think you were very brave.'

Connie was aware that she'd never *really* opened up to the other two about her marriage. They knew, of course, that she was divorced and had three children and that she'd been married for such a long time, a fact that plainly intrigued them.

'Why would a marriage go wonky after forty-one years?' Gill had persisted. She'd always been very vocal about her own relationships. 'The only decent bloke I ever had died on me,' she added, a fact that obviously still rankled.

Maggie, on the other hand, had asked more than once, 'If he wasn't beating the hell out of you, why would you bother to leave him at this stage of life? Or was there someone else?'

'No one else,' Connie had replied firmly. 'I told you about my trip.' But she'd never really explained much. It had all been too personal and she hadn't known these women well enough. But Connie had become very fond of them both, although at home they'd been merely acquaintances, not particularly her 'cup of tea'. And she still wasn't sure why she'd ever considered bringing them along. Nevertheless, over the miles and the metres, they'd grown close. And now, at last, she felt able to open up a little to them.

They were both looking at her expectantly.

'Well, I told you I was brought up with my uncle's family. Then I became a florist, and also did a couple of summers as a tour guide.' She thought fondly of Freddy, who'd been her fellow guide on both trips. Camp as a row of tents, but great fun. 'And then I married Roger. He was very handsome and very respectable, he got me pregnant and so we had to get married.'

'Yes, yes,' Gill said impatiently. 'And then you were married for a million years!'

'And you had three children,' Maggie added, refilling their wine glasses.

There was a pause before Connie said, 'I had *four* children.'

'Four?' they chanted in unison.

'Yes, four. There was Ben as well. He was born when Diana, my eldest, was nearly five, and before I had Nick and Lou. He was killed. An accident.'

There was a horrified silence before Maggie said, 'Oh, Connie!' and Gill said, 'Oh God!'

'It's a long time ago now,' Connie went on, 'but, do you know, I think about him every single day. He loved swimming and, every time I look at this beautiful sea, I imagine how he'd have enjoyed this.'

'I know I moan about my lot sometimes,' said Gill, 'but I can't bear to think about losing any of them.'

'You should never outlive your children,' Maggie said. 'However did you cope, Connie?'

'Well, you have to,' Connie replied. 'I had three other children to bring up.'

'And your husband, what's his name again?' Maggie asked.

'Roger.'

'How did he cope?'

'Roger coped by immersing himself in work and going to church on Sundays.'

'Not much help to you then,' Gill retorted.

'No, but I had a wonderful neighbour who helped enormously. But, you know how sometimes that kind of a tragedy can bring couples closer? Well, it didn't for us.'

'Was that where it all started to go wrong?' Maggie asked.

'I'm not sure,' Connie said truthfully. 'There were other factors involved.'

'Like what?' Gill asked.

'Roger was always a very "closed-up" sort of person, if you know what I mean,' Connie continued. 'Sad to say but I never felt, deep down, that I really knew him. And now, I know for sure that I didn't.' She paused. 'We never had a joined-at-the-hip type of marriage, so that may be why I didn't notice the indifference creeping in over the years. I just thought it was because we had different friends, different hobbies.'

'When did it come to the crunch?' Maggie asked.

'Well, one day I just decided I'd had enough. Not just of Roger and his endless golf, but I was expected to look after the grand-children three or four days a week. On my own. And then there was the bungalow.'

'The bungalow?'

'Yes, the bungalow. I hated it. Roger decided it was a sensible choice for our retirement.'

'Nothing wrong with a bungalow,' Gill murmured.

'No, there isn't,' Connie agreed. 'But I'd loved our old house and my lovely garden and didn't want to downsize. I'm sure it was the sensible thing to do but, for me, it was the final straw and I decided I needed to get away; recharge my batteries, leave them all to it. So off I went.'

'And what happened?'

Connie described her trip from Sussex up to the Highlands of Scotland and back again, and how it had changed her perspective on life. She reduced them to tears of laughter at some of her escapades.

'Things just happen,' Connie explained, 'when your car gets a puncture or breaks down, or you stop somewhere for a meal or a pee. But, you see, I was leaving myself wide open to new experiences for the first time in years.'

She spoke too about how she'd constantly thought about Ben, finally absolving herself from blame and finding some peace of mind. Gill wept openly when Connie said, 'Treasure your children, even when they drive you crazy. Because there's no love, or loss, like it.'

'I feel bad now thinking that I came on this trip to get away from them,' Gill said, wiping her eyes. 'I love them really.'

'Of course you do,' Connie said.

'I've just the one,' Maggie said sadly, 'and I don't see him very often, but he's there, in my heart, all the time. I'm not very religious but I pray for him every day.'

'And you found a lover?' Gill chipped in, eager to change the subject.

'Well, apart from Don, who I told you about, I had some other amazing experiences. In fact everything that happened to me made me realise that life is short and to be lived, not endured. So, after six weeks, I headed home to tell Roger I was leaving him.'

More gasps.

'I worried myself sick about how I was going to tell him, and how he'd react. I didn't want to hurt him, you see.'

'And?' Gill had moved closer.

Connie paused. 'Well, all I can say is that it was obviously time to leave.'

'And your children?' Gill asked. 'How did they take it?'

'Di and Nick were upset at first, but have taken it quite well. My youngest, Lou, hasn't. She's always been a real "daddy's girl" and he can do no wrong. According to Lou it's all my fault for going off and leaving him like that.'

'Have you seen Roger recently?'

'No, but I hear he's bought himself a smart little flat within walking distance of the bloody golf club. Anyway, I've gone on about myself for far too long, so time for a refill of vino, I think!'

CHAPTER FIFTEEN

NOT SO NICE

Connie woke early the following morning and idly flicked through the pages of Larry's *Times* as she drank her coffee. The edition was a week old, but she didn't mind; it was just good to read an English newspaper. And then the headline caught her eye. 'Criminal Gang Rob Bluett's Bank' it proclaimed, and underneath in smaller print, 'Police are seeking "Ringer" Bell'. Scarcely able to believe her eyes, Connie read that three of the gang had already been apprehended, and the fourth, Ringer Bell, their leader, had escaped and was believed to be on the continent.

Connie's hand was shaking so badly she had to put her mug of coffee on the table as it was spilling everywhere. She double-checked the date of the robbery; it would have been the night before they all left England. Did Maggie know? *Surely* Maggie knew? The gang had got away with over a million pounds from this bank in the City.

Connie felt a cold chill deep inside. Scratch-card indeed! *He'd* given Maggie that money! *Stolen* money, which they'd been blithely spending day after day! She could contain herself no longer. '*Maggie!*' she yelled.

A few minutes later a dishevelled Maggie tottered through. 'What's wrong?'

'*This* is what's wrong!' Connie snapped, thrusting the newspaper under Maggie's nose. 'And I'd like you to tell me that this money we've been spending like water was *not* given to you by Ringer.'

'No, it wasn't given to me by Ringer,' Maggie answered truthfully as she read the article.

'What's all the fuss about?' Now Gill had appeared on the scene, rubbing her eyes. 'Any tea in the pot?'

'Never mind tea, I think you should read this article, Gill,' Connie said.

Gill peered over Maggie's shoulder. 'Oo-ah,' she said.

'I want Maggie to tell me that this money was not given to her by Ringer,' Connie went on.

'No, it wasn't,' Gill said cheerily. 'She found it in the oven.'

There was a moment's horrified silence before Maggie snapped, 'Well, thanks very much for *that*, Gill!'

Connie felt sick. 'Am I the only person who doesn't know what's going on here?'

Maggie sat down opposite Connie. 'I was going to tell you today anyway,' she said. 'You were so honest and truthful with us last night that I thought it was only fair you should know.'

'Go on,' said Connie.

'Well, what Gill says is true. It was stashed in the oven overnight and he was snoring his head off in the spare room, so I helped myself.'

Connie glared at Gill. 'And *you* knew?'

'Only 'cos I found out from Raoul that Maggie had asked him to let her know if a man came looking for her.'

'Raoul!' Connie was becoming angrier and angrier. 'That was ages ago! And nobody bothered to tell me!'

'We thought you might go to the police,' Gill said.

'Damned right I would! Let me get this clear: we've been spending money that you, Maggie, stole from Ringer, which Ringer stole from the bank?'

'That's about it,' Maggie admitted. 'But don't go off your trolley, Connie, because that man *owes* me! He's never been generous with his money and, God knows, I've covered up for him and looked after him year after year after bloody year. And what thanks do I get? He finds himself a blonde bimbo and it would only have been a matter of time before I was shown the door.'

'That's not the point,' said Connie, wiping her brow. 'The point is that you have stolen money.' Her eye caught the picture of the idyllic French village scene on the wall. And then she thought about the five hundred euro dress hanging up in her cupboard. And what about the taxis, the site fees, the countless meals…? Dear God, what was she to do?

'And,' Connie continued, 'what's all this about him being on the continent?'

'He's after his money,' Maggie said bluntly.

'You mean he's trying to find us?' Connie wondered if she was going to faint. 'But surely the police will be on the lookout for him over here? Will he be in his own car?'

'Probably, but he'll have had the number plates changed. Let's face it, there must be thousands of maroon-coloured Lexuses on the roads. Don't worry, Connie, we'll be able to dodge him. Raoul told Ringer he'd never seen or heard of us.'

'He *found* Raoul's campsite?'

'Well, he probably tried all the sites in the area. And I think he was tailing us that time on the autoroute, which is when I dodged past the gendarme and managed to lose him.'

'And I think that might have been him chatting me up in Avignon,' Gill added.

'Oh my God!' Connie was rendered speechless. Then, after a minute, she asked, 'But how could he have known who you were?'

'Well, that's the thing, see, Connie,' Maggie said. 'My friend Pam forwarded on those pictures to him. You know, the ones of the three of us outside Bella?'

'But you've had your hair cut,' Connie said, turning to Gill. 'You look quite different.'

Gill shrugged.

'He's got a photographic memory, has Ringer,' Maggie said. 'He'll have memorised your faces. And of course Bella's registration was as clear as day in those photos.'

'So that's why you're always looking for out-of-the-way places to park!' It's all coming together now, Connie thought. 'Why didn't *you* tell me, Gill?'

'Because Maggie told me not to.'

'Please, Connie,' Maggie begged. 'Try to see it from my point of view. Look, it's a City bank and they'll be insured to the eyeballs; a million's nothing these days!'

Connie was still trying to make sense of it all. 'There were four of them,' she said, to no one in particular.

'They would have come away with around two hundred and fifty thousand each,' Maggie said. 'And I reckon I've got two hundred thousand of Ringer's share.'

'*Two* hundred thousand! But you said you'd won *one* hundred thousand on the so-called card!'

'I'm afraid I was lying,' Maggie admitted ruefully.

'So, we've got *two* hundred grand hidden all over Bella! Tell me you're joking!'

'We have spent a wee bit of it,' Maggie said.

Connie had no idea what to do. Should she go to the police here in France? Should she chuck Maggie and her wretched money out?

'Connie, the police are going to be looking for Ringer, not us,' Gill said.

'Are you telling me you *approve* of all this, Gill? Surely *you* could have gone to the police?'

Gill shrugged. 'It's not a case of approving, is it? It's done now. And Maggie didn't pre-plan any of this; it was a spur of the moment thing just as she was going out of the door. Anyway, I've had my hairdos and my dresses and you've done all right out of it too, so are the police likely to believe we didn't *know*?'

Connie tried to collect her chaotic thoughts. It was highly unlikely the police *would* believe them, with two hundred grand hidden all over the vehicle. And, as they'd all been happily spending it, what did that make them? Or her? Receivers of stolen goods? Aiding and abetting? The list was endless. And her dad had been a *policeman*! What would he think if he were alive now? Connie shuddered.

Nick and Lou were right. She should never have set off on this trip with two women she scarcely knew. She must have taken leave of her senses. They could all be arrested at any minute!

Maggie moved over to sit next to Connie and put an arm round her shoulder. 'Connie, we're going to be OK, trust me. Let's stay here today, have a lazy day in the sun, and we'll set off for Italy tomorrow. If the police over here are at all interested, they're looking for him, not us. And I expect they've got enough criminals of their own to keep them busy.'

The thing is, Connie thought, how could I abandon Maggie? I really do like her, and I like Gill too. And I'm loving our trip and how well we all get on together, against the odds. And we'll soon be halfway to Amalfi, so surely another week or two won't matter? Then perhaps we can go our separate ways and Maggie can decide what she's going to do and where she's going to go with that money. Sometimes you do just have to turn a blind eye.

They spent the rest of the day treating Connie like some kind of invalid, insisting she sat down while they did the cooking, the tidying up, the making of tea, the pouring of wine. Connie caught up with her emails – 'having a wonderful time on the Côte d'Azur'. If they'd any idea of what she'd got herself into she'd be snowed under with shedloads of 'I told you so's. And she got out all her *Teach Yourself Italian* stuff, because they were going to be needing that very soon.

It wasn't until they were eating dinner that it occurred to Connie twelve hours had passed since she'd learned the awful truth. And somehow things didn't seem quite so bad.

CHAPTER SIXTEEN

VIVA ITALIA

It was time to bid adieu to France. As they prepared to leave, Amélie, who spoke little English, made it plain that they were welcome to use her *salle de bains* to shower and wash their hair. They'd paid well for their stay, bought eggs and peaches and olives, and wine of course. Now Jean-Paul and Amélie insisted on giving them extra provisions for their onward journey, helping them to fill up their water supply and dispose of the waste into the outside toilet.

As they went about their tasks, Connie noted with wry amusement how very considerate the other two were to her this morning still, as a result of yesterday's conversation no doubt. There were lots of sympathetic smiles and remarks like, 'Don't worry, Connie, I'll do that,' and, 'You have a coffee, Connie, I can do this.' It wouldn't last, of course. But it made them feel better. Poor old Connie, who'd not only lost a son, but a husband too – even if she hadn't wanted him. And poor old Connie, who'd been kept in the dark about these criminal activities. Well, soon they'd be on their way and, doubtless, the everyday banter would continue. Thank goodness.

*

The road snaked its way round the rocky shorelines and tunnels, with tantalising glimpses of the sea and the mountains. The traffic was heavy, but orderly, and there were few hold-ups. Maggie had offered to drive again – probably part of the 'be kind to Connie' effort. Then again, she liked being at the wheel and she was a good driver. However, today was special, because they were going to Italy, and Connie wanted to be back behind the wheel.

Maggie sat in the passenger seat trying to make out the road signs from Connie's Italian phrase book, while Gill sat behind, leafing through a copy of *Elle*, which Amélie had given her. Occasionally she'd peer over their shoulders to see where they were going and admire some of the stunning scenery, before returning to study and duly report on how long or short skirts should be this year.

And there was no sign whatsoever of a dark red Lexus. Connie had never before even noticed Lexuses, dark red or otherwise, but now found herself studying every car on the road.

They bypassed Monaco and headed towards Menton, which, Connie remembered from family holidays of long ago, was a delightful place with a wonderful food market. It would be a good place to stock up on groceries.

'Are we still in France?' Gill called from the back.

'Yes, but only just,' Connie replied.

Menton was busy and, as usual, it was hard to find any parking space, far less one that would accommodate Bella's dimensions.

'Let's keep going,' said Connie. 'Perhaps we'll have more luck in Ventimiglia.'

The scenery was less attractive and less dramatic along the stretch of coastline as they crossed the border into Italy at Ventimiglia. Connie, as always, felt a little thrill at being in Italy again. She'd always loved the country, even before she knew of her Italian grandmother. There was something about the language, the music, the scenery, the history – or was it some distant ancestor calling out to her? Somehow or other she'd always felt she belonged here.

Andrea Bocelli was singing 'O Sole Mio'.

Gill peered over Connie's shoulder. 'Haven't you got any other CDs?'

'Yes, of course I have. What would you like?'

'How about Rod Stewart?'

'Well, I've probably got one of his in there somewhere,' Connie replied.

'I *love* Rod Stewart,' Gill sighed. 'I dreamed once that I met him at a party and my eyes met his across a crowded room. Like in the films, you know? And I was *so* excited! We got closer and closer towards each other and I just *knew* we were going to end up in bed together.'

Connie smiled to herself, trying to imagine Gill's beehive (that was) and Rod's upward spikes sharing the same pillow.

'And then I woke up,' Gill said sadly.

'I should think Rod was much relieved,' said Maggie.

Ventimiglia looked a little shabby, with litter blowing around, unlike the pristine Menton. But at least there was a parking space, which was fortunately down a side road and which, Connie hoped, would not be noticeable to anyone – i.e. Ringer – driving through. There was a market which, according to what Larry had told them, the French came to in droves because everything was a little cheaper, particularly alcohol. It was a hot day, overcast and humid, and the market was uncomfortably crowded. The prices weren't quite as wonderful as they'd been led to believe but, nevertheless, Gill spotted a pink leather handbag which she *had* to have. And they filled up with some vegetables, wine and Limoncello.

What was interesting, Connie noted, was the fusion of languages along this coast. In Nice, although most people naturally spoke French, you could also hear a fair amount of Italian spoken, and the waiters and shop assistants could switch from one language to another effortlessly. *And* speak English as well. Not for the first time Connie thought what an insular lot the Brits were, those few miles of water separating them from day to day contact with their neighbours and the incentive to speak their languages.

Now, here in Ventimiglia, the reverse was taking place, with French popping up periodically amidst the buzz of emotive, melodic Italian. She must concentrate on learning more of the lingo as, after all, if she were to find any relatives down in Amalfi, it would be an advantage to be able to converse with them.

Larry had instructed them, when he knew of their route, to follow the river down to the beach at Ventimiglia, where they would get a spectacular view back along the French coastline, and of Monaco in particular. But, as they got back to Bella under an ever-darkening sky, the heavens opened and so they decided to give the view a miss. Perhaps on the way back…? They decided to head for San Remo where, according to Maggie's literature, there was a large camping site. Connie felt sure they'd lost Ringer, if it *was* him in Avignon, but Maggie was still twitchy, particularly because there seemed little chance of finding a private, out-of-the-way spot around in which to park.

It rained non-stop until they arrived on the outskirts of San Remo when, suddenly, the sky cleared and the sun reappeared. They made their way through dense traffic to the camping site, which, Maggie said, was on the east side of the city. They discovered that *senso unico* meant 'one-way street', after a short, bald man waved his arms around while shouting at them.

The campsite was, fortunately, easy to locate and, even better, they had space available. It was well screened from the road by hedges and pines, so they wouldn't be very visible to passing traffic.

'It still early,' the woman in the office informed them. 'You come in August – no room.'

Connie was feeling, not for the first time, that they must reach their destination before these dreaded August holidays, when most of France and Italy seemed to shut down. In another week it would be July but, even if they dawdled everywhere, there was still time to get down to Amalfi by the end of the month. And then what? Would they drive all the way back again? Would they leave Bella behind and fly home? It was, as always, not spoken about because, Connie suspected, none of them really wanted this journey to end. And, one way or the other, they had to do something about all this money before they even contemplated driving back.

It could have been a disaster, it *should* have been a disaster, and it could still be a disaster. But at least they were having fun.

The campsite was quiet and, apart from one German family with teenage children, appeared to be child-free. They spent the evening quietly, eating a cassoulet of the vegetables they'd bought and using the laundrette facilities.

The following morning Connie studied herself in the mirror. 'My hair's a mess. It needs cutting and it needs colouring.' They'd been reliably informed that there was a bus into San Remo every half hour. 'Do you two fancy coming into town?'

Gill was painting her toenails and Maggie was fiddling with her phone.

'Tomorrow, maybe,' said Gill.

'I'm feeling lazy today,' Maggie said, without taking her eyes off the little screen. She seemed very concerned about her phone of late.

Connie pulled a strand of hair with distaste. 'Any further messages from dear Ringer?' she asked.

'Not for some time now,' Maggie replied shortly.

Connie turned away from the mirror. 'I can't see how he can possibly know where we are. He'd probably never have thought of going to Grasse and, if he did, he'd never have spotted us tucked away behind Claude's farm buildings. And the same in Cannes.'

'He's probably miles back, or miles ahead,' Gill added, replacing the top on the varnish bottle. 'He's most likely given up and gone home, and hopefully we can forget him now.'

'And no sign of him since Avignon,' Connie said. '*If* that was him, which it probably wasn't.' She glanced at her watch. 'Anyway, there's a bus in about ten minutes so I'm off. See you later.'

She remembered the routine: to buy the ticket in the *tabaccheria*, and have it date-stamped on board. The bus was on time and full of chattering ladies with empty shopping baskets heading for town.

Connie was looking forward to a few hours on her own to look round the city, and the shops, and the hairdressers. Although she'd become extremely fond of both Maggie and Gill, there were times when inevitably their company verged on the claustrophobic. And she was still reeling with the information about Ringer and the money. She'd refused Maggie's wad of notes this morning, and insisted on using her own money. But it was a bit late now, she reckoned, thinking of horses and stable doors.

Ten minutes later, having alighted in the city centre, Connie spotted a stylish-looking *parrucchiere*, from where a woman emerged with *the* most stunning haircut and terrific highlights and lowlights. That's exactly how I want to look, she thought, as she pushed open the door.

And, *si*, Gina would be available in five minutes if the *signora* would take a seat. Coffee? Oh, definitely, thought Connie. The espresso duly arrived in its tiny cup. Connie had always enjoyed an espresso after a meal, but knew she'd better get used to this ritual where no self-respecting Italian would dream of having a cappuccino after about 10 a.m. However did her Italian grandmother survive on milky instant coffees in Newcastle? Or worse, that Camp stuff that came in bottles! Had she brought her coffee pot with her from Italy?

'Buongiorno! Come!' Gina was tiny with a mane of lustrous black hair.

'What I'd like,' Connie said, speaking slowly, 'is a cut and colour exactly like that lady had, who left about ten minutes ago.'

Gina appeared completely mystified, until the young woman with the long blonde hair in the next chair came to the rescue with a string of fluent Italian.

'Ah, si!' exclaimed Gina. 'Capisco! Signora Mutti!'

'She understands, I think,' said the blonde, whose head was already half covered in foils.

'Oh, thank you so much,' Connie said, as Gina got out the colour chart. 'I've been trying to learn a little Italian, but I could never have managed that.'

'You here on holiday then?' the blonde asked. She was fortyish and unmistakably English.

'Yes, I am. What about you?'

'Yeah, me too.'

'Well, thanks again,' said Connie. 'Or perhaps I should say "grazie mille"!'

An hour and a half later, Connie and the blonde exited the salon at exactly the same time.

'Thanks again for the translation,' Connie said, patting her locks, 'I'm so pleased with the result.'

'It looks great,' the blonde confirmed. 'But look, I've got half an hour to kill before I'm picked up on the piazza here. Don't suppose you fancy a coffee or something?'

'I'm in no hurry,' Connie said. 'That would be nice.'

'Good. I'm Carol.'

'I'm Connie.'

'You travelling on your own, Connie?'

'No, I'm with a couple of friends. But I've come out on my own today.'

They found a little bar from where Carol could see her pick-up point, sat themselves down under the striped awning, and ordered drinks.

'You speak great Italian,' Connie said, sipping her freshly squeezed orange juice.

'Yeah, well, I lived out here for a year, looking after kids, to learn the lingo. Did the same in France. Fancied becoming an air stewardess.'

'And did you?'

'No, because when I got home Frank came along, and he was just drop-dead gorgeous. You know how it is when someone takes your breath away?'

'I'm not sure I do,' Connie admitted. She might have loved Roger once but, for sure, he'd never left her breathless. And, gorgeous though Don was, it had taken her a little time to appreciate his charms.

'Well, anyway, we had a great life together until his heart attack three years ago. I was gutted. And, sadly, no kids; it just didn't happen. How about you?'

'Divorced,' Connie replied. 'Three grown-up children, four grandchildren.'

'Oh, that must be lovely. Have you found a new man yet?'

Connie laughed. 'No, and I'm most definitely not looking for one. I'm loving my freedom too much. Have you found someone?'

'Well, here's the thing,' Carol said. 'Six months ago, I met this lovely bloke – a lot older than me though. And he's not short of a bob or two, which is always nice, isn't it? He's out here on a long business trip at the moment and I flew out to Nice to join him for a week. We're heading for Portofino. You ever been there?'

'Unfortunately not. Years ago we bypassed it on the main road heading south from Genoa.'

Carol drained her coffee. 'Well, he'll be here shortly. Can we give you a lift anywhere?'

Connie shook her head. 'That's kind of you, but it's only a short distance to where we're staying and there's a good bus service.'

'Are you sure? He won't mind. Are you on a driving holiday or what?'

'Yes, we've got a—'

'Excuse me interrupting, Connie, but here he is!'

A large, dark red Lexus had pulled up opposite.

Connie took a deep breath as she got to her feet. 'It's been great meeting you, Carol. You enjoy Portofino!'

'Oh, do come and meet Bill. I'm sure we can save you messing about with buses.'

'No, really, I won't, because I have to get some groceries before I go back. But thanks for the offer.'

Connie strained her eyes to see the driver, but could only make out short hair, a blue shirt and a cigarette dangling from his lips.

'Well, if you're sure? Bye then, Connie!'

And then they were away, Carol waving from the open window.

Connie, feeling a little wobbly, leaned against the table. Could it possibly be? Was Carol the bimbo? Highly unlikely. There must be no end of blondes in no end of red Lexuses round here. Did she say his name was Bill? Wasn't that the name of the guy Gill met in Avignon? Did this man haunt hairdressers or something? After Carol told him of her encounter with someone called Connie, would he come back looking for her?

She didn't plan to wait to find out, but ran towards the bus stop.

CHAPTER SEVENTEEN

LIGURIA

'We can't possibly stay here,' Maggie stated.

'But we don't know for sure it was him, do we?' Gill was filling the kettle. 'There must be millions of Lexuses…'

'I've got a bad feeling about this,' Maggie said. 'And I have a distinct feeling he's around.' She'd decided not to mention the telephone calls in Nice.

'But she didn't *look* like a bimbo,' Connie put in. 'I mean – sorry, Maggie – but she was *nice*!'

'Delightful, I'm sure,' Maggie said drily.

Connie had repeated every detail of her encounter with Carol several times. 'I only said I was travelling with friends. And that I was getting the bus. I said nothing about the friends or that we were in a motorhome.'

'You're sure?'

'Of course I'm sure. I *was* going to tell her, but he came along at that exact moment. So, just as well.'

'But he'll be told your name is Connie, and he's doubtless putting two and two together.' Maggie sighed. 'And there aren't that many caravan sites round here, so he'd have no difficulty finding us. We have to leave. *Now.*'

'But, if it is him, he'll only follow us along the coast anyway. So where do we go from here?'

Maggie thought for a moment. 'Genoa,' she said. 'It's a big city, with quite a few sites around. Perhaps we might even find a quiet spot where we can lie low for a few days.'

'But I haven't been into San Remo yet,' Gill wailed.

'And you aren't going to,' Maggie retorted. 'Let's get packing.'

It was nine o'clock and becoming dark when, as they passed the sign for Genoa, they also saw the sign for La Gioia, a *ristorante*, purely by accident. Connie made the diversion only because they were starving and, as they turned from the busy road into a quiet lamp-lit lane, she said, 'Perhaps we might even be able to find a layby round here somewhere.' She didn't sound hopeful. 'Just for tonight.'

'Well, he certainly wouldn't find us round here,' Maggie said, squinting through the windscreen at the dark foliage on either side of the road.

The restaurant was large, dimly lit, and packed with noisy Italians.

'Always a good sign,' Connie remarked. 'These people are fussy about where they eat.'

They had to wait ten minutes for a table but Stefano assured them, 'It will not be long.' He was one of two good-looking waiters, moving at speed around the tables; a point not lost on Gill.

'God, isn't he gorgeous!' she exclaimed. 'I have a feeling I'm going to love Italy!'

'Here's another one young enough to be your son,' Maggie muttered. 'Probably even your grandson.'

'The point is,' Gill replied, gazing at Stefano, 'he *isn't* either my son or my grandson. And there's no law says I can't enjoy looking.'

At that point a table became available and Stefano whisked tablecloths off and on, and replaced glasses and cutlery in a theatrical display of efficiency.

'Now, ladies,' he said, 'you come.'

'I'd have no trouble coming with him,' Gill whispered.

Connie giggled. 'You're incorrigible!'

They sat down, serenaded on all sides by the clinking of glasses, the rattle of cutlery and noisy animated conversation.

'Ah, for il secondo,' said Connie, 'they have fegato. Nobody cooks liver like the Italians.'

'Ugh!' said Gill, finally settling for *il pollo*, which Connie assured her meant 'chicken'.

'Probably battery-reared and scrawny as hell,' Maggie teased.

Nevertheless they waded their way through course after course, although Connie admitted defeat when it came to *il dolce*.

'Well, I'm having tiramisu,' Gill announced.

When Stefano appeared waving a second bottle of wine, Connie said, 'Better not; we're driving.'

He raised a perfect black eyebrow. 'Where you go so late tonight?'

'To be honest, I've no idea,' Connie admitted. 'We have a motorhome, caravan, er' – she struggled for the word – 'a *roulotte…*'

'No problem!' Stefano replied airily, deftly removing the cork. 'We have little place for ten caravans' – he held up ten fingers – 'behind here.' He waved at the wall. 'We have just finished the building of it.' He mimed ground-flattening motions. 'Soon we have big sign up on main road, and in tourist book. But you are the first! Il primo!'

The three looked at each other in amazement.

Connie could scarcely believe what she was hearing. 'And we could stay here tonight?'

'Si, si, no problem!' Stefano hesitated. 'There is toilet, but no shower yet. Is OK?'

'Is very OK,' Connie replied.

'It's more than OK,' said Maggie. 'And so is another bottle of wine.'

They woke the next day to find Bella the sole occupant of a large, cleared, grassy area surrounded by trees, where Connie had parked cautiously the night before, following Stefano's instructions but totally unaware of their surroundings in the dark. They'd used the toilet and collapsed into bed, knowing the chances were virtually nil that Ringer, or anyone else for that matter, would ever find them there. For the first time in days Maggie felt safe.

As she sipped her tea, Connie said, 'I wonder how far from the centre of Genoa we are?'

Maggie shrugged. 'Not so far, I would have thought. We were in an urban area when we saw the sign and you can hear the traffic in the distance.'

They both listened to the rumble, punctuated only by occasional snores from Gill.

'I've got used to her,' Maggie said, grinning. 'And these earplugs really work.'

Connie admitted to being very relieved that Gill had never again threatened to sleep on the narrow divan alongside hers at the front, particularly as she, Connie, didn't sleep deeply and wasn't as patient as Maggie. Maggie suspected that Gill – literally – liked to be on top of her make-up and beauty equipment, stored beneath her bunk, although lately she hadn't been using so much of either, and looked the better for it.

'When's her birthday?' Maggie asked as she made herself a second cup of tea.

'About four days' time, I think. Should we do something special for her?'

'Well, she's been going on about finding a beach, so perhaps we can find her some sand somewhere. But what on earth can we buy her?'

'A man!' Connie laughed. 'That's all she really wants!'

'A blow-up bloke!' Maggie snorted.

'We can have a lovely meal somewhere,' Connie said. 'Perhaps Viareggio – there's a beach there. But what about today? Shall we try to get to the station in Genoa and get a train to Santa Margherita and then the boat to Portofino? Well, on second thoughts, perhaps *not* Portofino!'

Maggie sighed. 'No, probably not a good idea.' She was silent for a moment. 'But you two could go.'

'Maybe,' said Connie, 'but Carol would recognise me, and he would recognise Gill. Sorry, I know I should call her "the bimbo", but she was really nice. And we're not going without you, Maggie.'

There was a further silence before Maggie said, 'We can't keep changing our plans because of Ringer; we'll take a chance. Come on, let's go! Bugger him!'

*

They decided to stay three nights at Stefano's hidden campsite. Maggie felt more relaxed than she had for days, probably because they were so far off the beaten track. She had offered up a little prayer to ask that they be kept safe. And it appeared to have worked. And, as a bonus, blond, green-eyed Bruno, Stefano's partner ('There's no justice in the world,' Gill had moaned), was happy to drive them to the station in Genoa.

'You phone me when you want to be picked up,' he instructed them as they got out of his smart red Alfa Romeo. Stefano and Bruno were a godsend in every way. Not only did they run a terrific restaurant and a mini caravan park, but they were in the process of building a little shop 'for you to buy your bread, next time you come'. In the meantime, Stefano delivered fresh bread and milk to Bella each morning, while Bruno chauffeured them to the *supermercato* and even supervised their purchases. 'You don't buy your pasta here – mamma mia! I take you to a much better place!'

Now the train wound its way round the rocky coastline towards Santa Margherita Ligure, where they navigated their way down a long flight of steps to the resort below. It was one of the loveliest places Connie had ever seen, with its little harbour and, opposite, hotels, restaurants, bars, shops and houses; cream, yellow, ochre and pale green, all with contrasting shutters and terracotta tiled roofs, and interspersed with palms, lemon trees and banks of flowers, set against the backdrop of the green-blue wooded hills and the unreal azure of the sea. There was even a small beach, densely populated with supine bronzed bodies.

'A beach!' sighed Gill.

'Too small, too busy,' Connie remarked. 'But we'll find a beach eventually, Gill.'

As they strolled along the main promenade, Maggie said, 'This is stunning. Like a film.'

Connie had spotted a particularly attractive bar across the road. 'What we need now,' she said, 'are Bellinis.' She turned to Gill. 'Peach juice and prosecco – you'll love it!'

Gill did. They all did. And later, three Bellinis apiece, they made their way somewhat unsteadily across to the little pier where the tourist boats loaded and unloaded, and bought three return tickets to Portofino.

'We are crazy,' said Gill as she scrambled onto the boat.

'Quite mad,' Connie confirmed.

Portofino was also picture-postcard perfect.

'Small, but perfectly formed,' muttered Maggie, as the boatload of tourist day-trippers made its way past the selection of yachts. Click, click, click went the cameras and phones. Again, there were gold and terracotta buildings, colourful awnings, and dinky little shopping lanes leading off the main street, which straggled up towards the hill with its pines and cypresses.

'You can smell money here,' said Maggie, suppressing a hiccough.

'You can smell food here too,' said Gill. 'And I'm ready for my lunch.'

'We'd better find somewhere off the beaten track,' Connie said. 'Just in case you-know-who should come waltzing along. I imagine they might have got here last night too.'

'Where do you suppose they'd be staying?' Gill asked, as they sat down in a suitable venue. She was studying the wine list. 'Think I fancy the Pinot Grigio myself.'

'We're getting pissed,' said Connie.

'We're already pissed,' Maggie stated.

'God, this is all so beautiful,' Connie said, glancing around at the well-dressed tourists and the pricey little shops. Even the waitress was a Sophia Loren lookalike. 'I'm beginning to feel inadequate,' she added.

'You are never inadequate, Connie McColl,' Maggie said slowly and clearly, glass of Pinot in hand. 'Never! And this idea of yours was the *best* in the world! The *best*!'

'The best!' echoed Gill, taking a large slurp from her glass.

'I love you both!' Connie said, feeling distinctly misty-eyed.

'I love you, too!' said Gill. And then, turning to Maggie: 'And *even* you! I love you too!'

'I'm loving you more with each gulp,' Maggie added, raising her glass. 'We're all loved-up!'

They felt marginally less inebriated after large plates of pasta.

After they'd settled the bill, they strolled back towards the harbour to await the next boat back to Santa Margherita. As they had some time to kill, they ambled around a couple of waterside boutiques.

'Beautiful!' sighed Connie as she gazed at a display of very simple, beautifully cut linen dresses.

'Two hundred quid!' Gill spluttered after finally finding a price tag.

'I've told you both before,' Maggie said patiently, 'that if either of you want one, you can have it. And I've already bought those two in Nice, so I've set the ball rolling.'

'And it'll soon be your birthday, Gill,' Connie added, winking at Maggie; but then she remembered she was determined not to buy anything else with Maggie's ill-gotten gains.

'Oh, I *couldn't*—'

Whatever Gill couldn't do was interrupted by a voice shrieking, 'CONNIE!'

Connie swivelled round to find herself face to face with Carol. Oh God! Connie was horror-struck; was the boyfriend around too? And what if it *was* Ringer? But there was no escape.

'Oh, Carol,' she said limply.

'Well, what a coincidence!' Carol exclaimed. 'So you got here after all?'

'Oh, we did.' Connie gulped and looked uncertainly at the other two, who were gaping open-mouthed at the new arrival. 'Where's, er, the boyfriend?'

'Oh, he's not much interested in shopping. He's having a beer up the road there. Say, why don't you all come and join us? You are all together, aren't you?' She looked questioningly at Maggie and Gill.

'Yes, we are,' Maggie got in quickly. 'I'm Edna, and this here is Violet.'

'Well, great to meet you, ladies!'

'And we're just about to leave,' Connie added, as she saw the boat approaching.

'Oh, what a shame! Never mind, perhaps we'll bump into you again somewhere,' Carol said cheerfully. 'Are you staying nearby?'

Before Connie could dream up a reply, Maggie said, 'Connie, Violet and I are heading for Venice.'

'Venice!' Carol exclaimed. 'Oh, wow! But that's right across the other side of the country, isn't it?'

'It is,' Maggie confirmed. 'It's a long drive, but we have a nice big Volvo.'

'Well, *enjoy!*'

'Oh, we will,' Connie said. 'But we must go now. Come on Edna, Vi!'

'That was a near-miss,' Maggie said later, as the boat departed for Santa Margherita.

'*If* it was him, or them,' Connie said.

Gill sniffed. 'After all, like Connie said, there must be no end of British blondes chasing around here with older blokes…'

'Yes, yes,' Maggie said impatiently. 'But I have a feeling about this one.' She tapped her nose.

'Anyway,' Gill continued. 'Even if it *was* Ringer with her, we've certainly put him off the scent. *Edna, Violet*, ha, ha! Venice! And a Volvo! That was quick thinking, Mags. I have to hand it to you!'

'If it *was* Ringer,' Maggie said sadly, 'he probably won't believe any of that.'

As the train headed towards Genoa, Maggie, deep in thought, was only dimly aware of Connie phoning Bruno to ask for transport from the station. She was mulling over how she'd certainly underestimated Ringer's charms if a stunning-looking woman like Carol had found him attractive. If it *was* Ringer, he must have spun her some sort of tale about being a business magnate, perhaps. Money always helped. And he must still have plenty of it if he was able to swan around France and Italy, and probably pay the bimbo's fare to come out to join him. She could just hear him. 'I'm bored down here on my own, babe! All business, no pleasure. Why don't you fly down and join me for a few days?' He'd be missing his nookie. And, if it was him, he was probably becoming bored, having lost sight of his prey since Avignon. And it might be difficult for Connie to think of Carol as the bimbo, but that was what she damned well was.

Unfaithful bastard! Maggie's feelings, originally of sadness, then anger and, lately, indifference, now rotated to her own inadequacy. Carol was thirty years younger, and a looker. With two breasts and great hair. What's not to love, and how could I compete? It was a no-brainer; of course he would choose the bimbo. Thirty-eight years of Maggie's support, devotion and covering up for him meant absolutely nothing. She was old and dull and needed to be replaced.

She scorned self-pity, but nevertheless she felt a tear rolling down her cheek. She dabbed at it and blinked furiously. She was not going to cry for that bastard, only for her lost youth. What she couldn't understand was why the police hadn't yet caught up with him. She listened to the BBC news daily and surely the authorities would have checked ports and airports. He was probably even driving his own car! How the hell had he got away with it?

Bruno and the red Alfa were at the station in Genoa to collect them. 'Is not far,' he informed them, 'but no bus.' As he drove along he told them that he and Stefano had been together for nearly ten years. They used to have a little bar in the centre of the city but they'd saved, and then Stefano's father had died and left some money just at the time that La Gioia had come on the market. It was surely meant to be! But it had been a dreary place, off the beaten track, with a terrible chef. There was a great deal of eye-rolling to illustrate this fact.

Now Bruno's brother was the chef and the place was full nearly every single night! And they were expanding; there was the little caravan park, and four bedrooms for letting also. And soon there would be showers, and the shop, and a swimming pool. Next year! And did they know that here in Liguria grew the best basil in all of Italy, and their pesto was the best in the world? They must try Stefano's pesto pasta speciality that very evening!

'I'm glad we're here for another day,' Connie said, glancing at Maggie as she kicked off her sandals.

'Great place,' Maggie agreed. She was doing what she always did whenever they returned to Bella: checking her stacks of bank notes. This involved lifting pieces of carpet, removing panels in the walls and poking around inside mattress covers. Sometimes she forgot, herself, where she'd hidden some of it and, even if Ringer did ever catch up with them, chances are he'd be unlikely to find it all, particularly the wad she kept in her bra.

Connie was still recovering from the shock of the encounter with Carol, and regretting that she hadn't had time to at least try on one of the beautiful linen dresses; she'd have used her own money, since her bank account had remained virtually intact since they'd left home. She'd come to accept that Maggie wanted to pay for everything but, now that she knew its source, she drew the line at accepting payment for anything unnecessary with stolen money. Who am I kidding? she thought. I'm enjoying every mouthful of food and every glass of wine, and it's *all* paid for with stolen money! But still.

The site was a perfect hideaway. They'd made friends with Stefano and Bruno, they had a great restaurant on their doorstep once again and, besides, Connie still wanted to visit the Cinque Terre, those colourful villages clinging perilously to the steep hillsides further down the coast. They could only be reached by train, or by boat from Santa Margherita and Rapallo.

And so, their final day in Liguria was spent on the Cinque Terre boat trip, with stopovers at two of the villages, where Gill flatly refused to even contemplate the flights of near vertical steps rising from the harbours to the houses above. Connie, with some relief, decided to keep her company at the lower level, while Maggie gamely headed upwards with the more agile passengers.

CHAPTER EIGHTEEN

VIAREGGIO

They were now on their way to Tuscany; Connie driving with Gill in the passenger seat, while Maggie opted to keep her feet up, still recovering from blisters acquired during the previous day's mountaineering. They passed the seaside resorts of Rapallo and Sestri Levante, before heading inland towards Massa, admiring the terracotta-topped villages, with their inevitable bell towers, which dotted the hillsides. Or perched perilously on top.

'That's where the marble comes from,' Connie said, when she saw the sign for Carrara. 'Up there in the hills.'

They re-joined the coast at Forte dei Marmi.

'Where exactly are we going?' Gill asked.

'Viareggio. We're giving you a beach for your birthday,' Connie replied.

'Thank God for that,' Gill muttered.

'Do you like swimming in the sea then?'

'Well,' Gill replied. 'The truth is I'm not a very good swimmer, but I like the buoyancy of the sea.'

Viareggio was a popular resort, and close to Pisa and Lucca. Connie liked swimming in the sea too but not so much in Italian resorts, with their endless beach clubs and military rows of sunbeds and sunshades. No chance of a nice secluded cove round here, she mused. We Brits again, she thought, always seeking isolation!

But tomorrow was Gill's birthday and she was going to have her precious beach. After all, Gill had escaped England and the threatened birthday party – which was probably her main reason for coming on this trip in the first place – and so the day had to be hers, and hers alone.

And Connie could see just how much Gill was enjoying the whole experience, and how good she was looking now. The awful beehive long gone, Gill's hair was stylishly layered and subtly coloured. She'd also lost a stone or so, wore far less make-up and, since she'd ditched the sunhat, even her face was now tanned. And she'd finally admitted to being seventy, although she looked younger now than when they'd left London. 'Better to be a youthful seventy than a knackered-looking old sixty,' Maggie had said bluntly.

But even Maggie, already seventy and the most agile of the three, had her limits. This insistence of hers on climbing to the top of the Cinque Terre villages had taken its toll with a puffy ankle and a selection of blisters. We still think we're young deep down inside, Connie thought. While a youthful mind is undoubtedly an asset, the body keeps reminding us otherwise.

'Looks nice here,' Gill remarked as they approached the resort.

Il Paradiso caravan park was well screened from the road by a row of cypresses interspersed with enormous hoardings advertising, among other things, the merits of various restaurants, car-hire companies, laxatives and suntan lotions. It wasn't the most picturesque location but it had a 'vacancy' sign and it was just across the road from the beach.

'I have space for two nights only,' the woman said.

Well, that would cover Gill's birthday and then we can move on, Connie thought, dreaming of a nice quiet layby. Gill seemed delighted.

'This looks ever so slightly naff,' Maggie remarked from the back, as she looked out of the side window.

'Well, I like it!' Gill yelled back. 'And it's *my* birthday!'

Il Paradiso, whilst not exactly heavenly, was clean and tidy with ample showers and toilets. It was also full of noisy families, wet swimsuits drying on makeshift washing lines, excited children running around everywhere, and a pervading aroma of onion and garlic signalling preparation for the evening meal.

'This had *better* be just for a couple of nights,' Maggie muttered as Connie reversed Bella into the allocated parking spot.

'But look, the beach is just across the road,' Gill said, 'and there were loads of restaurants and bars around.'

'Perhaps they'll go to bed early,' Maggie said, watching four infants chasing each other round the caravan next door while shouting at the tops of their little voices.

Connie decided not to shatter her hopes. Italian children did *not* go to bed early. They could be found out and about at all hours, some in pushchairs, some running alongside, as their parents socialised and strolled around. These little ones had plainly just woken up from their siestas and were now bursting with excited energy.

*

It was, they all agreed later, a very different type of evening, not exactly what they'd planned. It began when Connie, having showered and clad only in bra and pants, was trying to decide what to wear.

'Ciao!' said a little voice. And there, standing by the cooker, was a tiny, tousle-haired boy in a red T-shirt and nothing else.

'Well, ciao!' Connie replied, hastily pulling on a cotton shift. 'And who are you?'

'Posso nuotare,' he said, climbing onto the divan.

'I can swim,' Connie remembered. Perhaps he's only just learned.

'Bravo!' she said as he regarded her solemnly with enormous brown eyes. She remembered a little more Italian. 'Come ti chiami?'

'Marcello.'

'Buonasera, Marcello!' She tried to remember a few more stock phrases.

Suddenly there was some frantic yelling outside. 'Marcello! Marcello! Dove sei?'

'He's here!' Connie called out, shepherding Marcello out through the door, just as Maggie and Gill emerged from the rear to see what all the commotion was about. 'Is he yours?' she asked the anxious-looking young woman.

'Ah, grazie a Dio!' She smacked him soundly on his bare bottom and he started to howl. 'Mi dispiace…' she began, gazing at them all in turn.

'Non c'e' problema,' said Connie.

'You no Italian?'

'We no Italian,' Connie confirmed.

The woman tapped Bella's exterior. 'She Italian.'

'Yes, she is Italian,' Connie agreed, 'but we are British.'

'Ah, Inglesi! Fantastico! My daughter' – she pointed at the caravan next door – 'she five years and she learn English. You must speak with her.'

'Yes,' Connie said, staring in amazement at the large cloth-covered table, complete with cutlery, glasses and a carafe of wine, which had suddenly materialised between their two vehicles.

'We eat later,' their new neighbour explained. 'You like eat with us? How many you?'

'No, no,' Connie said hastily. 'There are three of us, and we're going out to find a nice restaurant.'

'I Silvia. Who you?'

'Well, I'm Connie, and—'

'You like Italian food? My husband he cooks il pollo.' She made clucking noises.

'Yes, chicken, very nice,' Connie agreed.

'Pasta too. We have too much, so, you eat with us!'

'This,' said Connie as the other two appeared, 'is Maggie, and Gill. Gill has a birthday tomorrow, so that's why we're going to find a nice restaurant.'

Gill beamed at Silvia, now joined by Marcello, who had recovered from his smack, and a little girl with a mass of dark brown curls who looked a couple of years older.

'Franco!' Silvia yelled. Franco dutifully appeared from the interior of their caravan, bare-chested and wearing a towel tucked into his shorts.

'They English,' she informed her husband. 'And that one' – pointing at Gill – 'have birthday. You cook for birthday, eh, Franco?'

'Certo! We have too much,' Franco replied in near perfect English. 'We like to share. Nadia likes to try English, non è vero?' He nudged his little daughter, who was gazing at them with saucer eyes.

Connie blinked as an exact replica of Marcello appeared at the door, stark naked and sucking his thumb.

'This Carlo,' Silvia explained. 'He been sleep.' She saw the women looking from one child to another. 'Si, they twins! They have three years.'

The new, naked one headed towards Gill and said, 'Nonna!'

'He thinks you are grandmother,' Franco explained. 'She look like you. She has, er, the big…'

At this point Silvia took over. 'These!' She waved her hands in enormous semi-circles over her front.

Gill looked pleased. 'I'd pick him up,' she said, 'if he was wearing a nappy.'

'I do nappies,' Silvia said. 'You do wine.' She indicated the large carafe on the table. 'Sit!'

'We might as well,' said Gill, obviously flattered. 'Just for one drink?'

Maggie sighed.

'Look,' said Connie, 'we can't go drinking their wine. Let's put a bottle of our stuff on the table too.'

'Yes, let's!' agreed Gill. 'Come on, Mags, it's nearly my birthday! And they're nice people.'

'Just one glass then,' Maggie replied, looking resigned.

*

Coming up to midnight, Marcello was fast asleep on Gill's knee, Carlo was fast asleep on Connie's knee, and Nadia was wide awake and keen to practise her English with anyone who would listen. Everyone had eaten pasta and chicken and strawberries, washed down by copious amounts of wine, and they were now on the Grappa.

The family came from Barga, up in the Tuscan hills, and liked to come down to Viareggio for a few days so the children could play in the sand and learn to swim in the sea. When Franco discovered Maggie was Scottish, there was instant rapport. Everyone in Barga had Scottish connections, he said. Their fathers and grandfathers had all gone to Scotland to find work; even his very own Uncle Angelo in Glasgow, and he had lots of Scottish cousins who came to visit every year. In fact he, Franco, had spent a year in Glasgow too with the family there before he married Silvia. Maggie could recall so many Italian families from her youth in Glasgow. They all had great restaurants, fish and chip shops, and made the best ice cream in the world, she told him.

Three elderly British ladies, well fed and tipsy, had attracted some curious neighbours. They'd driven all the way from England! And that lady would be seventy at midnight! More gasps! More wine!

The children finally in bed, Franco found a Rod Stewart CD, 'Sailing'. Connie found herself jigging with a tiny ancient man, sadly lacking teeth and English, but light on his feet. She'd no idea where he came from. Maggie was dancing with some lanky teenage boy, and Silvia was doing a little dance all by herself. Gill had, in her usual fashion, overindulged, and had latched onto Franco who, also having overindulged, didn't seem to mind too much.

'Isn't he gorgeous?' she mouthed to Connie.

'Don't forget the "grandson" bit,' Connie reminded her.

At midnight a cheer went up, more drinks were dispensed, and everyone sang 'Happy Birthday' or some translation of it, after which Gill sat down on a chair and promptly passed out.

'I only just dozed off,' was how she put it later.

CHAPTER NINETEEN

IL COMPLEANNO

Gill, in her shocking-pink swimsuit and awash with Alka-Seltzer, didn't begin to feel human until around midday. Connie and Maggie regarded her with amusement as they stretched out on their sunbeds on the crowded beach.

'I didn't pass out,' Gill snapped at them. 'I just dozed off.' She donned the sunhat and her dark glasses and slapped on vast quantities of suntan lotion. Then she picked up her phone to tackle the mountain of emails and e-cards in her inbox. 'God!' she groaned. 'I didn't know I had so many offspring!'

Connie and Maggie were taking her shopping later when they left the beach, because she'd seen some fantastic leather handbags on her way from Il Paradiso. They weren't exactly cheap but they were in the most mouth-watering colours. She'd never be able to choose just one, she'd said, to which the reply was, 'Well, we'll each buy you one! After all, it is a special birthday!'

She'd been told by Connie that it was her *compleanno* and she was *settanta* years old. It sounded much more musical than 'seventieth birthday', but then everything over here did. Now Connie was waving the prosecco bottle at her and Gill felt her stomach give a tiny heave.

'Later, perhaps,' she mumbled, swigging from her bottle of water.

And Maggie had opened up some little cartons of olives and mini-pizzas.

'Not just yet,' sighed Gill, ignoring their giggles.

'Go on! It's your big day!'

Gill felt her stomach give another little lurch. 'No thanks,' she muttered, trying to avoid looking at the pots which Maggie was holding out in her direction.

It was uncomfortably hot and noisy; their neighbours yelling lustily for children to come back as they dispensed drinks and snacks and suntan lotion.

'I'm not used to having loads of kids around,' Maggie said. 'Alistair had his kids in Australia and I hardly ever saw them when they were wee.'

'Lucky old you,' Gill murmured. 'It's just like being at home, but at least I can understand what my lot are talking about.' She declined Connie's further offers of panini, salami and cheese. 'Are you trying to get me to throw up?' she asked crossly.

'So, when are you going for this swim of yours?' Maggie asked.

'When it cools down a bit,' Gill replied. 'And after I get a chance of some shut-eye.'

A few minutes later, Gill's snores could just about be heard above the screaming of children, the yelling of the mammas, and the blare of pop music from some youngsters a couple of rows in front.

Maggie groaned. Connie dreamed of a secluded little cove.

'Let's go for a swim,' Connie suggested.

They pushed their bags under Gill's sunbed and raced, the sand blisteringly hot beneath their feet, towards the blissful cool of the water.

Gill woke up as they were drying themselves. She felt much better.

'You should have waited for me,' she yawned as she eased herself off the sunbed.

'We weren't sure how long old bats of seventy would need for their afternoon nap,' Maggie said.

'Well, you *should* know!' Gill was adjusting the heavily laden bra top of her swimsuit. 'Can't have these falling out, can I?'

The hot sand beneath her feet had Gill emitting little squeals as she ran towards the sea and blissful relief. Mediterranean or not, the water still felt unexpectedly cool as she waded in with caution. Then, aware that the other two might be watching and having a giggle at her expense, she plunged in. When she regained her breath, she commenced a careful breaststroke, concentrating on keeping her hair as dry as possible, and keeping within her depth. She'd never yet had the courage to brave the deep end of a swimming pool, but now the buoyancy of the sea was boosting her self-confidence. If only she lived by the sea, Gill was convinced she'd be a good swimmer. A confident swimmer. Now she fancied a little float, although it would doubtless wreck her hair. Aw, what the hell! Nobody knew her here, or cared, and she could always pay a visit to the hairdresser on her way back to Il Paradiso. And, after all, it is my birthday!

Gill gazed up at the sky as she bobbed up and down on her back on the gentle waves, thinking about her family and their emails and e-cards, all full of good wishes. She loved them all dearly and she missed them – but only a little. And she certainly wasn't sorry to be missing the bloody party they'd planned. In fact, she had to admit it, she was enjoying herself more than she had in years! She was enjoying the company, even Maggie's caustic sense of humour. And, more and more, she wished this journey would never end; one beautiful place after another, endless sunshine, delicious food and, even better, Maggie footing the bill for everything!

Come to think of it, where *was* this journey going to end? Rome? Amalfi? Gill just wanted to keep going on and on but of course they couldn't. They'd have to go home eventually, but she wasn't going to think about that just yet. She was going to enjoy every hour, every day.

Gill realised she'd been daydreaming for some time, and she really should be getting back. As she turned over to swim, she realised she'd drifted a fair way out from the beach, and she was most definitely very much out of her depth.

Stay calm, Gill, she told herself. Just do your breaststroke and keep going; it's not that far. There were a few other swimmers around. Strong swimmers, diving under the waves like bleedin' fishes, she thought. Knowing what they're doing. Well, I mustn't panic because I *can* do this. I *must* do this. She was swimming and swimming but the shore didn't seem to be getting any nearer. Oh, please, God, she prayed. I know I've said I don't believe in you, but I do really! Now the salt was stinging her eyes and she couldn't make out if she was any closer to the beach or not.

Keep going, keep going! But I'm out of condition and I'm getting tired. And I don't want to drown! Should I call out? Would any of these swimmers hear me?

How long would it be before Connie or Maggie got concerned? After all, they knew she wasn't much of a swimmer.

Don't cry, you silly cow! That'll do no good at all!

'Signora! Va bene?'

Gill was aware of a masculine voice alongside and felt relief flooding through her veins. She gave a strangled sob. 'I think I need help!'

'Ah, Inglese!' he said, as if that explained everything. He encircled her with one hairy arm. 'Relax, Signora!' And he swam powerfully towards the beach with Gill hanging on. They had reached the shallow water before Gill was able to have a good look at her hero: stocky, grey-haired and balding on top, but covered with hair everywhere else.

Almost sobbing with relief, Gill found her feet and waded alongside him. He wasn't a lot taller than her and sported a pair of very fetching emerald green trunks.

'Thank you so much!' She tried to control the trembling of her lips as she wiped her eyes with the back of her hand.

'No problem!' He regarded her gravely with his velvety brown eyes. 'No go so far next time, no?'

'No,' Gill agreed. 'I won't.'

God, she thought, what must I look like? Why the hell did I put mascara on today? It will have run all down my face, and my hair's wrecked. She looked down in horror to see both boobs bouncing towards escape, and frantically she attempted to push them back into their stowage.

'Where is your husband?'

'My husband?' Gill wiped her eyes again. 'I don't have a husband. I'm here with a couple of friends.'

'Ah,' he said. 'So maybe you like a drink?'

'Yes,' she agreed. 'I think I would. But I must buy you a drink because you saved my life.'

'No, no, no!' he protested modestly. 'You just needed a little help. Come with me up to the bar and we get nice drink.'

Gill could see him clearly now. Rather nice, if abnormally hairy.

'I'll just pop across to tell my friends where I'm going,' she said, scanning the rows of bronzing bodies before spotting Maggie, who was standing up adjusting her sunshade.

'So, I wait here.' The drops of water glistened like tiny crystals on his chest hair.

'We were beginning to worry about you,' Connie said. 'You've been gone for ages.'

'Yes, well.' Gill towelled herself dry. She wasn't going to admit to having to be rescued. 'I'm going for a drink with this guy I met in the sea.'

'A guy?' They both regarded her with astonishment.

'Yeah, we're going up to the beach bar.'

'You don't waste any time,' Maggie remarked. 'Chatting up blokes in the water!'

Gill donned her dark glasses and hoisted her bag over her shoulder.

'Honestly, Gill,' Connie said, 'we can't trust you on your own for more than five minutes!'

*

He was waiting at the entrance to the beach bar, now clad in a pair of white shorts. 'Ah!' he said, smiling.

He had nice teeth. Gill hoped they were his own.

'You need a little brandy!'

'No, no!' Gill said hastily. 'Coffee's fine. Really.'

'I Alfonso,' he said solemnly, holding out his hand.

'Gill,' she said. 'An Americano, please.'

They shook hands and then he pulled out a chair for her. 'I go to bar.' He returned a few minutes later with one Americano and one espresso.

'Thank you, Alfonso. You're very kind.'

'I call you Geelee,' he said. 'Like the singer.'

She looked at him blankly. 'That's nice,' she said. 'And I'm sorry I caused you so much trouble. I'd been floating, you see, and hadn't realised how far I'd drifted out. And I'm not a very good swimmer.'

'I give you lessons,' he said. 'How long you are here for, Geelee?'

'I think they want to move on tomorrow,' Gill said gloomily.

'"They"?' Alfonso raised his still dark eyebrows. 'Who is "they"?'

Gill took a sip of her coffee and began to give him brief details of the trip.

'All the way from England? Three ladies? Dio mio! Where you here?'

She told him.

'Il Paradiso.' He gave a disdainful grunt. 'You stay more long. I find you better place.'

He was gazing at her with such intensity that Gill felt some unfamiliar stirrings deep within, quite different from her normal responses. He had nice hands, square and capable looking with neatly cut, clean nails. You could tell a lot about a man from his hands, even if the backs were hairy. And shoes. In the absence of these, Gill cast a look at his feet, surprised to see that even the tops of his feet were hairy. She didn't think she'd seen such hairy feet before; there wasn't a lot of it about at home.

'How far you go?' he asked, downing his espresso in one gulp.

'How far?' Gill pondered anew their probable destination. 'I think we end up in Amalfi – near Naples, you know?'

'Si, I know where is Amalfi.' He winked at her. 'So, why stop in Amalfi? You go to Sicilia too?'

She wanted to tell him that she'd be more than happy to carry on to Sicily, Greece or anywhere else with cloudless skies, blue seas and hairy Mediterranean men. Instead she told him about Connie's grandmother and how she and Maggie had 'just come along for the ride'.

He was bound to be married.

'My wife,' he said, as if reading her thoughts, 'come from Sicilia. Palermo.'

I knew it!

'She gone, so I no go often now,' he said sadly.

Gill cleared her throat. 'Has she passed on then?'

'Passed on? No, she dead.'

'Oh, I'm sorry!' No, I'm not.

'Five years.' He held up his fingers. 'You have husband in England?'

'No, he's dead too.' For a moment she fondly visualised Peter with his buns and his bagels.

'Ah.' He paused. 'What you do in evening?'

'This evening? Oh, we're going out somewhere for a nice meal. It's my birthday.'

'Il compleanno!' he exclaimed. 'How many years?'

No Englishman would dare ask such a question. For a brief moment she wondered if she should try for sixty again, but then thought, what the hell!

'Today I'm seventy,' she admitted reluctantly, wondering if she'd wrecked her chances with this lovely, hirsute man.

'Settanta! Mamma mia, you no look it!'

'Thank you!' she said graciously.

'I seventy-three. But you want to eat dinner with ladies, and no with me?'

'Oh no!' she said quickly, hoping she didn't sound too eager. 'It's just that we sort of arranged…'

'You can un-arrange?'

'Yes, I can un-arrange.' Certainly I can, she thought. Not half.

'What?' Connie stared at Gill in disbelief. 'You want to go out tonight with some old lothario who's been chatting you up in the water?'

Gill had decided against mentioning the rescue. 'He's nice. And, for your information, he's a widower.'

'Oh yeah?' said Maggie.

'Yes, he is!'

Connie laughed. 'Well, it is your birthday!'

'You don't mind, do you? Because I really want to go. He's meeting me at the gates of Il Paradiso at seven.'

'No, of course we don't mind,' Connie replied. 'Just make sure he doesn't whip your knickers off up some dark alley or other.'

'Connie, he's *seventy-three*!'

'But he's Italian,' Maggie reminded her. 'Full of geriatric lust.'

I do hope so, Gill thought. 'And tomorrow,' Gill added, 'he's going to take us somewhere else where we can park Bella.'

'We sort of thought of heading towards Pisa and Lucca tomorrow,' Connie said.

'Couldn't we have just one more day?' Gill pleaded.

'She certainly sounds happy but I hope she knows what she's doing,' Connie remarked later as she listened to Gill singing in the shower.

Maggie was chopping onions. 'I doubt it,' she said.

'I mean, he could be *anybody*!' Connie went on. 'She knows nothing about him.'

Maggie snorted. 'Well, he's hardly likely to have got her lined up for the white slave trade!'

'No, but she strikes me as being quite gullible. I don't like the idea of her being molested down some dark alley.'

'He's the one in danger of being molested, if you ask me.' Maggie wiped her eyes. 'These onions are really strong.'

'Seriously, Maggie, I think we should keep an eye on her. Just to make sure. You know?'

Maggie turned to stare at Connie. 'And how do you propose we do that?'

Connie thought for a moment. 'We could follow them. At a distance, of course.'

'You've been reading too much cloak-and-dagger stuff, Connie. I should think Gill is well able to take care of herself.'

'Well, I'm going to follow them anyway.'

'OK, OK, I'll come with you. If only to make sure he doesn't bundle her into a truck full of other desperate old biddies. For auction in some dodgy country.'

They both giggled.

There followed an hour of Gill trying to decide which dress to wear, which shoes, which bag, and which perfume, before she was finally ready to meet her date at the gate to Il Paradiso.

'It really is the gateway to paradise!' she said gleefully before setting off.

'What if he's got a car?' Maggie said a few minutes later, as she and Connie locked Bella's door and, having waited until Gill rounded the corner out of sight, prepared to follow.

'We could at least get the registration number,' Connie said.

As they got in sight of the gate, they saw Gill stop and look in both directions but, fortunately, not behind. And then they saw a smartly dressed, stocky man appear from nowhere and kiss her on both cheeks.

'He doesn't look much like a white slaver,' Maggie muttered, as Gill and the man set off down the street towards the restaurants and shops. 'Then again I don't suppose they ever do.'

'Well, at least they're walking. Come on, let's see where he's taking her.'

Everyone in Viareggio appeared to be out taking their evening *passeggiata* and Connie hoped that, by keeping some distance behind, even if Gill turned round she wouldn't spot them. There were tables and chairs outside each restaurant, full of people enjoying drinks and food in the evening sunshine.

'Hey, they've disappeared!' Maggie said suddenly.

'They've got to have gone inside one of these restaurants,' Connie said. 'Come on, we'll just have a peep through the windows to make sure.'

It was as they drew level with the third *ristorante* that they realised Gill and her companion were standing in a doorway right in front of them, studying the menu. It was too late to retreat.

'Keep walking!' Connie whispered.

But, just at that moment, Gill turned round. 'What the…!'

'Oh, hi Gill!' Maggie said airily. 'We just thought we'd have a little stroll before supper!'

Gill's eyes narrowed. 'Is that so? Last I heard you were preparing a casserole and having a lazy evening.'

'We changed our minds,' said Connie.

'Fancied a walk,' added Maggie.

Gill's date looked from one to the other in total confusion. He was quite good looking, Connie noted, but excessively hairy.

'This,' Gill said, 'is Alfonso. Alfonso, this is Connie and Maggie, my travelling companions, who've suddenly decided to have an evening stroll.'

There was handshaking all round, with Alfonso looking even more confused. 'You are eating with us also?'

'No, no!' Connie said hastily. 'We just came out for a stroll.'

'That's a little *walk*,' Maggie explained to a still mystified-looking Alfonso.

'Well, don't let us stop you,' said Gill. 'You'll want to build up an appetite for that casserole of yours!'

'Such a coincidence to run into you like this,' Connie said, taking Maggie firmly by the elbow. 'We'll be on our way.'

'Damn me!' Maggie exclaimed as they resumed walking. 'She must *know* we were following her.'

'Well,' Connie said, 'she should be pleased to know we were just making sure she came to no harm. And he seems OK, doesn't he, this Alfonso?'

'Yes, but you know what Gill's like. We're never going to be able to get her to move on now.'

Connie laughed. 'There's still that guy in Rome she goes on about. We should get her that far at least. Now, I think we should go back to our supper.'

CHAPTER TWENTY

ALFONSO

Connie awoke and eased herself up on one elbow to check the time. Only half past six. She wondered how Gill had got on and then, to her astonishment, she saw that Bella's door was open and Gill was sitting on the step gazing out at their still sleeping neighbours. In the distance a dog was barking.

Connie swung her legs out of bed. 'Gill, are you OK?'

Gill, in her nightie, took a sip from her bottle of water. 'Did I wake you?'

'No, not at all. But it's not like you to be up so early.'

There was a big sigh. 'I just couldn't sleep.'

'Why ever not? Was the dinner date a disaster or something?'

'Oh no,' Gill replied. 'That's just the problem.'

Connie scratched her head. 'Tell me all!'

'He's so lovely,' Gill replied dreamily. Then, getting to her feet: 'Can we have some tea?'

'Of course we can!' Connie yawned as she filled the kettle. 'Hope you didn't mind us tailing you last night, but it was only because we wanted to make sure you were safe.'

Gill settled herself down on the small divan. 'No, and I'm really touched that you cared. Anyway, we went to this great restaurant. And everyone seemed to know him – lots of hugging and handshaking and all that. "This is Gee-lee," he told everyone. That's how he *says* it! And he told them all it was my birthday.'

'And the food? Did you like the food?' Connie asked as she dropped the teabags in the mugs.

'Yes, the food was delicious.' Gill paused. 'And he's got two daughters.'

'And definitely no wife?'

'Definitely no wife. And Connie, dare I say it, but I think he really fancies me!'

'And do you fancy him?' Silly question, Connie thought.

'Oh, I do!' Gill said as she accepted a mug of tea. 'I really wanted to stay with him last night but I knew you two might be worried.' She took a gulp. 'But I'll stay with him tonight.'

'You will?'

'Would you mind?'

Connie grinned. 'Gill, you're seventy years old! You hardly need my permission!'

'He's so lovely.'

'Yes, you already mentioned that. But why couldn't you sleep?'

'I just couldn't get him out of my mind. God, Connie, I haven't felt like this in years!'

'Well, he sounds very nice. But Gill, you're on holiday, the sun's shining, the wine's flowing and Mediterranean Man has always been around to add a little spice to the mix.' Connie recalled long-ago holidays in Italy and Greece enlivened by these bronzed, dark-eyed lotharios.

At this point a bleary-eyed Maggie emerged from the rear. 'What's going on? Why's everyone up so early?'

'Gill's hormones have been keeping her awake,' Connie replied. 'Tea?'

'Yes, please.' Maggie sat down next to Gill. 'I heard you creeping in late last night. Just as well you had the spare key.'

'Yeah. It was gone one o'clock, I think.'

'So, how did you get on with the hairy old Italiano?'

'He's lovely. And his name's Alfonso, if you don't mind.'

'Well you *did* introduce us!' Maggie winked at Connie.

'And I call him Alfie. He likes that. And he pronounces my name "Gee-lee", isn't that sweet?'

'As in "strawberry jeely with custard",' Maggie teased. 'That was once considered a sophisticated pudding in my part of Glasgow!'

'Like a singer, Alfie said.'

'What does he do, apart from chatting up British ladies?' Connie asked.

'He was a policeman,' Gill replied. 'He was the police chief for this area before he retired.'

'Dear God!' Maggie muttered. 'Just what we bloody well need! I don't suppose you mentioned in passing that we had a criminal pursuing us for a load of stolen money?'

'Somehow or other that didn't enter the conversation,' Gill replied drily.

Alfonso appeared a couple of hours later, clad in a well-fitting navy blue T-shirt and pristine white slacks.

'You've met Connie and Maggie,' Gill said.

'Buongiorno! I am pleased to meet again! Now, you follow,' he ordered, 'and I take you to nice place for parking.'

'Well, perhaps for just one night.' Connie wondered what they were letting themselves in for now. She didn't think she'd ever seen anyone quite so hairy – even the very tops of his feet! Must all be a bit hot in bed. But she could see that he had a certain hirsute charm, and very nice velvety brown eyes.

'I park at gate,' he said, pointing towards the entrance. 'Gee-lee, you come with me. We wait in my car and they follow us.'

Gill, who'd spent the last couple of hours doing her face and hair, and deciding what to wear, said, 'Yes, Alfie,' and beamed at the other two. 'Do you need me to help you pack everything away?'

'No, we'll cope,' Connie replied.

As she began to stow away the kitchen stuff she noticed the tense expression on Maggie's face.

'We're doing this for Gill,' she muttered once Gill was out of earshot. 'Just to let her have some more time with her Alfie.'

'Lord only knows where he's taking us,' Maggie groaned. 'And why on earth did he have to be a bloody policeman!'

'He's not a policeman *now*,' Connie reminded her.

'Maybe not, but he'll still be a suspicious bastard. Once a cop, always a cop. I only hope Gill doesn't let something slip out in their conversation.'

'Like what?'

'Like avoiding red Lexuses, just for a start.'

They followed Alfonso's black BMW for about a mile before he turned into a narrow lane, passed an olive grove and finally pulled up at a square terracotta-coloured villa, with dark green shutters drawn across all the windows. After he parked his car he signalled Connie, who was driving Bella, to follow him as he walked round to the rear of the house, where they found an open area bordered by cypresses and with a large swimming pool on one side.

'Wow!' said Maggie, as he waved them to stop.

'Not bad!' Connie agreed as she applied the handbrake.

'You like this place?' Alfonso asked through the open window. 'My house.'

Gill emerged, beaming, from the front of Alfonso's car.

'Like the cat that stole the cream,' Maggie murmured.

'You stay here,' ordered Alfonso. He opened a small cupboard attached to the wall. 'Here is electric.' He waved at the seductive turquoise water. 'You like swim?'

'This is OK,' Connie conceded as she jumped out of the vehicle.

Gill joined them. 'This is better than Il Paradiso, isn't it?'

'You did well for us, Gill,' Connie admitted.

Alfonso had unlocked a large carved wooden door and beckoned them to follow him.

'La cucina!' he exclaimed, as they found themselves in a cavernous kitchen. From the tiled floor to the high-beamed ceiling the atmosphere was cool and calm after the blistering heat outside, with free-standing dressers and cupboards round the walls, and one enormous wooden table in the centre.

'And you're here all alone?' Connie asked, unable to imagine cooking a solitary lasagne in this enormous space.

'Now, si,' he said a little sadly. 'But I have many friends who come to eat here, you know? And is warm in winter.' He indicated a giant stone fireplace at the far end.

'Well, I think it's lovely,' said Gill, walking slowly around and running her hand along the fronts of the cupboards. 'I could cook in here!' She glanced at Alfonso. 'You don't bother so much for yourself, do you?'

'Esatto!' he beamed back at her. He opened a door, which led into a hallway. 'Come! I show you my salotto!'

The sitting room was formally furnished and very dark, the shutters closed firmly against the outside heat. Obviously no one had done much sitting in here lately, Connie thought, as she gathered a layer of dust on her forefinger from the ornate sideboard.

They moved in procession into a dark-shuttered dining room, a dark-shuttered study and, finally on the ground floor, an enormous dark-shuttered bathroom, complete with roll top bath.

'You can use,' Alfonso announced, 'because I have another upstairs.' He indicated the staircase as they emerged again into the hall, but declined to lead them upwards. He held up four fingers. 'Four rooms for sleep.'

'It's a big house, Alfonso, for just one man,' Maggie remarked as they re-entered the kitchen.

'Si, si, but I lazy to move. And I like to swim. And to care for my olives.' He produced a glass jug containing a golden liquid. 'You like try? Is my oil.' He dug four tiny glasses out of one of the cupboards.

'You *drink* oil?' Gill asked in horror. 'Out of a *glass*?'

'Si, si, buonissimo!' Alfonso said as he poured. Then, glancing at Gill's face, he uncovered a container on the table, withdrew a loaf and chopped a thick slice into small chunks. 'Now you try!'

Connie was no expert on the merits of olive oil and she sipped the liquid gingerly, surprised to find it had an almost fruity, peppery flavour. Gill and Maggie both dipped the bread into their glasses and agreed that the taste was indeed very acceptable.

'Tonight,' said Alfonso, 'I wish to take Geelee out again so, if you like' – turning to Connie and Maggie – 'you can use kitchen.'

'No, no, we're fine,' Maggie said hastily. 'We have a great kitchen in our Bella. But we'd love to use your bath.'

'And can we have a swim in your pool, please?' Connie asked.

They spent the remainder of the afternoon swimming, sunbathing and dreaming of the large free-standing bath in Alfonso's downstairs bathroom.

'I can't remember when I last had a bath,' Maggie sighed. 'I just hope to God his toilet doesn't need cleaning.'

'He has someone who comes in to do all that,' Gill informed her loftily. 'Some old crone in the village.' Well, she hoped Giulia *was* an old crone. Anyway, she had better things to think about, such as what she might wear this evening, and which handbag would suit best. Connie had bought her the green, Maggie the blue, and both were gorgeous. Would Connie be offended if she chose the blue one tonight? And she must wash her hair and have a lovely soak in that bath. She'd wear one of the Cannes dresses, and definitely the matching lacy bra and knickers. She'd begun to wonder if she'd ever have an opportunity to wear these or, better still, an opportunity to have them removed! She felt quite giddy with anticipation. What a seventieth!

*

Connie and Maggie had leisurely baths in the evening, soaking in Alfonso's bubbles from a bottle he'd conveniently left on the shelf.

I can't remember the last time I saw my fingers so prune-like, Connie thought as she dried herself while letting the water run away. She was relieved to see the water was still hot as she ran a bath for Maggie. They then took the opportunity to have a good look round the house, in particular Alfonso's bedroom, fascinated by the painting of cherubs on the ceiling above his bed.

'Imagine waking and staring up at that lot,' Maggie mused.

'Gill will look up and think she's gone to heaven,' Connie said.

Maggie laughed as she looked through the contents of Alfonso's wardrobe. 'I must say everything's very neat and tidy, all colour-coordinated too. And a smell of cologne to boot. Ringer's wardrobe was a shambles, full of sweaty T-shirts and a jumble of shoes in the bottom.'

There was a photo of a woman beside the bed, presumably Alfonso's late wife. She gave them a stern glare.

'On the other hand, Gill might open her eyes and meet this lady's stare,' Connie said. 'Very disapproving, I would have thought.'

It was mid-morning the next day, and there was still no sign of Gill and Alfonso. Connie and Maggie, sunning themselves by the pool, were contemplating where to go next.

'Tuscany is so beautiful,' Connie remarked. 'You must see Pisa and Lucca, the walled city where Puccini was born. And then there's San Gimignano and Volterra and Florence…'

'That's if we can ever prise Gill away from her hairy Romeo,' Maggie said, gazing at the shuttered upstairs windows.

'You don't suppose…?'

'What?'

'You don't suppose,' Connie said, 'that this could blossom into a real romance?'

'What? Gill and Alfonso? Of course not; they're both just desperate for a bit of nookie. She'll forget all about him when we move on.'

Connie looked thoughtful. 'I wouldn't bet on it.'

'Well, we certainly can't have him chasing after us. He's *police*, Connie! And Gill's bound to say some stupid damned thing about wine-coloured Lexuses and avoiding their drivers.'

'We must give her a talking-to, I suppose.' Connie sighed.

'We must move on, pronto,' said Maggie.

Gill emerged at eleven, with no sign of Alfonso. She waved cheerily at her two friends as she headed for Bella to change out of last night's crumpled blue dress, and then, fifteen minutes later, clad in a multi-coloured floral swimsuit, she joined them by the pool.

Maggie raised her eyebrows. 'Nice restaurant, then?'

'Restaurant?' Gill had to think for a moment. 'Oh yes, the restaurant was great. Lovely nosh.'

There was a short silence before Connie asked tentatively, 'What time did you get back?'

'Time? No idea. Late.'

Connie cleared her throat. 'Well, the thing is, Gill, we should be moving on. There's a lot of Tuscany to see.'

'Well,' said Gill, 'Alfie's happy to take us anywhere we want to go, and so we could leave Bella here for a while.'

'A *while*!' Maggie sat up suddenly. 'Just how long is *that*? Look, we need to distance ourselves from Alfonso, delightful though he may be. He's a *policeman*, Gill!'

'So what? He *was* a policeman but he's an olive farmer now.'

'Once a cop, always a cop,' Maggie said drily.

'Cobblers! Anyway, you can do what you like but I'm staying right here.'

'You are joking!'

'No, I'm not, Mags. He's a lovely man and he fancies me, and I fancy him, and I'm not about to bugger up any chance of happiness.'

Maggie rolled her eyes. 'You've only known him a couple of days, for God's sake! The heat's got to your brain!'

'And he's Italian,' Connie put in. 'Do you honestly think you're the only British woman he's chatted up on the beach? Come *on*, Gill!'

'Randy old thing!' Maggie added. 'Well, he's got your knickers off and you've had a nice birthday. And now it's time to move on – pronto!'

At that moment Alfonso, clad in a brief pair of blue trunks, emerged from the house, smiling broadly.

'Buongiorno, ladies!' he said. 'It too hot, nearly time for siesta. All Italy go to sleep then.' He winked at Gill, then turned to the other two. 'Tomorrow I take you to Pisa.'

As he and Gill sauntered off, his arm round her shoulders, Connie said, 'Not much sleep likely to be going on there!'

'They've only just got *out* of bed!' Maggie exclaimed. She was wearing her anxious face again. 'I'm not happy at the thought of leaving Bella here all day tomorrow.'

'Why ever not?' Connie asked. 'She's perfectly safe here.'

'What if Ringer…?'

'How can Ringer possibly find us *here*, Mags? We're not on a site, we can't be seen from the road; what's the problem?'

'Yes, but I just have this feeling he's around. And he always seems to know where we damned well are.'

'That's nonsense, Maggie. And we really can't be one hundred per cent certain that any of these incidents and sightings were anything to do with Ringer. And anyway, we've left Bella before when we went into Paris and Avignon and—'

'But those were caravan sites with proper security and everything.'

'And now we're hidden away in the back garden of an ex-police chief! Nobody, but nobody, is going to break into a dusty motorhome on private property and start taking it apart looking for hidden money they don't know we have!'

Maggie sighed. 'Except Ringer. OK, OK, I take your point. We'll let him take us to Pisa.'

Alfonso appeared to know every second person they met in Pisa and, to Maggie's consternation, he kept stopping to chat with members of the Polizia and the Carabinieri. Everyone knew Alfonso as well. As Maggie was becoming increasingly agitated, Gill was wittering on about getting to the tower.

'I've never seen so many good-looking cops,' she murmured to the other two. 'And have you seen those sexy uniforms, and the way they fit round their bottoms! They must be individually tailored, not like our lot!'

'Now,' Alfonso announced after one of these encounters, 'we go to the tower. But' – he paused for effect – 'it is not only the tower. We have the beautiful Battistero di San Giovanni and the Duomo also.'

'That,' translated Connie, who'd been before, 'is the baptistery and the cathedral, alongside what is actually the bell tower.'

On arrival at the Piazza dei Miracoli, they were all silenced by the beauty of these famous marble buildings. Like carved ivory, Connie thought, or a gigantic wedding cake with intricate white icing, against the blue of the sky. What she didn't like, as before, were the stalls on the road directly opposite, selling souvenirs, bags, scarves and cheap jewellery. Gill plainly had no such objections to the stalls, seeming to be torn between gazing at the tower and deciding which necklace she should buy, whilst ignoring Alfonso's warning that they were no good, and he would buy her a better quality one in a shop he just happened to know and where he would get a good discount.

They went into the baptistery first. 'It leans also, you know,' Alfonso informed them. He stamped his foot. 'Because here the ground is too soft.' In the cathedral, he crossed himself and slid into a pew for a few moments. The three followed, grateful for the cool interior, and to sit down to rest their weary feet. They'd already walked a long way from where Alfonso had parked his car and Connie wasn't relishing the prospect of climbing to the top of the tower, even if Alfonso did have the wherewithal for them to avoid waiting in the queue. The last time she'd come to Pisa the tower had been closed for some 'straightening' – not that you'd notice.

They emerged again into the blazing sunshine and crossed to the tower.

Alfonso continued his commentary. 'They build him on sand, you know. So, after three floors he starts to lean and they must leave him for one hundred years to, er…'

'Stabilise?' Connie suggested.

'Si, si, to stabilise. For one hundred years. Then they build four more floors, and make one side higher than the other to – how you say – balance?'

'And it's still wonky,' Gill said with some satisfaction.

In his usual style, Alfonso got them to the head of the queue but resisted the temptation to climb the tower himself. 'Many times I do this,' he informed them, as he lit a cigarette and headed for an inviting patch of grass. 'I wait.'

Gill got as far as the third floor before she removed her sandals. 'These straps in this heat are killing me,' she groaned as she shuffled on upwards in her bare feet. Maggie, as usual, was way ahead and Connie, also as usual, wondered where someone who looked so frail got her energy from. The longer she knew her, the more Connie realised that Maggie was tough, inside and out, despite appearances to the contrary.

It was worth the climb and the views from the top were breathtaking, if you could manage to push your way through the hordes of snap-happy tourists brandishing all manner of phones, tablets and cameras.

As they finally limped out they found Alfonso asleep on his patch of grass, emitting soft snores.

'He's got the right idea,' Maggie muttered.

'Enough sightseeing for today,' Connie added. 'I could murder a glass of something.'

Gill was gazing admiringly at her lover. 'Alfie, Alfie, wake up!'

He opened his velvety browns and looked confused for a moment. 'Oh, ladies, I sleep! I sorry!'

He got to his feet, brushing the back of his trousers with his hand while twisting around trying to see his bottom. 'No grass on there, no?'

'No, no, Alfie – you're perfect! Now, can we find a nice glass of something somewhere? We're parched, and we need to rest our weary feet.' Connie shook a stone out of her sandal.

They limped after him into a relatively quiet side street with a welcome 'Bar' sign and a collection of metal tables and chairs alongside a potted vine. They ordered beer and water and Aperol with soda for Connie, who was flexing her toes against the cool metal of the table leg.

Alfonso gulped his beer. 'Where you wanna go tomorrow?'

'Maybe a day off tomorrow?' Connie said, thinking of her aching feet. 'And I wonder if you could help me to make a call to Napoli? I'm trying to trace some relatives, and I only have one phone number for reference, which I looked up before I left home, but couldn't find anyone who spoke English. And perhaps you could look at some of these letters in my box, which are written in Italian, but very faded.'

'Of course. Then I take you to Firenze,' Alfonso said.

CHAPTER TWENTY-ONE

IL RANDAGIO

Connie had dug out The Box again, looking for any clue that might lead her to finding out more about the elusive Martiluccis. She'd bought a magnifying glass in Genoa, which enabled her to decipher more of the faint squiggles in the letters, and which also magnified the detailed carving of vine leaves on the door of the house in the background of the group photographs. Might she be able to find this door somewhere? Perhaps in Amalfi? And Alfonso had been able to translate a few of the contents of the Italian letters, all of which appeared to be to Maria from her parents: *We pray daily for your safety*; *Can you eat the English food?*; *We are glad your husband is no longer at sea*; *We are thrilled you have a baby boy!*

She'd spent hours searching websites before she left, but could only find pages of complicated Italian. The name of E. L. Pozzi had cropped up again and again and, when she'd finally located what might be the phone number, she'd got through to that woman who spoke the rapid Italian, without pausing for breath, for about thirty seconds, and then abruptly hung up.

Connie couldn't believe that, in this day and age of electronic miracles, she couldn't find a satisfactory answer. Perhaps she hadn't been clued-up enough; modern technology frequently moved too fast for her. But Maggie had come up trumps regarding the photograph of the man in uniform. 'Merchant navy,' she said. 'I'm almost certain it is. My maternal great-uncle wore something similar to that. My ma always kept the photo on the landing wall; she was very proud of it, and of him. He was the only one of the family in those days to venture forth and see the world.'

That, of course, made perfect sense. Her grandfather had most likely been in the merchant navy at one time and that would explain how he might have met Maria in Naples. And Maria would not have relished being on her own in a foreign country while he travelled the world, which might explain why they ended up with that stall near the docks in Newcastle.

'I'm trying to find anyone with the name of Martilucci who might be related to me,' Connie informed Alfonso, when he and Gill finally emerged the following morning. 'I tried to trace the family on some websites before I left home, but they were all in Italian. And now all I can find on Google is the name of one E. L. Pozzi in Naples somewhere.'

'You have number for this person?' Alfonso asked.

'Yes, but I've no idea who he or she is, and I'm worried they won't speak English.'

'I try.' Alfonso took over and, as he held the phone to his ear, Connie waited anxiously. He spoke some rapid Italian, then listened for a moment before handing the phone back to Connie. 'He speak English. He talk to you.'

'Hello?' Connie asked tentatively.

The voice that replied was deep and very masculine. 'You are?'

'I am Connie McColl. My grandmother was called Maria Martilucci, from somewhere around Amalfi, and who went to live in Newcastle, England, presumably when she married my grandfather around a hundred years ago. Your name came up as the only reference when I googled her name.'

The man sighed. 'I am Eduardo Pozzi, and I am a lawyer, as my father and grandfather before me were lawyers. My grandfather might have dealt with this family and the papers will be stored in our vaults somewhere. Since many years.'

'I was just hoping to find some relatives,' Connie said. 'Is there any way they could be traced?'

Mr Pozzi sighed again. 'Si, probabilmente. It takes time to find these files.' He hesitated. 'And time is money, you understand?'

'Oh, I understand perfectly,' Connie replied. 'And I am quite willing to pay, Mr Pozzi. I'm on my way from England but it'll be a week or two yet before we get to Naples.' She looked across at Gill and Maggie splashing about in the pool.

'You are sightseeing?'

'Oh, indeed I am.' Connie stared in disbelief as Gill emerged from the water minus the top half of her bikini, which was floating around in the middle of the pool.

'If you will come to see me in my office when you arrive in Napoli, I will be happy to help you then, Signora. I shall calculate the amount I will need from you, and send an email. I will then check our records and then we can make an appointment for you to come here.'

Well, Connie thought as she turned off her phone, that's the best I can do for the moment. And nobody down there is prepared to blow the dust off any old files until they see the colour of my money. But what other choice do I have?

As Connie replaced the phone into her shoulder bag she saw Alfonso appear from nowhere and plunge into the pool, heading towards the bikini top that was floating around like two large pink blancmanges in the middle. Meanwhile, Gill stood waist-high in the water, her arms folded modestly across her mammaries.

'I don't know how that happened,' she wailed.

'I do,' said Maggie. 'That top is too small for your big boobs.'

'Cover yourself with a towel,' Alfonso ordered as he swam back to the side, towing the top. 'Somebody might see you.'

'We've seen them before,' Maggie muttered. 'And I imagine you have too,' she added, glancing at Alfonso before returning to her sunbed.

Connie, laughing, sank onto the sunbed next to Maggie.

'You couldn't make it up,' Maggie said, rolling her eyes.

'We really should be moving on,' Maggie said later, as they sat eating pasta in Alfonso's kitchen. He had insisted on cooking, and the ravioli was delicious, as was the tomato and red onion salad.

'No, no, you stay – no hurry!' He refilled their glasses with Chianti. 'Tomorrow we go to Firenze. And then' – he turned, beaming, to Gill – 'I have tickets for a wonderful concert at the weekend, under the stars!'

'A concert?' Gill looked at him over the rim of her glass.

'Si, si, is the famous Andrea Bocelli! You like?'

'Oh, you *lucky* thing!' Connie exclaimed.

'Connie likes,' Gill replied. 'I've had to listen to him warbling most of the way here. You take Connie!'

'Oh, I didn't mean—' Connie began.

'OK, OK,' Alfonso interrupted. 'We no go. Connie go with Maggie.'

'Fine by me,' muttered Gill.

'Oh, I *couldn't*, Alfonso!' Connie said, desperately wanting to go.

'Why no? I have two nice tickets near the front. You go with Maggie.'

'Yes, I'll come with you,' Maggie said.

'Is at Lajatico, where Bocelli is born. Every year, big concert, al fresco.' He looked back at Gill. 'We will have romantic evening with music you like, no?'

'Rod Stewart,' said Gill, gulping her wine.

They offered to pay for the concert tickets but Alfonso would have none of it. 'I go every year,' he said, 'I have friend, you know?' He tapped his nose. 'Not important for me. I glad you like.'

Connie was thrilled. She had only seen the singer that one time in London and the very thought of seeing him in his natural habitat was unbelievable! Good old Alfonso! She felt quite shivery with excitement – wait until she told Di!

And at long last she'd have an opportunity to wear that beautiful Parisian designer dress. Connie knew it would be imperative to look good amidst those hordes of Italian concertgoers because she'd seen what Italian women looked like, dressed up for the evening. Even the older, chubbier ladies had such great style, such beautifully cut clothes, such elegant footwear. And to see and hear the wonderful Tuscan singer underneath the Tuscan stars!

Gill decided she couldn't possibly go somewhere as beautiful as Florence without a nice new sundress. And all the more important now that she wanted to look good for Alfonso. And particularly with all the well-groomed Italian ladies that were bound to be in Florence. And Alfie, of course, knew exactly where to find a good boutique! How many Englishmen, she wondered, would have the first clue as to where a boutique might be, even if it was bang next door to their local? That was just one of the things she liked about this man. He noticed what she wore! 'That colour so nice,' he'd say. 'It match the blue of your eyes.' Once, and only once, had Peter said, en route to the pub, 'I haven't seen you in that dress before, have I?' when she'd had the damned thing for ten years. No, there was little point in dressing up for most men back home because they didn't notice. Or they only noticed when she didn't want them to. 'Is that new?' Peter would ask suspiciously when she'd overspent. 'Oh, what, *this* old thing?' But these Italian men were something else. There was so much more than the Channel that separated Englishmen from their continental counterparts, Gill reckoned.

Connie and Maggie had opted for a restful day by the pool. In spite of all their wittering on about getting to Florence and Rome and God-knows-where, Gill thought, they were happy enough to park for free in Alfonso's garden and swim in Alfonso's pool.

Gill couldn't bear to think of moving on. Yes, she'd like to get to Rome and all that, and she loved the nomadic lifestyle with Connie and Maggie, but now there was Alfonso, and she loved him too. Well, she was pretty sure she did. And she had a feeling that he felt the same. But what if they were to move on and she was never to see him again? She'd probably regret it forever. Gill was being pulled in every direction. No one but me and my old cat for years, she thought, and now all this!

Gill and Alfie were strolling along the main shopping street en route to the boutique when she saw him. He was alone and heading straight in their direction but, mercifully, he hadn't seen her yet. He was wearing shorts again, and this time she could see the long scar down his left leg.

Gill froze. She grabbed Alfonso's arm. 'Quick! Quick!' she muttered, turning abruptly into the first available doorway. Alfonso followed her in, looking confused.

'You are hungry?' he asked, nearly colliding with a tray of cream cakes being transported to the window by a white-clad baker. 'You want cake?'

'No, no!' Gill peered over his shoulder through the window to make sure the street was clear. 'No, I just needed to avoid someone.'

'Avoid?'

'Yes, someone I didn't want to see. Not important, Alfie,' she added, her heart thumping. 'Let me buy you a little cake.'

Still looking confused, Alfonso chose a strawberry concoction and Gill, still shaken, chose the first cake she laid her eyes on, which was some kind of éclair. They were paid for, prettily boxed and, as they left the shop, Alfonso asked, 'Who you no want to see?'

'Oh, not important, Alfie.'

He stopped abruptly. 'Is *very* important! Is a man? He Italiano?'

'No, no, nothing like that.'

'Is a woman?'

'No, Alfie! Please don't concern yourself. It's just someone from England…'

'England? Englishman? He looking for you? Lover? Husband?' Alfonso stood rooted to the spot, cake box in hand, refusing to move.

'I haven't a husband or a lover! No, he's a friend of Maggie's who she doesn't want to see any more.'

'So why he following her here?'

'I don't know, Alfie. But he seems to know we're travelling together and I don't want to meet him.'

They strolled along, Alfie still carrying the beribboned box of cakes. 'Why she no tell him go away?'

'Yes, well it's a little more complicated than that. And he's very persistent.' And Maggie's going to kill me, Gill thought, but what was I to say? 'Anyway, *please* don't say anything about this to her, Alfie! I don't want to worry her.'

'How he know she here, in Viareggio?'

'I don't know.' And I truly don't, she thought. How come he always seems to know exactly where we are? She suppressed a shiver. She wouldn't tell Maggie; no point in worrying her. She'll only want to be on the move again and what's the point? That Ringer will find us sooner or later, wherever we are.

They stopped outside the boutique. 'I wait for you in the bar,' he said, pointing across the street. 'I hope you find pretty dress,' he added, kissing her on the cheek.

Gill was very pleased with her sundress. It had blue, mauve and white vertical stripes and made her look slimmer. Not only did she look slimmer, she *was* slimmer! She hadn't weighed herself since she left home but she knew she'd lost weight.

Now the ever-obliging Alfonso insisted on taking the three of them to Florence to see the Duomo and the Uffizi, and Gill, in particular, wanted to see the famous statue of David because she couldn't believe that such a famous, virile male should have such a little willy. 'Well, of course, he hadn't seen *you*,' Maggie commented drily.

It was another day of soaring temperatures. The queue for the Uffizi snaked round the courtyard and beyond; 'four to five hours' wait' they were told, so they consoled themselves gazing at the replica statue of David, where Gill duly commented on his private parts, before they wandered into the Duomo.

It was as they emerged again into the blistering heat that they came across the dog. He appeared to have been waiting for them and fell into step with the four of them as they wandered along the bank of the Arno to the Ponte Vecchio. Small, scruffy and very determined, he was not at all on the agenda for their day in Florence.

'Who does he belong to, I wonder?' Maggie asked as she mopped her brow.

Alfonso shrugged. 'Who knows?'

'He's so sweet,' said Gill, stroking him. The dog licked her hand and looked up at her adoringly.

They had a late lunch on a street leading to the San Lorenzo market, the dog sitting at Gill's feet. They all fed him some titbits, much to Alfonso's disapproval. 'He *never* go away now.'

'He's very thin, poor little thing,' Gill said. 'But he must belong to *somebody*, surely?'

Alfonso shrugged. 'Many dogs like this. He randagio.'

'Randagio?' Gill repeated.

'How you say – dog of the streets?'

'Do you mean he's a stray?' asked Connie.

'Si, si, a stray.'

'"Randagio" sounds much nicer,' Gill commented, passing a small piece of bread to her new friend.

After the pasta and the wine they trudged towards the market, where all three fell upon the clothes, the bags and the belts. It was very crowded, very hot and very uncomfortable, but Gill spotted a cotton top which she had to have and, after haggling and then buying it, realised that she'd lost the others. There were so many stalls, and so many people, and she couldn't remember in which direction they'd all been heading. She looked around, feelings of panic beginning to rise in her chest, and then she looked down, and there was the dog. The *randagio*. He met her eye and wagged his tail.

'I'm lost, dog,' she informed him.

He cocked his leg, peed against a nearby lamp post and then, casting a look back at Gill, trotted on a few yards and waited. Gill was totally confused. Should she follow the dog or head the other way? The dog appeared to be waiting for her so she slowly followed him. After a few more yards he stopped again and waited for her.

The only sensible thing to do was get her phone out and call Connie or Maggie. Fumbling in her bag, she continued following the dog, and then she saw them: Alfonso, Connie and Maggie, looking agitated and scanning the crowds in every direction.

When he saw her, Alfonso opened out his arms and enveloped her in a hug. 'Cara! I worry! Where you go?'

'I've no idea,' Gill said, 'but this little dog has led me back to you.'

Maggie snorted. 'Nonsense! Just coincidence!'

'No,' said Gill, bending down to stroke the little animal. 'He definitely led me back to you. Didn't you, dog?'

Dog seemed to agree, wagged his tail and then had another pee against the wheel of a parked Fiat 500, before waiting expectantly for them to move on.

'I think he plans to stay with us,' Connie observed.

'Vai via!' Alfonso ordered the dog, pointing back the way they'd come.

The dog cast soulful eyes up at Gill.

'He's taken a fancy to me,' said Gill. 'Poor little dog!'

Alfonso sighed, put his arm round Gill's shoulders, and began to lead the way back to the station where they'd parked the car. The dog trotted happily along behind Gill.

'You not coming in my car!' Alfonso hollered at him.

'Oh, *Alfie*!' Gill was stroking the dog again. 'He needs a home!'

Alfonso sighed some more. 'I tell you, he a randagio! Many round here.'

'Yes, I know. But couldn't he come with us, *please*?'

'No,' said Connie. 'We are not travelling with a dog.'

'Definitely not,' added Maggie. She turned to Alfonso. 'Isn't there some sort of home for stray animals? Like we have Battersea?'

Alfonso shrugged. 'Best leave him here where he belong.'

Gill's eyes filled with tears.

'Oh, please, Alfie! *Please* can we take him with us?'

Her lover looked helplessly from one to the other. 'What I do?'

Connie put her arm round Gill's shoulders. 'He's a street dog, Gill. He'll survive; he'll adopt different people each day, get fed, move on. These dogs are really streetwise, you know.'

Connie and Maggie got into the back of the BMW while Alfonso stood holding the passenger door open and looking at Gill. Gill was looking at the dog. The dog jumped up and licked Gill's hand.

'I want to keep him,' she announced, picking him up.

'I don't believe this,' Maggie muttered.

'And he's probably daft enough to let her do it,' Connie said, staring at Alfonso.

'OK, OK, we bring him to my house,' he conceded. 'Then we find some place for the dog tomorrow.'

'Or *he'll* be in the doghouse,' Maggie said to Connie under her breath.

'It must be love,' Connie said.

As Gill strapped herself in, the dog jumped eagerly onto her lap.

'Here,' said Alfonso, brandishing an old towel from the boot, 'put this round. He full of fleas.'

'Aw!' Gill said, stroking the dog. 'You poor little thing. You look just like a little teddy bear! Don't you think so?'

'A mighty scruffy one,' said Maggie.

'He'll be fine when he's had a nice bath,' Gill went on. She patted the little dog's head, which caused much tail-wagging. 'I might just call him Teddy.'

'What's the Italian for teddy bear?' Connie asked Alfonso.

'Orsacchiotto,' Alfonso replied.

'Oh, I'd never get my tongue around that,' said Gill. 'Say it again, Alfie.'

'Orsacchiotto.'

'I could use the last bit, Otto, couldn't I?' Gill turned to look at her two friends.

'Toto would be nicer,' Connie said. 'And it's an anagram of Otto.'

'Oh, I like that! Toto!' Gill turned back to the dog. 'Buongiorno, Toto!'

Toto appeared pleased.

'No, no, no!' Connie exclaimed when they got back and were sitting by the pool. 'He can't possibly come with us.'

'Let Alfonso take him to the dogs' home,' Maggie said. 'He'll be looked after there.'

Gill was close to tears again. The dog had been washed, fed and watered, and was now happily asleep at her feet.

'And he won't be house-trained,' Connie added.

Alfonso appeared brandishing a bottle of Chianti. 'Tomorrow I take him to dog place at Pisa.'

'No!' Gill said vehemently. 'This poor little dog has taken a fancy to *me*!' She thought of her lonely life at home now that the cat had died, and she had visions of walking Toto on the nearby common.

She'd take him to the vet, make sure he had all his jabs, and she'd feed him up. Then she wondered how difficult it would be to bring him into the UK. Would they welcome an immigrant dog? Might he be allowed to stay? Or could she smuggle him in somehow? She'd dreaded the thought of going home, but this would make it better.

But there were groans all round.

'Alfie!' she said. '*Please!*'

Alfie looked confused. 'Please what?'

'Please could you keep him here? At your house? Then I know he'd be safe. Oh, *please*, Alfie!'

Alfie looked at Gill, who had tears in her eyes. Then he looked down at the dog.

'OK, for now,' he said at last. 'To make you happy, Geelee.'

As Gill threw her arms round his neck, Maggie murmured, 'Damn me, she's got them *both* on a lead!'

CHAPTER TWENTY-TWO

IL CONCERTO

After a not altogether successful visit to Florence, Maggie thought that at least there was still the concert to look forward to. Alfonso knew someone near La Sterza, close to the concert venue, where they could park Bella overnight. He and Gill would lead the way with the car, they'd all spend the day together in Volterra, and then return to Bella in time for them to dress up for the concert. He would even transport them to the venue before heading back to Viareggio with Gill and the dog. His friend, Alvaro, would collect them in his taxi at the end, and bring them back to Bella.

'How will he know when it'll finish?' Connie asked anxiously, with visions of being stranded in the Tuscan hills in the middle of the night.

Alfonso shrugged. 'No one knows. Everyone go there midnight, and wait. One o'clock, two o'clock, no problem.' Nothing appeared to be a problem for Alfonso, or else he knew someone who could take care of it.

An hour and a half later they arrived near the village of La Sterza, where Alvaro, as well as being a farmer and a taxi service, had a pitch for three caravans. Well, *normally* he had a pitch for three caravans but today, being so special, he could squeeze in *four*! '*Non c'e' problema!*' This necessitated some very tricky manoeuvring as Connie reversed into her allotted space.

Alvaro did not speak English, so Alfonso translated. 'He apologise. No much room. But people come from all over the world for Bocelli.'

'It'll only be for one night,' Connie murmured as she switched off the ignition.

'Just as well,' said Maggie, extending her hand out of the window to touch the hot corrugated surface of the German motorhome next door.

'At least we're well off the beaten track so Ringer isn't likely to find us here,' Connie added, as they locked up and prepared for a ride up to Volterra in Alfonso's car.

Maggie wasn't so sure. Her ex-lover appeared to have some sixth sense. But there had been no sightings of him since San Remo and possibly Portofino, if indeed it had been him accompanying Carol, the blonde. And it wasn't necessarily him either picking up Gill in Avignon. Perhaps they were imagining the whole thing! But the phone call in Nice had been real enough although, she supposed, he could have been calling from London just to frighten her. And he had done a good job. But she could have sworn that was him right behind them on the French autoroute, unless he had a doppelgänger! OK, so it wasn't his registration, but he'd have had that changed without any problem. No, she felt sure that he was around somewhere and that sooner or later he was going to catch up with them. I should be making escape plans, she thought.

*

The road leading to the beautiful medieval hilltop town of Volterra snaked its way upwards, round and round the hairpin bends and steep drops. Connie noticed that Maggie looked uncomfortable at times and, with memories of the gorge, she asked, 'You OK?'

'I'll be glad to get there,' Maggie replied, 'but just look at these views!'

Looking down across the sunbaked Tuscan landscape beneath, Connie reckoned it was one of the most spectacular and beautiful views she'd ever seen. The rolling hills and undulating countryside had been heated by the jewel-like sun to amber, gold and amethyst. A few farms were dotted here and there, and scatterings of cypresses, and there were miles and miles stretching to the horizon.

Finally, they ascended into the town and the golden stone of the ancient buildings, the turrets, the campanile. As they emerged from the underground car park into the piazza, even Gill was mesmerised. 'Wow!' she exclaimed, tugging Toto along on his new blue lead. Toto didn't know what to make of this; he'd never encountered a lead before and kept running in circles trying to catch the strap.

They had to wait for a table in the Piazza dei Priori, which was full of tourists of every nationality. 'All here for Bocelli,' Alfonso informed them. When they were finally seated Maggie became very excited because she could hear Scottish accents at the next table.

They put away several courses and three bottles of wine, for which Maggie insisted on paying.

'No, no!' Alfonso argued. 'Is not right. You no pay.'

'I insist,' said Maggie, removing a wad of notes from her shoulder bag. 'Never argue with a Scotswoman who offers to pay.'

Alfonso looked confused again.

'You've been so good to us, Alfonso,' she continued. 'You've given us parking, and the use of your lovely pool. Not to mention all these expeditions. *And* the concert tickets! So, don't argue!'

'Grazie mille,' Alfonso said. 'You very kind. No wonder man wants to follow you.'

There was a stunned silence.

'What man?' Maggie asked at last, glaring at Gill, who was looking distinctly uncomfortable.

'The man in Viareggio,' Alfonso replied, gulping his espresso down in one. He turned towards Gill. 'The one we see on the street, no?'

'Um, well, I'm not sure it was him…' Gill began.

Maggie narrowed her eyes. 'What's he talking about, Gill? What man on what street?'

'I didn't want to worry you,' Gill mumbled. 'Sorry, Maggie. I *told* him not to tell you!' She turned towards a troubled-looking Alfonso. 'I *told* you, Alfie, didn't I?'

'Sorry! Sorry!' He looked suitably contrite. 'I never say again.'

Maggie turned to Gill. 'Tell me.'

Gill told her. 'It just looked like him, Mags – the one I met in Avignon. *And* he had a scar on his leg! But I didn't want to risk it so we dashed into the cake shop.'

'Why did you have to say he was anything to do with me?' Maggie persisted.

'Well, because Alfie was getting all funny about him being my lover or something. I'm sorry, Maggie!'

'OK. OK!' Sensing Gill was close to tears, Maggie patted her shoulder. 'I just wish you'd told me.'

Alfonso put his arm round Gill. 'No worry, now we go to alabaster museum.'

The shops were full of beautiful, delicate alabaster figurines, bowls, carvings and lamps. They had a brief wander round the museum, Gill unusually silent, Maggie deep in thought. Only Connie and Alfonso carried on a conversation of sorts.

This Ringer business is getting to us all, Connie thought, constantly spoiling our blissful getaway. Perhaps now was the time to face up to him, give him his bloody money and give them some much-needed peace. Maggie, of course, would not agree. But how could it possibly end? They couldn't be on the move forever and Maggie would have to go home eventually to face the music there, if not here. And now Ringer had managed to blight their visit to one of Tuscany's most stunning hilltop towns.

Connie vowed she'd come back one day on her own. There was so much to see here. In the meantime, they needed to stock up with prosecco, having been informed by Alfonso that it was a necessity to have some refreshment for the interval in tonight's concert.

When Alfonso had dropped them off back at Bella, and Toto had had a pee, he, Gill and the dog set off for San Gimignano.

'We'll be back to take you to the concert!' Gill shouted as she placed Toto on her knee again, and they roared off.

Connie could see that Maggie's day had been ruined by the supposed sighting of Ringer.

'I just wish Gill had told me,' Maggie sighed for the umpteenth time.

'She wouldn't want to worry you.'

'Well, she *has* worried me! Gill saw his scar, so it *must* be him! And now Alfie's got wind of something going on. I knew she couldn't keep her trap shut!'

'We'll be moving on again soon,' Connie said.

'And so will Ringer,' said Maggie, as she lifted her dark brown dress out of the wardrobe.

But Connie was determined that thoughts of Ringer were not going to ruin tonight's concert.

The concert venue on the Bocelli family land was set among the rolling hills where, in isolation, the Teatro del Silenzio was situated. Only once a year did the theatre come to life, drawing an audience from all corners of the globe. There were thousands of seats in numbered rows, a huge platform, an enormous orchestra and, not least, the wonderful voice of Bocelli. They were fortunate enough to be seated only a few rows from the front, which must have cost Alfonso a fortune, Connie thought, *if* he paid for them.

Connie wore her Parisian dress, and Maggie wore the dark brown number from Nice, along with the necklace and the sandals.

The concert was an hour late in starting which, they were assured by a seasoned concertgoer, was quite normal. This gave Connie and Maggie ample time to study their surroundings and the audience in particular. Connie had never seen so much glamour condensed into one comparatively compact area.

'Get an eyeful of *her*!' Maggie said, nudging Connie as they watched a tall woman with impossibly red hair, clad in a floating orange number, gliding along on what must have been six-inch silver heels.

'And just look at *this* lot!' Connie put in, as a group of very polished and immaculate women, dressed in what had to be designer outfits, all embraced one very suave man in a white suit.

Connie sighed. 'I felt really good when I arrived here, but feel positively dull now in comparison!'

'You don't look at all dull,' Maggie said, adjusting her necklace. 'But, God, don't these women know how to dress up!'

'Not to mention the men,' Connie added. 'And we are in the best seats after all. Good old Alfie!'

Amongst the Italian glamour were dotted more ordinary mortals from every corner of the world. Maggie found herself next to an elderly Australian couple on their second visit to the concert.

'We come over to Europe every couple of years,' the woman said. 'And this is the highlight of our visit!' They came from Melbourne. 'We save up for the best seats.'

'My son and his family are in Melbourne,' Maggie told them. 'He's been out there for years and years. He's even got an Aussie accent now.'

'You go out often to see him?'

'No,' Maggie admitted. 'I'm terrified of flying.'

'Aw, that's a shame.'

'It is. He only comes back to the UK every few years, and I really miss him.'

Now daylight was fading, the stage was illuminated, and overhead the moon and stars appeared in the darkening sky. And then the orchestra's introduction rose to a crescendo to herald the arrival on stage of the renowned tenor.

Connie could scarcely believe how close she was to her idol. And, looking back at the thousands of seats behind, she realised how very lucky she was. Time and time again she felt the hair rise on the back of her neck as he sang arias from the Italian operas, along with other popular numbers. Spellbound by the entire performance, it wasn't until Andrea Bocelli had rounded off the evening with 'Nessun Dorma' that Connie and Maggie came back to earth. It was a magical night. A night to remember. All thanks to Alfonso – and thanks to Gill for meeting Alfonso! And thanks to Maggie for their beautiful dresses and just for being there! In spite of Ringer, it had been the best decision ever to bring these two along!

Connie woke at nine o'clock, having got back from the concert at 2 a.m. She was still on cloud nine and longing to play one of the CDs. But there was no movement from Maggie, just silence everywhere as last night's audience caught up on their sleep. She made a cup of tea. The teabags were running low and she hoped that somewhere they'd find a grocer who sold boxes of Twinings or something. They'd soon be in Rome, where there was bound to be a great selection of everything. That was if they could ever persuade Gill to leave Tuscany. What with Alfonso and the wretched dog, Gill had taken root in Alfonso's house. She wondered, not for the first time, if Gill fell for every man she met. And what about the famous Fabio in Rome?

Nevertheless, Alfonso did seem besotted by her. Maggie dismissed the romance as Gill being 'just desperate to get her knickers off one last time before she has to start wearing incontinence pads'. Connie wasn't so sure.

Maggie, a lapsed Catholic, was keen to go to the Vatican. Gill wanted to see the Colosseum by moonlight, hand in hand with a Latin lover, although she hadn't specified which one. And Connie just wondered if they'd ever be able to find a parking spot somewhere reasonably close to the city. And would Ringer find them there? If not there, then he probably would in Amalfi, their final destination. No doubt Pam had told him that.

It would be the end of the road, with nowhere left to run. They could be in big trouble. Ringer might be the villain, the robber, the baddie, but nevertheless they were all the receivers of stolen goods. They could end up in jail. Connie looked at her beautiful sea-green dress hanging up on the outside of the wardrobe and shuddered. She'd never enjoyed wearing anything quite so much as that dress.

They'd lived well, eaten well, drunk well and bought anything they fancied, so surely they were all criminals? They'd probably be arrested when they set foot back in the UK, if Ringer didn't finish them off first.

And they'd soon be in Amalfi or somewhere in the area. She had forwarded some money along with all her particulars and made an appointment with Mr Pozzi, so she hoped that he might have some good news for her.

Connie was on her second mug of tea when Maggie surfaced.

'God, it's hot!' she said, as she filled up the kettle. 'It'll be like an oven in Rome. When are we leaving by the way?'

'When Gill gets back,' Connie replied. 'Alfie said they'd be here around lunchtime.'

'What's the betting Gill doesn't want to leave?'

'Your guess is as good as mine. It wouldn't be the same without her though, would it?'

'No. She drives me nuts half the time, but I'd really miss her,' Maggie admitted.

'He said he'd come to see me in Naples or somewhere,' Gill said later, drying her eyes as Alfonso, following a tearful farewell, drove away with the dog barking out of the window. 'And I'm going to stay with him on the way back.' She looked at the others, expecting some reaction. 'And he's going to keep Toto for me,' she added.

'Perhaps you won't want to see him after you meet up with Fabio in Rome again,' Connie said.

Gill sniffed. 'I'm not that bothered about Fabio any more.'

'Ah, but you won't really know for sure until you see Fabio again, will you?'

'It's just that I love Alfie so,' said Gill, dabbing her eyes again. 'And Toto.'

Maggie groaned and rolled her eyes.

'He thinks I'm lovely.' Gill blew her nose. 'It's centuries ago since anyone thought I was lovely.'

'Due in no small part to me hacking off that awful busby you used to call a hairstyle,' said Maggie. 'You owe me; I should be chief bridesmaid or something.'

'You *have* to get a dig in, don't you?' Gill looked as if she was about to start weeping again. 'Can't you just be pleased for me?'

'Dear God!' Maggie placed a comforting arm round Gill's shoulders. 'I'm only teasing! Honestly! But it's true, you look one hundred per cent better with your new short hair and your tan. No wonder he fancies you!'

There was silence for a minute before Gill, blowing her nose lustily, said, 'That's the nicest thing you've ever said to me!'

'Well, you're not such a bad old bird!' Maggie conceded.

CHAPTER TWENTY-THREE

THE ETERNAL CITY

The signs flashed past. Follonica, Grosseto, Civitavecchia. Even on the coastal road, the drive south towards Rome was manic after the relatively quiet roads of rural Tuscany. For the first time in days Connie felt nervous. She'd got this far without mishap, but could their luck hold out much longer? Although she'd got used to driving in Europe again, she still hated heavy traffic, with drivers all hooting each other, changing lanes every few seconds – most driving with one hand and clamping a phone to their ear with the other. Furthermore, they were unlikely to find a leafy layby in which to park anywhere near the Eternal City, and they hadn't pre-booked a site. Now it was late afternoon and still very hot.

Then Gill, who was in the back, leaned forward and piped up. 'Alfie thinks we should head towards Ostia, because it's on the coast and we're more likely to find somewhere to park up there. And there are trains into Rome.'

'I reckon we're going to need at least three clear days in Rome,' Connie said. 'So we need at least four nights somewhere.'

'Alfie said we should have booked,' Gill added helpfully.

'Now you tell us!' Maggie snapped. She was sitting in the passenger seat and had been studying the list of campsites on her phone, having little idea of where they were or how to get there. 'Looks like it might have to be a roadside stop for tonight as no one seems to have any vacancies.' She continued tapping.

Half an hour later Connie saw the sign for Ostia.

'I'm following Alfie's advice,' she said to Maggie as she turned off.

Maggie wondered if Ringer could possibly find them in Ostia. If he was on their tail then he'd be likely to head for Rome, as he knew they were heading south. Rome was a huge city so it was unlikely he'd ever find them there. She'd said nothing to the other two but she'd wondered from time to time if he might have fixed some sort of sensor onto Bella, so that he could trace their whereabouts. She'd even surreptitiously checked the outside of the vehicle, realising at the same time what a crazy idea this was since, if he ever got close enough to fix a sensor, then of course he would have found them! I must be going nuts, she thought. Was the rest of her life to be spent on the run?

It was dark when they finally found a site close to Ostia. The place was fully booked but someone hadn't shown up and the manager insisted they wait until midnight to make absolutely sure that they didn't. Fortunately the people concerned eventually phoned to say their plans had changed and they weren't able to come, and so Bella, at half past eleven, finally found a home. Connie, exhausted, backed into their allotted space and managed to hit the wall behind, which she couldn't see in the dark. She prayed she hadn't done too much damage to Bella, but was too tired to go looking.

All three were exhausted. Connie and Maggie hadn't got back from the concert until the early hours and sleep had plainly not been one of Gill's priorities. After a long, hot and dusty drive, followed by a lengthy wait for their pitch, they all collapsed. It was the first time in days that all three were sleeping overnight in Bella.

Connie woke at nine. It was already hot, she had a headache and, more than anything, she'd have liked a quiet day, somewhere in the countryside, doing nothing. But it was not to be. Rome beckoned, the other two hadn't been before, and there was a lot to see. She ventured outside to see if she'd damaged Bella and found, to her relief, only a small dent.

When Maggie emerged she said, 'Gill's snoring at full throttle again.'

'Wonder how Alfie coped with that?' Connie mused.

'Don't suppose they did much sleeping,' Maggie muttered. 'Or perhaps he was even louder. Now, where's Rome?'

It was nearly midday before they emerged from the Termini station in Rome and, having had little breakfast, their first priority was to find somewhere to eat. There was going to be a lot of walking involved and Connie said she hoped Gill's sandals were up to it.

Gill had spent most of the morning on the phone to Alfonso. 'I wish he was here!' she moaned.

'What about the famous Fabio?' Connie asked.

'Who knows, you might fancy him even more,' Maggie added. 'So why don't you phone him? He might even have a nice big car like Alfonso had, and we could do with some further chauffeuring around.'

'I'm feeling very nervous about this,' Gill admitted. 'It's been such a long time, and maybe his number's been changed.'

'Well, there's one way to find out,' said Maggie as she perused the menu. 'What the hell is a "gamberetto"?'

'It's a shrimp,' said Connie. 'I think I'll have the veal. That's "vitello".'

'It's ringing, I think,' Gill said with the phone to her ear. 'It's a different sort of ringing tone to what we have at home. Oh, *hello*, yes, buongiorno! Um, can I speak to Fabio? *Fabio Moroni?*' she repeated loudly. 'Is he there? I'd like to speak to him.'

'Many peoples would,' said the woman at the other end. 'He is important man. He has been retired for several years and right now is on his yacht in the marina close to Ostia.'

On his *yacht*! Near *Ostia*! Oh my God!

'Ostia!' Gill could scarcely believe what she was hearing. 'But that's where *I'm* staying! I'm an old friend from London, you see. So, could you tell me the name of his yacht and I'll pop along to see him?'

'No, I cannot do that.'

'Oh, *please*!'

The woman sighed. 'I will telephone to ask if he wishes to see you. Are you a business colleague from our London branch?'

'Yes, yes!' Gill said impatiently. 'From London.'

'What is your name? Please hold.'

Gill gave her name and waited anxiously. Would he remember her? Probably not, but it was worth a try anyway.

'What's happening?' Maggie asked.

'Shhh, I'll tell you later.' Just wait, Gill thought, until I tell these two he's only got a *yacht*. And, much as she fancied Alfie, here was a very important man with a yacht, a very rare species indeed and non-existent in Gill's social circle. Anyway, Alfie was away up in Viareggio, so it would do no harm whatsoever to renew an old acquaintance. With a *yacht*!

'Signora?' The woman's voice cut into Gill's reverie. 'Signor Moroni will see you tomorrow briefly before they sail. One of his crew will meet you at the entrance to the marina at 11 a.m. You understand?'

'Oh, yes,' said Gill. And, hey, she thought, Fabio wanted to see her before he sailed, so he must remember her even after all these years! Of course he remembered her! They'd had such great sex day after day!

'You look like the cat that's stolen the cream,' Connie said.

'Let me tell you what's happening tomorrow!' Gill said, and then proceeded to give them both a detailed account of her conversation, and how she was going to see Fabio, in his *yacht*, the very next day.

After they oohed and aahed at her good fortune, they walked to the Colosseum, where Gill had once dreamed of walking in the moonlight with Fabio. Instead, she had her photo taken, at vast expense, with a 'gladiator' who pinched her bottom and made her day complete. They were too late for the English guided tour, but paid to go inside anyway; they were overwhelmed by the sheer size and structure of the ancient arena with its underground cells and tiers for spectators. In their imaginations they were transported back to the world of ancient Rome with its gory gladiatorial triumphs and the so-called 'entertainment' of mass slaughter.

'I can just see that lovely gladiator facing a lion down there,' said Gill, still pink-faced from her flirty encounter.

'That so-called gladiator out there couldn't scare a pussy-cat,' Maggie said. 'He's probably a student on a holiday job and doesn't get paid unless some idiot comes along to have a photo taken with him.'

'And another idiot pays for it,' Gill retorted.

Connie bought a guide book and they gave themselves a brief tour of the Forum, where they all had photographs taken amongst the pillars, before heading towards the Vittorio Emanuele monument, known locally as 'the wedding cake'.

'It's just like walking around in a film set,' Maggie remarked. 'All these ancient ruins! All that history! I can't quite believe it's real!'

Almost everywhere they went they came across an ancient excavated cave, a pillar or an archway, presided over by the magnificent, lofty Mediterranean pines.

'It's the most fantastic place I've ever been to,' Gill agreed. 'If only it wasn't so damned *hot*!'

'It is high summer,' Connie reminded her. 'And if you were in London right now you'd most likely be sheltering from the rain. Take your choice!'

'Even the ordinary streets look like theatre scenery,' Maggie observed as she photographed a square of ancient buildings in terracotta and gold, with their shuttered windows and tiny wrought-iron balconies filled with potted geraniums and the inevitable washing lines.

Connie found her Twinings teabags, Maggie found a postcard to send to her friend Pam, and Gill sampled three different flavours of ice cream.

'Tomorrow,' said Connie, 'we'll do the Spanish Steps and the Trevi Fountain.'

'And I'd like to go to St Peter's one day,' Maggie said. 'I may not be a good Catholic these days but I couldn't come to Rome and not see St Peter's and the Vatican.'

'Tomorrow,' said Gill, '*I* shall be on board a luxury yacht.'

On their return in the early evening they found their campsite heaving with families and the aroma of cooking smells permeating the air. Gill was inside washing her hair and Connie was preparing to shower, while Maggie collapsed on one of their folding chairs, which they'd erected outside, with an Aperol and soda, which was fast becoming her favourite drink. She put her feet up on one of the other chairs and lay back listening to a mother shouting at her child in the next-door caravan. The child answered back and then a male voice, presumably the father, joined in the general discord, before another child started crying. In spite of the cacophony she decided it would be an opportune moment to call Pam to see if there was any further news of Ringer in the media. She fished her phone out of her bag and switched it on. Almost immediately the phone started ringing and she saw a number she didn't recognise.

At first she didn't recognise his voice either. Then, with horror, she realised who it was.

'Don't hang up!' Ringer begged. 'Please, Maggie! I *need* you to listen to me!'

'I'm listening,' she said icily.

'I'm in hospital,' he said.

'Oh yeah? And where might that be? And what's wrong with you?'

'I've had a big heart attack, Maggie. I collapsed in the street a couple of days ago, here in Rome.' He sounded breathless and very subdued but Maggie remained suspicious.

'And what exactly were you doing in Rome, Ringer?'

'I was hoping to see you, Mags. I guessed you might be here. It's not *just* the money, you know.'

'Oh, really?'

'Yes, really.' He coughed. 'I was in intensive care for twenty-four hours. They've put it down to stress because I've been very *very* stressed. I know, I know, I've been unfaithful, and I'm really sorry. That's all over now, but she wasn't a patch on you anyway.' He was breathing heavily. 'They say I could have another heart attack any minute, which most likely would carry me off. I miss you, Maggie, and I just want to see you again. One more time. Please come to see me!'

'Where are you, Ringer?'

'Oh, Santa Maria Something-or-other. Nuns everywhere. Hang on and I'll get the proper name and the address. He shuffled some papers. 'You got a pen?' He read out the address. 'And I'm in Ward Eight, "numero otto", that is.'

Maggie was silent as she wrote it down.

'I don't care about the money,' he said. 'What good's money to a dead man, Mags? Mind you, I don't know exactly how much all this is going to cost me, so I may need a euro or two. But Maggie, I *need* to see you! It might be the last time – *please*!' Maggie said nothing. 'Oh, hell, I have to go – there's a tiny wee nun heading my way with a bloody great syringe!'

'I'll call you tomorrow,' Maggie said, and clicked off as she saw Connie emerging from Bella's doorway clutching a bottle of prosecco.

'Who were you chatting to?' Connie asked, sitting down opposite and pouring herself an Aperol topped up with prosecco.

'Oh, just Pam,' Maggie replied. 'Weather's lousy at home.'

Maggie cried off the supper they'd planned to have at the local pizzeria. 'I'm still full from lunch,' she lied, 'and I've got a bit of a headache. It must be the heat. I think I'll have an early night if you two don't mind.'

Connie produced some paracetamol and Gill appeared with a glass of water. 'Take a couple of these,' Connie said, 'and do have that early night. Are you *sure* you don't mind us going out and leaving you?'

'Quite sure,' Maggie replied, longing for some time on her own.

When they'd disappeared from view she poured herself another drink. He *had* sounded poorly. She was inclined to believe him; she knew him so well, every intonation of his voice, and he'd always been a bad liar. And she didn't like the sound of that weird cough. I wish I had a cigarette, she thought. I could do with one now even though I stopped smoking forty years ago!

There was no point in worrying Connie or Gill about any of this. They'd tell her not to go, that it was probably a trap and, if he really was as ill as he made out, then at least he wouldn't be forever following them. But Maggie wasn't so sure. What if he really *was* on his last legs? Could she live with herself if she ignored his plea and then found out that he'd died? After all, she'd been with this man for nearly forty years, they'd had some great times together and they'd loved one another once. She wasn't sure that she still did love him, because in fact she was loving her new-found freedom even more. But that didn't alter the fact that he might be dying in a foreign hospital and she was only a short distance away. She'd never be able to live with herself.

She'd sleep on it.

She didn't, of course. She tossed and turned, tormented by her conversation with Ringer, and further disturbed by Gill snoring loudly underneath. Normally a tidy little sleeper herself, the top bunk had suited Maggie fine. Now, apart from her turbulent thoughts, she felt restricted by the noise and the heat.

Maggie crept noiselessly down the ladder and tiptoed towards the door. It was 4 a.m. and all around was silence except for the distant sound of a dog barking. She'd sit outside in the cool and try to gather her chaotic thoughts together. The glass of water was still half full on the table, so she drank that.

He'd given her the address of the hospital. If she left early she could claim sleeplessness, say she'd decided to take a taxi to St Peter's, and that she'd meet up with them somewhere. The Trevi Fountain, perhaps. She'd keep in touch by phone. Later she'd phone Ringer to let him know she was on her way, that it would be a brief visit, that she was meeting friends. She might even be able to squeeze in St Peter's as well, and pray for his heinous soul. She hoped that Connie wouldn't ask too many questions.

'I couldn't sleep,' she informed them a couple of hours later, 'so I thought I might take a taxi to St Peter's this morning and meet up with you later.'

'Has she suddenly got religion or something?' Gill murmured to Connie.

'We can postpone the sightseeing until later,' Connie said, 'now that you've both got other plans for today.'

'I'll meet you by the Trevi later, after my visit to St Peter's,' Maggie said. She had a wad of money in her bra, as usual, but hadn't taken much in her bag, just in case. She'd tell Ringer that she'd banked it all and that there had been no point whatsoever in him tailing them, although he probably wouldn't believe her.

Half an hour later she phoned him from the taxi. 'I should be with you in about ten minutes.'

'Thanks, Maggie. It means so much to me.' If anything he sounded even more feeble than yesterday.

The taxi driver said, 'It beeootiful 'ospital, your friend lucky because I think I hear nearly everyone move out now.'

'Hmm,' said Maggie. 'Have they indeed?'

It was a long way but nevertheless the fare still seemed exorbitant and, as she paid him, she wondered if he'd extended the journey. She'd used up most of the notes in her bag, so just as well she had a bra-full. She suddenly remembered she'd left her passport in the pocket of the jacket she'd been wearing last night, so hoped she wouldn't need it, if she had to produce identification.

The hospital was situated behind large wooden gates and surrounded by well-tended lawns and flowerbeds. There was even a little fountain at the front. The building was large, square, and painted pale yellow with green shutters. It looked restful. So quiet, in fact, that she wondered if it *was* still open. The whole area seemed deserted. What had the taxi driver meant?

As she approached the gates Maggie was aware, from the corner of her eye, of someone racing towards her, holding something. It took a split second for it to register; she froze only momentarily, then turned and ran. She ran and she ran, having no idea where she was going, but only aware that he was catching up with her. There were few people around, but the ones who were stopped to look on in amazement at the two racing figures.

Maggie ran like her life depended on it, which it probably did, down a residential street with large imposing houses set behind walled gardens. She thought she could outrun him but he was moving surprisingly fast and rapidly gaining ground. She wished she had some sort of weapon.

He had almost caught up with her when, gasping for breath, she stopped, turned and swung her shoulder bag at him, hoping to catch him on the side of the head. With a deft movement, he grabbed the bag, but lost his balance and fell flat on the pavement. He'd dropped something that clattered on the pavement, but she didn't wait to find out what it was.

Then she saw the bus. It was only a few yards ahead and had stopped to disgorge two elderly ladies. The doors were still open, and she leapt on board just as they began to close. She saw the driver hesitate, looking back at Ringer in his mirror.

'Go, go!' Maggie yelled. 'Per favore!' She was terrified he'd open the doors again.

The driver shrugged and moved on. Maggie, breathless and with her heart racing, collapsed onto the first empty seat, aware of the stares of amazement from the other passengers. She hadn't got a ticket and she looked guiltily at the ticket-stamping machine. She should probably disembark at the next stop.

Ringer had got her bag but her mobile was in her trouser pocket. And thank God she'd left her passport behind! But he'd got her bankcards, her diary, her reading glasses and a very expensive lipstick that Connie had persuaded her to buy in Volterra. And thank goodness she'd spent most of the cash!

The bus stopped. People got off and people got on, all obediently stamping their tickets in the machine. They seemed to be getting closer to the city centre so Maggie decided to stay on for a bit, praying that no official would come round to check the fares. Two stops later she decided it was time to get off. Her luck couldn't hold out much longer, and Ringer wouldn't find her here. She found herself in a busy street full of shops, cafes and bars, and she badly needed to sit down with a coffee and something stronger. She stopped at the first bar she came to, resisted the temptation to sit outside, and instead settled for a dark corner in the interior. She ordered a coffee and a large brandy and, ensuring that no one was looking, lifted up her T-shirt and pulled some notes out of her bra, which she transferred to her pocket. It felt strange not having a bag.

Maggie couldn't believe she'd been so stupid as to fall headlong into his trap. He'd taken advantage of her better nature, knowing she was a bit of a softie underneath. She remembered how he'd always laughed when she dabbed her eyes during sad films. 'You're not as tough as you make yourself out to be!' he'd taunted her. 'You're just a wee softie!'

And today she'd been a bloody great softie and an even greater idiot. And he was a bloody good actor.

CHAPTER TWENTY-FOUR

THE ETERNAL TRIANGLE

Connie could hear the sound of gushing water well before she arrived at the Piazza di Trevi where, as usual, there were crowds surrounding the fountain. She was entranced again by the magnificent rococo extravaganza of rearing sea horses and conch-blowing tritons cavorting below the wall of the Palazzo Poli. Then she spotted Maggie.

'Hi! How was St Peter's?' Connie asked. 'And where's your bag? Maggie, are you all right?' Connie could see that something was wrong. At this, Maggie dissolved into tears. This was unheard of – Maggie never cried. Connie delved into her bag and handed her a tissue. 'Maggie…?'

Maggie gulped. 'I got mugged.'

'What, in *St Peter's*?'

'No, no, on the way there.' Maggie had practised her speech. 'The taxi had to drop me a little way off. There was no one around, and this guy just appeared out of nowhere and ripped the bag off my shoulder.' Well, that much is partly true, she thought.

'Oh, Maggie! Have you been to the police?'

'No, I haven't. What's the point? I didn't see him properly so couldn't describe him. And they'd never find him anyway.' Maggie didn't enjoy having to lie to Connie, but there was absolutely no way she could spoil Connie's trip now. Perhaps she'd tell her when they reached their final destination. Perhaps.

'But—'

'But nothing, Connie. There wasn't anything in my bag except a few bits and pieces, and my bankcards. Fortunately my phone was in my pocket and I had the bank details on there, so I rang up and cancelled all the cards while I was recovering with a brandy. It doesn't matter, I've plenty of cash. I couldn't actually face St Peter's after that, so I'll probably go tomorrow.'

'Oh, that's awful!' Connie hugged her. 'Are you sure you're OK for a bit of sightseeing?'

'After I've bought myself another bag!' Maggie replied with a ghost of a smile.

Rome was hot, vibrant, crowded. After Maggie bought her bag she followed Connie towards the Piazza di Spagna and gazed in disbelief at the crowds thronging the Spanish Steps. She said she remembered Gregory Peck and Audrey Hepburn sitting there in splendid romantic isolation on their 'Roman Holiday'; they wouldn't stand a chance of finding a few spare inches today.

Then, a stroll down the Via Condotti to gaze at the displays of (almost) unaffordable clothing in the designer shops, before heading back towards the Via Nazionale.

'Tomorrow, the Pantheon,' Connie promised. 'And the Piazza Navona with its lovely fountains. And we really need another day to go to the Vatican.' She cast a glance at Maggie. 'Are you sure you're OK?'

*

Maggie knew she was in a world of her own. She was looking at all these famous landmarks but they weren't registering. Her trip lay in ruins amongst the ruins of this amazing city. Not only that, she hated lying to the other two, but she didn't want to worry them. Why spoil their visit too? They'd want to move on, go to the police.

She should have left Ringer some of that money; it might have calmed him down sufficiently to keep him at home. He obviously had plans for it or he wouldn't be following them so manically. Perhaps she should phone him, split the remaining cash with him and get him off their backs. Then she remembered she'd heard the crash of whatever it was he had in his hand when he hit the pavement. Could it have been a gun? She knew for sure now that she could never trust him again and, for the very first time, she was beginning to wish that this trip was over. And now she was fearing for the safety of her two friends. Because, against the odds, they *were* friends. She'd really come to love them both and she'd miss them like hell when this was all over.

Perhaps she should leave them here in Rome and let them head south on their own? But he'd still tail the motorhome if he thought she, or any of the cash, was in it. And Connie was so keen to have them both with her on this final lap of their journey.

She'd think of something.

Gill looked round nervously. She'd arrived at the marina five minutes early and she'd no idea who might be coming to meet her. She hoped she looked good, and sufficiently jetsetter-ish, having chosen her pink cotton trousers and the nice white filmy top she'd bought in Nice. And she wore her one and only pair of flat sandals, because she remembered the fuss that poncy Pietro, or whatever his name was, on the yacht in Cannes, had made about high heels and decks. And then she saw someone who looked just like the poncy fellow in Cannes, still wearing tight white jeans with a billowing blue shirt knotted just above the waist to display a taut brown belly. And he was heading towards *her*!

He stopped and stared.

Gill stared back.

After a moment he said, 'You are here for Signor Moroni?'

'Yes,' Gill said, 'I am.'

He continued to stare at her. 'We have met before?'

'Yes,' Gill replied drily, 'in Cannes. There was a chef problem.'

He clapped his hand to his forehead. 'Mamma mia!'

'Yes, quite. Are you working here now?'

He didn't bother to answer her, just saying, 'Come this way.'

She followed him for some distance along the jetty and then she saw it, *Il Delfino*! The yacht from Cannes! What an unbelievable coincidence! She wondered if that old biddy was still the chef, but it had been on hire in Cannes so they probably had an Italian crew now.

Pietro had stopped.

'This is quite a coincidence,' Gill said, 'this boat, and you being here too.'

'This,' Pietro said, 'is the boat of Signor Moroni.'

Gill was dumbstruck. This was *more* than a coincidence! Fabio was the owner of the boat she'd boarded, supposedly as a chef, in

Cannes! This *must* be fate! And now, here she was, the guest of Fabio Moroni and not a bloody cook! And time this lackey showed her more respect.

'Well, thank you, Pietro,' she said graciously. 'Now be so kind as to take me to Signor Moroni.' She wanted to add 'and then you may go', but perhaps that was overdoing it. Poncy bloke, poncy shirt.

Without meeting her eye he led her across the gangplank onto the boat and into the salon, where she remembered quaffing champagne with Lord-what's-his-name while they headed back to the marina. It had been full of people then, but it was empty now.

'You wait,' he ordered and then promptly disappeared.

Gill looked around at the sumptuous sofas, the polished mahogany, the cocktail bar. This surely was the life she was destined for!

She heard someone approaching. What would he look like now? she wondered. He must be in his late seventies. Gill ran a hand over her hair, pulled in her tummy and took a deep breath as the door opened to admit a very attractive elderly lady, slim, tanned, elegant, bracelets jangling on her wrist.

She smiled at Gill. 'You have come to see my husband?'

Gill felt everything drop and droop: her hopes, her spirits and probably her face. She rearranged her mouth into a smile. 'I met Fabio in London many years ago and he said to get in touch if I was ever in Rome.' She cleared her throat, feeling more idiotic by the minute. 'And here I am!'

'And remind me of your name?'

'Gill.'

'Piacere, Gill. I am Silvana. I assume you were working for our company in London?'

Gill nodded mutely. How else could she explain it? There was no escape now.

'You will see a difference in my husband. You know, of course, Fabio has been retired for some years. It will be interesting to see if he remembers you.'

It certainly will, Gill thought, wondering if she could make some excuse, any excuse, to get out of here. But there was no way out, and she could only hope that Fabio would play along with this charade. All at once she felt shabby and sweaty next to this graceful, charming woman.

'He will be with us shortly,' Silvana continued, bracelets jangling. 'Would you like a drink?'

It was far too early in the day, but God, she needed a damned drink. 'Oh yes, please! Could I have a gin and tonic?'

'Of course.' Silvana headed towards the door and called out, 'Pietro!'

Immediately Pietro appeared. 'Signora?'

'Could you do this lady a gin and tonic, please? And just a glass of wine for me – the Pinot, I think.'

'Certo, Signora!' He slid, snakelike, behind the bar and began to make a big production of shovelling ice into a silver bucket, slicing lemons and perusing the array of gin bottles.

'I think, perhaps, the Bombay Sapphire, Pietro,' Silvana said. 'Our guest is English and the English like Bombay Sapphire – no?' She looked enquiringly at Gill.

'Oh, lovely, yes,' Gill muttered.

With a flourish Pietro placed the glasses on a tray and presented them to Silvana.

'Our guest first, please,' she ordered, indicating Gill with more jangling of bracelets.

Without meeting her eye, Pietro thrust the tray in front of Gill.

'Thank you, Pietro,' Gill said as grandly as she could. Conversation was becoming more and more difficult as, apart from anything else, her lips had now stuck to her teeth with nerves. She needed a sip badly.

They waited until Pietro retreated and then Silvana raised her glass. 'To old acquaintances!' she said.

'Oh yes,' mumbled Gill, taking a welcome gulp.

Still no sign of Fabio. Perhaps he was doing business in his office. They were bound to have an office on board this thing and, after all, these old executives – or whatever he was – never *really* retired. He was plainly still in constant touch with the company because they'd known exactly where to find him. Then Gill heard more footsteps approaching.

After what seemed like an age, the door opened and a small, withered old man shuffled in, leaning heavily on the arm of a white-clad woman who was obviously a nurse. Gill stifled a gasp.

'Come, Fabio,' Silvana said, 'and meet our guest.'

Fabio stood shakily in the middle of the salon, still leaning on the nurse's arm and staring down at the floor. *This* was Fabio! Dear God! Gill could see little she recognised. A minute passed in total silence and then he lifted his head and stared at Gill blankly. No sign of recognition whatsoever.

'I'm Gill; remember me? We met years ago in London.'

He ignored her outstretched hand and continued to stare blankly at her, then lost interest and let his gaze drop to the floor again.

Silvana sighed. 'I wanted him to see you as I so hoped you might, how you say, jog his memory. Sometimes a face from the past will get through to him and he will come alive again for a few minutes.'

Gill had no idea what to say. That the gorgeous Fabio should end up in this unbelievably cruel state! And it was fortunate that Silvana thought she was a business colleague because she could hardly say, 'Remember me, Fabio? We shagged non-stop for five days and you told me I was the sexiest woman you'd ever met!'

Silvana placed a hand on Gill's arm. 'I'm sorry he doesn't recognise you. Most of the time he doesn't recognise me either and we've been married for fifty years. We are about to have a little cruise to celebrate our golden wedding anniversary, but he has little idea of what's going on.'

'I'm so sorry.' Gill gulped her gin as the nurse helped Fabio to collapse onto one of the sofas. 'I'm sorry too that I bothered you, but I had no idea.' No idea that he'd been married for fifty years either. And no idea that he'd been married when he bedded her in London. She had to get out of here, and fast.

'You've taken the trouble to come here, so you must stay to have some lunch with us before we sail,' Silvana said.

'No, no, that's very kind of you, but I really must go,' Gill said hastily. 'I'm meeting friends for lunch.'

'Oh, that's a pity. You'd be most welcome.'

'Thank you, and it's been lovely to meet you, Silvana. And I'm so sorry about Fabio.' Gill drained her glass rapidly. She laid the glass down on the table and gazed at her ex-lover for a brief moment, then said, 'Arrivederci, Fabio.'

He didn't move. Silvana escorted her out onto the deck. 'Would you like Pietro to take you back to the gates?'

'No, thank you,' Gill said, wobbling slightly as she stepped onto the jetty. 'I'm fine, thanks.'

The two women shook hands and Gill, trying not to cry, headed back the way she'd come. It wasn't until she was outside the gates that she let the tears flow.

Gill returned to a deserted Bella. Connie and Maggie were sight-seeing in Rome and, for once, she was glad to have the place to herself to collect her chaotic thoughts. What had she expected, for goodness' sake! Had she honestly thought that Fabio would be single, in perfect health, and welcome her with open arms after all these years? She should have left well alone. In her stupidity she'd imagined meeting him in the city for a coffee or a drink, strolling past the Colosseum, having a little flirt perhaps? She'd suspected, of course, that he'd be married, but widowed or divorced maybe. And she was genuinely shocked that he'd been married when they were shagging away in London. And he was still very much married. To the charming Silvana with her immaculately coiffed steel-grey hair. And the bracelets. She'd never visualised Fabio growing old, other than in an elegant and distinguished way, and she'd certainly never imagined him with dementia.

Gill made herself a salad and poured a glass of wine. It wasn't as if she'd planned to be unfaithful to Alfie, because she loved Alfie, and prayed that he'd keep his promise to fly down to see her in Amalfi or wherever. All she'd wanted was to satisfy her curiosity about Fabio.

But then there was the yacht! She'd no idea Fabio had become so rich and successful. And, she had to admit, just for one teeny-weeny moment back there, she'd imagined cruising the Med, clad in designer clothes, bracelets on her wrist, and not even having to pour her own drink! She'd get rid of that poncy Pietro though.

Life could be cruel. Look at poor, poor Fabio. No amount of money or success would improve his condition. And here was she, seventy years old, fit and well, looking better than she had in years, with a new admirer and two great mates. What an amazing trip this was turning out to be. Gill finished her salad and decided to lie down.

When Connie and Maggie got back at about five o'clock they found Gill fast asleep, and snoring, on the settee. She awoke with a start as they came in.

'Sorry to disturb you,' said Connie, sitting down opposite and kicking off her sandals. 'We're knackered. And poor Maggie's been mugged and didn't even make it to St Peter's.'

Maggie was pouring herself a glass of water.

Gill, fully awake now, said, 'Oh, I'm so sorry, Mags. Are you OK? What did he take? Have you been to the police?'

'Yeah, I'm OK,' Maggie said. 'And he didn't get anything of major importance. And I'm not going near the police. Not that they'd find him anyway.'

'What about you?' asked Connie. 'Did you manage to locate the famous Fabio?'

Gill sighed. 'Yes, I did.'

'And?'

'And he's got a yacht, a wife and dementia.'

'Oh, Gill!' Connie grimaced. 'But you didn't honestly think he'd be waiting for you, arms outstretched, did you?'

'Not really.'

'OK, so let's hear it all.'

Gill told them of her visit to *Il Delfino* and found they were more amazed by the incredible coincidence of it being the same yacht as she'd inadvertently boarded in Cannes, than they were about the wife and the dementia.

'Just as well you've got a spare Italian up your sleeve,' Maggie said with a grin, before taking herself off to her bunk for a lie-down.

'That mugging has really taken the stuffing out of her,' Connie said.

Later, when Maggie was inside showering and Connie and Gill were sitting with cool drinks outside, Connie said, 'I'm quite concerned about Maggie.'

'Well,' Gill agreed, 'it must have been a scary experience.'

Connie sighed. 'I wonder if she's telling us the truth?'

'What *do* you mean?'

'Well, she was very evasive about everything when she left so early this morning, and she's been so morose all afternoon.'

'So, what's on your mind, Connie? You don't think she's heard from Ringer, do you?'

'I wonder.'

'Surely she'd have told us?'

'Maggie wouldn't want to worry us. I'm only guessing though. But we'll soon be at the turning point of this trip and I can't imagine he's just going to obediently turn round and follow us all the way back. *Something's* got to happen.'

'Alfie wants to come down and join us in Amalfi. Perhaps I should tell him what's going on?'

'Oh Gill, you *know* Maggie would go ballistic!'

'Yes, but we could all be in some danger, couldn't we? We've spent the last few weeks looking over our shoulders every five minutes, and this is *our* trip as well as hers.'

Neither spoke for a moment.

'We'll make a decision when we get to Sorrento,' Connie said. 'Maggie's found a tiny offbeat site there on the internet, so we should be safe. She's booked it for the end of the week.'

'And then there's your Italian cousins.'

'I'll have to see the lawyer in Naples. I've got copies of everything I could find, and I've even got my grandmother's wedding certificate. I've sent on the money they wanted and have an appointment for the beginning of next week. It's probably a wild goose chase, but worth a try.'

'You might find you're heiress to a fortune. You could end up richer than Maggie!'

'Mmm,' Connie said thoughtfully, watching Maggie, with her hair wet, coming towards them. 'I'm not at all sure that's any guarantee of happiness.'

They skipped breakfast the following day and headed into the city for an early *aperitivo* and lunch on the Piazza Navona, background music vying with the sound of gushing water from Bernini's famous fountain.

So many beautiful people in this city, Connie thought. She watched two teenage girls, arm in arm, golden-skinned, chestnut-haired, casually but immaculately clad in tight jeans and crop tops, as they sauntered by. She remembered the youngsters she'd admired at the Sacre Coeur in Paris, which seemed like a lifetime ago. I'd like to be young again, she thought. Somewhere like this. If Maria had married a fellow countryman I might have been born here. Even so, I am one quarter Italian, so perhaps that's why I feel so at home in this country.

She'd had a call from Don, who had a rotten summer cold and wasn't going to be able to make it to Rome, but he had every intention of seeing her in Amalfi, or wherever she ended up. Summer cold? Well, perhaps, but more likely some romantic tryst. You never quite knew with Don. Connie was used to his erratic ways, and now it suited her free spirit.

She watched one of the artists sitting in the middle of the piazza, between the fountains, sketching an overweight tourist. The locals came here to ply their art and sing their songs. A young tenor was serenading the customers in the *ristorante* on their right with a rousing rendition of 'O Sole Mio'.

'Not quite in Andrea's class,' Maggie murmured.

But he wasn't at all bad. Nor were the couple of gymnasts somersaulting in front of the restaurant on their left. You could spend most of the day here, Connie thought, lingering over a drink and watching the world go by. And, in the evening, there would be *la passeggiata*, the nightly ritual of parading up and down, looking your best, admiring and being admired. Stopping for refreshments, exchanging coy smiles, starting conversations. Beats internet dating any day, she thought.

En route to the Pantheon, Gill bought a pair of gold leather trainers, which she put on immediately.

'I never liked trainers before,' she informed the other two. 'But I'll be able to walk as fast as you now. Do you think Alfie would approve?'

Alfie dominated her every conversation. Would Alfie like this? Would Alfie like that? Did they think Alfie would *really* come down to join them in Amalfi or somewhere? Yes, he'd said he would but still… Should she stay on in Italy if Alfie asked her to? Would that be crazy? Should she learn some Italian? Did Connie and Maggie really *really* like him?

Gill was on the phone to her lover several times a day. She knew that when he called her 'cara' he meant 'dear' or 'darling', but couldn't get her head round the fact that she had to call him 'caro'.

'In most European languages you have to alter the word ending depending on whether you're referring to a man or a woman or a masculine or feminine noun,' Connie endeavoured to explain. Gill looked blank.

'Didn't you do French at school?' Maggie asked.

'Yeah, but I didn't pay much attention. It's such a long time ago.' Gill grinned. 'But I've just remembered Bobby Carter who sat right behind me in French. He was so good-looking and we all fancied him like mad! He groped my boobs once when I was coming out the toilet.' Her face lit up with pleasure.

'I can see you had a very rounded education,' said Maggie. 'And do you know,' she continued, reading from the guide book, 'that this is the largest unsupported dome in the world and they reckon it was built around 2000 years ago.'

They were standing inside the Pantheon and gazing upwards at the famous hole in the top of the dome.

'And,' Maggie continued, 'nobody knows the exact composition of the material but it's structurally very similar to modern-day concrete. How about that?'

'And lots of famous people are buried here, including Raphael,' Connie added.

Gill was still gawping at the hole in the dome. 'What happens when it rains?'

'You get wet,' Maggie said.

The following day they arrived early at St Peter's Square for their half-day walking tour of the Vatican. Much to Maggie's relief they'd paid to skip the line, which was much better than waiting for hours in a queue in the heat of the day.

They began with the Vatican Museum, where the young, good-looking guide regaled them with tales of saintliness and scandal, and explained how the Vatican popes had put together one of the world's greatest collections of private art. There were Raphael's Rooms, the Cabinet of Masks, the Gallery of Maps, and finally the Sistine Chapel. While all around people marvelled at Michelangelo's frescoes, Gill complained about having a crick in her neck with all the looking up she was having to do.

And, finally, St Peter's.

Maggie was glad she'd come. She felt a definite sense of peace as she genuflected, found a pew and sat with her head bowed. Dear

God, she thought, I don't know if you exist or not. But, if you do, I really need your help now. Please tell me what to do.

Connie and Gill had moved on to admire Michelangelo's early sculpture of the Pietà – the Pity – showing Mother and Son, with Mary holding the body of Christ after the crucifixion. Connie said she'd been moved to tears when she saw it first many years previously, and she was moved to tears again now. She thought of Ben, and how she'd seen his poor little body after the accident. No mother should have to endure that.

Gill, rarely sensitive, must have guessed, as she put a comforting arm round Connie.

All three were completely exhausted, physically and emotionally, as they emerged into the heat and noise of the outside world again.

There was so much more of Rome to see, but Maggie had booked the site in Sorrento, so they headed off, promising to see more on the way back. They sang 'Arrivederci Roma' as they set off from Ostia, Maggie driving and Connie in the passenger seat, on the road to Naples and Sorrento and Amalfi. And goodness knows what else? Connie wondered. At least she'd made an appointment with the lawyers in Naples. And then what? Would the three stay together? Would they all turn round and drive all the way back to the UK? The thought did not appeal, particularly with Ringer on their tail. There hadn't been sight or sound of him for some time now so perhaps he'd finally given up the chase, Connie hoped. Even so, he was unlikely to be waiting with his arms outstretched to welcome Maggie home. What would she do?

She glanced across at Maggie, marvelling how the three had become such friends on this journey. Not for the first time, Connie had discovered that you could never tell about people just by looking at them; you could mentally write them off before you knew the first thing about them. Let's face it, she thought, I'd never have chosen these two as friends, not in a million years! But friends they had become, and she already dreaded the thought of parting with them at some point, because sooner or later they all had to get back to the real world. And of course they could all remain friends in London. If they all went back to London. Connie had a feeling some sort of crunch was coming.

They reckoned on a four-hour drive if the traffic wasn't too bad. But the traffic was horrendous; everyone in Italy appeared to be going on holiday and the first part of the journey, which was inland, was slow and tedious. They lost sight of the sea until they got to Terracina, and then decided to lunch in Gaeta, a small city at the southern end of the Lazio region, about fifty miles from Naples. Gaeta was situated on a promontory surrounded by water on three sides, where they discovered that everyone in Italy had decided to lunch as well. They finally managed to locate a parking spot for Bella and a space in a busy restaurant near the harbour for themselves. They ordered salads, which arrived liberally sprinkled with the dark oval olives for which the area was famous.

They set off again, Connie in the driving seat, to tackle what they hoped would be the final hour.

'Whatever happens,' Connie said, 'I do not want to be driving into Naples. It's manic at the best of times from what I remember.'

Maggie was studying the map and looking out for signs while Gill, sitting behind as usual, could be heard talking to Alfonso on her phone. 'Oh, caro, that would be *wonderful!*'

'What's she up to now?' Maggie muttered.

'I bet he's coming down here to see her,' Connie said.

'Do you think he's as keen as she is?'

'I wouldn't be surprised.'

'Really?' Maggie was gazing out of the window but almost missed the turning to take them round the bay. 'Quick, take the first right!'

'Thank God!' Connie sighed with relief as she turned off, glad to escape the slow-moving chaos ahead, the tooting of horns, the yelling of drivers at each other, and the never-ending heat. It was even hotter here than in Rome, and accompanied by an assortment of smells, few of them pleasant. And Andrea Bocelli was singing 'Funiculì, Funiculà'.

Gill was humming as she poked her head forward. 'Guess what? Alfie's flying down tomorrow, with Toto, and he's booked us into a little hotel in Positano for five days! That's near Amalfi, you know?'

'Yes, I know where it is,' Connie said.

An hour later, still in heavy traffic, they arrived at the little park near Sorrento, having pulled in several times to admire the beautiful Bay of Naples, Vesuvius lurking above.

'What a stunning coastline!' Maggie exclaimed. 'And what a fabulous part of the world! And your poor old granny left all this lot behind for Newcastle!'

'Love conquers all,' quoted Gill from behind.

The camping site was tiny, but very orderly. There were generous spaces for four large vehicles, and it had a small shop, a toilet and a shower. It was also very expensive, but Maggie had insisted on booking it from Rome, mainly because it was 'off the beaten track', and it was only a ten-minute walk into Sorrento. Maggie, of course, was paying. Connie had long since given up worrying about such extravagances and was only too relieved to switch off the ignition, stretch her aching limbs and peel the shirt away from her sweaty body. There was a slight breeze from the sea but it, too, was hot. Everywhere shutters were drawn, shops were closed, fans whirred and locals slept. Shortly it would cool down a little, shops would reopen, and people would reappear.

Gill had already collapsed onto her bunk and Maggie had a wander round to check on the facilities.

'I don't want to drive again for a long time,' Connie said when Maggie came back in. 'We can get the train from the station in Sorrento which will take us back round the bay to Pompeii and to Naples. And we can get a bus to Positano and Amalfi.'

'We've done damned well to get here in one piece,' Maggie remarked as she poured herself a cold drink.

'And with only a couple of dents,' Connie said. 'And this is the end of the road, geographically at least.'

Maggie nodded. 'Well, I've booked for a week, while we decide where we go from here.' She looked around. 'You'll doubtless be staying with relatives anyway.'

'I'm not counting on it,' Connie said.

All three fell in love with Sorrento, perched on the cliffs above the marinas, even though it was buzzing with tourists. They ate dinner in the Piazza Tasso, the cafe-lined square, admiring the lemon and orange trees all around, laden with fruit. It was the home of Limoncello, which was Connie's favourite liqueur, and their kindly waiter refilled their glasses several times without charge. As a result they tottered unsteadily as they explored the narrow cobbled streets full of artisan shops.

'Tomorrow,' Connie said, as they meandered back down the lamp-lit street, arm in arm for support, to where Bella now resided, 'I've booked to see a Signor Eduardo Pozzi in Naples at eleven o'clock. If anyone can help me trace these elusive Martiluccis, apparently he can.'

'Well, I'll come to Naples with you,' Maggie said, 'because I'd like to look round a bit.'

Gill sighed romantically. 'And I'll wait right here for my Alfie.'

CHAPTER TWENTY-FIVE

THE LEGAL EAGLE

Connie and Maggie took the Circumvesuviana, the train that circled the bay, stopping at all the small towns and at Pompeii, before taking them into the heart of the city. Maggie wanted to explore the dock area, while Connie headed towards the centre.

'Be careful!' she warned Maggie. 'This city can be a bit dodgy.' She remembered feeling slightly threatened on her previous visit.

'Och, I can look after myself,' Maggie retorted as they parted company. 'Go find those relatives of yours and we'll meet up later.'

As Connie set off alone towards the busy central area, she began to feel unsure of herself in this city, where everyone and everything felt more intense and more foreign than anywhere else she'd visited in Italy. Becoming increasingly confused, she stopped in a shop doorway to consult her map but couldn't work out her own position. She needed to ask someone how to get to the Via dei Pellegrini but the woman she stopped looked at her blankly, shrugged and continued walking.

Connie's confidence faded further. What on earth was she doing here? So far all she'd done was forward money to an unknown lawyer in the feeble hope of finding a few relatives. Perhaps any relatives might also look at her blankly, shrug, and walk away.

Pull yourself together, Connie, she scolded herself. You've not come all this way to be so easily dispirited! She saw what looked like a businessman approaching. 'Scusi!'

Yes, he knew where the Via dei Pellegrini was, and directed her down a narrow side street with the promise that 'you'll see a big wide avenue at the end'. Five minutes later Connie found herself lost in a labyrinth of narrow streets and alleyways with tiny open-fronted shops, lines of washing overhead and everyone shouting their wares. 'Hey, lady, you Eenglish?' 'You like nice shoes?'

The heat was stifling. And it was some minutes before Connie, in desperation, asked directions from one of the shopkeepers. Taking her by the arm, he marched her back to a narrow passageway she'd already passed and dismissed as leading nowhere. 'You go there,' he ordered, 'and then you see!'

Feeling ever more anxious Connie obeyed, trying to resist the temptation to run along this dark, deserted alley. But then she rounded a corner and saw, with relief, light and noise and traffic ahead. The Via dei Pellegrini.

The lawyer's offices were situated over two floors above a bank, just off the main shopping street. Eduardo Pozzi, straight out of Italian *Vogue*, Armani-suited and immaculately groomed, ushered her into a large book-lined office, having first ordered his secretary to bring them coffees, *pronto*. He was tall for a Neapolitan, had a hooked nose, and looked to be in his mid-forties.

'Allora, Mrs McColl!' he said, as they sipped their espressos. 'We meet at last! But first, I must see your documentation.'

Connie handed over the marriage certificate, plus copies of local records, her father's birth certificate and her own birth certificate. He studied them carefully for several minutes.

'I will need some time to verify these and check them against our records,' he said. 'Perhaps you can come here again tomorrow?'

'Tomorrow!' Connie exclaimed. 'Can't you tell me *anything* today?'

Eduardo Pozzi shook his head sadly. 'Everything in the legal world takes time, Mrs McColl. Particularly in Italy. But, if you can be here at three o'clock tomorrow afternoon, I should be able to answer some of your questions.'

He's had my money for over a week now, Connie thought. Surely he must already have checked his records? And then she began to worry about handing over her precious documents.

'You are not happy?' he asked. As if sensing her doubts he added, 'Let me photocopy your documents so that you can keep them with you. Please don't worry!'

With some relief Connie watched him set off in search of a photocopier. Five minutes later, feeling somewhat deflated but at least in possession of her documents, she was shepherded down to street level and given detailed instructions on how to get back to the station.

The route was much more straightforward than the one she'd chosen to get there, and Connie was relieved to find not only the station but also Maggie, already seated outside the small bar opposite drinking coffee.

She looked up as Connie approached. 'How did it go? And where are all these cousins of yours?'

Connie sat down with a sigh. 'I've to come back tomorrow. Apparently he needs time to check this and that.'

'Surely he's had time already?' Maggie asked, signalling the waiter. 'You want coffee or something stronger?'

'Coffee's fine,' said Connie, and proceeded to tell Maggie about her meeting with Eduardo Pozzi. 'Anyway, what did *you* get up to?'

'Oh, I just had a stroll around,' Maggie said. 'But I'd like to come back tomorrow as well.'

'You *would*?' Connie stared at her friend. 'What, to look at the shops or something?'

'Or something,' Maggie replied with a grin.

Connie continued to be mystified by Maggie's eagerness to return to the city. But Maggie was saying nothing other than she found the dock area interesting. And the following afternoon, as they sat together again in the train, they chatted about everything and nothing, other than what Maggie was going to be doing. They agreed to meet at the bar opposite the station again later before setting off in different directions.

This time Connie found the lawyer's offices without any trouble and was welcomed again by a dapper Eduardo Pozzi in yet another designer suit. That's where my money goes, Connie thought wryly. And again he organised coffee and asked about her health, her family, her sightseeing and how she was coping with the extreme heat.

'Signor Pozzi…' Connie began.

'Oh, call me Eduardo, please!'

'Have you found out anything at all?'

'Well,' he said, gazing out of the window. 'I have some good news and some bad news.'

'Can I have the bad news first?' Connie asked tentatively.

He studied her over the top of his glasses for a moment. 'Well, the bad news is that I cannot find a single Martilucci to whom you might be related. Not one.'

Connie felt her spirits plunge. She had so hoped to find someone, however distantly related.

'It seems,' he continued, 'that they were a very small family. We have practised law here for two hundred years and, in the late 1880s, we handled the affairs of one Marcello Martilucci who had a *ristorante* here at the docks. He came from Amalfi, he was married there and he had his children there, before he came to Napoli. There was one son and one daughter, but the son, Gino, died of tuberculosis in 1887.' He spoke perfect English.

'And the daughter?'

'The daughter, who was called Maria, worked in the *ristorante*, but all reference to her seems to have disappeared from the turn of the century.'

'I think my grandfather was in the merchant navy at that time,' Connie said, 'so I'm guessing that he met her here in Naples.'

'Most probably. And, if so, then it is likely that her parents would have disapproved. They would not want their daughter to be taken away from them.'

'Particularly as they'd lost a son,' Connie said with feeling.

'Exactly! And is it likely your grandfather would have been a Catholic?'

'I don't think so,' Connie replied.

'So, another reason why the parents might not approve. But' – he shrugged and smiled – 'she was Italian, she was in love, and so she went to England to be with him.'

Connie sighed. 'Poor Maria! And the poor parents too, to have virtually lost both their children. I don't suppose they ever saw Maria again.'

'Probably not. Travelling was a slow and expensive business back then and the Martiluccis were not rich people.'

'So it looks as if my father was the only grandson, and only survivor of that family.'

'Correct. I will have my staff double-check all the records to make quite sure.'

'Oh, please don't go to any trouble,' Connie said, feeling utterly deflated. 'I realise now that there's probably little chance of finding any relatives.'

'Would you like the good news now?' He drained his espresso.

'There's *good* news?'

Signor Pozzi smiled again. He had beautiful teeth. 'Well, the good news is that there is a property involved – their property, near Amalfi. Perhaps they went back there sometimes, who knows? But no one has ever claimed the place.'

'What sort of property?' Connie could feel a little excitement fizzing its way up through her disappointment.

'Probably around three thousand square metres. And there's a pile of stones where the house used to stand. But the view is wonderful! Meraviglioso!'

'Could I see it?' Connie asked.

'Yes, of course. But I must emphasise that there is some legal work to be done before I can confirm that it might be truly yours, although I cannot see too many problems.'

'This is *incredible*!' Connie wondered for a moment if she was in shock. 'I can't believe that nobody has claimed it over all these years.'

Signor Pozzi sighed. 'I can tell you now that, in all of Italy, there are countless unclaimed pieces of land. Italians have always emigrated – all over the world, to North America, South America, Australia, everywhere! And they have left behind land, and houses, with no one to claim them. The house has fallen down, the land is overgrown, and local farmers have let their sheep and goats graze there for years. Because it belongs to no one. Yet.'

'How did it go?' Maggie asked, as she and Connie met in the bar opposite the station.

'It was a tad complicated,' Connie said. 'Some good news, some bad news.'

'Well, don't tell me till we've ordered a drink. I'm parched! Are we ever going to feel cool again?' Maggie gasped as she collapsed against the back of the metal chair.

'England awaits,' Connie reminded her as they ordered beers.

'Right, let's hear about these relatives then.'

'Disappointing news,' Connie replied.

'What, they all went to Newcastle with your granny? And are dishing out ice cream to this very day?'

Connie laughed. 'No such luck.'

'They're all Mafioso then?'

'No, they just don't exist. Maria's brother died when he was young and her parents didn't appear to have any siblings.'

'But that's ridiculous! Italians had huge families in those days, Connie!'

'Well, the Martiluccis didn't.'

Maggie thought for a moment. 'And you're sure this lawyer's on the level?'

Connie nodded. 'Yes, I think he is.' She was feeling incredibly sad. She'd told herself all along there was very little chance of finding anyone but, now that this had turned out to be the case, the finality of it was quite devastating. There was an echo of losing family all over again. 'I would so like to have found somebody.'

'So you've come all this way for nothing?'

'Not exactly, Maggie. I just might have somewhere to park Bella for free.'

Maggie looked mystified.

'It seems there's some unclaimed family property,' Connie continued. 'A plot of land with the ruins of a house, halfway up a hillside. Near Amalfi. Great sea views apparently.'

'My God, that's *fantastic*!' Maggie raised her glass. 'Hey, I'm sitting with a landowner! When will you see it? What will you do with it? Oh, Connie…!'

Connie laughed and took a gulp of her beer. 'I don't know anything yet. And I don't want to get too excited until all the legal stuff is sorted out. The lawyer reckons there should be no complications but reminded me that there's lots of bureaucracy in Italy and nothing gets done in a hurry.'

'Oh wow, Connie! I'm so pleased for you! You've come all this way to find the pot at the end of the rainbow!'

Connie laughed. 'Well, I hadn't thought of it like that!'

'And you deserve it. You've had some rough deals, and this looks like great news. Do you have any details about the place?'

'Only that it's completely overgrown and the house, like I said, is a pile of stones. Seems funny when you think of all these buildings surviving for thousands of years, and my great-grandparents' house hasn't lasted two hundred years.' Connie consulted a scrap of paper. 'Apparently there's about three thousand square metres.'

'Gosh, Connie, that's more than half an acre!'

'Is it? I'm hopeless at maths.'

'You could build the house again and forget about buying a home in England.'

'Oh, I don't know that I'd want to do that. But I really have no idea, Maggie. I haven't got my head around this yet.' Connie wondered if this might change her life, or would it simply be a possible holiday escape for her and the children? 'Anyway, what about you? Did you explore?'

Maggie drained her beer. 'Yes, the dock area here is fascinating. Some weirdos hanging around, mind you, but I just walked quickly and avoided eye contact. Like being on the Tube!' She glanced at Connie. 'I may even come back again.'

'What, just to see the docks? If you fancied the shops I'd come with you.'

'No, I really fancy the docks,' Maggie replied. 'Now, shall we be on our way?'

CHAPTER TWENTY-SIX

JOURNEY'S END

When they got back to Bella, they found Alfonso making himself a coffee while Toto ran round excitedly and Gill packed.

'This could take some time,' Connie informed him. 'Gill isn't known for travelling light.'

Alfonso had flown down to Naples with Toto and hired a car from the airport, with which to transport Gill to their love nest in Positano.

'The thing is,' Gill called out, 'the hotel won't take Toto. Sorry and all that, but could you have him here, *please*? Just for a few days? He seems to be house-trained too, so he must have belonged to somebody once.'

'He very good dog,' Alfonso confirmed.

'Oh my God,' said Maggie, 'we need a dog here like a hole in the head!'

'We could probably manage,' Connie said, stroking Toto's head.

Maggie sighed. 'Well, he'll be all yours!' she told Connie.

Then Connie told Alfonso about her visit to Naples.

'Is *wonderful!*' he exclaimed. 'When you find where is this place, I shall drive you there.'

'Grazie mille, Alfonso! I have some directions written down, so maybe in a couple of days…? Signor Pozzi has said that it may take some months to get any sort of legal certificate of ownership, or deeds, or whatever they call them here.'

'Maybe years,' Alfonso said cheerfully. 'But, non importa! It give you time to decide what to do.'

At this point Gill appeared dragging two enormous bags.

Alfonso looked at her and then at the bags. 'Cara, I only here for five days!'

'Yes, well,' said Gill. 'Anyway, what's all this about a house or something?'

The following morning Connie and Maggie – and Toto – headed for Pompeii. A welcome breeze had sprung up which made exploring the ancient ruins much more enjoyable.

At first, both were silent as they absorbed the magnitude of the disaster and tried to imagine the horror felt by the residents, knowing there was no escape from the deluge of ash and pumice descending upon them back in AD 79. They marvelled at the amphitheatre, the Temple of Jupiter and the House of the Tragic Poet, with its elaborate mosaic floors and frescoes.

But it was among the humbler streets that they could better imagine how it might have felt that fateful day.

'These were ordinary folk, just like us,' said Maggie.

'With young families,' Connie added. 'And dogs.' She kept Toto on a tight lead, having carried him in as surreptitiously as she could, unsure of whether dogs were permitted entry or not.

She also carried some plastic bags as she wasn't too sure of his toilet habits.

Maggie was wandering round what must once have been a living room. 'At least it would have been quick.'

'Yes,' Connie agreed. 'Doing the washing-up one minute, solidified forever the next.'

Maggie grinned. 'And just think of all those goings-on in the bedrooms! I bet you'd never have thought, as you were banging away, that you'd end up as a museum piece!'

Connie, with Toto on her knee, and Maggie were on the bus the following day, heading for Positano to meet up with Gill and Alfonso. Connie double-checked to make sure that she still had the precious piece of paper, with directions from Amalfi to the property, in her purse.

Connie stared out of the window, beguiled by the view of the Amalfi Coast, stretching from Sorrento in the west via Positano to Amalfi in the east, one of the most beautiful coastlines in the world. The road snaked its way round the cliffs, a sheer drop to the sea on one side, the rugged shoreline beneath dotted with tiny beaches and pastel-coloured fishing villages. Above were the terraced vineyards and cliff-side lemon groves for which the area was famous. It was a sightseer's dream, provided you're not driving, Connie thought, when you daren't take your eyes off the road, or provided you're not inclined to motion sickness.

Connie glanced across at Maggie, who was looking a strange colour underneath her tan.

'Are you OK?'

'I'm hoping to make it,' Maggie groaned, clutching a plastic bag in readiness.

Signor Pozzi had apologised profusely that the pressure of work this week prevented him from being able to accompany her to the property personally. But by the end of the week it should be OK. Connie couldn't wait that long – she wanted to see it *now*! And, after they met up for lunch in Positano, good old Alfonso would ferry them there in his hired Fiat.

Connie could hardly contain her excitement, unable to believe that a little patch of this glorious terrain could be hers! And that her grandmother had been born there, and that her great-grandfather must have bought it, or built it, or inherited it. Now that she had some more information about the family she would definitely be investigating her ancestry further.

As they got off the bus in Positano, Maggie wiped her brow and took a swig of water. 'That was a near thing!' she said. 'And I so wanted to absorb those fabulous views, but I didn't dare look anywhere except at a fixed point at the back of the driver's head – otherwise I'd have been a goner!'

'Well, you can look now!' Connie said, gazing up at the houses and shops in terracottas, pinks and creams, which cascaded down the steep narrow streets to the small, pebbly beach.

'Oh, it's beautiful,' Maggie agreed, looking in the window of one of the many boutiques. 'But you'd need to be a jetsetter to afford anything here. Or a thief.' She grinned wickedly.

There was only time for Maggie to admire the church of Santa Maria Assunto with its colourful majolica-tiled roof, while Connie stayed outside with the dog.

When they met up with Gill and Alfonso in the piazza, Connie thought that she'd never seen Gill look so happy. As if reading her thoughts, Maggie murmured, 'Talk about the cat who stole the cream!'

Both Gill and Alfonso made a huge fuss of Toto.

'Has he been a good boy?' Gill asked, looking nervously towards Maggie.

'Bloody pest,' Maggie muttered.

'Yes, he's been fine. Only one little accident on the kitchen floor, but no problem!' Connie had been quite smitten with her little lodger. 'And he slept on my bed all night.'

They lunched al fresco with stunning views over the rooftops to the sea beyond. Her fish was delicious but Connie's excitement was such that she could hardly eat. Eventually, bundled into Alfonso's Fiat with warnings about not driving too fast because of Maggie's delicate equilibrium, they headed further along the coastal road towards Amalfi.

'I have to admit it beats Southend,' Gill said, as Amalfi came into view with its dramatic setting and its cliff-hanging abodes.

'Bellissima!' Alfonso agreed, as he waited patiently for a parking space. 'But too many tourists!'

They should see the Sant'Andrea cathedral in the middle of the town, Alfonso said. At which Gill rolled her eyes and murmured to Connie, 'This could be another ABC day.'

'ABC day?'

'Another bloody church. Alfonso likes churches.'

This church held the crypt of St Andrew who, Maggie informed Alfonso, was Scotland's patron saint, and she was pleased that he was so well represented in these parts. And, of course, Connie was very well disposed to the name 'Andrea'.

It was 3 p.m. before Alfonso had studied Connie's directions thoroughly over coffee, and they made their way eastwards out of Amalfi looking for a left turn to somewhere called Lamara, which could only be found by driving slowly and incurring the wrath of countless irate drivers behind, all tooting madly. 'Farti fottere!' he yelled back at them as they turned into a well-hidden, narrow road. It was well surfaced and they drove steadily upwards, looking for another left turn. This was so badly overgrown that they drove right past it and had to reverse to double-check that it really was a road.

'Mamma mia!' Alfonso nosed the car gingerly into the tiny opening and it was then that Connie spotted the sign, carved into a stone and just visible through the grass. *Marigino.* That was the name of her *property*! Of course! Maria and her brother, Gino!

'That explains it!' Connie exclaimed.

They trundled along what was little more than an overgrown lane with a stony, bumpy surface and all manner of vegetation brushing the car on every side.

'It's for sure no one's been up here in a very long time,' Maggie remarked, as Connie wondered if it was humanly possible to drive Bella up this precarious pathway. It would be a challenge.

They rattled on for a few minutes before the lane flattened and widened a little, goats scattering in every direction, and there seemed nowhere further to go.

'Looks like we've arrived,' Gill said, emerging from the front seat where she'd been holding Toto on her lap.

Connie stepped out into a wilderness of trees, bushes and waist-high clumps of grass, interspersed with pink valerian and trailing asparagus fronds, all fighting for survival. It seemed such a tiny space that she wondered how a house could ever have been built here. But Alfonso was already ploughing his way through the surrounding jungle. 'Look!' he shouted.

But the three paid scant attention as they stood transfixed by the view they could see through the trees, a panoramic vista of the Gulf of Salerno sparkling in the sun, while Toto ran round in circles, lifting his leg at every tree.

'Oh my God!' Connie exclaimed. 'Will you just look at *that*!' The emotion of the moment had got to her; not just the glorious view but also the feeling of 'coming home'. She felt as if this little place had been waiting all these years for her to come and claim it. Perhaps there were no living blood relations in Italy, but she could almost feel the presence of her ancestors in the air around her. She was connected to this place; she belonged here.

'That,' said Maggie, 'is one of the most fantastic views I've ever seen.'

'Out of this world!' agreed Gill.

'Look *here*!' Alfonso yelled from behind as he extricated himself from a jungle of bushes and weeds. 'I have your *house*!'

Stumbling through the undergrowth, Connie could decipher what was left of a wall, and then noticed that this wall formed a large erratic square. She noticed further stones strewn everywhere, many covered in tenacious rock plants, but hardly enough to form walls.

'You clear this,' Alfonso shouted, waving his arms around, 'you find stones everywhere. Maybe some taken away though.'

'Do you mean stolen?' Connie asked, looking around in awe. She spied some wild lilies and wild thyme with its tiny mauve flowers and reckoned she could make a wonderful garden here.

'Sure. People take nice stones. This land not belong to anyone, they think.' At this point a stray goat emerged from the background and shot past them.

This house, Connie thought, looking towards the sea, must have had the most stupendous view, particularly from the first floor, if they had one.

'Why on earth would my ancestors ever have wanted to leave this idyllic spot?' she wondered aloud.

Alfonso sighed. 'Work. Always work. To make money they go to Napoli.' He continued kicking around amongst the stones. 'You also have many ancient olive trees here.'

'And Ringer would never find us here,' Maggie said.

'Stop worrying about that man!' Connie ordered. 'He's obviously given up the chase weeks ago!'

'You are being troubled?' Alfonso, flattening down some of the surrounding bushes, plainly had excellent hearing.

'No, no,' Maggie said hastily. 'Not at all.'

'The area isn't very big, is it?' Gill said, looking around.

'Ah, but when it is cleared, you will see!' Alfonso stretched his arms out wide.

'I can quite see why they wanted to build here.' Connie looked down at the sheer drop through the trees towards the sea. 'There'll need to be a wall here,' she said, imagining grandchildren tumbling into oblivion. Then, turning to the others: 'Oh my goodness, this is doing my head in!'

'Take it easy, Connie!' Maggie placed a soothing hand on Connie's shoulder. 'You have plenty of time to decide what to do.'

Connie was taking photo after photo on her phone. She'd email them to the kids, bearing in mind that Nick, the architect, in particular would be fascinated. As she took photos of the ruins of the house, she wondered why it had fallen into such disrepair. Perhaps it hadn't been built very well in the first place or perhaps there'd been an earthquake. After all, earthquakes were common in Italy. And then she stumbled on a piece of wood, half buried in the undergrowth. And there, still just visible, was carved an elaborate arrangement of vine leaves. A piece of the door of the house that she'd seen in the old photograph! She had definitely arrived at the ancestral home!

Alfonso was now squinting upwards. 'I can see houses up there,' he said.

Connie followed his gaze and could make out the roofs of buildings further up through the trees.

'Is good,' he said. 'So there is electric and maybe water, not too far. Or there may be a spring here. We must look.'

Connie sat down on a patch of dry, dusty grass, totally overwhelmed. The ever-thoughtful Alfonso had produced four cans of beer from the boot of his car and, as they all gulped thirstily, Gill asked, 'So, Connie, was it worth coming all this way for this?'

'Oh yes!' Connie replied with feeling. 'It was! It was!'

CHAPTER TWENTY-SEVEN

ALTERCATION

There had been rain overnight. Connie, sleepless, could hear the drumming on Bella's roof as she went over and over the visit to Marigino in her head. She knew she shouldn't get excited yet; there would be endless red tape involved. But, deep down in her very soul, she felt a certainty that the place was hers. That she would be reclaiming the land of the Martiluccis. Yes, she'd been bitterly disappointed not to have found any relatives, but this unexpected inheritance did do something to compensate. Then she worried again that she'd be unable to get Bella up that narrow track. After that she worried about the other two, because now she was in no great hurry to return to England. Perhaps they wouldn't mind flying home from Naples? But that would mean driving Bella home on her own eventually. Then she remembered that the things you most worried about were the least likely to happen. But she worried anyway.

Last night she and Maggie had discussed the day's events over a bottle of prosecco and far too many Limoncellos. Now she felt dehydrated and, at six o'clock, she gave up on the idea of sleep, got up, let the dog out for a pee, and filled the kettle for a cup of tea. She was looking forward to a blissful day here on her own. Well, with the dog. Gill, of course, was still in Positano with Alfonso, and Maggie – for no apparent reason – wanted to go to Naples again. She wasn't interested particularly in shopping or sightseeing, so Connie assumed that she, too, needed her own space. Maggie, still enigmatic at times, would have her reasons. And she, Connie, had not had a day to herself for what seemed like months. She might have a wander round Sorrento, or she might just sit in the sun, or she might even go for a swim if she could tie Toto up somewhere.

Maggie sat down at the little bar, close to the station, where she and Connie had sat a couple of days earlier, and considered the enormity of what she had done. And now she urgently needed to make some calls back home. The third number she needed to call wasn't listed on her phone. Bugger! It was probably in her diary though and she started to rummage in her new shoulder bag before she remembered. Ringer had the damned diary.

Then she remembered.

Maggie sat up with a jolt. She'd scribbled the address of their little site in Sorrento and directions on how to get there in the diary when she made the booking in Rome, prior to entering it in her phone. She felt a chill creep through her body; now she knew what it meant when something made your blood run cold. Because Connie was there on her own, in the motorhome. Two of their neighbours had moved on that morning and the remaining one was normally empty during the day when they took themselves off in their car.

Funny then that there had been no sign of him so far. He would have had ample opportunity to find Bella yesterday when they were out, but he hadn't. Probably because there had been a lot of people around yesterday. Maggie knew her money was still intact because she'd checked it again this morning, as she did every day.

But, without a doubt, he knew exactly where they were. And here she was in Naples, with Connie on her own in Sorrento with only a stupid hairy little mongrel for company.

Maggie slammed five euros on the table and, without finishing her drink, bolted to the station.

Not only did Connie have Bella to herself, but she had the site to herself. Two of their neighbours had moved on earlier, and the Dutch couple at the far end had taken off for the day in their Smart Car. She looked at the dog. 'You stay put while I have a shower,' she instructed Toto as she closed the outside door.

After she'd dried herself and got dressed she contemplated walking up to the town. She wondered how the dog would behave himself, because she couldn't very well leave him shut in here. Connie poured herself a cold orange juice, opened the outside door again, put her feet up and dreamed again of what she might do to her inherited property.

She could hear what she thought was a scooter. Then she heard footsteps approaching and saw a shadow fall across the doorway. 'Hi, Maggie, is that you back already?' So much for my peaceful day, she thought. Then she froze as the stockily built crew-cutted male came slowly through the door and turned into the kitchen.

He had steely blue eyes and a menacing smile and she saw, with horror, as the blade glinted in the sun, that he was carrying a knife.

'Where is she?' he asked calmly.

'Who?' Connie tried to keep her voice steady as she set the tumbler of orange juice onto the table with trembling fingers. The dog, who'd been sitting on the settee with her, started to growl.

'You know bloody well who!' His Glaswegian accent was still strong. 'Where's Maggie?'

'She's not here,' Connie replied. 'As you can see.'

'Then I'll wait, and I'll start looking for some of my money while I'm waiting.'

Connie thought quickly. 'No, she's gone. Away. On a plane. And there's no money here.'

'Lying cow!' He pointed the knife at Connie as he walked backwards towards the bunks. Then, with one deft movement, he slit through the sheet and mattress cover on the top bunk and slid his hand underneath, retrieving some twenty-pound notes as he did so.

'Thing is,' he said, casually popping the notes into the pocket of his shorts, 'she'd never go away and leave her money behind. Not Maggie.' He glared at Connie. 'And I know how her mind works. They'll be stashed in every bloody place where she thinks I won't look.'

Connie gulped. There was no way she could make a run for it because he was now standing between her and the door. And there was no one around if she yelled. Toto, in the meantime, continued to emit a low growl. All she could think of was to let him take all his bloody money and go. Go out of their lives and leave them in peace. She watched as he sliced an area of carpet alongside the bunks, and then began to feel cold fury welling up inside her. How dare he mutilate Bella like this! *He's going to rampage his way through my precious Bella, cutting anything he thinks might contain money.*

She had a sudden idea. *Would it work?* At least it would give her time.

'If you want to know where most of the money is,' she told Ringer, 'I can show you, if only you'll stop wrecking everything.'

He bundled some notes into his rucksack and studied her through narrowed eyes. 'Oh yeah?'

'I never wanted this money here in the first place,' Connie said truthfully. 'And now I just want you to find it, get out, and leave us in peace.'

He hesitated for a moment.

'There's a panel behind the toilet,' she continued. 'It's down there near the floor and I think it's used for accessing the pipes. You'll need a screwdriver though.'

'Behind the toilet?' Ringer considered for a moment. 'That sounds like Maggie,' he muttered as he walked towards the front. *Thank God he seemed convinced.* Connie had no idea if Maggie had hidden notes in there or not as she rummaged in the kitchen drawer for the set of screwdrivers. In the meantime, the little dog, his hackles up, was still growling at Ringer.

'Here!' she said, handing him the set. 'One of these should do the job.'

He stared at her for a moment, then said, 'Don't get any bloody ideas about running away.'

'I won't,' Connie said calmly. 'I just want you and the cash gone.'

He snatched the screwdrivers and studied them for a moment, before he delivered a kick at Toto, who yelped.

'You don't have to hurt the dog!' Connie shouted.

He ignored her. 'There's no bloody room in here!' he snapped as he got down on his hands and knees in the shower room.

'Not a lot,' she agreed.

She watched as he crouched down at an awkward angle to best access the panel, accompanied by much grunting and swearing. She bent to stroke the dog, who continued growling, plainly a good judge of character. He'd most likely been mistreated in the past and could smell trouble.

She couldn't close the door because one sandalled foot of Ringer's still protruded out into the corridor. That wouldn't do, and this was her only chance. Perhaps she could hit his foot with something heavy, but that was the thing with motorhomes; you tried to keep the contents lightweight. There was the fire extinguisher, of course. Then, just as Connie wondered if she could lift it from its bracket and crash it down on his foot with enough force, the dog, still growling, sank his teeth into the back of Ringer's ankle.

Ringer screamed in pain, automatically retracting his foot and yelling every obscenity he knew, and he was well versed. And then Connie slammed the door shut. Not only was he wedged tightly inside and it would take him some time to stand up and turn round, but he wouldn't be able to open the door either. He would, of course, be able to knock it down comparatively easily, but it did give her some precious time. Connie grabbed her keys, called out for the dog, and dashed out of Bella's door, locking the vehicle behind her.

Forgive me, Bella, she thought; I'm leaving you in the hands of a madman but I don't know what else to do.

Then she heard footsteps approaching from the road. Someone was walking fast. Oh God, who's this? she wondered, and almost cried with relief when a breathless Maggie came round the corner.

Connie, in tears, ran towards her friend. 'Oh, Maggie! You won't believe—'

'Oh, I *do* believe,' Maggie interrupted, hugging her. 'I should not have left you here on your own today.'

'I've locked him in, and he's going to take a few minutes to get out of the loo as well,' Connie said. 'And when he does get out he'll be hobbling, I hope. Thanks to this brilliant little dog.' The brilliant little dog wagged his tail. 'But he's found a lot of your money, Mags.'

In the background they could hear muffled thumping and shouting.

'Don't worry, Connie. I took lots of it with me today and I've still got a bra-full. I'll tell you everything later. Now, let me handle that bastard.'

'No, Maggie, no!' Connie panicked as she watched Maggie heading towards the door. 'Let me call the police now, *please*!'

'Not until I tell the bastard what I think of him,' Maggie said calmly. She inserted her key in the door, then stopped as they heard a car approaching. Probably the Dutch couple returning, or perhaps it was one of the new visitors who'd booked in for the night. This little scenario should send them packing pretty quick, Connie thought.

When the Fiat came round the corner and screeched to a halt Connie couldn't think for a moment who it might be. Then Gill got out from the passenger door and bent down to fuss over an ecstatic Toto, who'd made a beeline for her. 'What's up?' she asked, picking up the dog.

'It's Ringer!' Connie said. 'I've got him locked inside Bella.'

'Oh my God!' Gill turned towards Alfonso, who was still in the driver's seat on his phone. 'He's *here*!'

Connie turned her attention back to Maggie. 'Please don't go in, Mags, *please*! He's got a knife, *please*!'

Maggie hesitated for a moment, staring at Gill and then at Alfonso, who'd now got out of the car, still clutching his phone to his ear, and was striding purposefully in their direction.

'I deal with him!' he said.

Gill caught his elbow. 'No, Alfie, he's got a *knife*! Didn't you hear what Connie said?'

'Yes, I heard. Please open the door, Maggie.'

Oh Lord, thought Connie, what's going to happen now? Alfonso will get himself knifed for sure, and probably Maggie will as well.

The door open, Alfonso stepped inside and there followed a commotion of shouting, swearing and crashing, while Bella swayed alarmingly, and all the time Maggie, at the doorway, was directing an impressive string of obscenities at Ringer. Connie could see that Ringer had broken down the shower-room door and that the two men now appeared to be wrestling in the lounge area. My poor Bella! Connie thought.

Gill was in tears. 'My poor Alfie!'

Connie placed a comforting arm round her shoulders. 'He'll be OK, Gill; he's a policeman and he'll know how to handle this.'

At that moment Alfonso appeared in the doorway, his arm locked round the neck of a swearing, kicking Ringer, and hauled him down the steps. 'Stand back!' he ordered, as the dog went into paroxysms of barking.

It was then that Connie heard the police cars. How on earth had they known to come here? Alfonso, of course. She didn't know whether to feel relieved or fearful as the cars screamed round the corner and pulled up abruptly behind Alfonso's Fiat. Four policemen swung open the car doors and ran to assist the struggling Alfonso. Much shouting in Italian went on for several minutes while Ringer was handcuffed and paraded, limping – Connie noted with satisfaction – towards one of the police cars where he was pushed unceremoniously into the back seat.

'This man,' Alfonso translated for their benefit, 'I tell them he wanted by police in London for bank robbery. He go now, and you not see him any more.'

In the meantime, Maggie had followed Ringer and continued her tirade. 'The blonde bitch ain't going to get you now!' she concluded.

One of the policemen was taking copious notes. 'He follow this lady,' Alfonso said in English to the policeman, 'but she not want him any more.'

The policeman turned to stare, somewhat incredulously, at a scruffy, perspiring, furious Maggie.

'These ladies on holiday!' Alfonso continued loudly in English.

One of the policemen, also in English, said, 'He says she stole his money.' He pointed at Maggie.

'Pazzo!' Alfonso gave a dramatic sigh. 'He crazy. Maggie has no money – *look* at her!' They looked at her. 'Does she *look* like rich lady? She's in caravan, not hotel.' There followed further conversation in Italian, with a great deal of gesticulating, before the police appeared satisfied. And Connie noted, with relief, that he'd talked the police out of going inside Bella, which was just as well as there were liable to be twenty-pound notes lying all over the place.

'Tell them, Alfie, that he'll likely need a tetanus jab,' she said. 'Toto had a taste of his ankle.'

Alfonso nodded and turned to Maggie, who'd quietened down. 'We go to police station to make statement. You come with me.' He beckoned towards the Fiat.

'Must I?' Maggie looked close to collapse, her earlier anger appearing to have drained her.

'Yes,' said Alfonso, 'you must.'

She shrugged and followed him to the car. 'I'm so relieved this is over,' she said to the other two. 'For your sakes more than mine.'

'Oh, Maggie!' Connie said as she and Gill both hugged her. 'It's going to be all right. And I have to say I'll sleep better tonight!'

'Me too!' echoed Gill.

CHAPTER TWENTY-EIGHT

TIME TO SAY GOODBYE

Connie felt as if a great weight had been removed. She and Gill stood silent and still for a moment as the three cars drove off. Then Connie said, 'But how on earth did you two manage to appear at this exact moment?'

'I told Alfie the truth about Ringer,' Gill admitted. 'I know I promised Maggie I wouldn't, but I had this feeling that Ringer would show up sooner or later. Alfie was worried and said we should come over each day to make sure everything was OK. He reckons that Ringer was able to work out where we were, or had been, by tracking Maggie's phone, every time she switched it on. But, poor you! You shouldn't have been involved in any of this! And what damage has that lout done to poor Bella?'

'There's one way to find out,' Connie said as she headed towards Bella. As she entered, she saw the shower door hanging sadly by one hinge.

'Never mind,' said Gill, still carrying the dog. 'We can get that fixed.' She turned right towards the sleeping quarters. 'Oh my God!' She stared at the ripped mattresses and the butchered carpet. She put her hand on Connie's shoulder. 'Maggie'll buy you new ones, you know she will. And who needs a carpet anyway? The floor's not damaged.'

'I could get a nice little rug instead,' Connie said. 'More hygienic anyway.' She turned towards the front. Fortunately he hadn't had time to do much damage here although there was evidence of the struggle between the two men, with cushions strewn around and the glass of orange juice she'd been drinking lying in smithereens on the floor. There were also some streaks of blood, presumably from Ringer's injured ankle.

'Here, take the dog for a minute, in case he cuts his feet.' Gill passed Toto across to Connie and proceeded to dig out the dustpan and brush. 'First thing is to get rid of this glass, and then we'll give the floor a good wash. It could be a lot worse.'

'Thanks, Gill. But I wonder how Maggie's getting on? Do you think she'll be in trouble?'

'No,' Gill replied firmly. 'Alfie will sort it out.'

Such faith, thought Connie, such love! And, for the first time, she considered that Gill might really be in love.

It was two hours before Alfonso and Maggie reappeared, looking remarkably unperturbed.

'Let's see the damage then,' Maggie said.

'Oh, Maggie!' Connie hugged her. 'Are you all right? What happened at the police station?'

'Ringer's in custody,' Maggie said. 'He's to be sent back to the UK in the next few days. Apparently he's been staying in Naples and driving a Vespa.'

'A *Vespa*!'

'Yup, a Vespa. He hired a Vespa because the Lexus broke down and is having a new clutch fitted somewhere in the city. Which is probably why he didn't appear yesterday.'

'Everything OK now!' Alfonso announced, and then turned to survey the bunk area. 'I measure and we get new…' He waved his arms around.

'Mattresses,' Gill put in.

'I get new mattresses for you, but maybe not today.'

'We can cope,' Maggie said, peering over his shoulder at the devastation. 'The top one doesn't look too bad. I can sleep on that.'

'And we have the other divan at the front, Gill, because you can't possibly sleep on yours,' Connie said.

'Not important,' Gill said airily.

'She stay with me,' said Alfonso. 'Now, I go back to police station. I come back' – he consulted his watch – 'after one hour, for to take Geelee back to Positano.' He kissed Gill, waved, and was gone.

'We need a drink,' said Connie, putting away the mop after sponging and disinfecting the floor.

'Large ones,' Maggie agreed.

'Several,' added Gill.

Connie withdrew the remaining bottle of Bombay Sapphire from the cupboard and poured out hefty measures while Gill sliced a lemon and got tonics out of the fridge.

When each had a glass in her hand, Connie raised hers and said, 'Here's to us!'

'Here's to us!' they repeated.

'Tell me,' Connie said after they'd all had a gulp, 'did the police not suspect you'd taken that money, Mags?'

'I don't think so. They were all going at it in Italian so I hadn't a clue what was being said. But, so far as I can gather, Alfonso convinced them that Ringer was a bit deranged because he thought I'd taken off with another man. I think they were mainly interested in getting Ringer deported back home.'

'Good old Alfonso!' Connie said with feeling. She looked at Gill. 'I wonder what he *really* thought though?'

Maggie shrugged. 'Who knows?'

'I know,' Gill said. 'Alfie will believe what he thinks is best for us all because, let's face it, we're *all* involved in this.'

'Ringer found a lot of the money,' Connie remarked.

'Well, he won't be having it for long,' Maggie said. 'Anyway, he won't have found *all* my hiding places.'

'As a matter of interest, was there money behind that panel in the shower room?' Connie asked.

Maggie shook her head. 'There won't have been much. I've been taking it out from there over the past few weeks, so he'd be damned lucky if he got a hundred or two. Anyway, your Alfie's been great, Gill, and I shudder to think what might have happened if you two hadn't come along when you did.'

'He's a lovely, lovely man.' Gill cleared her throat. 'On the subject of which, I have some news.'

They both looked at her expectantly.

'I'm sorry, girls,' she went on, 'but I think we've come to the parting of the ways. Alfie's asked me to move in with him.'

Connie gulped. 'What, permanently?'

'Yeah, I hope so.'

'That's great news!' Maggie raised her glass. 'Here's to Gill and Alfie!'

'So, will you ever be honouring us with your presence here again?' Connie asked.

'Just tomorrow night,' Gill replied. 'Alfie's flying home in the morning and then he'll drive straight back down again to pick up me and Toto, and all my belongings.'

'He'll need a bloody big car,' said Maggie.

'Will you get married, do you think?' Connie asked.

'Who knows? Does it matter at our age? It's enough, for the moment, just to be together,' Gill replied with a faraway look in her eyes. 'Me and Alfie, and Toto.' She bent to stroke the dog.

'What will your family think?' Connie asked. 'Will they try to talk you out of it?'

'Probably. I don't care. And are any of them really going to want to look after me when I'm dribbling and incontinent?'

'You're not far off that now,' Maggie said with a grin.

'Aw, shut up!'

'So let's hope Alfonso's well stocked up with incontinence pads!'

Gill ignored her. 'And no more awful British weather!'

'It does get very cold in Tuscany in the winter though,' Connie said. 'I hope he's got central heating in that great big house of his.'

'Well, she can cuddle up to Alfie,' Maggie said. 'It'll be like sleeping with a rug.'

'What,' Gill asked, grinning, 'are you going to do when I'm not around to have a go at?'

'God only knows,' Maggie said sadly.

'So now there'll only be the two of us,' Connie remarked, looking at Maggie.

It was a few moments before Maggie spoke. 'Not for long, Connie. I'm leaving too. It's an idea I've had for a while now, and probably well timed just in case the police might start to believe there's some truth in what Ringer's been saying.'

'*What!*' Connie nearly choked on her gin. 'And where might *you* be going?'

'Australia,' said Maggie.

'*Australia!*' Connie and Gill chorused.

'Australia,' Maggie confirmed.

'But – but you said you couldn't fly all that way…' Connie said.

'I'm not flying. I'm sailing.'

'Sailing!' Gill looked at Maggie, then at Connie who seemed dumbfounded, and then back at Maggie again.

'Yes, sailing.' Maggie paused for a moment. 'I'm leaving on a freighter from Naples the day after tomorrow, in the evening, bound for Sydney, with hundreds of cars on board. They have four passenger cabins and I've got the last one.'

There was complete silence for a minute.

'Oh, Maggie!' Connie said at last, tears visible in her eyes.

'How long will that take?' Gill asked.

'Around six weeks. That boat will stop at places I've never even heard of, so it'll be quite an education. And I'll be eating at the captain's table every night!'

'Just as well you bought yourself a couple of decent dresses then,' said Gill.

Connie was refilling their glasses. 'So *that's* what you've been up to in Naples!'

'Will you be coming back?' Gill asked.

'Nope. This is a one-way ticket to my new life with Al and his family.'

'Oh, Mags!'

'It just feels like the right thing to do.'

'Of course!' Connie agreed. 'But what about your flat and all your stuff?'

'It's Ringer's flat. And there's not a lot there that I'd want to take with me anyway. But I've rung Pam to say I'll send her the key and she'll pack up the stuff I want and freight it on to me. I won't need much, only personal bits and pieces, because I'm going to be starting again. New life, new country!'

'My God!' Gill took a large slurp of her gin. 'And I thought *my* news would have you both gasping!'

Connie remained silent.

Then Maggie said, 'The thing that bothers me most, Connie, is will you be OK driving back to England on your own?'

'Don't you worry about that,' said Connie. In fact, she hadn't given the return journey any thought. Perhaps she wouldn't be driving back at all.

Alfonso flew home the next morning, having deposited Gill back in Sorrento and leaving the three to spend their final twenty-four hours together. True to his word, he'd ordered two new mattresses and they arrived mid-morning.

'Well, at least you'll both get a decent night's sleep,' Connie said, although Maggie had spent the night without complaint on her top bunk. The deliverymen from Naples had been instructed to remove the two slashed mattresses, which they duly did with exchanged glances, but asked no questions.

'Let's have a nice lunch at our lovely restaurant up in the square,' Maggie said. 'My—'

'*My treat!*' the other two mimicked.

'How often have you said that over the weeks, I wonder?' Connie mused. 'You've been treating us ever since we left home. It'll be a shock having to dig into our own bank accounts, won't it, Gill?'

'I shall be digging into Alfie's,' Gill said with a giggle.

'And Connie,' Maggie said, 'you'll probably still find a few quid hidden in here from time to time because, to be honest, I can't remember exactly where I hid it all. But I'd like to leave you some cash to get yourself and Bella home.'

Connie shook her head. 'No, Maggie, please don't give me any more money. I've hardly spent any of my own since we left, and anyway I plan on staying out here for a while.'

'You're going to see what happens about Marigino, Connie?' asked Gill.

'Yes,' Connie replied. 'I thought I might try to get Bella up there, and stay for a bit.'

'And decide what you're going to do with it?'

'Something like that.'

'Just as well we're going then,' said Gill, attaching the lead to Toto's collar. 'Come on, Toto, let's go for a nice walk around Sorrento, and tomorrow we'll go home to Viareggio.'

*

It was their last evening together. After a long, leisurely lunch at their favourite restaurant, having taken Toto for a walk round some of the little narrow streets and down to the marina, they'd sat in the sun for a couple of hours.

Now, windows and doors wide open, they sat sipping wine and chatting quietly.

'You'll come and visit us, won't you, Connie?' Gill asked.

'Of course I will.'

'Don't suppose you will, Mags?'

'No, Gill, I don't suppose I will. But we can Skype and all that. I'll need to keep an eye on you in case you're ever tempted to that bloody awful beehive again. And now you'll both have an excuse to make a trip to Australia.'

'You might end up marrying the captain of the boat,' said Gill. 'Have you seen him? What's he like?'

Maggie laughed. 'And end up living back here in Napoli again? Not bloody likely!'

Connie was deep in thought. 'You're not the world's best traveller, Maggie. Do you think you might be seasick?'

'Very probably,' Maggie admitted. 'But they say you get your sea legs after a while. I've bought lots of pills, just in case.'

Connie sighed. 'This time tomorrow night you'll both be gone and I'll be sitting here talking to myself. I'm going to miss you both so much! And Toto too! That's one feisty little dog, and a great judge of character!'

'He's a streetwise little guy,' Gill said, lifting him onto her knee. '*He* knows who's who.'

*

Maggie and Gill spent the following morning packing, a procedure that took Maggie about fifteen minutes, and Gill two hours. Connie took Toto for a walk, leaving Maggie in peace to check any remaining hiding places for forgotten notes. She'd need them all to start her new life in Australia, and Connie would be relieved to be rid of them.

Tomorrow she would attempt to drive Bella up the narrow track to Marigino. Eduardo Pozzi had, much to her relief, offered to follow in his car in case there was a problem, and besides, he said, he was really curious to see the place. This evening she would send emails to everyone to let them know she planned to stay on for a little. And she'd keep the middle door closed so that she didn't have to look at the two empty bunks with their new mattresses.

Alfonso arrived in his BMW at three o'clock. It was a long drive and he was keen to set off again as quickly as possible. After he'd lugged all of Gill's belongings into the boot and the rear seat he said, 'We must leave, cara.'

'Yes,' said Gill. She turned, moist-eyed, towards Connie first. 'Thanks, Connie, for everything.'

'Oh, Gill, it's been fun!' Connie tried to swallow back her tears. 'I shall miss you.'

'I shall miss you too. But we're not far away so promise you'll come to see us? And thanks again for bringing me here, and for my new life.'

'You're very welcome,' Connie said, hugging her.

Gill turned to Maggie. 'I'm even going to miss *you*! Who's going to sort me out and rubbish my hairstyles?'

'Heaven only knows,' sighed Maggie. 'I expect you'll go to wrack and ruin. But, Gill, you've found yourself a good guy there.'

'Yes, I have,' Gill agreed. They hugged each other, and then Gill picked up Toto and rushed for the car, wiping her eyes. Alfonso kissed them both, wishing them much luck, much happiness, and 'thank you for bringing me my beautiful Geelee'.

'Just as well he didn't see her with the beehive,' Maggie murmured as, with much waving, Gill and Alfonso and the little dog drove away.

Maggie's boat was sailing at 7 p.m. She'd flatly refused to take a taxi because, 'I've only got these,' she said to Connie, indicating one holdall and one backpack, neither of which were full.

'You certainly don't *look* like an emigrant,' Connie said.

'I must give you some money to have that fixed,' Maggie said, pointing to where the shower door was dangling from one hinge and refused to shut at all now.

'No way!' Connie protested. 'It's only me who's going to be using it and I shall keep it as a memento of our trip together. I shall think of you every time I have a pee.'

'Quite right too,' said Maggie.

They were strangely silent as they sat opposite each other on the train, each engrossed in their own thoughts. Connie was trying to imagine what it might feel like to even contemplate a new life on the other side of the world at the age of seventy. But Maggie had a son there, and she was a brave little thing anyway. She looked across and tried to mentally photograph her, so she could remember her like this. Maggie had put on some weight, she was deeply tanned and, since Ringer's arrest, she'd already lost some of that nervous edginess that once defined her.

Yes, it had been wrong to steal the money, Connie thought. But I'm beginning to appreciate why she did it. There's right and there's wrong, and there are innumerable shades of grey in between. And thank God for Alfonso! As an ex-police chief himself, he had obviously been able to convince the local police that these three *inglese* were totally innocent. Maggie had gone along with the story that Ringer had been pursuing them because of his great love for her, and because of his suspicions that she'd taken off with another man. *Passione* was a word that was used a lot, Maggie told them later, and one of the only words she understood in the police station. Perhaps the Italians would empathise with that more easily than their British counterparts.

Now, as the train pulled into Naples, Connie contemplated returning to Sorrento alone, and how strange that was going to feel.

As they walked towards the docks, Connie said, 'Oh, Maggie, this is all so final. Unless you can overcome your fear of flying, it's unlikely you'll ever come back to the UK again.'

'No, I won't be back,' Maggie said. 'I won't see London again, and I won't see Glasgow again. But just as well I didn't know that I was seeing those places for the last time because I'm rubbish at saying goodbyes.'

'Me too,' said Connie, feeling tears prickling behind her eyes again.

'I'm going to have so many lovely memories of this trip,' Maggie said. 'Remember that gay bar in Paris? You couldn't make it up!'

'Claude and his lavender,' Connie prompted.

'And lecherous Larry! And that concert in Tuscany; that was one of the best nights ever.'

They stopped outside the customs area.

'You won't be able to come any further,' Maggie said, removing her backpack and fishing out her passport and paperwork.

They stood smiling at each other for a moment before they hugged.

'I shall miss you, Maggie.'

'I shall miss you too. And thank you, Connie,' Maggie murmured. 'Thank you for letting me come along. Thank you for the fun we've had on the way, and thank you for my future, because you've given me a future.'

'No, Mags, you've given yourself a future. I've just transported you towards it.'

'Promise you'll keep in touch and maybe visit sometime?'

'Of course I will,' Connie said.

They stood apart, then Maggie picked up her bags, blinked furiously and, turning abruptly, disappeared into the customs building.

And Connie, tears streaming down her face, turned the other way and headed back towards the station.

CHAPTER TWENTY-NINE

MARIGINO

It had been a struggle to ease Bella up what amounted to little more than a rough track. Eduardo, true to his word, folded himself into and led the way in a Fiat 500, which arrived relatively unscathed, while poor Bella ploughed and scraped her way behind, scattering stones and branches in her wake. But at least they'd got here, even if Bella had acquired some scratches and Connie some near heart attacks. Bella was now resting in front of the olive trees next to the ruins of the house, and Eduardo could see no reason why she couldn't be left there for the time being, but recommended that Connie had the vehicle stored in a safe compound when she flew back to the UK. That, he said, was if she intended to keep it, otherwise he could arrange for it to be sold.

For the moment it was still home. Of course, if she did eventually decide to rebuild the house, then in all probability Bella would have to be sold, but she didn't want to think about that. The legal side, Eduardo informed her, could take some months, so there was no need for any hasty decisions. Best of all, Connie discovered a footpath of sorts which zigzagged its way down to Amalfi. It was a fifteen-minute walk but at least it gave her access to the bus to Sorrento and the train to Naples if necessary, as she had no wish to subject Bella too often to the tortuous drive back down to the main road.

Now Connie felt she belonged here. Her great-grandparents had built this house, and Maria and her brother had been born here. Connie would try to restore the place to its former beauty, in their memory, for Maria and for her own family as well. But the view needed no improvement; it was as it always had been. She was looking out at exactly the same vista as her grandmother had.

Connie stretched out on one of her canvas chairs and poured herself some wine. She watched the sun slowly dipping towards the horizon and noticed several boats out there. She wondered then how Maggie was getting on. She'd been gone several days now; would she be in the Suez Canal yet? Connie knew she'd hear from her, and Gill too, eventually. They'd promised to keep in touch. For now this was enough.

Andrea Bocelli was singing 'Che Gelida Manina'. Connie's hand wasn't very tiny, and it was far from frozen. She took another sip of wine and raised her glass to the future.

LETTER TO READER

Dear Reader,

Thanks so much for reading *The Getaway Girls*, and I hope you enjoyed sharing in Connie's run to the sun. If you haven't yet read *The Runaway Wife*, I'd love it if you did, and then you'll see why Connie's been enjoying her independence so much!

And, if you've enjoyed this book, and want to keep up with Connie or similar publications, you can sign up to the following link:

www.bookouture.com/dee-macdonald

Your email address will never be shared and you can unsubscribe at any time.

Also, if you feel like writing a review, I'd love to know what you think, and feedback is invaluable. You can get in touch via Facebook and Twitter.

Dee x

 AuthorDeeMacDonald

@DMacDonaldAuth

ACKNOWLEDGEMENTS

Many thanks to my brilliant editor at Bookouture, Natasha Harding, and to my wonderful agent, Amanda Preston at LBA Books, for their invaluable help and expertise and, not least, their faith in me.

Thanks too to the Bookouture team who put it all together: Kim Nash, Ami Smithson, Alex Crow and Jules Macadam, Ellen Gleeson, Lauren Finger and Claire Gatzen (with apologies to anyone I've unwittingly omitted).

I'm particularly grateful for the patience, support and encouragement of my husband, Stan, and my son, Daniel, and his family. And a special thanks to my clever friend and critic, Rosemary Brown, without whose help the book would be knee-deep in unnecessary adverbs and clichés, to name but a few.

Finally, a huge thanks to the women friends who've always been there for me over the years: Sylvia Morrell, Margaret Perkins, Maggie Boucher, Silvia Gridley, Jan Hunt, Sue Thomas, Carol Barnes, Angie Obbard, Sylvia Vaughan-Stanley and Linda Flynn. Where would I be without their humour, advice, wine, fun and encouragement? (And I won't mention the shopping trips.) But I must admit none of them are anything like Maggie or Gill…!

Made in the USA
Middletown, DE
14 December 2023

45670958R00203